Reset

New Dawn Challenge

Jay Warren

This novel is a work of fiction.

Any resemblance to actual persons, living or dead, events or places, is purely coincidental

Cover design: More Visual Ltd, Leicester
Formatting for print by LionheART Publishing House

Dedication

I dedicate part of this novel to my late father, Raymond Harris, who was so desperately 'ready for his box': the rest, to this delicately balanced orb we call home.

Acknowledgements

My special thanks go to Claire, my neighbour in Spain, whose words of encouragement my book was worthy of publishing and suggestion to attend an Amazon Author Academy came at the right time. And for recommending Reset to her good friend, one of Amazon's most popular author's. Her honest review I truly value. To Jackie, Kev, Stef and Amie who read parts of the story in its infancy and enthused about its disturbing appeal. To my daughter-in-law Claire, who proofread the completed novel. You all lifted my hopes maybe I was onto something.

I send my gratitude to Karen Perkins, Lionheart Publishing, for diplomatically pointed out my glaring errors and saved me from making a complete arse of myself. If I could have afforded your acclaimed editing skills as well as your formatting service, I would have jumped at the chance, saving my frequent Amazon Author account revisits!

And last, but not least, I'd like to thank my husband, Brian. Who, after realising perhaps she *can* write, has smoothed my technology frazzled moments and suffered the most throughout this lengthy process.

Reset

Mutatis Mutandis

'The necessary changes having been made.'

Chapter One

Alberta, Canada

Through the front passenger seat window, a cleansing waft of vegetation invigorated Morgan's senses, as the station wagon sped past blurs of vibrant green countryside providing a much-needed contrast to the stale rancidity of greasy bedding; unwashed bodies; the stifling odour of shared air: his usual cell block existence.

It's good to get out of that damn hell hole, he reflected.

Sat in the front, Cecilia, a prison guard, tilted her head, so he could see her profile, but not enough to make eye contact, before scoffing, 'Not long now, fat boy.'

She was the worst at making him feel like scum; her expressions of distaste wilted him like a chastised puppy. Although common: he hated the look of pity or disgust he attracted; only his long dead mother ever looked at him with a fondness.

Smiling in perverse pleasure, Morgan awaited the reaction to his silent, fetid release of gas as the hue of what he'd ingested engulfed the interior of the car.

'Filthy bastard,' Cecilia exclaimed in disgust — turning her head to the open car window.

Her colleague chuckled bloke-ishly.

Driving into suburbia, the normality of life tantalised Morgan with the unobtainable. He sighed, as a smell of warm tar awakened childhood memories of riding his yellow bike, struggling to pavement dodge shiny new patches of the gooey substance, and the tacky noise as it had grabbed his tyres.

The sound of children in a playground: their high-pitched laughter, screaming and shouting, drifted on the breeze. A

1

strong smell of school dinners: of stewed meat pervaded his space. Morgan pictured infants, in matching uniforms, sitting in a line on benches stuffing food into tiny mouths; innocent, over stimulated eyes darting around them. Relenting to his callous needs, holding this image turned his blank expression to one of sadistic cruelty. As counselled, closing them helped erase the scene conjured by his subconscious.

Handcuffed incapable of evasion, to unsuspecting pedestrians they passed, he was just a fat bloke in the rear of a car may be travelling to a play-off with his family. That's unless they peered closer: prison uniform shirts and epaulettes relaying the true intent of their journey: taking him to a place where they'd help him with his bad headaches.

Having heard rumours of inmates disappearing — moved to other wings, other institutions, and knowing he fitted the profile of the no hopers: the ones not visited now absent from the daily rituals of penitentiary life; he had nagging doubts today's mission was bona fide.

'Shall we cut him a break? Get him a Big Mac. It might be his last?' Cecilia suggested.

Concentrating on the road ahead, the other guard shrugged his shoulders, giving her a playful shove on the arm with his free hand, saying, 'You going soft in your menopausal years girl? How's that sound? If you behave, we'll give you a treat for lunch. What the heck, a KFC sounds better. I'll stop at the next drive through. We'll feed Chump in the back before dropping him off.'

Drop him off! 'Why are they not staying with me?' Morgan wondered; the guards phrasing doing little to pacify his uncertainty, deciding it pointless asking, they'll only lie, best sit still and stay quiet, else I might not get that KFC.

Reflecting about when he last felt in control of his life; was asked how he was; what his hopes were, Morgan remembered June: a prison volunteer who'd been the only reason he'd tried improving his appearance. He'd also started reading and writing classes, which only encouraged more ridicule from the wardens and inmates: 'Dumb, fat boy piece of shit,' their favourite phraseology he'd mumble himself when shaving his pomegranate coloured, acne marked skin while gazing into his piggy eyes exuding hopelessness.

Morgan gave religion a go: ten Bible reading, or listening in his case, sessions which only made things worse. He never understood what the preacher meant, or been able to add to the discussions. He'd got confused, angry: which the others fed on. What was he supposed to do: let them poke fun all the time? His attempts at finding God led to two weeks in solitary confinement, and a good beating from the friends of the prisoner he'd hospitalised; recollecting everyone's astonishment, a Bible *could* fit into some-one's mouth.

'What happened to June?' Morgan asked.

'June. Whose June? Oh yeah, I remember. Your pretty little pity friend. She got a proper job. You were part of her psychology thesis Chump. Don't beat yourself up about her, she's long gone. You weren't getting sweet on her, were you, Dick Head?'

Morgan ignored the condescending answer from the guard driving. Closing his eyes, mulling: I've the strength to overpower them, and so want to, but if I survive the crash, I'll stand out like a sore thumb in this bright orange boiler suit. I'll spend a few nights in the woods drinking stream water before getting tracked by dogs.

'What's the fucking point of anything?' he muttered.

'What's that? You want nothing?' the driver goaded — glancing in the rear-view mirror — catching Morgan's look of sorrow.

Bumping up the kerb under a KFC sign sporting Colonel Sanders grandfatherly smile, lifted his spirits as his nostrils filled with an essence of Southern fried chicken.

Chapter Two

The car slowed as they turned into a ranch, awaking Morgan from an upright nap. Stretching his back, groggily absorbing the new vista, this seems a nice place: it can't be where the doctor he's seeing works? he thought, surmising a visit here looks expensive, knowing it unlikely the system would waste decent money on him: a murderer of young children — an unacceptable risk to society not eligible for parole for another fifteen years.

'Come on. Out you get. We've a surprise for you. These nice people are going to make your life a whole lot better from now on, my son,' the male guard announced, preparing his Taser as Morgan eased himself from the car.

Watching Cecilia walk away, hips swaying casually, as she chatted on her mobile to whoever was meeting them. 'We're out front. Ready when you are,' Morgan heard her confirm, feeling calm, contemplating whether this was it? Maybe his time's up?

Earlier, as they'd driven through multiple prison gates, he'd an inkling he might not return. Recollecting his march with the jail wardens — ignoring the usual verbal barrage spewing from behind cell doors — rounding the first corner, he'd glanced backward as two guards, unfolding plastic bin bags with a rustling flourish, strode into his vacated space. Assuming they were after contraband: Morgan knew on the grape vine no raids were due.

This recollection fuelled more doubt. 'Maybe he was out of there: moved on like the others?' Having no-one on the inside willing to tell him of a decision about his future. And no-one on the outside concerned about his fate — he felt very alone.

Enjoying the relative freedom, taking in the mountain scenery, Morgan inhaled a lungful of the sweet scent of horse, hay and meadow. Savouring the pleasurable moment, he felt becalmed, realising whatever was in store, he didn't care. If today was to be his last: so be it.

Hearing footsteps approach, Morgan glanced behind, seeing three men in white laboratory coats stride towards them. A pretty woman, with glossy dark hair tied in a ponytail catching the sunlight as she moved, trailed in their wake. Her flawless skin exuded a radiance; she'd an energy; an aura captivating Morgan, who expected her to open a pair of wings and fly skywards like an angel.

'Don't get any ideas there, my son. She's way out of your league,' the male guard sarcastically whispered in his ear, bringing him back from his pleasing reverie with a predictable put down.

Lead towards a low-level building, through a large glass door, down a flight of concrete steps past laboratories bustling with activity, then into a consultation room with nothing more than bare walls and a wide examination couch: onto which they settled him.

Still handcuffed to his minder, struggling to make sense of a mumbled conversation the men in white coats were having outside the room, but failing, Morgan relaxed, tapping his fingers against the spongy warmth beneath him in time to a melancholy tune the guard hummed. A rumble in his stomach reminded Morgan of the bastard guards' final words: 'No tasty chicken for you, my friend. Nil by mouth. Doctor's orders.'

The clatter of footsteps and clinking of metal alerted him something was about to happen.

Morgan observed the angelic woman come into the room. She didn't glance at him, just picked up a syringe from the array of medical implements on a tray and wandered over.

Exchanging a knowing look with the guard, her neutral expression changed to one of remorse. Forcing a fleeting dose of eye contact made his heart race with the realisation she wasn't comfortable.

Cleansing his arm, glancing to her right — at the huddle of doctors — before back at him, 'Don't worry. You're being sedated while we do scans. The results should help us find out what's wrong with you,' she said, in a reassuring tone.

Morgan smiled, without exposing his crooked, greying teeth. Focussing on her dainty hands nimbly eliminate trapped air from the hypodermic. Positioning the needle millimetres from his pale freckled skin, as it broke his flesh, she mouthed, 'Sorry,' he was positive, making him frown and glance towards the doorway, as the guard yanked away the handcuffs.

In a stupefied daze Morgan heard the other doctors say, 'Let's get started,' as restraining straps were callously placed across his limbs.

Transferred onto a gurney, the wheels squealed in complaint as he juddered forwards.

Pushed along a corridor, Morgan watched bright fluorescent lights pass above him. Then everything went black.

When Morgan came around, he'd no idea where he was? Or who he was? Strapped, in a vice like grip, to a flat table raised off the ground, he felt hot; tried moving, only able to arch his spine causing perspiration to run down his back muscles.

Feeling no pain, but in some way violated, he pushed against the restraints as a physical urge to stand overcame him. Shouting: only a feeble wheeze filled the quietness.

A woman, looking through a glass panel at him, was speaking, but he couldn't make out her words. She looked very sad. Her hand pressed flat against the transparent wall clutched a ball of tissue. She kept glancing at a group of men in the room's corner, then back at him, before creeping in, taking a rectangular piece of metal from her pocket.

Morgan so wanted to see that angelic face, but she kept the object at arms-length obscuring his favoured view.

A flash of light caused him to blink.

In that moment, she slipped away; he saw her white coat flit out the door.

Morgan tried again to speak: the gurgling sound emitted, alerted the men.

Sauntering over, one took his arm while the others consulted clip boards, talking amongst themselves.

'Doing well. Ready for the next phase,' the eldest one directed.

'What do they mean?' he wondered, before losing consciousness.

Morgan *was* being helped. He was being transformed in a way he'd never have thought imaginable.

Chapter Three

Paris, France

'Professor Brockman! I've a message from Mr Josh Hall: he apologises, says he's running half an hour late,' the concierge called to Milo as he hurried through the foyer.

'Thanks Hugo. Realised my mobiles off,' he answered, raising his eyebrows to emphasise his annoyance — fingers dancing over the phones surface, disturbing it from slumber. The lurid pearlescent device chirped to life with a jaunty rap number his daughter Jolie downloaded: the tune always made him smile, sometimes with embarrassment, in the high-profile company he kept.

Striding towards the revolving doors, opting to make a return call to his wife Marie. Milo's eye a drawn to the hypnotic prisms of dancing colour created by the ostentatious crystal chandelier hanging overhead, chirped, 'Hi Hun. I'm running late. Are you alright?' Bursting from the calm of the hotel to join the rude explosion of noise on the Rue de Rivoli.

'Yes. Fine Mi. We've been up most of the night with Jolie pony issues, *again*. A colicky Caramel this time. She's a fat waste of space. I'm tempted to have the vet send her on her way, so I thought I'd give my beloved a call before getting my head down,' Marie chuckled.

'You don't mean that. You love her. Listen, Hun. I've found out why Josh has been off kilter. It's not good news, Penny's got pancreatic cancer with only months to live. He offloaded, after a few Armagnacs last night, was in a proper state. Made it hit home how horrible my life would be without you in it. So, stop riding that crazy bloody horse of yours, let Oliver risk his neck. Agreed?' Milo barked — manoeuvring between pedestrians exuding cheap perfume scents; a noisy group of skinny, brightly dressed Japanese tourists slowing his progress. Stepping off the pavement, he passed them, again finding his pace.

'No. Not agreed. Poor Josh. How awful, she was so full of herself when we last saw her. But thinking about it, I wondered. Just something she said when we left.'

'I remember you mentioning. Glad we squeezed in that weekend. Josh says she's not seeing anyone: getting too hard. Best call her when you can. Oh, before I forget, as instructed, I've got Jools' present's: a snow shaker thingy with an Eiffel Tower inside and one of those Tour de France yellow t-shirts. I hope it fits? How's things in the laboratory? You didn't sound very happy the other day.' Milo knew he'd not glean much: Marie being guarded about her work with her father, Donald.

'Same old. Same old. I'm trying hard to leave what I see behind those doors. We'll talk more when we go to the lodge. We've had loads of rain. The grass is a quagmire and the lower laboratory has flooded again. Nothing vital lost, thankfully. I'm meeting the builder tomorrow—,' Marie paused. 'Pops is asking after you Mi. He's sleeping a lot and ready. Keeps chanting. Gives me the heebie-jeebies, to be honest. ... I love and miss you like crazy Mi. Only two more sleeps, can't wait.'

'Back at you Hun. Don't get me started. I've the metro to negotiate. Could get embarrassing squashed up against the wrong person.' Milo disguised a knot of trapped emotion with humour. 'This is such a farcical waste of energy Hun. I know I keep saying it, but we're banging our heads against an intransigent brick wall of arrogant pig headedness. Right, I'm at the underground, losing my signal. I'll text when boarding. Can't wait to see you. Give Jools a clip round the ear and save some Merlot for me. Bye Marie. Love you,' he shouted — unsure whether she'd caught the sentiment, stashing his phone in the pocket of his Harris tweed jacket.

Trotting down the stairway into the subterranean world of

the *Louvre Rivoli* metro line, Milo's mind returned to Marie: who at times, amazed and equally, disturbed him. In awe of her pragmatism, intellect and uncanny ability to assimilate and act on facts in seconds, these attributes bringing her worldwide acclaim in her field of Neurosurgery and Molecular-Biology.

Annoyingly, like a malevolent nightmare, an image of Donald manifested in his subconscious. As a frown emerged, Milo's raw memories of their strained conversations; the man's frequent, judgemental put downs, came to the fore. 'Was he still good enough for their Child Prodigy?' he wondered, mulling the man's past: the rumours he frequently heard of his involvement in controversial Eugenics programmes and other unsavoury dealings.

'All history, no changing it,' he muttered, never feeling the moment right to raise a challenge; knowing for certain: Donald was, '... the founder of the Osborne Trust, and main sponsor of the Institute for Bio-demography, Human and Social Biology.' The times he'd heard the man spout this with pompous pride were innumerable.

These sour moments tainted Milo's favoured recollections of the city where he'd meet the love of his life. His first sight of Marie's little turned-up nose and pink cheeks; the rest of her face covered by a purple pom-pom hat as she'd stood admiring the *Sacre-Coeur* bronze horses. That fated encounter when he'd asked her to dinner. Eighteen years on — with a cheeky thirteen-year-old daughter and a rewarding career as head of the Earth Watch Institute — life's great, he thought, reflecting, let's see what today brings, then I'll know what lays ahead.

Pushing and shoving, joining the flow of travellers approaching the turnstiles, he mumbled, 'And get back to Marie, my beautiful scary visionary. That sums her up nicely.' Before Donald popped back to mind. 'Was he where he was because of him?' He thought not, but couldn't erase the persistent doubt his swift promotion, so soon after their marriage, was arranged. No: his hard-earned pedigree and persuasive charm had made him the perfect candidate to head the organisation recognised as the research leader in green sustainability.

Although Milo's attendance at the bi–annual conference for Participating Nations — where he was heading — was expected; in his opinion these conferences were good PR opportunities held to satisfy environmental protection bureaus; energy coalitions; health organisations and lobbying groups that Global Warming and its planetary impact *was* being taken seriously.

Having endured the preliminary days — filled with empty words and false achievements — Milo, and his team, needed to work harder to gain the committee's agreement to their touchy, politically incorrect stealth measures in order to achieve their agenda. Encouraged by the attitude of half the delegates; they needed full backing to sanction his organisations far-reaching, surreptitious plans, putting politics, commerce, and the cosseting of society on hold.

Milo hoped today there would be no need convey a signal for action to his other vital cogs.

His heart: fearing this outcome highly likely.

Patiently queuing, shuffling towards to the barriers, Milo committed to memory his main arguments; a strong smell of garlic tinged body odour, oozing from a scruffy man by his side, forcing him to hold his breath and dash in front of the offensive source to be next in line for automaton acceptance into the labyrinth of tunnels, bedlam and darkness.

Access granted, Milo retrieved his ticket as it shot out the turnstile, resembling an impolite paper tongue, and ran to the platform.

A powerful draft of warm air engulfed his face, announcing the start of another bustling journey.

Milo found travel by underground odious. To pass the time he'd categorise passengers into groups; tourists, gripping guide books, bursting with animated chatter. Students cramming, scribbling notes, using a crossed leg as an anatomical support. Lone men and women: the worker bees of society, functionally dressed with scuffed shoes, listening to music through dangling white plastic spaghetti. Milo supposed they hankered for this temporary encapsulation to help them endure their repetitive cycle of drudgery. The sinister shifty types, staring coldly ahead, or at everyone around them with contempt, concerned him the most; stereo-typically the ones behind well-planned atrocities. The notion often crossing his mind: What impression did *he* give others?

For sure: no one in that carriage would have the faintest inkling about his plans.

Not one of them understood he, literally, carried the weight of the world on his shoulders.

After the oppressive stuffiness of the metro journey, energised by the chill on the air and crisp morning sunshine, Milo slipped on his Ray-Bans and strode along the tree-lined avenue. A slight breeze overhead rustled the leaves, detaching a few which fluttered to the surrounding pavement, swirling in a vortex created by passing traffic.

Signs of the recent development were clear: from unused building materials; heavy plant idle, gathering litter around huge tyres; to the fresh concrete and pristine kerb stones.

No sign of weeds or moss gave away the infancy of the area.

The hypocrisy exasperated him — recalling his handout at the last seminar: 'Global Warming. The Link with Construction.'

Taking the marble steps two-at-a-time into the venue, Milo visualised the other delegates cocooned in their limousine's, unaware of this disgraceful misuse of resources, tutting, 'Give me strength.'

Sat on a black leather couch in a quiet corner of the lobby, Milo waited for his most trusted friend: Josh Hall.

Nonchalantly watching the to-ing and fro-ing, his mind drifted to when they'd first met. Then, a field campaign manager for the Governor of New Jersey, and now US Secretary of State for Global Affairs: Milo's best pal — who'd have thought from his humble beginnings. So much water under the bridge since their ice breaking jog through the cherry blossom in Newark park.

'Come on Mr Busy Bee,' he mumbled with impatience, frantically jiggling his leg.

As the queue for the trade stands grew, Milo recalled his earlier dawdle around the exhibitor's emotive displays. Encouraged by their enthusiasm; their depth of feeling about the effects our anthropogenic selfishness was having on their chosen cause, the commendable slogans, plastered on billboards in the foyer, printed on calming pastel backgrounds, grabbed his attention: ... The journey to tomorrow begins with small brave steps. The collective interests of humanity. Living in harmony with nature. Governing for sustainability.

A forcible blow to the shoulder announced Josh's arrival, making Milo spill the Evian water he was sipping.

'You were away with the fairies, Mi. How's your head?' he barked.

'Hi. Noisy bugger. You look better than I expected. Coffee saturation obviously did the trick. You need a mint though; stale Armagnac and garlic are not pleasant my friend.'

From the depths of his briefcase, Milo found a blister of spearmints, offering them to Josh as they approached the escalator. He hastily devoured two of the refreshing pastels.

'Thanks for listening last night. ... When Pen's gone — not the right way to put it, but you understand — I'm jacking in this politics lark and putting my energy into bee conservation: Colony Collapse Disorder, to be precise. I read up on it early this morning. Helped my future fall into place. ... Just wish I'd spent more time with her. Pointless dwelling.'

Milo glanced at Josh with empathy.

'Today's the day, Josh. Make or break. Whatever tomorrow holds, we can at least move forward,' Milo's determined gaze remaining fixed at the top of the escalator as he spoke.

The auditorium was packed when they entered for the final session.

Chapter Four

During a coffee break, in a side room, out of earshot of the other delegates, Milo engineered a moment to work on the committee. One last time, before I set my pit bull on them, he thought, settling in his seat.

It didn't take long for Milo to send Luca Kielholz — his second in command at the institute — the look. On cue, the hot-headed Viking stood, launching into a predictable rant: 'How can you be so short sighted. We're making no progress, just suffering further procrastination,' he shouted, throwing a chair forcefully against the wall, the clunk of impact startled everyone, drawing their eyes to a fresh dent in the plaster, before again focussing on the bear of a man. 'It's imperative we act as a collective to make drastic change. The planet dominated by our human presence with every breathing soul adding to the carbon overload every damn second, the time bomb is ticking. And you, my friends, by not giving serious consideration to our proposals, are allowing it to tick faster. Half the global population is living in abject poverty, decrepitude, and dysfunctional turmoil. As the chosen representatives in our field of expertise, we must grasp the responsibility and implement the uncomfortable decisions. Environmental sustainability cannot cope with our numbers as they stand, let alone in five-or-ten years. I need not remind you we've exceeded the tipping point. We have to take action, not pussy foot around creating the right noises—' Luca 's voice trailed away.

Mopping his brow gave Milo the chance to assess the committee's reaction: an air of forbearance hung as Luca resumed his aggressive diatribe. 'Here's the unpalatable truth.

The planet's only hope of sustaining life, for the longer term, will be lost if we don't halt our toxic destruction *now*.'

Milo monitored the room: as predicted, only two of the fence sitters were onside. The rest: they'd no chance of winning over.

'Sixty per cent of the world's ecosystems have degraded,' Luca hissed, continuing, 'With the latest estimates of thirty-five per cent of plant and animal species likely to face extinction by 2050 — your target date for halving carbon emissions. It'll be too damn late. ... Do you want your grandchildren to live in a world filled with 10 billion souls. To have to wear breathing apparatus, and swim in acidic oceans?' Luca — red faced and sweating — slumped into his chair, drank a glass of water, adding nothing further.

Josh harrumphed, letting Milo know he was ready to give support. Milo stood. 'I'd like to thank my colleague for his emotive words, we trust, haven't fallen on deaf ears. ... With genuine sincerity, we do recognise the positive progress made over the past weeks. We're encouraged by The Breakthrough Energy Consortium's innovative approach: they're passionate, refreshing, making the right noises. And heartened there's an overall acceptance our main carbon sinks: the oceans, are reaching saturation point. The funding for swift production of pioneering carbon capture techniques is great news. But these agreed measures won't be enough. And whilst I acknowledge my close colleagues, and my own suggestions are provocative, radical, even revolutionary, we only have the best interests of the planet and all non-invasive life upon it, at heart. ... I'll also take this opportunity to decline the committees offer to join their team in facilitating the present ratified changes.'

Knowing he couldn't commit himself, or the institute to a remit of non-punitive action, Milo studied the perplexed expressions of the conference President, the French ambassador, and other members of the implementation group.

'We commend the international cohesion attained and assure those present we will continue to offer support and data analysis when required. We wish you luck, until we meet again,' Milo concluded, before sitting down, sipping a glass of luke warm water, and raising his eyebrows to Luca, whose beetroot complexion had lost its fiery glow.

The board members humoured them; acknowledging their solutions had a dark age appeal. But, the realities of present-day society meant they'd never be acceptable, or achievable.

Milo knew they'd hit that solid brick wall in negotiations.

As briefed, his team said nothing further, just sat, restraining their outrage. Milo didn't want to ring alarm bells, giving the impression they had their own agenda. Looking around the room in exasperation, he thought, it will only be a matter of time before these procrastinators reach that conclusion.

Composed, back in the assembly hall, running his hands through his hair, Milo checked to see if his key players were back in their seats. During a lull in banal statements spewing from the main stage, choosing his moment — with the slightest of nods — Milo communicated his message. Reciprocating the gesture, in turn, they acknowledged his unspoken intent.

To the sound of applause and false rejoicing, Milo and Josh left the auditorium, walking from the ineffectual nonsense without a backward glance.

Proactively they'd taken charge; were the ones about to make a difference. Their plan of action — a goer.

Encased between Milo's palm's, Josh's skin was clammy.

'Is that a tear in his eye?' Milo wondered, watching him duck into his waiting car, drive away, leaving Milo frozen to the spot, one arm raised in farewell.

'My God, what have we started?' Milo pondered, with a heavy heart — inner doubts running overtime — persuading his legs to function, watching the last glimpse of Josh's showy cavalcade disappear.

Chapter Five

Human nature possessed a strange trait of recapping dramatic life changing moments; a form of Post-Traumatic Stress Disorder, to justify; come to terms with a recent event, Milo supposed, wishing he'd a stronger character — could move on without the need to press replay.

To steady himself, Milo planted his feet, countering the sudden lurch of the metro train droning and hissing to a halt. Grabbing a vacated seat, he watched two men hesitantly step on, overtly gay, their gestures relayed. Reassured, after catching Milo's eye, they plonked onto the seat opposite with exaggerated bottom wiggles as they settled. 'Did they want to leave impressions of their backsides?' he wondered, resuming his habit to observe.

Both wore stone-washed jeans with matching floral shirts, buttons gapping under strain. A strong stench of cheese and onion billowed from the crisp packets opened with relish; trite chatter accompanying their loud snack chomping analysis of the passengers, before it was Milo's turn for appraisal. In bizarre unison, like bloated Lewis Carroll incarnations, they threw him a beaming smile as they munched.

Milo broke eye contact, preferring the carriages motion blur out the window, juggling with the notion where humanity heading? And, like Donald, did he *also* have a deviancy aversion? Deciding not. He didn't find the apparent closeness of these Cheshire cats abhorrent: unusual, amusing; their hormonal imbalance a result of mankind's obsession with oestrogen mimicking chemicals, making him further ponder what state the human race will be in by the turn of the century?

Much better, *if* our plans are a success, he thought,

visualising a steaming hot bath — longing the journey to end.

Chapter Six

Holding his breath, Milo slid under a layer of effervescing bath oil, embraced by the soothing heat flushing away an abundance of contaminating city grime and his brush with false hope. Losing its penetrating intensity, Milo banged his heel on the pressure plug, allowing the water to drain with a gurgling glee. The bubbles, trapped in his pubic hair, fizzing as they dissolved. After a brisk towel dry, slipping on lounging trousers and a fleecy top, a call of: 'Room service,' came from the other side of the door.

'It's OK. You can come in,' Milo called, as the lock release mechanism clicked.

'Good evening. Did you have a good day sir?' the cheery girl asked — breezing in with a salmon baguette, coffee and fruit: all he fancied. She's new, Milo thought, watching her sashay through the room, place a stain-less steel tray on a side table, his attention drawn to her pert behind enhanced by a close-fitting black velour skirt. It *was* time to get back to Marie, he realised.

'Sorry. No, not really. Can't always win them,' he answered, his gloomy expression relaying his mood.

With a quirky downward mouth expression, the girl finished laying out his supper, lilting, '*C'est la vie, Monsieur*. Enjoy. *Au revoir*,' as she left.

Cutting the massive piece of crusty bread in half, eating loose segments of flaky fish with his fingers, without much appetite; the snack would see him through the night, he surmised, using his other hand to scroll his phone contacts for Josh's. Not wanting to hold a negative, futile conversation, Milo texted: 'Be in touch in two days. Take care. Luv to Pen.'

The greasy residue washed from his hands; with heavy eyes, Milo sprawled onto the bed, his memory going back ten years, to an evening he'd spent with Marie at her parent's ranch house. 'Milo, read this, the time is right,' Donald had said.

'My circumstances now: is this a coincidence?' he wondered, remembering flicking through Donald's manuscript: *'New Dawn'*, 'Mutatis Mutandis' written on the last page, Medieval Latin he'd not understood Donald educated him meant — the necessary changes having been made. Milo recollected re-reading the document the following morning and how disturbed he'd been, wondering then whether it was plausible fact; a thought-provoking vision of the future or just a work of fiction? Knowing he'd been given a peak into Donald's mind; his desired intentions, most of which Milo had understood.

Falling into a fitful doze, tsunami's, earthquakes and a recurring nightmare of being lifted by a malevolent force and thrown from a great height, awoke him — drenched in sweat and gasping. Turning on the TV; the time, half-past five Fox News informed him. The sultry tones of the presenter keeping him company with news of US citizens caught out by the latest cold snap. Choosing a classical music channel, better suiting his mood, Milo made a coffee, then sat starring at the screen saver; one particular swirling pattern conjuring an image of Crispin Brockman, Pops, his eighty-nine-year-old father. Milo pictured him confused, skeletal, with advanced dementia and going down-hill fast, having not coped after the death of his wife four years earlier.

Fate: it's fickle hand and the irony, Mum walked everywhere. It would have been quicker rather than appease her friend by accepting a lift that night. At least when the drunk driver had ploughed into them, she'd been killed out-right, Milo again reflected.

'And now we've Pops' wanderings to contend with along with everything else,' he muttered — deciding to pack ready for his flight as further slumber was proving elusive.

Chapter Seven

Red Brook Ranch, Alberta

Milo never tired of the stunning views. From the bedroom window a distant backdrop of the Rocky Mountains, in all their snow-capped glory, being especially appealing this morning.

Sipping a steaming hot coffee, he wandered, barefoot, to the frameless glass wall that made up the front of their cosy pine log cabin. Viewing the rest of the wintry vista, imagining Marie hard at work behind the stone-clad walls of the laboratory block beyond the meadow. Twisting his spine one way, then the other, it already felt better back in his familiar bed. Marie's horse related injuries, and his skiing mishaps playing havoc with his lumber region; the pair of them needed the restorative effect of their orthopaedic mattress.

Re-filling his mug, Milo smiled at Jolie's hap-hazard display of red Dogwood twigs, topped with crepe paper flowers scattered with silver glitter in a vase on the kitchen table.

'Bless her,' he mumbled, reading her note, brushing fallen sparkle from the checked tablecloth, *SOOO glad you are home. Riding Ziggy. Up for that game of chess you promised? Luv you Jools xxxx.*

Milo re-read the greeting Marie had leant against the kettle: *Let you sleep in. You were out like a light last night and twitched a lot! Want my fill of you later? luv M x.*

'Good plan,' he thought, before Pops, and the un-enviable task, dampened his mood.

Giving himself a mental kick start, running through his 'to do' list as he headed for their study. 'Let's get this show on the road. Ring Pops' neighbour check she's sorted the bungalow for next weekend, then the doctor to confirm he's received the med's', he muttered.

Settled in the comforting mould of his worn leather office chair — the only item he couldn't part with when they'd married and moved from his Edmonton apartment — Milo studied the lap top Donald had placed on his desk. Considering the role it was about to play, a childish Smiley sticker on its casing added a rather distasteful touch.

Lifting the lid, the machine hummed a greeting.

With a new mail option open, Milo chose pre-set addresses and typed a one-word message, before hesitating — looking around the normal environment from which to despatch such a controversial trigger. His eyes falling on a gold framed family photograph of their Christmas skiing trip. Happy smiles and rosy cheeks. Even then, he could see the dark shadows lurking in their eyes. Only Jolie was the relaxed innocent in that captured moment.

He must spend time with Pops; make a flask of coffee, with brandy, how he likes it. We'll fish in the brook before sunset.

'Stop stalling. Come on,' Milo chided, picturing his contacts, recapping what he knew of their families, thinking I wonder what they'll be doing right now.

It's taken the collective two years of planning to reach this point. We're committed. In unanimous agreement: there's no other course of action, he reasoned, manoeuvring the cursor over send. His index finger still poised over the touchpad, Milo chewed his bottom lip, focussing again on those snowy peaks, to the fluffy clouds floating high above without a care in the world.

Trusted as the key player — the linchpin — only he had the authority to start the programme. Tapping the key fulfilled his part of the agreement, conjuring an adrenaline surge: the same a nuclear missile commander must experience controlling the destiny of nations with a launch code.

Here goes. No going back. God help us, he thought — relaxing into the chairs comfortable hold.

Milo's communication, sent via Tor software would travel the anonymity network through multiple digital layers, reaching his catalysts: who he hoped will altruistically play their part.

After shouldering the responsibility for so long, feeling perversely elated, Milo observed with envy those careless clouds be pushed by a tropospheric breeze.

Calling Pops' doctor: they went firm with their arrangement for Tuesday.

In London, Cologne, Bonn, Amsterdam, Melbourne, Quebec, and Philadelphia, Milo's email subject: 'Change', arrived. Seconds afterward, at locations in Kampala, Lagos, Harare, Brazzaville, Agadez, Bamako, Lusaka, Hyderabad, Bangkok and Brasilia, one which read: 'Go,' was received.

His one basic word — having reached far more destinations than they had led him to believe — meant Milo was unaware the extent of events he'd set into motion.

Chapter Eight

'Right. Time for *my* life and *my* fitness,' Milo murmured, tying the laces of his Adidas trainers. Drinking a large glass of water, flinging open the kitchen door, he ran, unburdened, out into the crisp daylight — feeling as if nothing could stop him, setting off on his regular running route.

Taking in the scenery: his visual acquaintance for these morning bursts of energy, relishing the dry mountain air, finding his pace under the summer shade providers of lodge-pole pine and spruce. He'd appreciate that warmth today, he thought, shivering, driving himself out into the winter sunshine.

At a bend in the perimeter track, glancing up into the dense branch cover, making out the roosting shape of the male great horned owl always settled there, hoo-hooing his customary greeting. The bird — rudely awoken from its daytime slumber — snapped its bill, throwing Milo a menacing, golden eyed glare.

Turning downhill, the haunting hum of the ranches wind turbines; stripy fluorescent blades spinning, grabbed his attention. Their bright modification: a result of Jolie's emotive presentation: 'A visibility issue and the harm caused to our birds.'

Smiling, recalling the afternoon in Donald's study when she'd wheeled in a clothes rail with macabre avian corpses, vacuum sealed in plastic, dangling from it: 'So that's what she's been doing with the hoover, not cleaning her room,' Marie had whispered. Millicent had muttered her frequent, 'Oh!' in disgust. Milo could see and hear them as if it were yesterday.

The next half a mile took him to the bottom of the hill, past the lake and awe-inspiring main house protruding from the hillside. Tendrils of greenery draped from exposed areas of the roof, giving the impression of an organic waterfall tumbling over the stone work.

With tired legs slowing his pace, drawing a few deep breaths, Milo grinned at their big horn sheep mulling under nearby willow trees; shimmering prairie grass creating a suitable back drop to the scene; realising his weeks away had taken their toll on his health. The sight of Jolie exercising her pony in the corral brought a spring back to his step, waving as he neared the paddock. She's wearing the yellow t-shirt he'd left on her bed late last night. Bless her, he thought.

'Hi Dad. Soooo glad you are here,' she called, tugging on her pony's reins to slow his pace, leaping off and squealing in protest at the tightness of Milo's embrace.

Kissing the top of her unbrushed hair, inhaling her musty, sweaty odour, 'How's things Jools? Was that a three-footer I saw you going over?'

'Yep. She's doing really well. Mum says I can enter her in the advanced class at school, so Hollie Smith had better try harder this year, as that trophy will be mine,' she said — punching above her head in emphasis, before cooing, 'Thanks for my presents.'

She was changing. Her face had matured, her cheeks a little hollowed. 'Have you been eating properly, young lady? Has mum not been feeding you?' Milo pushed with a stab of concern.

'Yeah, Dad. Snacking on cereals, sandwich's, when I'm hungry. My fav' jeans are getting a bit tight, and Mum's always in the lab.'

'What about grandma? Have you done much with her?'

'No. She's busy all the time. And weird. So, I've hung in my room. At the stables. I've been fishing with Pops. Dad, watch me jump the biggy again, Mum doesn't believe me and you can back me up. I'm exercising fatty Melly in a minute. Do you know, the other day I tied her to the fence and cantered Ziggy round and round in front of her thinking it might remind her of how she used to be — give her a kick up the jacksy — but the lazy moo fell asleep. Can you believe it!' Jolie exclaimed in one excitable breath.

Jolie jumped Ziggy over a few fences. Milo cheered as she cantered past, pondering their unnecessary dread in sending her to boarding school; the routine and companionship had definitely boosted her confidence. Resting his arms on the wooden fencing, letting his chin drop onto linked fingers the mental exhaustion caught up with him, and any remaining physical strength drained. Imagining his counterparts probably doing the same. 'Let's hope it's worth it,' he muttered, closing his eyes; the moment broken by a sharp tap on his left shoulder from Jolie's riding crop.

'Daaaad. You're supposed to be watching me,' she scolded.

'Sorry Jools. I'm tired,' enthusing, 'You look very professional. Well done.'

'Right. Off to the lab' to find your mother. See you in an hour for daddy brunch. Sound like a plan?' he suggested — setting off at a slow jog; creating a reminder to have words with Marie: in his opinion Jolie wasn't eating enough.

'Can I have three honey coated waffles, scrambled eggs, and loads of crispy bacon, pleeease,' she squawked.

Milo offered a thumb's up, his attention drawn to a flurry of straw hurled from a stable door by their full-time ranch hand: Oliver. On cue, he stepped out, sweat gleaming on his forehead, patting down the fresh addition onto a loaded wheelbarrow. With his usual doffing hat action, threw Milo a greeting, which he acknowledged with a touch of his forehead.

Milo respected the healthy, muscular chap; actually, envious of his stress-free lifestyle. How hard can it be to manage a bit of land and a few animals? he considered, pitying his mother Betty: housekeeper and general dog's body for Donald's wife, Millicent. The poor woman earned every penny having to deal with the woman's constant mood swings.

'Ah. The water problem,' he surmised, stretching his

hamstrings outside the laboratory block, noticing a film of green moss had returned on the north-facing wall, adding a contrasting touch of nature he appreciated. Oliver, you better get cracking with the old pressure washer, he thought: knowing Donald hated to see the offending residue.

Striding towards the glistening tennis court sized pond on the opposite meadow; sickly blades of submerged grass, like anaemic alien fingers, moved in a current created by the breeze. The unnatural movement looked out of place, Milo felt, visualising the vast underground network beneath his feet. A huge resilient ant's nest bustling with concealed life.

Checking his pocket, realising he'd forgotten his swipe access card, Milo cussed: although it made no difference, he'd not been into the below ground laboratories for months. When challenged, Donald and Marie spouted their customary excuse — a temporary electrical glitch must be the cause. Milo didn't bother pushing the point, convinced they wanted to keep him in the dark about their secretive research.

Forcefully thrusting his bulk against the massive glass door: it didn't yield. 'It's Milo. Could someone let me in please?' He shouted through the intercom.

Trying the buzzer again after a few minutes, using his hands to block the sunlight, he saw no movement inside, picturing a distracted worker glimpse at the entry monitor, dismissing his request of no immediate concern, a crucial stage in their work taking precedence. 'Thanks,' Milo mouthed to the camera, turning towards the eastern section of meadow, to the observation room window where Pops recently moved.

Through gaps in the semi-closed vertical blinds; the gentle rise and fall of white bed linen confirmed Pops was sleeping.

Milo stopped himself tapping on the pane, pointless confusing the old fella, he'll bring Jolie after lunch to spend time with him.

'Now for my neglected daughter,' he mumbled, heading back to the cabin.

The instant warmth of their cosy abode embraced him. Kicking off his trainers, Milo strolled to the office, alarmed the laptop was missing from his desk. Assuming Donald — a quiet player in the events to come — received feedback Milo had played his part, he must have already taken it for disposal: as was the plan. Before the thought crossed his mind: maybe an opportunist thief helped themselves. Due to habitual complacence, he'd left the cabin unlocked.

'Best ring Millicent, she may have seen him with it,' he murmured, with the phone tucked under his chin, rummaging through the sparsely stocked fridge.

'Oh Milo. So glad you're back safely. Don't forget tonight, around seven, the little *soiree* for Crispin. Betty's preparing a finger buffet. Is that fine with you?'

'Yes. You know it isn't necessary. Thanks anyway, Millicent.' Milo pictured long suffering Betty getting her precise instructions. 'Is Donald there?' he continued.

'In the laboratory as usual, my dear. He mentioned he'd visit you this morning.'

'OK. Not to worry. See you later.'

On edge, after hanging up the phone, Milo looked over his shoulder, expecting to see a cashmere clad shape suddenly appear. The man tended to do that: shape shift, as if by magic. Monitor him when it's a full moon, Milo often joked with Marie.

Jolie barging in the back door, bringing a clatter of noise, closely followed by Scamp — one of the ranch dogs who never left her side — broke his unease.

'Something smells good,' she said, grabbing a lump of cheese from the chopping board.

'Get showered. It'll be ready in five. And chuck that smelly mutt out, you can save him a bit of bacon.'

Milo smiled at her scruffy image: baggy leggings, hair sticking out all over the place. Her new yellow t-shirt now smeared with green pony drool.

'What am I going to do with her?' he mumbled.

Their laughter filled brunch and playful washing up liquid bubble fight, made Milo laugh until his sides ached. Jolie's squeals were infectious. She was a joy to be around: her exuberant nature always gave him a boost. Excited by the racket, Scamp continually pawed at the wooden barrier blocking him from his soul mate. Dodging another cupful of bubbly water, Milo lifted the receiver of the trilling house phone. 'Sounds like you two are having fun. Save some laughter for me. I could do with cheering up,' Marie began.

'Hi Hun. How long will you be?' Milo ignored her tone — fending off Jools with his free hand.

'Not sure yet. Have you seen Pops?'

'I was there an hour ago. As expected, I couldn't get in. Why's the outer door locked, *again*?' Milo asked, his annoyance plain.

Silence ensued.

'Never mind. Let us in in ten please.'

'Yeah. OK,' Marie barked with irritation, before the phone went dead.

'Welcome back Milo,' he muttered, tickling Jolie who he'd pinned to the floor. 'Say it. The password to freedom.'

'Merci-merci-Muggins,' she succumbed in a fit of giggles.

Chapter Nine

'Is Lucy coming to my party?' Crispin blurted, his voice along with his hand of cards, trembling.

'Who's Lucy, Pops?' Milo asked, pouring a glass of wine for himself and Marie.

'He keeps saying that name. We assume he means Ruth, the new day nurse,' Marie answered, taking a sip of the ruby red fluid.

'Not her. She's cruel and pinches me,' Pops made his point with a gnarled grimace.

Marie threw him her look, adding, 'I'm sure it's accidental.'

'You would say that. You probably tell her to, so I behave. You both say I'm a nuisance.' Crispin starred coldly at her with a child-like pout.

'Whatever,' Marie hissed — raising her eyebrows in frustration.

'Lucy's a little under the weather Pops. She'll see you later. That's OK, isn't it?' Jolie consoled: as usual the one to calm the waters, Milo reflected, as Crispin began a habitual, ritualistic chant.

The haunting sound resonated. Milo studied his dealt hand, pretending not to hear.

'Oh God. Here we go. Does he *have* to do that, Mi?' Marie barked — scowling at Crispin, none the wiser eyes closed, he continued his wistful lament.

'Stop it, Pops. Come on. Let's get this over with. Everyone ready?' Milo dictated — finishing his wine in one gulp.

Chapter Ten

'I'm proud. Well done for seeing things through to the end,' Donald whispered in Milo's ear, by his side, clutching brandy glasses in front of a grand fireplace, before adding, 'I've dealt with the laptop.'

Milo didn't react.

He should trust the man, but his prickly manner and overt falseness: never made it easy. Neither was the evening turning out to be with uncomfortable silences and insinuation riddled conversation. After two hours of awkwardness, with Crispin and Jolie happy in their own world playing juvenile patter-cake games, Milo hinted they'd be on their way.

Marie's eager nod of agreement confirmed she felt the same.

Sentiments of apology, 'For not being particularly good company, and thank you for coming my dears,' accompanied Millicent's coat handing out. Helping Crispin with his, she gave him a lingering hug and a peck on the cheek.

Donald — ill at ease around senility — offered only a firm handshake, before Millicent escorted the old man down the front steps to join the others in their car.

'All aboard,' Milo announced, releasing the handbrake, rolling forward — jumping out of his skin in alarm, as Crispin croaked, 'There!' — followed by the whirr of motor noise as he opened the passenger door window.

Milo broke hard, watching his father lean out and point to the house; the warmth of his breath, combined with the chilled night air, creating a spooky ectoplasmic swirl around his wrinkled lips.

But no one stood where Crispin gesticulated with an outstretched finger. 'Lucy. You came. Come in here out of the cold,' he chided to the empty darkness — beckoning to a figure of his imagination.

'Don't worry. She wants to walk back Pops. I'll stay as well. I can sleep in the spare bed. It'll be fun. We can natter about my spirit guide,' Jolie comforted Crispin from the back seat — placing her small hand on his shoulder.

Milo looked behind to share his bafflement with Marie: but met with her puzzled expression — her line of sight settling on Donald and Millicent's faces, eerily lit by sunken floor lighting mouths agape, conveying horrified recognition.

The hairs on Milo's arms rose.

'Come on, Pops. Let's get you warm and tucked up,' Jolie suggested.

Once again, Milo was grateful her perceptive old soul had taken charge, picturing her: an emotional crutch for girls at her school. His eyes brimmed with the tears he'd tried controlling as the purpose of the evening's *soiree* hit him hard.

Through water blurred vision, Milo drove towards the twinkling lights of the laboratory block, allowing errant droplets to run down his cheeks.

Having lit scented candles, banked up the fire, and poured large Pinot Noirs, Milo fell into a sofa embrace beside Marie; cradling wine, warming their feet, enjoying the stillness of the cabin without Jolie clattering around. 'Bliss,' he muttered, sipping room temperature burgundy.

'Not sure what that was all about Mi? I've never seen them so unsettled. And, what is that smell?' Marie scrunched up her nose.

'Vanilla and cinnamon,' he read from cardboard packaging on the side table.

'No. The candles are nice. There's an undertone of—' She didn't finish.

'Washing up liquid, damp dog, and unclean child. And Jools keeps sneaking smelly Scamp into her rather stinky bedroom. Seriously Marie, she should eat more. I know you've been up to your eyes, but she needs nourishing. She's growing fast, and from the lack of stuff in the fridge, no shopping's been done for days. And have you seen the state of her fingernails? The girls gone feral,' Milo scolded.

'You're right Mi. Don't worry. Things will be quieter during her next school break, and you'll be around. We can ride. Or go to the lodge,' Marie answered, staring vacantly into the flickering flames.

Milo pulled her close.

Resting their heads together, they continued enjoying the wine — mesmerised by the dancing blaze.

'That's it. I've waited long enough. Professor Milo Brockman get your trousers off, I want to carry out a rather pleasant experiment in front of this fire,' Marie blurted, making him spill splashes of red onto his jeans.

Milo took no persuading.

Chapter Eleven

The screech of the great horned owl awoke Milo with a start. 'Why do they have to be so bloody loud,' he whispered. But it wasn't the nocturnal bird — something else had roused him: shuffling noises coming from the back of the cabin made a surge of adrenaline course through his veins.

Marie, still in a deep slumber, softly blowing on the sofa, partially covered by the blanket he'd draped over her. 'Nothing wakes you,' Milo mumbled — pulling the fallen edge of the soft fabric over her shoulders.

Taking the poker from the hearth, creeping to the kitchen, he froze on the spot when the white plastic handle of the back door waggled as someone tested the lock. 'I can hear you. I've got a weapon,' he shouted — flicking on the light ready to strike the first movement he saw with the ornamental iron rod; his heart leapt into his mouth when it flew open.

'Oh, for goodness' sake, Jolie. I nearly clonked you with this. Is everything OK?' Milo vented in panic, before noticing Crispin outside in his wheelchair covered by a blanket.

'Hi Pops. Do you need a doctor?'

'He's fine. It's just way too spooky down there. I couldn't sleep. Pops could, and he snores. I've laid there for hours listening to creaks and groans, and Pops,' Jolie said, throwing him a look.

'Little Madam, why wake him and drag him up here too?' Milo chastised — stepping into the cold to wheel his confused father in the warmth.

'It's sooo dark Dad. I didn't find a torch and felt it best safety in numbers. If a wolf was lurking, I planned shoving Pops' wheelchair at it, giving us time to run away. ... I brought Scamp as our guard dog.'

With the mention of his name, the scruffy mutt appeared from the darkness, head hung low, wagging the tip of his tail for acceptance.

'What's going on?' Marie, wrapped in the blanket, mumbled from the living room doorway.

'It's fine Hun. No drama. Jools freaked out and dragged Pops back here.'

'What *is* the time,' she asked — wearily rubbing at her eyes.

'Four o'clock. Past the witching hour,' Jolie answered with a wide mouthed yawn.

'I'm off to bed then. And don't forget to lock up, Mi.'

Marie shuffled away, trailing an edge of fleecy fabric.

Huddled on the floor, in front of the fires dying embers, Jolie sipped her hot juice drink. 'Sorry I woke everyone, and for being a dingbat,' she said, guiltily.

'Quite funny really Jools. Pops can't run fast, could have ended up as wolf supper—'

'No. He'd have been fine. You'd have saved him. You always make things right,' she interrupted in a purr.

Milo grinned.

'Dad ... the lab' is scary. You hear all sorts of noises ... Has Mum got monkeys in there? Because I'm sure I heard screeching, and something stroked my hair. Honest to God. And Pops' rocking chair rocked itself too. I swear. I saw it in the moonlight, moving. That didn't freak me out much and make me nearly wet myself. And I smelt an odd, herbal tea kind of smell. I know I wasn't imagining it. Look, my hands are still shaking. I think Pops has been seeing things. I believe him, Dad. He says Lucy reads children's stories to him at night.'

Milo watched Jolie out the corner of his eye as she regaled events, realising her genuine fear.

'It's your overactive imagination getting the better of you, young lady,' he chided — comfortingly rubbing her arm.

'Come on, we need sleep. We've got to get going early to make the best of the weekend. I bet I catch more fish than you and beat you at bowling.'

'No, you won't. My next school history project will be about the ranch, and who's Lucy? Woooohhhhh,' Jolie blabbered — waving her arms around for effect.

'You're on the sofa, vivid imagination girl.' Milo played light of her worrying re-collections: for the best, he decided.

'It felt like someone walked over my grave earlier at Mums. Do you think your dad does see stuff we've put down to his senility? It could be just us who can't, because we lack the ability?' Marie offloaded to the darkness, as Milo slipped into bed beside her.

'Perhaps? He's a spiritual man. Not religious, but follows the Seven Philosophies. Do you remember, the Commandments for a Native American in a frame on his wall? I meant to bring it when we moved him. His dad was part Swan Creek, Black River Chippewa, one of those unrecognized tribes; it's natural Pops would follow the old ways. Pity more don't, with their respect for the planet. Right. Sleep,' Milo said, in a noisy yawn — pulling Marie towards him for a spoon's embrace, settling their souls.

Chapter Twelve

Maryville, Canada

'How long's Dad staying?' Jolie chirped, frantically waving through the closed car window to Milo and Crispin silhouetted against the bungalow's hallway light.

'Five days, Jools. He's got some stuff to deal with. Why?'

'Do you think we'll see Pops alive again? I don't think so,' she stated matter-of-factly. 'The other night, he told me about my strong spirit guide, Neville. No Nathaniel, that's it. Pops reckons it was him who slammed the door when those bully girls started picking on me and I shouted at them. Whatever. It worked. They leave me alone now. Did I tell you about Mary Fraser? She tried committing suicide. I do know what that is, even though you keep whispering about Pops and his attempts. I know people sometimes just have enough of life. Anyway, she climbed above our classroom. She was supposed to be sick, and we only realised she was up there because a roof tile nearly fell on Mr Parkinson's head and we ran out and saw her Mickey Mouse slippers hanging over the guttering. ... She didn't jump Mum, and two of the horrible girls got expelled. It was quite funny really. She laughed afterwards. That's good isn't it. Why did Pop's take Storm?'

'Not sure, Jools. Probably because he's never liked him, or me come to that. And he didn't take him. The silly old fool just went for a gallop. No harm done, other than Storm bit the gas station bloke before we caught him. Upset me, I was livid. Still, all water under the bridge.'

'Blimey Mum. Is this what it's like to rally? You drive much faster than Dad.'

'Don't tell him. I'll get in trouble again.'

Marie glanced at her daughter — eyes fixed on the road

39

ahead, grinning from ear to ear, gripping part of the front seat and grab handle to steady herself. Although playing light of her need for speed, Marie wanted to get back, concerned about Donald's activities in the laboratory in her absence; but reminding herself it was her duty to be with Milo, support him through the weekend: his last few days with Crispin.

'What did you enjoy most with Pops, Mum? I enjoyed the fishing. I love the way the small fish shimmer in the sunlight on the line, then disappear in a flash when I put them back in the water. I'm going to paint that. I wonder if there's any silver coloured in the art room. Can you actually buy it, Mum? Jolie babbled. 'Did you see Pops' picture of a woman he drew for me? It's in the back somewhere. ... He says it's Lucy. Could be I suppose? Visiting nanna's grave made me cry. The verse on her tombstone: 'Beloved wife. A day of rest begun.' That's so sweet. Why do some people get buried, and some cremated?' Jolie continued to prattle.

'Their choice Jools. Sketching bison in the park and getting drunk at Pops' local with his old mates,' Marie eventually answered.

'Yeah. That was funny. I've decided, I'm never trying alcohol. It makes people funnier, but then sadder. I'll stick to strawberry milkshakes and apple juice.'

Marie said smiling, 'Good idea. I've seen what it can do to your insides. It's not pleasant.'

While stuck in a queue of traffic, Marie studied Jolie — who'd fallen asleep with her head resting against the window — everything from her fresh air induced enviable skin; to her freckles, tousled brown locks, and pony inflicted bruises on her arms made her a bundle of vibrancy. And she was developing fast. She needed new tops, and bigger bras, Marie realised, deciding an internet shopping spree was necessary, trying to remember the last time she'd wandered around a shopping centre: something she hated.

The traffic flow still stationary, gave Marie ample time to

study her own sallow complexion in the rear-view mirror. Even after a weekend in the sunshine, her skin looked ghostly white. All those hours in the lab' aren't doing me any favours in the looks department, she thought, reminding herself to buy vitamin D supplements.

Tasked by Milo to broach the plan for Crispin as she drove Jolie back to school, Marie knew he'd be annoyed she'd chosen not to; feeling it best let events take their course. She'd hear soon enough. Her recent fun memories of Pops were good ones. Marie was glad of that, she mulled — nearing the main accommodation wing, all red brick and imposing.

Gently shaking Jolie's leg, 'Wake up, Jools,' Marie whispered.

'Whoa. That was quick,' she yawned — ruffling the sleep flattened side of her hair.

Returning Jolie to school always made Marie reflect on what she'd missed as a child; having loved to have boarded, to have got away from home and had fun times with girls her own age.

Gathering Jolie's things from the boot, memories of getting off the bus, lonely dawdles up the ranch drive would come to mind. Her love of reading and beautiful ponies — these two things helped her through a sad childhood.

Loaded with Jolie's bags, Marie watched her skip ahead, recalling: 'That Saturday', as she'd named it: the day two classmates had been invited to tea. Having methodically planned the event, Donald's foul mood had soured Marie's joy — remembering the sight of her mum crying, and poor Betty telling her, '... It's best your friends don't come today, my dear.'

With a struggle, making it to the top of the oak staircase, Marie blew from the weight she was carrying. Plodding along the echoey corridor to Jolie's dormitory, imagining her younger self, out of sight, hiding on her parent's landing listening to her dad shouting about a funding problem: 'Can't afford prying eyes and strangers around the place.' Millicent reprimanding him: 'You're over reacting Donald. That girl needs normality.'

That comment hurt Marie the most; was the one she'd never forget, having made her feel like an object — a desk or a chair — not like a cherished daughter.

Dumping Jolie's heavy weekender bag on top of her cartoon horse adorned quilt, Marie focussed on her tulip lipped, juvenile mouth moving, knowing she wasn't absorbing last-minute pony instructions.

'OK. Got that. Get unpacked and head for supper. And tie your hair back,' Marie called, as Jolie skipped away to greet her friend, whose socked feet jiggled in time to music off the end of her bed.

Such a perfect childhood, Marie again reflected.

Chapter Thirteen

Marie relished the thought of not making conversation, or worrying about anyone else's emotional needs for the remainder of her journey back to Red Brook. But — encapsulated in the solitude the car provided — her conscience kept reminding her she had to confront those niggling doubts muddying her temporary freedom.

In the grand scheme of things, Marie knew her research *was* playing a crucial role; but to help her make sense of her place in all of it, she needed to share more with Milo. She trusted him completely; for her own sanity would welcome his impartial views and knew he'd never divulge anything that may put them in danger.

Reacting to the bright glow of taillights, she broke sharply; the momentum making her head rebound off the seat restraint. 'Ah,' she moaned — rubbing at her neck.

Stuck in a queue, realising the sudden jolt fractured her dam of worry — with no one to judge her — Marie dropped her steel guard, allowing her pent-up emotions to flow and wept for the first time in an age: about her sad memories; Pops; Milo; her mother, lately so forlorn; what she'd seen, and heard, over the past few months in the laboratory. Sobbing for her own well-being, wondering, 'Why didn't she show her feelings? Why did an instinct dictate she shut people out? Why was she so odd, having to always think about what she should do for her family, when for others, it came naturally?' These character flaws were damaging her relationship with Milo and Jolie.

Marie harshly assessed herself, crawling the SUV forward, keeping pace with the traffic, deciding — that's it — enough of the old Marie; she wasn't a lost cause; had recognised her faults, and would change. Finally, having clarity to her future.

Back at the ranch, craving Storms calming magic — like her ponies as a child, always comforting and consoling with their soft muzzles nuzzling her pockets for treats — she wandered to his stable, recalling how she'd often fall asleep in her favourite equine companions stall, waking hours later covered with a blanket. Either Betty or Winston would have made sure she was warm.

Poor Winston: her gentle giant of a bodyguard. No one spoke about his Downs Syndrome; his soft, caring soul was all that mattered to Marie. Millicent warned her he wouldn't live long. Marie remembered her short-lived sadness, thinking: oh well he's gone, like they told her, as she'd skipped away from Betty in tears after breaking the news he'd died.

'Hi fella,' Marie spoke in a soothing voice, flicking on the stable light, offering Storm a mint on her palm.

Waking with a start — lifting his head with a snort — the powerful animal, recognising her, relaxed, welcoming the attention of Marie burying her face into his luxuriant black mane.

Stroking his muscular shoulders, 'Tomorrow, my friend, we'll go for a blow-out round the cross-country circuit,' Marie's voice muffled by his bulk, before the comforting moment was lost, noticing white smears of antiseptic cream on his dark coat covering fresh cuts on his nose and knees: a tell-tale sign he'd freaked out in his stable.

This had happened before and meant one thing: they'd used the helicopter landing pad.

Marie recalled over-hearing comments: 'It's Utah—' as someone handed a mobile to Donald, gathering another move imminent: the main reason she'd wanted to get back sooner.

'Bloody Donald,' Marie muttered, knowing over the weekend Philip Oldman, and his team from the National Brain Institute, must have collected their latest Graphene guinea pig.

Donald having timed the pickup just right — away from her doubting, judgemental gaze.

Chapter Fourteen

Maryville, Canada

Milo sat with his father, enjoying the warmth from his tiny log fire, chatting, drinking ale, reminiscing through old family photographs. He'd jog Crispin's memory who the little boy in blue shorts, arm in plaster was: Milo, aged nine, after falling from the neighbour's wall. The pretty lady in a red and white polka dot dress, legs dangling in the water: his wife Juliet.

Turning to face Milo, with a penetrating stare the black voids of Crispin's eyes seemed to awaken; a brief moment when his trapped soul seemed to claw its way from a narrowing tunnel of hope. So sad, Milo thought.

Closing those failing eyes, Crispin began singing, *Heya-Hee*: the song to stop the rain, one of the easiest for him to remember.

Milo felt his shoulders relax in reflex to the reverberating sacred melody.

Satisfied his father was ready for his next journey; Milo had no reservations about the scheduled event for Tuesday.

Lulled to sleep by his own ancient chant, Crispin's chin dropped to his chest. Milo took the blanket from the back of the brocade armchair, wrapping it around the man's wasted, bony limbs, noticing the sharp creases in his classic fawn trousers added the only definition to the fabric.

Carefully placing his veiny hands, splashed with age spots, on top of the warm tartan cloth, Milo went through to the kitchen to get a colder beer.

Encouraging the fridges tatty compact door shut with a shove of his foot, convinced it was the same ageing appliance he remembered from his childhood; they made things to last back then, Milo pondered, looking around the worn, faded room.

Pulling a chair from under a cluttered pine table, brought back memories of hasty pre-school breakfasts, cereals with full cream milk he'd rush to eat before running to catch the school bus. He could still see his mum, stood at the sink, scrubbing a greasy pan, the motion making her round bottom wobble; flowery blue frills of her apron, like fluted clown's ears, peeping from either side of her thighs.

Remembering he had to ring Josh, Milo plucked his mobile from the back pocket of his jeans. 'Hi Bud. How's things?' he asked, upbeat.

'Fine thanks. Listen, I'm glad you've called. I've had encouraging news. Been talking with Tom Wood, you remember him? The professor from Harvard whose working in collaboration with NIBIE.'

Milo didn't answer.

'Word is we've secured the Robobee funding for next year. Just the i's to dot with the grant, and we're on track. Until we find the cause of this Colony Collapse Disorder, at least the right steps are being taken to help these crucial little guys. ... You still at your folk's place? No WIFI, can't have the latest stats—? Worst case, two million and counting. Granted, it's a drop in the ocean, but by Friday, who knows?' Josh paused.

Milo remained quiet, knowing his friend was on a roll.

'The icing on the cake though Mi. Pens decided to help the cause.'

Milo caught the emotional tremor in his voice.

'She won't take pain relief, wants to go out on a positive and thought why not send a high-profile message? ... Mi, it's not sunk in yet. Don't get sentimental on me.'

'Christ. Not sure what to say. All good news. That doesn't sound right, but you know what I mean. So, the big six have delivered. Must admit I had my doubts. Shows how well distribution logistics can work. ... We'd love to hear from her. No pressure. I'll ring Wednesday evening. Give her a hug from us. Take care my friend.'

Milo ended their conversation became too maudlin or incriminating.

Chapter Fifteen

London, England

The sheet under Chris's cheek was damp with saliva. To stop his head spinning, he again closed his eyes, stretching an arm to the other side of the bed, praying it was vacant: groaning when his fingers met a warm, podgy leg. Oh, shit. You've fallen off the wagon. You fucking Muppet, he thought, deploying the other hand to prise his mobile from the tacky bedside table.

Needing to know what bloody day it was: the device was dead — devoid of life — the same as he felt inside.

'You damned idiot,' he whispered — screwing up his nose — sheepishly looking around the room, surmising he'd ended up in a cheap dump, with filthy carpets, curtains, basically everything had seen better days. And it was rank and airless — with an odour of rotten onions, or fruit: he wasn't quite sure of the unpleasant source.

Turning his attention to his bed mate: a bush of bleached blond hair attached to dark roots peeped from the top of the duvet. With a kick to his crutch, the memories flooded back.

'Oh, fucking Christ. I didn't?' he muttered into the firm mattress, reasoning at least what's visible *has* hair, isn't bald as a coot like bisexual Steve: last months, unplanned passion mate. It's bloody Stella, must be. She was lurking around yesterday evening at Doug's boozer. She's always trying it on with me: probably with every drunk bloke in the hope of getting laid, he reflected.

'Why didn't the plonker stop me,' he mumbled, picturing the landlords 'pie-hole' laughing at him, pissed as a fart, getting dragged out his hovel by the elated old whore.

I'll get my own back: report him for late-night bloody lock -

ins. Bastard, Chris silently mouthed, as other memories emerged from the fog of his mind. Downing disgusting shots; sliding off a bar stool and banging his chin; passing out, coming to on a wooden floor with crisps stuck to his cheek next to a pair of ugly feet in tatty black stilettos. Then being dragged by the arm up steps that stunk of piss to the sound of thumping music, before getting plonked onto a shabby leather sofa by a crocheted blanket smelling of baby sick. Oh, and singing Happy Birthday to someone called Steve. Vomiting outside a kebab shop was the last of Chris's sordid recollections.

Some night, he thought, using his hands to explore his body, finding the tough fabric of his jeans reassuring. And, from which, concluded he must have passed out before he'd given her one. 'Phew,' he sighed.

Stealthily slipping from under the stale smelling, black and grey skyscraper printed bedding to the floor, staying on all fours, he crawled to, what he hoped, was a bathroom, avoiding discarded shoes, empty cigarette packets, and a very hairy dog-less dog bed. Perhaps it'd died? What wouldn't, living here for long, he thought.

With the gentlest of clicks, locking the fist dented door behind him, he listened: no sounds. He'd made it without waking Stella, the nymphomaniac psycho hose beast.

Using the stained loo seat to pull himself upright, looking at his wretched image in the smudgy mirror, hung above an untidy vanity unit, 'Christopher fucking Manning. What the fuck have you done, *again,* you bloody idiot,' he murmured, to the puffy eyed, bruised chinned half-wit, starring back at him on this pain in the arse of a morning, before vodka tasting bile rose in his throat, exploded from his mouth, joining the congealed soapy water already in the sink. A pink G-string comically floating to the surface, its discoloured crutch twisting in the unsavoury brew, reminding him of its wearer.

Chris shut his eyes to block the unpleasant image, wondering whether his retching had woken 'The Beast'. Luckily, still no sound came from behind the damaged barrier.

Pulling the blackened chain, releasing the plug, slowly turning on the tap flow washed away the revolting sludge. A scrunch of pink elastic settled in the outlet, keeping effluent scuds in its folds.

Sloshing his face under running water, squeezing a blob of toothpaste from a screwed-up tube, using his index finger to freshen up his stale mouth. A loud grumble then resonated from his bowels, signalling the need for an urgent dump.

Going through his noisy motions, giving his manhood the once over: it appeared unchanged: no dried sexual fluids or ED rings were apparent. It just hung — limply.

'Phew. Lucky escape this time. Knob head,' he chided, focussing on his immediate aim — get out of this shit hole avoiding Ever Ready Stella.

Goading himself into action, surmising all that hanging around in night clubs must have taken its toll on her hearing, should give him the advantage. And she had to be knocking on a bit. He remembered at least three of his school mates lost their virginity thanks to her.

But could he leave the pungent toilet bowl of excrement for her to find? Sussing the moment: yes, unacceptable risk of waking her by flushing. Serve her right, he thought, washing his hands, gulping down more water straight from the tap, running over his departure options.

Out the bathroom window was a possibility.

He'd fit through, and there was a flat roof below with lumps of loo paper; a hairbrush and a nappy. 'But bugger. My mobiles still in her lair,' Chris mumbled to his less dishevelled reflection in the splashed mirror. He couldn't risk leaving his media contacts behind: far too sensitive. He'd no option but to slink out the front way.

Here goes. Deep breathe. Not a good idea in here, he realised, gagging.

Gingerly tip-toeing, picking up his phone and clothing en route, Chris surveyed the off-white, nicotine stained door, cussing, 'Where the fuck's the bloody key?' Running his eye around the framework and scratched bottom half covered in dried dog snot. 'Ah-ha,' he mumbled, noticing one on a pile of curled up Hello magazines in a corner.

Tentatively trying to slide the bolts in their housing, the resulting harsh rasp made his heart sink. Oh Crap, he thought.

'Where are you sneaking off to Big Boy,' came a croaky voice.

'I didn't realise the time. Sorry. I really have to get going,' he said, struggling to wiggle the locks free.

'That key in your 'and ain' t the right one, luv. Don't y'er fancy a coffee and a cuddle before you bugger off?' Stella cackled, erupting into throaty coughs.

She must have flicked on the TV as she'd watched his befuddlement, Chris went on alert as BBC news presenter reported, '*Further breaking news following the events of the last few days...*' making him stop his frantic escape attempt and turn to face his tormentor.

'OK. Just a coffee. But no hanky-panky. I've got an itchy cock, to be honest. Want a peek? Perhaps you've a tube of cream that'll do the job,' he chuckled.

'Cheeky blighter. What do y'er think I am? A knocking shop, Madam. You're no use to me. You might as well sod off then,' she scolded, lighting a cigarette.

Chris watched the white object bounce up and down, clinging to her lips as she chastised him. 'Fine by me. But I need to watch this,' he scoffed — focusing on the grubby portable TV perched on an oak dining chair at the end of her bed.

'Suit yourself. Pass that ashtray,' she snapped — aiming a plume of smoke at the ceiling, gesticulating towards a coffee table.

Chris was appalled by the sight of her battling to pull a baby pink negligee over her head, before manhandling saggy breasts into place, hoping this disturbing scene *would* stay with him as a cautious reminder to sort his shit out, having, once again, compromised his occasionally driven nature to follow scoops.

Keeping his eyes glued to the tiny TV screen, Chris robotically obliged, passing the full of fag ends glass object in her direction. Bugger. What on earth has kicked off? And how much time have I lost? he thought, absorbing the news; knowing he'd been out of circulation for two, maybe three days, having pissed off his boss and been told to get from under his feet.

'According to spokespersons for the British, American and Canadian Medical Associations, the recent events, which have gone viral on all social media sites, were part of a planned, synchronised stand against the archaic ending of life laws still enforced in some countries. The people involved were willing participants. In some cases, left video diaries as evidence it was their choice and they were of sound mind.

For those of you who may not be aware, a mass, international, medically supervised suicide, or "peaceful voluntary release programme" the term used by those who agreed to be part of this protest by action, has taken place over the past few days, with reports of more coming forward who also wish to find release and be part of this terminal demonstration of human will. It is reported, The Participants, as they are being referred, their families, care staff and GP's had been secretly selected, counselled and given full information on the drug assisted options open to them. We've learnt Nembutal, manufactured in Denmark by the pharmaceutical giant Beckglax-Proctor, was provided at cost only, and administered either in the normal liquid medium, or multi-pill form, now called The Release Pill. It is believed the current figure of successful suicidal deaths from this, it is thought, private pharmaceutical and medical science backed and led programme, is near four million people. So far, the Crown Prosecution Service has declined to comment, pending further investigations, but speculation is with the hundreds of thousands of doctors and medical workers who cooperated, it could take years to prosecute and worldwide health organisations would grind to a halt if arrests were presently authorised. Given the numbers involved, the question being asked is: How was this movement kept secret? And is the statement now made by thousands, strong enough to open serious debate by governments and church leaders to reform the present laws?

It would appear the worldwide population has spoken with action and is demanding change. Many are speculating the operation received back door government funding. With so many health services and age-related illnesses crippling the NHS, and its worldwide counterparts, were these souls coerced into taking their own lives as a way of reducing the global population, and by so doing, decreasing human carbon emissions? ... Some of you may find the following footage disturbing, as you will see people being administered the drugs prior to their deaths and immediately after they pass away.'

'Holy crap,' Chris blurted — dropping his head into his palms, rubbing his temples — as the newsreader announced, *'The Secretary of State for Health and the Justice Secretary will be live on air at three to give their joint statement. Please join us then for their views on this unprecedented event. Now over to the regional newsrooms for your local news and Bob for the weather.'*

'Ave you seen your mum lately. 'Per'aps she's one of them that did it?' Stella squawked.

Chris threw her a scowl. 'Can I use your phone? It's important,' he asked — refraining to look her in the eye.

'Sorry love. I ain't got one. Dropped it down the 'lavvie' the other day. It's fucked,' she clucked.

'God, you're foul,' he hissed at the soap opera script debauchee — checking his pockets again for his dead phone, wallet and keys.

Being thrown the right door key, he tackled the ageing blockade to his freedom with renewed vigour.

Chapter Sixteen

Chris, overwhelmed with trepidation, tore down the steps for the underground to get to his office at The Daily Reporter, jumping on the tube train thinking, Christ almighty, what's going on? Was he playing a role in a black comedy? That's what it seemed like. Was he actually awake? I bet awful bloody Stella has played a prank showing me a B-rated DVD. Probably gets a kick out of alarming her conquests. Most of them stoned out of their skulls wouldn't realise, and she'd have the last laugh. But the newscaster was real enough: he'd met him at a book launch recently, Chris pondered, trying to stay calm, convincing himself it had been a cruel joke, reasoning, I expect she's back there laughing her disgusting baggy drawers off.

Looking around at the other tube travellers, deciding to test the truth with a throwaway remark. The woman sitting by his side would do. 'It's unbelievable what's happened, don't you think?' Chris broached — hoping her reaction would be: 'Excuse me. What do you mean?' To lift his spirits.

'It's been a surprise. Long overdue. Do you know, my poor granddad has been saying for months he's had enough. He can't feed himself, wears a nappy. It's disgraceful not being able to help someone end their misery. He's suffering. Says he wants that pill. I say good luck to them, and their families. In my opinion, they've done the right thing.'

'My thoughts too,' Chris answered, mortified, thinking, Christ, it's real. And I'm seriously in the shit.

'Where the Jesus H have you been? You complete fucking wanker,' was Ian Pendleton's expletive, as Chris barged into his editor's office.

'Sorry Boss. I've had the flu. And I *was* off at your suggestion. I forgot to charge my phone. My neighbour told me what'd happened when she brought me soup because I looked so ill,' Chris breathlessly lied.

'Liar. Why do you stink of booze? And you've not washed, waster,' Pendleton shouted. 'Anyway, you're here now. Get your arse to this Golden Leaves Care place and the other one near it. It's in this brief,' he said — slinging a bundle across his desk. 'The juicier places are being covered by your, on the ball, motivated colleagues. See if you can get their doctors to comment. I want a half decent, above the fold within 24. Got it. Good.'

'Right on it, Boss.' Chris backed out the door — looking down, wondering whether he'd left spare clothes in his locker. Coffee, eggs, soiled nappies, bastard blokes pee, or something worse often came your way, so you had to be prepared. All in a day's investigative journalism, he reflected.

Showered and smart — Chris was en route to his assignment in twenty minutes flat. Petrol blue wording on a sign, poking from a well-trimmed stubby hedge, confirmed he was at the Golden Leaves Care Home.

'You're in luck. The Manager told us, no comment, to any of you vultures. I can only think she felt sorry for you, your grandmother being one of those who departed?' the care assistant Beryl, said with dismissive sarcasm, before marching him along a low-ceilinged corridor.

Chris avoided old people's homes. He found them disturbing; hating the combination of acrid medicinal smells; unstable souls scuttling around, or corpse like in chairs, enthralled by the sight of youthful demeanour; the envy apparent in their rheumy washed-out eyes.

'Give me a release pill, rather than end up in here,' he muttered, striding past a gang of them, unable to hold their gaze, focussing instead on how much static electricity could be generated between the thighs of large lady's sheathed in nylon? Judging from the swish swishing sound coming from Beryl's — quite a lot, he mused. Perhaps he was onto something. Maybe Brad, his geeky mate, could invent a device to charge mobile phones while on the move. Conductive fibres in the hosiery. A port at the waist band. They could get funding from an entrepreneurial programme where you give a pitch, Chris reflected for distraction.

'This is Albert. He was friends with Robert Ackroyd who chose to leave us,' Beryl stated, signalling with the flattened palm of her hand to a frail man sat alone.

'Hello there. How's things? That chair looks comfy. I bet you're one for the ladies with those blue eyes. I'm Chris. Do you fancy a chat if you've got the time?'

'No. This chair is bloody uncomfortable, and what else have I got to do other than watch old bags shuffling around in flipping slippers. I'll tell you what you want to know, if you bring me a crispy portion of fresh bloody cod and chips,' he retorted.

'I think we'll get on just fine, my friend,' Chris said — smiling at the poor, abandoned old bugger.

Chapter Seventeen

'For Christ' sake, hasn't anyone got anything better! This is a major bloody event. Surely one of you losers can offer more than this tripe!' an incensed Ian Pendleton bellowed — throwing articles around his chaotic desk. 'The other rags will be crawling all over this. I don't want to resort to churnalism, so get me some meat folks. Not this predictable crap. ... It's taken a lot of organising. Someone must be willing to spill the beans on who masterminded this bloody mess. Someone must have doubts. What about the funeral homes, insurance companies, solicitors? Get their spin on how they'll cope ... did none of your grannies taken the plunge?'

One reporter left the room in tears.

'Oh crap. Julie. Sorry. Come back.'

'She'll be all right. I'll find her in a minute. Her auntie ... well, died,' Chris informed him.

Pendleton shrugged his shoulders with a who gives a shit expression. 'I want splash. I know door stepping is pants, but this is a fantastic HI opportunity. Raise skeletons, excuse the pun, and bring me objective, investigative fucking journalism to fill our front page with compelling strap lines, make our competitors look pathetic. Work in packs, but on the record. Keep your minds open for any tenuous links. There could be a trend. You can beg, steal or borrow, but no hacking. That's an order. I'm giving you another twelve. Chris. Stay put. The rest of you — fuck off. You're on a mission to save your arses!'

Jumping from their chairs — a few stumbled as they left.

Being lazy at heart, Chris found most of his assignments lame: they didn't fire his lack-lustre rockets. Already in the poo for his constant deadline surfing, most of his stuff was spiked: basically, he was a crap journalist. Sinking in his seat, expecting the worst. 'I'll clear my locker,' he mumbled.

'What? You fucking idiot. No. I like where you're going with this piece of shit.' From Pendleton, this was a compliment, Chris thought with relief.

'This nurse from the home. You think she's legit?' asked a calmer, enthused Ed.

'She started a blog with a huge following. Loads of nursing staff, NHS and private, are coming out of the woodwork with their experiences. Now, according to her data, there were seventy per cent more life support switch off's, and the 'gyny' wards are booked solid for D & C's because that deformity virus has women scared shit-less their kid won't be right ... If you're looking for a trend, this could be it. I don't believe one word those lying politicians say, there's no cover up, or government funding, that's bullshit. I think it's a conspiracy to reduce the population by fair means, or foul. I mean, what better form of birth control, at your own risk, take the chance, normal or not for the rest of its life. And who's to say the docs haven't encouraged all these abortions and killing off's? Patients will believe them they're likely to have a phlid' kid, or granddad only has two weeks to live.' Chris eagerly made his point, noticing the veins in Pendleton's neck subside: a good sign, he thought — folding his arms — relaxing back in the bright red plastic chair.

Silence prevailed as Pendleton contemplated.

Chris realised in his attempt to impress with his over the top theories, the penny had dropped: he could be onto something.

'I'm surprised no one's blabbed for the dough by now. ... Get solid proof, Chris. Real news, not a personal take.' Pendleton massaged the back of his portly neck, saying, 'You met this nurse for the first time at the old people's home. Is that right? Or, is she a new nursey conquest?'

God. He can read me like a book. Chris grinned at his boss,

59

answering, 'Yeah. She gave me her number. Told me she needed to share her findings and wanted to know if she could trust me as she's picked up more intel'.'

'OK. If she wants money, I'll authorise a monkey. What about your toilet bloke? What's he given you?'

'Bog? A few urinal dropped names from that big-wig conference in Paris. Said their VIP loos had great WIFI. He's credible. Speaks six languages, doesn't miss a trick ... I went to uni' with him, in case you're interested. Bought a flat in Amsterdam and a yacht in Spain, it pays him well enough. Plus, my Danish contact has a way in at the death drug manufacturing place. Bear with me Boss, this time, I won't let you down. But I'll need two economies to Canada, as I've a gut about one of Bogs snippets.'

Ian Pendleton winked.

Chapter Eighteen

Kampala, Uganda

'Today will be a good day,' Okoth Nalule muttered — waving to his wife stood in the doorway of their little tin roofed hut. Okoth's beautiful butterfly, wearing her favourite turquoise blue and lime green dress, with their three-year-old son Akia, standing between her legs, beaming like a cherub. His two precious gifts — vibrant splashes of life and colour in stark contrast to the dark interior of the soon to be vacated mud dwelling. Last night the professor let him drive the institutes Nissan Navarra home ready for his house move: a rare treat he was enjoying, feeling vain pride slowly cruising through his neighbourhood.

Although given a few days off, Okoth felt it only right he touched base with the professor at the institute, also giving him an excuse to spend more time using the car. Baingama would be getting their things together, saying her goodbyes. He'd only get in the way, he reasoned — crawling in low gear past his neighbours' shabby homes.

Unable to hide his elation; their envious stares didn't worry him. He'd gone to school with these people: these under achievers who'd wasted their education. Okoth had been top of his class, often praised: 'Your Oxford English is perfect.'

Slowing to negotiate ruts in the red earth tracks outside his brother's hut, Okoth's body swaggered in unison with the chassis, as he shouted, 'Mayanga. Come look. I'm an important man. You should shake my hand it will bring you good luck.'

Okoth grinned at Mayanga waving back from his crude, frameless window.

In the wing mirror, seeing the small running figure of Mayanga's daughter, Sabiti, in a bright orange dress, giggling and calling after him — waving to her, continuing his showy crawl, elbow resting on the door frame, throwing self-assured greetings to those who knew him.

How quickly his fortunes had changed: promoted to chief research assistant with a hefty pay rise. Given an interest free loan for their new home by the professor, all within the last three weeks. 'Was he dreaming?' he checked, pinching himself.

Okoth's only concern *was* the professor. They'd become his surrogate family — his only family. And he'd been working longer hours; was subdued. Okoth often found him asleep, slumped at his desk in two days' worn clothing.

'Perhaps he's ill and wants to keep it a secret?' He was thinner: paler. Perhaps his work is troubling him?' Okoth wondered, just knowing they were: '... helping the community fight diseases.' Recalling the Professor's spiel.

Okoth never felt comfortable asking too many questions while they worked. He couldn't always follow the professor's explanations, more than happy to do as instructed. He knew his limits.

Approaching the centre of Kampala, the volume of traffic built before grinding to an inevitable halt. Stuck in the capital's notorious commuter jam, Okoth ate a bag of sweet cinnamon coated mandazi doughnuts he'd bought earlier from a street seller — licking the excess sugar from his fingers, not wanting to make the Nissan's steering wheel sticky, before phoning the estate agent to find out if there were any problems with their house move.

Happy everything was on schedule, Okoth rang the institute to get hold of his assistant, Irumba. Oddly, he didn't get a reply. So tried the security guard, Kasozi. But again, no response. Trying the professor's phone: the same.

A sense of foreboding rose, dulling his cheery mood.

As a distraction, flicking on Radio Simba, the sound system sprung to life, lifting his spirits. Accompanied by the constant bleat of car horns, he opened his lungs in song, drumming rhythms on the dashboard, smiling to drivers around him doing much the same.

A child's hand thrust a carton of orange juice through the open window, making him jump. Slapping coinage into the small palm, he held the chilled drink against his forehead to ease his dull headache: a reaction to antibodies he'd received two days earlier.

Okoth felt proud his family were amongst the first to benefit from a new immunisation programme funded by the institute. Although Akia hadn't thought so. Okoth recalled his son's cry as the needle penetrated his fragile arm.

Finally gaining more speed, Okoth narrowly avoided a collision with a man on a push bike balancing a kitchen unit on the seat. And another, moving a back axle in the same fashion, muttering, 'Crazy.' As he steered around the steady stream of erratically ridden motorbikes weaving in and out of the traffic.

Armed police on street corners; brightly coloured political banners flapping in the breeze: Okoth's usual sights for his morning commutes he'd usually see from his aged Vespa. But today, as the proud driver of a powerful vehicle.

Clear of the suburbs, opening the throttle filled the car with the stench of cow dung, wood smoke, ditch water and warming earth, as he sped past banana plantations to the institute.

Okoth felt concerned seeing the entry barrier raised, and the sentry box empty. The professor had mentioned break-ins at their laboratories in Brazil and Colombia, resulting in their genetically modified insects being released too early. Fearing they'd also been targeted would confirm why he'd not been able to raise his colleagues.

Driving slowly past the hangar, noticing one of the Fletcher light aircraft was missing: the one he'd adapted as a dropper, Okoth's frown deepened. He did the pre-flight checks, even for the professor, and knew none were scheduled for today.

'What's happening?' he wondered, his gaze drawn to the side door of the laboratory, wide open, swinging in the warm breeze.

Accelerating hard, the roar of the engine made a flock of Marabou storks take to the sky, their wet droppings splattering on the windscreen.

'I thought my day was starting too well,' he grumbled.

Cruising around the perimeter, passed the institutes many buildings, still with no sign of his colleagues; Okoth's sense of unease heightened.

'Should he call for back up now, or continue to check?' he wondered, before chiding himself for overreacting, sure once he found Kasozi he'd explain everything.

With the Nissan parked in a sheltered spot, armed with the lug wrench from the boot, tucking his mobile into his shirt pocket, Okoth entered the laboratory — pushing a rock against the pounding door to stop the irritating sound.

Seeing droplets of blood on the normally pristine white tiles, Okoth's heart missed a beat. Backing into a recess under the stairwell, he looked around — forcefully exhaling to calm his nerves.

Most of the specimen tanks had been shattered; the containing nets ripped.

This wasn't good. With the door open, their test specimens were now loose. 'We're nearly there, Okoth. In a few more months, we'll be A-OK.' The professor's words invaded his mind, unsettling him further. But, as he'd suspected, they'd been targeted. 'Ndi mweraliikirivu, ndi mweraliikirivu?' he muttered, listening for sounds: nothing, apart from the gentle hum from the refrigeration units broke the silence.

Creeping into the professor's office, he wasn't surprised to see documents strewn everywhere; filing cabinet drawers yanked open. 'Maybe he got away, or didn't come to work,' Okoth mumbled, praying the professor was safe, wondering, 'Where are Kasozi and Irumba? Whose blood is on the floor?

And where's the plane?' What if I'm being watched?' His eyes darting around him.

Contemplating calling the police, deciding he felt safer keeping quiet, he crawled under the professor's desk. Sat in the gloom he checked his mobile for calls he may have missed during his commute. None he'd made during his drive had been returned. But he found a message from the professor, sent three hours ago.

'How had he missed that?' he muttered, remembering the ping of receipt as he'd charged the phone while parading the status symbol past his brother's home. He'd chosen to ignore it. Fool, he thought.

'Look in your locker. There's an envelope for you, Okoth. Take care, have a good life. You and your family deserve it. Thank you so much for being my trusted companion over the years. Keep the car. Regards Norman.'

What's happening? Okoth whispered in alarm, crawling from his hiding place, finding the envelope which he quickly stuffed in his trouser pocket.

Retracing his steps, he panicked at the sight of more blood on the floor outside the washroom.

Fighting the urge to run, knowing his friends may be in there on the brink of death, Okoth changed his hold on the wrench; listened, before tentatively approaching the closed door.

Staring at the white flatness; waiting for adrenaline to make his legs obey, finally booting it open, standing tall and forceful in readiness to fight, he gasped at the sight of Kasozi sprawled on the tiles, tied up, a bloody weeping gash on his temple.

A muffled plea penetrated the black tape across Kasozi's mouth as he gestured, with wild rolling eyes, to behind the door.

Okoth reacted by slamming his back against the wall — turning — ready to take a swing.

But he didn't see a strapping intruder waiting to kill him: only Irumba, lifeless, in a crumbled heap. His lips a deadly shade of blue. Okoth's voice trembled as he cried, 'Irumba. Kasozi. What happened? Were they children after drugs?' As he carefully removed the tape from Kasozi's face, pressing a wodge of toilet paper against his head wound.

His mouth freed, he ranted, 'Okoth, we must get out of here. They will come back. Not kids. I think they knew the professor and about your work. They were telling each other what to do with the scientific things. It wasn't for drugs.'

'OK. Let's work this out, my friend,' Okoth said, gently pushing Irumba's limp body against the closed door.

'Can you walk Kasozi?'

'Yes. I was hit coming into the laboratory. They made Irumba ring to tell me to open the barrier as he was expecting a delivery, and could I help him prepare equipment as he was on his own. He said it would only be for a few minutes. What a fool. Why didn't I think something was wrong? He sounded different, strained. We must get the surveillance camera to the police, but I don't know if they've gone?'

'Did you hear the plane leave?'

'Yes. I don't know how long ago. ... Okoth, how long does it take someone to die? Irumba was still alive when I heard the engines. I thought they'd stolen it and left, but one came back, I heard squeaking trainers on the tiles outside the door, but it didn't open. I think that's when you showed up. We've got to go, Okoth.'

'Yes. Yes,' he agreed, looking around the small room for options: through the false ceiling, along the ventilation ducts was a possibility.

Standing on the hand-basin, lifting a tile, Okoth peered into the darkness, searching for leverage. With a shove up from Kasozi, he could use the toilet waste pipe from the floor above. But how would Kasozi get up? If he hauled him, the plaster-board ceiling around the gap wouldn't support their combined weight. Okoth needed to help Kasozi into the void, to get out wherever he could, leaving him to chance it through the laboratory. This was the only chance for one of them to make it out alive.

Checking his mobile, Okoth hoped to phone for help — but no signal penetrated the concrete stairwell. To stay put — in what may turn out to be their washroom tomb — wasn't an option.

Helping Kasozi up into the recess, he wished him good luck, popping the tile back into place.

'Sitegeera. Poor Irumba,' Okoth crooned, sat next to the chilling body of his friend. 'What here is so valuable to make people do this?' he wondered, surmising we've no street drugs. But the equipment's specialised: this must be what they were after.

Making the most of the calm before the storm, he read the professor's letter, hoping it may provide an answer to the mayhem.

Dear Okoth,

Here is a copy of my will lodged with Angualia Advocates. You know the office's; you drove me there last month. A copy is also in the mail box of your new home, so should anything happen to you, your family will be provided for. You do not have to worry about money anymore. My loan to you dies upon my death, which could be soon. You may have guessed; I've not been well. They diagnosed me with multiple sclerosis over a year ago. The signs of its progression have started to affect me. I do not wish to live any longer. My work has been fulfilling — preventing me from having a normal family life, so I thank you, Baingama, and little Akia for providing such joy to me and filling that gap in my latter years. And for all your support and kindness. I pray no harm comes to you and that you go on to enjoy the thrill of being a grandparent many times over.

Best wishes. Norman.

Okoth, racked by the truth, sobbed uncontrollably — pulling Irumba's corpse towards him in reflex. Cradling, stroking his cold floppy head, Okoth's mucus and tears dribbled into his dead colleagues wire wool hair, before collecting himself; putting a stop to his pitiful release.

Regaining focus, composing a text to Baingama telling her how much he loved her, and if he wasn't home in time, she must go to the new house to meet the agent, as planned. And check the letter box. Sent. Okoth hoped she receives it, knowing he'd done all he could to make his final farewell.

'For once, Baingama, charge your phone,' he quietly mouthed, as a loud thump and cry made his heart race. 'Oh no. Kasozi,' he whispered, to the sound of swilling fluid, a dull clonk of something against metal, and a strong smell of petrol filling the room.

Kissing Irumba's chilling skin, lifting the forlorn head from his lap, he carefully laid it on the floor, then readied himself, wrench raised, knowing he had to face what was on the other side of the door, or end up a crispy corpse with Irumba.

In one swift movement, he was out running — losing impetus at the sight of a lifeless Kasozi, dragged by the armpits, be unceremoniously dumped in the middle of the corridor.

'Noooo,' he cried out, running to where Kasozi lay.

The intruder nearest Okoth — turned.

He was not African. Scandinavian, Okoth presumed as the man's penetrating blue eyes assessed him with a calculating evil. He knew he was a dead man.

The first blow to his shoulders came from behind, knocking him off balance. Okoth felt another to his skull, before falling to the floor, listening for his phone to ping assuring him his message had reached Baingama.

After a barrage of kicks to his head and body, Okoth's consciousness ebbed. His mind started playing tricks: he was watching Akia riding a blue bicycle around a mango tree in their new garden. Baingama was shouting at them — be careful, which made him smile, before the dull impact of a third blow ensured he'd not view the world in the same way ever again.

Chapter Nineteen

Busily folding clothes and wrapping their few belongings into boxes Okoth had brought home, Baingama curled up her nose at the smell of the damp cardboard and stale vegetables: glad they'd be emptied soon, poking fresh camphor basil leaves into gaps to improve the packaging. Sealing the last box with brown tape, she watched Akia crawling around the floor on a blue fleecy blanket, making brumming noises, loading his favourite bright green tractor with broken twigs.

Invited to Monic's for a farewell lunch of matoke, rice and fish, Baingama was looking forward to a few glasses of her neighbour's special blend of Waragi; the inviting aromas wafting in the hut, making her stomach rumble in anticipation of the feast.

But before relaxing, having already charged her mobile with their Firefly lamp, she had to phone Okoth to remind him to buy Akia's present. He'd left too quickly that morning, not giving her chance.

'Showing off in that big car,' she muttered, grinning at the prospect of electric and running water at the new house. 'Always so busy, and in a hurry. Even today. He works far too hard. I'll have words with the Professor when I next see him,' she mumbled, firing up the phone.

Okoth's message made her frown.

'Oh dear. Let's hope everything's all right?' she chuntered — glancing at little Akia.

Chapter Twenty

Dropping his game changing pay-load from the plane's hopper, the professor mulled over the last six months, knowing his existence was short lived: whether or not he chose to end it.

Having underestimated quite what he was getting involved in or the steps his so-called colleagues would take to cover their tracks; it should've dawned on him the recent, informal chat at the institute had been a psychological assessment, to delve — uncover his deepest thoughts.

His conscience had battled with their reasoning; the scientific sense behind their plans. But, although he understood their logic, unlike those working with him, he didn't possess psychopathic tendencies, and didn't have the stomach for the extent of what lay ahead.

Satisfied the future was secure for those who meant the most to him; he'd not be able to live with the consequences of his actions and was taking the coward's way out.

He'd lied to Okoth about his illness, wanting him to remember him as a good man — to believe he'd taken his life before the disease became too debilitating.

The agreement was Okoth, and the others, wouldn't be harmed. Kidding himself this was the case, in the depths of his heart knowing what end truly awaited them.

'What are we doing? How could we have agreed to this pogrom?' he cried out, weeping as he deposited the rest of his deadly cargo.

Watching a herd of elephant's amble majestically below, resembling land locked whales their grey hulks contrasting against the savanna with tiny infant forms hurrying to keep pace, small legs working double time. And at the stunning scenery, 'Good luck my friends,' he said — feeling detached from the moment; like an audience member enjoying the final scene of a film. And yet he — along with the others — were the players; the catalysts creating a changing the world.

Expected to rendezvous with the rest of the carefully chosen scientists, surgeons, and IT specialists gathering at the institute's remote outstation near Kasese: this wasn't Professor Norman Goldings intention.

The planes fuel gauge showed nearly empty. Its audible alarm giving him a start, urging him towards the next stage in his plan; recognising the spot on the equatorial line where he planned to go down. Perversely, wanting to hit the earth at its mid-rift — to split it open like an egg — merge his remains with the soil. This final act suited his frame of mind.

His resolve enhanced with the remaining brandy from his hip flask; the fluids sensation numbing properties calmed him as he ascended.

There'd be enough fuel left to obliterate the plane on impact: of that he was sure.

Professor Golding bellowed, starting his rapid descent.

Chapter Twenty-One

A plane en route from Kampala to Johannesburg settled into its flight path. Sat in a window seat a young boy tugged urgently tugged at his mother's sleeve. 'Mummy. Look at the big eposion down there,' he said, jiggling up and down with excitement.

'Oh yes. Let's hope no one's hurt, darling. And the word is explosion. Exxxplllosion,' she emphasised, stroking her child's arm.

Five minutes later, pointing out the porthole, he cried: 'Look, Mummy. Another little exxpoosion.'

'It's probably the start of a bloody military coup. Good job we left today,' the father grumbled.

Chapter Twenty-Two

Alberta, Canada

'For goodness' sake', you can see I haven't got much oomph,' Milo shouted to an inconsiderate lady driver, starring defiantly ahead, refusing to let him join the slow flow of traffic. Matching the quickening pace of the following cars, embarrassed by the plume of black exhaust gas ejected from the rear of the faded blue Dodge, he sank lower in his seat, noticing the car behind hang back.

Caressing the steering wheel, mingling the moisture from his palms with any residue left from his father's. 'Don't worry. If we're forbidden to use her, I'll park her in the sun stacked with hay bales for the dogs. She'll be cherished. ... Remember our summer holidays? Hurriedly packing, setting off on a whim. Rigging a makeshift cover for the pickup as a tent. Happy days,' Milo consoled an absent Pops.

Jools will love this old banger. I'll teach her to drive around the ranch. Take the track through the brook up the hills to the woods, he thought; admitting however environmentally green his ethics, the sound of the engines thunderous roar couldn't be bettered; its mud claw tyres and ram's horn emblem adding to the whole Dodge experience.

Half an hour from Red Brook, Pops' last request for his bungalow: 'Just planks and old rusty nails. Sell it. Give the money to Jolie...' sprung to mind. Milo, sad the cosy link to his childhood had to go, decided he'd spend the evening with Marie looking through the photos and mementos from the boxes sliding around in the back.

Pops eagerly drank the two bottles of Nembutal while holding Milo's hand. They'd chatted before downing his third shot of brandy, calling out, 'Juliet.' Then peacefully slipped away.

Pops' time was up; he'd wanted release.

His lasting image of his father was a peaceful one.

Milo warmly thanked Doctor Lundy for his part in their common-sense campaign; the man having helped twenty more on their way that day, along with thousands of collaborators releasing millions of grateful, trapped souls.

Over-zealous sheriffs had made a few arrests. Countless medical professionals told not to leave their locations argued they had to continue their work. The care they provided for their living patients couldn't be compromised.

Law enforcement agencies, globally, were undecided how to deal with the numbers involved. Much debate ongoing. Judicial advice awaited.

Raids and seizures of Nembutal dosages: countless. A Danish pharmaceutical company — the main producer issued a statement: *'They were legally manufacturing a sedative. Anecdotal evidence confirmed that just having the drug in a patient's possession was proven to improve the quality of life for the terminally ill's last few days, weeks, or months. Once prescribed — what a patient did with that drug was, ultimately, their business.'*

Morally: who could argue? Surely it was against an individual's human right *not* to allow them release from their flesh and blood prison.

The demand for the release pill was higher than ever: which spoke for itself.

The UK, USA, much of Europe and regions of Australia, having blocked the Danish company's website meant the black market was rife. With five producers of a derivative product openly declaring their support, and the media hype, many more souls had been educated there was a liberating solution to their dilemma.

Milo, humbled to have been part of the process from the start. And grateful the collective's true intent had been accepted, with humility and dignity, by the collaborating families; many opting for greener funerals, choosing willow or wool caskets over wasteful wood. Or that they're buried in shallow graves, so their decomposing compounds could feed the wildflower seeds lovingly scattered above.

Browsing through social media posts, Milo was impressed, and inspired by the resolve; the attitude of the families left behind. The strongest emotions displayed: understandably sadness, but relief and closure.

The collective had shown a new approach to the death of a human being. Families having embraced the opportunity to plan; to celebrate the peaceful passing of their loved ones. The birth of a baby could be planned — even the exact emergence of that new life — so why not the ceasing of an exhausted one?

It was now socially acceptable for the millions to express gratitude for their release from burden. Perhaps the release programme *will* prove to Governments' they'd have the public's support to make a drastic change? Parents' of disabled, or brain-damaged children, locked in a gruelling drudge of care, torn due by the love for their impaired offspring may welcome an acceptable end to their dutiful plight, he pondered.

'As a species, we need to toughen up and whittle down. As the saying goes, cut the wheat from the chaff,' Milo muttered — driving under the ranch's archway; mounted wavelets of copper lettering appearing to shimmer a sunlight wink of approval to his sentiments.

A fast-moving black streak hurtling across the meadow to his right then attracted his attention. 'Aha! That's why she hasn't answered her phone. She's at a full paced gallop,' he chuckled — speeding up to reach the stable block — parking to the sound of clattering hooves on tarmac.

Milo leant against the Dodge, adopting an I've been waiting ages stance, arms folded, as Storm — covered in patches of white lather — appeared around the bend with Marie astride, smiling broadly.

They both felt it: a fusion of emotional release as they embraced. Their silent closeness conveying what they'd discussed during lengthy phone calls: their need to re-connect. Their professional lives no longer allowed to dominate their relationship. Already planning to leave in the morning, nothing would stop them spending time at their lodge in Kicking Horse — desperately needing distance from Donald's analytical nature — his mood dictating manipulation.

To Milo: it seemed there was a hidden agenda Donald feared may become exposed. I'm probably being paranoid, he thought — clinging to Marie.

Chapter Twenty-Three

Mid Atlantic & Canada Bound

Chris reread his article, smiling to himself, remembering the genuine wallop on the back from Pendleton knocking him sideways: 'Knew you had it in you. Tosser,' his accompanying expletive. But however ruthless Chris believed he was: he'd a pang of guilt, as the gist of the piece had come from the sexy kissable lips of Julie during his comforting between the sheet's activity after the Ed's insensitive barrage. Her tearful embrace, his cheeky blue eyes and reputation for satisfaction guaranteed: the outcome was inevitable. What was he supposed to do — resist? Chris continually chastised himself.

His other article: '*Earn their benefits. Grave digging and beyond*' — an envelope-sized addition to page fifteen, wasn't bad. He'd prompted a lot of debate, and seriously couldn't see what was wrong with his suggestion. There were loads to be dug. Council workers weren't coping, and most of their readers agreed. What was wrong with them pulling their finger out, filling potholes; municipal gardening; clearing up graffiti before being paid their benefit? It made sense to kick start a work ethic; stop them sitting around getting fat, stoned and drunk.

Chris knew he'd ruffled politically correct feathers. But the malignity flowing his way had knocked him off kilter. This trip *had* come at the right time.

'Bastard. F---ing bastard.' Julie's last text loomed into his conscience, as his eyes returning to his *pièce de résistance* on the front page of yesterday's Daily Reporter.

She should've got cracking instead of going off sick. In the dog eat dog world of journalism, taking your finger off the pulse won't get you anywhere. He'd discussed his article with her too: she could have run with it, achieved page fifteen and nationwide hatred, Chris reflected, nodding his head, agreeing to his ruthless guilt.

'What's with the moronic head thing?' Bog scoffed — nudging him sharply on the elbow.

'Sorry. What? Oh, just thinking about something.' Bit worrying, Chris thought, not aware he'd actually been moving his head.

'You sure you wrote that?'

'It's my style. Unmistakable. The Ed's not daft. Look at the speed of that other plane.' Chris faced the porthole, choosing to hunt polar bear shapes in the fluffy clouds, preventing Bog from seeing the sudden flush of pink to his cheeks.

Their flight to Calgary was on schedule. After a bit of nattering and watching films, Chris noticed Bog's head drooping in jerky spasms. Settling it against the head restraint, his snoozing friend began a wheezing snore, giving Chris the opportunity to delve further into Bog's background. Carefully extracting his passport — from the top pocket of a pale pink Dolce and Gabanna shirt — flicking through the pages, reading: *Julian Fletcher Reynaud Spalding*. Birth registered at *SBA Akrotiri, Cyprus*. He'd been around arrival entry's to *Venezuela, Peru, Panama, Trinidad, Cuba, The States, Bali, Botswana*, showed.

'Perhaps he's a spy?' Chris wondered — giving his intriguing, dozing companion a quizzical glance.

Other than Bog was born with a silver spoon in his mouth; received a sizeable allowance from his retired Brigadier father, and only worked for the socialising, travel and buzz: he'd not learnt not else, slipping it back into place.

Kicking Bog's ankle to rouse him, 'Wakey, wakey. Lunch is coming, you Toff,' Chris whispered into his neat, well-bred ear.

Landing at Calgary airport, Chris frowned with

disappointment at the view, expecting the place to be greener: not the depressing, barren landscape panning out below.

'Must be the worst time of year to visit,' he muttered, as they circled.

Their rental car ran well. Had a nifty stow and go seating arrangement, ideal for securing their photographic and technical equipment being two blokes on a sight-seeing tour: their story, if questioned.

Speeding past flat bleak terrain, peering higher into the sky in perfect parallel to the ground, as if one element was repelling the other; Chris's impression of the place didn't improve, passing mile after mile of monotonous brown tundra. Perfect for cycling and running, he supposed, fancying a muffin — passing patches of snow clung to verges resembling sugar icing on a coffee coloured one.

Using a cuff to rub a greasy forehead mark from the window, his stomach creating a loud rumble, and feeling disappointed, like a kid looking forward to his holiday only to get there and realise he might as well have stayed at home as this is crap, made Chris want a comforting Big Mac — right now. Although, to be fair, leaving the claustrophobia of London life to reach the vastness of the place, freed your mind, creating an urge to run for miles and miles, arms spread wide. 'To infinity and beyond,' he mumbled, finger flipping his top lip, giving Bog a prod on the arm. Getting thumped in return, confirmed Bog was in the land of the living — hadn't falling asleep at the wheel by the lack of motivating scenery.

'Deliverance,' they said in unison, pulling up outside their motel in Conraine: a heritage town caught in a provincial time warp.

The mumsy reception lady, Ashley, her badge confirmed, gave off a flowery scent as her podgy fingers flew over a keyboard. The cuffs of her mustard coloured blouse under strain, encasing her chubby wrists, as she handed them their room key.

What an awful coloured blouse. Maybe she put it in the wash with her old man's Y-fronts? It does nothing for her complexion, Chris critically evaluated — picking up a tourist guide from the counter predictably adorned with a chuck wagon photograph.

Chapter Twenty-Four

Alberta, Canada

Chris's face lit up in a boyish grin, marvelling at the awesomeness of the snow-covered Rocky Mountains dominating their early morning drive through the wilderness of Mountain View County to hunch location number one. For his benefit, Bog again ran through his theories to convince him they *were* onto the man behind the suicides, and his assumption those who'd died *weren't* willing participants, wasn't that far-fetched. From Chris's nursing home informants blog, they'd solid proof at least a third of The Participants had no immediate family. And *if* they'd written letters of consent, they'd proved to be forgeries.

'Yeap. OK. And just remembered the letter written by the dead friend of the old bugger I interviewed at that Golden Leaves place: 'Worried he would be-dun-in.' Good job he made a note in his diary where to find it. That's vital evidence safely stashed with our other bargaining tools in big sis' attic. ... She's not back for another month. Shouldn't be an issue.'

'Glad to hear. Seriously though, we've got to be careful. You're the journalist: matter of opinion, but assess and describe. Prep' your piece without me planting ideas. Fresh eyes should reap rewards —'

'Bloody cheek! Just happy to get from under the Ed's feet, to be honest. But, Christ!' Chris shouted in alarm as they passed yet another bear warning sign. 'Never thought about grizzlies when we planned camping. Best re-assess that option, don't you think? And, it's frigging colder than I imagined. So apart from freezing my nuts off, I don't fancy getting them chewed off by half a ton of smelly fur, with sharp teeth and claws.'

Bog ignored Chris's latest immature outburst.

An hour past before he slowed. Judging from his meerkat stance, Chris assumed they'd arrived at their destination as they cruised past an imposing wooden boundary fence.

The road, being quiet, meant they could drive at low speed to assess the land. 'I take it we're at hunch number one then?' Chris questioned, eagerly absorbing the new vista, noticing a name — Red something, in rusty coloured wavy letters above an entrance. And, through the dense tree cover, a high barbed wire enclosure.

'I saw a picnic area three hundred metres back. I'll park up so we can suss the place.'

'As we're supposed to be bird watching tourists, do you want me to rig up the camping seats under the trees? Want some crisps and a coke mate?' Chris suggested as they pulled over.

'No,' Bog said sternly. Grabbing binoculars from the glove box; getting to work straight away making sense of the magnified images with frantically scribbled notes.

'I assume that's a no. Good luck then. I'll grab a snooze. Wake me if there's a problem or you want a break.'

'Did I miss much?' Chris asked, rubbing sleep from his eyes.

'Nah. Nothing vital. But pucker bird watchers park further down. We could blend in with them. They walk along a track running parallel to the perimeter. Do something useful, get your gear on — silly hat, camera round your neck — you know the score.' Bog suggested, working on his own disguise with sunglasses, a padded lilac jacket, thermal trousers and a wide brimmed wax hat with a blonde plait attachment.

'What are you doing mate?' Chris chuckled.

'Listen, Knobhead. If the bloke I think lives here does, the chances are he'd recognise me from the Paris venue. I was all over the place, keeping an eye on him. Caught me a few times. Anyway, that's how I came up with the hunch he's the key player. His demeanour. Lots of furtive glances. The urinal goss' and the way a group of blokes gathered around him.'

'Whatever,' Chris smirked, setting off along the well-defined track skirting the southern perimeter leading uphill to a thickly wooded ridge: the perfect place for decoy bird watching.

Bringing up the rear, Chris realised what small feet and mildly feminine features his super-sleuth accomplice had. The altered appearance was effective, but couldn't help himself jest: 'I'd keep quiet if I were you. Your bloody voice will blow your cover. And, you need to take girlier steps mate.'

'Get serious, you prat. If we raise suspicions, you've no idea who you're up against.'

Chris playfully smacked Bogs back-side to shut him up.

Through gritted teeth, he swung his false hair in annoyance.

The ridges forest cover provided the ideal shelter for their surreptitious learning of the land. Deciding upon their first target: a sizeable log cabin nearest to them. Their second: a contemporary building, perhaps a large garage, or workshop.

Their third: an impressive ranch house in the distance.

Tucked into a depression at the edge of the woods, Chris deftly set up his Nikon D5. On open ground — within whispering distance — Bog placed their decoy camera on a tripod, facing the treetops away from the ranch.

With no sign of anyone — only distant barking dogs and horses neighing, they settled into their task. To a casual observer, doing nothing suspicious.

'Chris. How's it going —?'

'Nothing *yet* out the ordinary. Give us a chance. There's a bloke working at the stables. An old woman brought him grub from target three. They chatted, and a guard walked up the drive to the garage place. Must have come from a security hut we haven't seen. Should find that on our way back. I've shots of their security cameras. There are bloody loads, mate. For just a ranch, seems overkill. Unless they've got fancy horse-y blood lines. Can you look how far back this fence goes? If I can get further round, I might get a shot of the front of the garage-y building with vent thingy's coming out a bank ... I reckon there's stuff happening underground.'

As instructed, hands stuffed in pockets, Bog followed the fence line to the fading accompaniment of a camera's burst shutter mode, his breath creating puffs of moisturised mist in the dank atmosphere.

'This is going to take some time. We spy with our little eyes,' he mumbled, feeling hyped — yet vulnerable.

Chapter Twenty-Five

Early on day five, after spending the night in their rental car — they got lucky. As a black SUV left the ranch, Chris recorded the licence plate, and, through their contacts, made the link: Bog's man did *live* there. The woman who drove it was the same one they'd seen walking from the log cabin to the underground place and definitely connected to their prey. Also, judging by the volume of white coats, coming and going, they deduced it was either a laboratory; a research facility, or a small hospital.

Two days before lucky day five, had been lots of dog's day: one which heightened the mystery further. The place had been crawling with security — plus the dogs.

Ten minutes after Bog had left to warm up the car, Chris captured a shot of the old white coat from target three, talking with two suits who'd arrived by helicopter. Knowing there was odd stuff happening and not wanting to hang around, get caught red-handed, Chris scarpered, using a way through the woods they'd recce'd. Luckily for him, the furry snarlers got trapped the other side of the fence.

These vital shots, along with their others, were analysed, magnified and catalogued on Bog's lap-top, which he was studying in the back en-route to hunch location number two: Edmonton.

'Eureka-ka-ka-ka. Struth. I know that noggin. He's aged a bit. But I've seen him at some sensitive sneaky beaky places. Blimey Chris, I think the US military are in the loop, or the non-existent organisation with more funding. Unless he got the boot. But a leopard doesn't change its spots. What did you make of the black bloke? Looks drugged. Shoulders all droopy in a boiler suit wearing some sort of face helmet. He's definitely not right.'

'I thought he might be under arrest. Or disabled, or something, which made me think perhaps it's a correctional facility for serious nut jobs. Or, a terrorist interrogation unit. Dunno really. Just my take.' Chris shuddered.

'Possibly? We could do with a car upgrade. A limo with a rear seat tray would be better. Oh, shit. Spilt my water. Not on the keyboard, luckily. Must back this lot up again. Where are the memory sticks? Alright. Found them.' Bog mopped up his spillage with a near to hand dirty t-shirt.

'That chopper was a Mil Mi-8. They're used by the military for air ambulances. Perhaps the bloke's infected with a new virus. Or, they're testing chemical weapons. But none of the others were wearing protective masks, or wellies, so that can't be it ... Perhaps he's a Hannibal Lector type bloke? Dangerous. Unpredictable. Could bite your nose off in a second. It's a possibility? God knows, Chris. But I've decided, change of plan. Forget Edmonton. Stop at the next gas station. We need WIFI to book flights so we can check out hunch number non-bloody existent, which I'm upgrading to number two. We're Utah bound.'

Chris glanced in the rear-view mirror, concerned by the new fire in Bog's eyes. This assignment is getting worrying, he thought — putting his foot on the gas.

Chapter Twenty-Six

Rocky Mountain Resort, Canada

Marie loved coming to their lodge at Kicking Horse. Humming, inhaling the cabin's pine scent, she fired up her favourite feature: the central wood-burner, like a fire-y glass box of comfort dominating the middle of the living room. The aroma worked its sedative magic, creating a psychosomatic link to relaxation, putting her at ease within minutes.

They'd bought their sanctuary — their love shack — when Milo sold his apartment. Plus, used all their savings. It was so worth it, she reflected, watching him stood at the kitchen island scrubbing potatoes.

'You were right Marie not to have told Jools about the plan. I'm sorry I made you feel bad,' Milo said, sporting an am I forgiven face.

'It didn't make sense alarming her, so, yes, I ignored you. Best scold me later. Big fella,' Marie chuckled, washing salad leaves under running water — sticking her bottom out teasingly. 'She wasn't alone: ten more from the school lost grandparents. ... I expected her to get mad I'd not warned her. I tell you Mi, she's something else. I heard others in the background crying. She was sniffing, but composed and said: "It's OK Mum. I'd a feeling I wouldn't see him alive again, that's why I spent so much time with him when I was home." Then ended with, "Mum. I've got to go; the other girls need me. I'll call you tomorrow." And hung up. To be honest, I was taken aback, but thought, good for you, girl, let's hope you handle the rest of your life so pragmatically.'

As Marie turned towards him, he noticed droplets of water drip from her hands onto the wooden floor: a no-no at the ranch. Another positive affect of the cabin. Her irritating hang-ups faded, he reflected, throwing her a warm smile.

'Bee's. Goddamned bees. Josh is using his influence to make sure, "...these undervalued little creatures are given all the help he can muster." His first crusade after sorting Penny's affairs.' Milo quoted his friend as he laid dinner plates onto the raised breakfast bar, the action interrupted by Marie grabbing his hips, twisting him around to face her.

'So, my sexy husband. We eat, drink, sleep, ski, play in the snow, plus, partake in impromptu sex. Is this the aim for the weekend, so I'm clear?'

Milo winked suggestively, pulling Marie towards him for a tight embrace.

Savouring the reassurance of his strong steady heart beat against her cheek, her gaze drawn out the window, to the setting sun casting a dimming baby pink blanket hue over the snowy mounds, keeping them warm until morning.

Marie's momentary peace didn't last. Invasive worries of her disturbing work revelations, and other destabilising development tainted the otherwise comforting moment.

Chapter Twenty-Seven

Edmonton Highway, Alberta

'What do you think the link with the ranch *is*? If the bloke you were hoping to see *is* a climate expert, how's he linked to drugged up terrorist convicts?'

'No idea, Chris. But his Mrs's is into ... hang on ... microbiology and genetics.'

Bog noisily flicked through his notes, sat in the rear as Chris drove, before blurting, 'Stop. Pull over. I need a moment.' Throwing the door open as he slowed — leaping out — stumbling as the soles of his shoes met the soft verge.

Watching his friend pace along the side of the road, leaning into the strengthening wind, raking his fingers through dishevelled hair, Chris chuckled when he plonked back in, ranting, 'Hear me out. On reflection, it's pointless heading to Utah. We'd need different visas. And apart from *possibly* seeing the same faces at the main entrance, in all seriousness, we wouldn't get in any further as long as I've got a hole in my arse. Plus, my noggin might set off facial recognition alarm bells and I don't want to be arrested. And, besides, to get close to the underground hangars, you're getting into X-files territory, being stalked by bloody Apache helicopters. I've learnt from experience. So, it's a waste of our finite budget, Chris. I'm certain there's a top-secret military link between the two locations. I've worked out, that 'copter could get to Fairway, the Utah place, with three refuels at air force bases en route. It figures that's *why* Red Brook is being used, it's low profile. I reckon they've teams of scientists working on something sensitive. You will ask: what that's got to do with our climate bloke? Answer: I don't have the foggiest. So, here's our new plan. We go back to the Red Brook, into the log cabin, and the lab' place. I'm confident we'll find our answers there.'

Bog rubbed at his temples with a fury, awaiting a Chris inanity.

'Have I heard you right? We're going back the way we've come, just as the bloody scenery's improving.'

'You're such an arsehole, Chris. I'm driving. Your turn reviewing,' Bog ordered, launching himself out — dragging his annoying colleague by the jumper from the driver's seat.

'How do you know all this stuff about helicopters and secret locations? What *were* you doing at that Utah place to get tagged as a Mulder threat?' Chris quizzed after half an hour of self-absorbed silence.

'A long, boring story. But with my cousin following one of his crazy conspiracy theories.'

'Well go on, fill me in,' Chris pushed, convinced his idea of Bog being a spy could get credence.

'Daft gap year stuff with Sputnik. Real name, Michael. We had the time and money, so went off in search of the truth. Didn't find any. Got chased a few times. All water under the bridge. I've had no problems with visas since. That's a bonus.'

'What's this Sputnik cousin doing with himself now?'

'Not sure, actually. He disappeared off the radar five years ago. I don't think his family have a clue either. Last I heard, he went to Indonesia, or somewhere Asian. I expect he's shacked up with a subservient Thai chick, eating rice and following Buddhism.'

'Shame. Sounds a useful sort and explains one thing: why you enjoy living on the seat of your pants when you needn't. It's in your bloody genes, mate,' Chris chortled.

Chapter Twenty-Eight

Red Brook Ranch, Alberta

Apart from the ranch hand, laboratory admin staff — who came and went like clock-work — with no black SUV, or guard dogs, plus no movement from either house, the intrepid duo concluded: conditions perfect. Today was the day.

Although Chris had done a fair bit of sneaking around: he felt anxious crawling under the wire fencing using a wildlife free-way named Jolie's Gap: a small signpost read next to the sodden, scooped-out patch of mud. Noticing tiny footprints of the creatures who travelled via the empathic route, he pictured alarmed critters instinctively hesitate, noses twitching, detecting his unfamiliar scent. 'Don't worry. I'm just a big friendly rodent not waiting to kill you, my little friends,' he mumbled — straining his bulk under sharp edges of wiring, wiping a blob of repugnant scat from his hand onto the undergrowth.

The perfectly located way in led them behind the log cabin with no security cameras to capture the early stages of their fact-finding mission. If detected, they'd found a well concealed rabbit hole to stash their footage and claim they were lost hikers. Also, armed with doped meat in case snarling Alsatians re-appeared.

'Crap. I need to go again,' Chris exclaimed — losing his footing on the wet soil.

'Take more bung up tablets or stay behind. You're becoming a liability,' Bog barked — eyeing him with disdain.

'Fingers crossed they're not on their way back from where-ever they've been. Just our bloody luck, getting caught red handed,' Chris chuntered, imagining them getting dragged, kicking and screaming into the laboratory.

'Mask at the ready, Chris. We're there.'

If they'd overlooked any surveillance, bizarrely, David and Victoria Beckham lookalikes would be seen suspiciously wandering.

'Shit. I'm covered,' Chris cussed, rubbing at his buttocks after slipping down a bank, a log pile breaking his ungainly descent.

'Shhhhhh. Buffoon! As forecast, the winds blowing in our direction. Great start, 'Bog enthused, plucking a lock picking tool from his back pocket. Working its magic in a second. 'No alarm. Thank goodness,' he said with relief.

Tucking their muddy trainers in a recess outside the door, they tip-toed into the kitchen.

'Right Chris, put everything back exactly where you find it. Probably best we stick together. And follow my lead—'

'I *have* done this before, Bog. No need to preach,' he barked — the shape of a desk chair catching his eye across the hallway.

Starting his search in the living room, Bog heard Chris call, 'It's not locked.' A cause for concern, Bog felt, rushing into an office, pushing Chris aside.

Delving into a filing cabinet, Bog flicked through files, keeping them meticulously in order. Amongst the musty odours, an occasional burst of fresh printer ink alerted him to recent correspondence. 'This is good. Strong links to Brockman and his institute, but just routine stuff you'd expect — stats, climate data, nothing juicy about the suicides,' he whispered, cam scanning useful finds.

Chris, head tilted, leaning against a pine book cabinet reading faded science journal spines, emitted a girly squeal as reams of paper slid from a fax machine feeder. With a beep and a creak of plastic moulding, the machine resumed its peaceful slumber tucked in a corner.

Bog softly mewed at the sight of fresh material, chuckling at his accomplice's silently mouthed expletive.

Carefully lifting the delivery from its tray, 'A report from the Planet Watch Institute office in Stockholm. I'll speed read, Chris — *Fletcher FU24. Registration — 5X-LPQ. The aircraft collided with the terrain on a 30-degree rising grassy slope at a forward high speed and low rate of descent. The engine was producing high rotational energy at the time of the impact. No evidence of mechanical failure prior to the impact. An autopsy of the pilot proved no fire had begun in the air and a blood alcohol level of 160mgs. This being a speculative assessment taken from the pelvic red bone marrow with correction being made for the lipid content. The fire confined to the engine bay and cockpit. Milo, report just in from Kampala for info as the ATI now closed. Copied to Edmonton HQ. The POC will be in touch re the accident the lab issue, and will forward the ex-ante psychiatric assessment on Golding. Pleased to know, a confirmed break in. Bodies of two local workers found. Regards L.* Not sure if this is any use. Must be from a field station. A light plane crash and break in. Not unusual for Africa, I suppose. It was probably doing air quality analysis, flying over lakes and rivers. Perhaps conducting rhino or elephant counts. Let's cam scam and do some Googling. I'll hold it flat, Chris. You take the shots.'

Chewing gum, contemplatively stood at the cabin's picture window, Bog broke the moment, 'We've found no clues here. There's no getting around it, I have to get inside that mysterious building. I'm certainly not breaking in. There must be keys in here somewhere. Let's take a peek upstairs.'

Chris dutifully followed, padding behind him.

A security swipe card attached to a length of red cord protruding from the pocket of a white doctor's coat, discarded on a wicker chair, provided Bog's access solution. 'Ah-ha. This could be useful,' he chirped, turning to catch Chris rummaging through a bedside unit drawer. 'Her arse must be as cute as it looks through my lens, mate,' he chuckled, holding up a pair of tiny black panties.

Bog grimaced in disgust, moving through to a dressing room. Sliding open a large wardrobe door, 'I recognise that jacket and shoes. Definitely my man.'

'Blimey. How do you remember this stuff? Have you got a photographic memory?' Chris asked in awe, replacing the underwear before heading downstairs.

'Yes. Yet another of my talents,' Bog confirmed.

Stood back at the window, Bog dictated, 'I'm doing this alone, Chris. Can't risk you bumbling around. If you suspect a problem, leave with what we've got, and raise the alarm. I'd rather get charged and live to tell the tale.'

Trying to look offended, Chris was relieved, more than happy to stay in the cabin's safety with a toilet to hand.

The best route was to the south of the laboratory block where the ground dropped from a rise, blocking the view from the big house and stable block. With no cars parked to the east, and the ranch still quiet, it was now or never.

Persuading an undersized lab' coat, plucked from a kitchen hook, over the breadth of his shoulders, Bog tugged a looser fitting waterproof one over the top with the swipe card hung around his neck.

'Can you move your arms, mate? You're well trussed up,' Chris tittered.

'Not much, but I'll manage. Hopefully I won't stand out like a sore thumb. I feel sick. Is there any brandy around to take the edge off?'

'Will this do?' Chris offered, grasping a bottle of Madeira he found in a kitchen cupboard.

'I normally enjoy adrenaline kicking in, Chris. But risking a close encounter with the wrong kind; a prison sentence or being a guinea pig for a military experiment is making *this* mission is a different kettle of fish.'

Swigging the fortified wine, Bog wiped his mouth with the back of his hand. 'Those humungous burgers, at that diner — they're on you Chris if I get out alive. ... Psyched. Here goes,' he mumbled, setting off into the unknown with an expression brimming with fear, before masking it as a male Beckham.

'He who dares wins mate,' Chris shouted, attempting to lighten the mood.

Chapter Twenty-Nine

Drive-By Diner, Edmonton

'I can understand the Vikings urge to rape and pillage. This high calls for a bloody good blow-out. I'm getting pissed as a fart later. You can be a bore, sit and study your finds. But you know what they say: all work and no play makes Jack a very dull boy,' Chris chortled — taking a large bite of double whammy burger. 'Bog. You're a one-off. How you kept your cool. I'd have been a gibbering wreck. Do you think she'll notice your stink on her coat? Then, I suppose you thought of that.'

'I squirted it with fabric freshener. Shouldn't have left a trace, unless we missed a camera?' Bog slurped from a bucket of coke as Chris rattled on. 'When that guard turned up, my heart seriously upped the ante. He wasn't due for another two hours. I shouted through the window, inconsiderate moron, and I'll admit panicked, thinking, Christ, do I stay and wait for you, or run. Let's see what you've got then.'

Bog glanced around, making sure the tables nearest were empty. Satisfied they couldn't be overlooked, he thumbed through his phone images — throwing his head back in manic laughter at the anxiously captured moments. Chris grinned at his companion, still pumped after his brush with danger.

'Accidentally took these when the door opened and I ran for the locker. Nice ones of a desk, my legs, a flapping lab' coat and the palm of my hand. Close shave or what. Her notes should prove useful,' Bog narrated — turning the phone towards Chris — gazing over his shoulder robotically devouring stick thin fries. 'Anyway. Enough here. Let's get going.'

'I'll need the loo again first mate,' Chris said, jiggling in his seat.

'I suggest we find you a bloody chemist,' Bog jested.

Chapter Thirty

'Where's my effing story? Get your arse back here, asap!'

Slouched on the small couch at the motel, Chris read his Ed's text out loud. It helped, voicing the man's animosity to the room, his impending one-way conversation, dissolving any euphoric high spirits. Who'd have thought monsters like him still existed in today's workplace, he pondered, mumbling, 'I wouldn't put it past the bastard to stop my pay. Got your message. Going well this end. Be there in three days max',' Chris conversed with his voice mail, relieved not having to talk with the odious little man.

Slumped, watching Bog laid on his bed thumbing through photos, Chris sipped a chilled beer, clicked his neck, as his mobile suddenly vibrated against his leg inducing a wave of anxiety: which abated when he saw the caller ID.

'Bog, got a message from my contact in Denmark. He's another lead about medication meddling. Reckons, a hypertension pill called Lisinoprit is now being investigated. Could be linked. Best add that to my research list for tonight ... Still nothing from my nursey informant. She's not even answering my texts. Do you think they've got to her? May have I suppose.'

Bog blocked the sound of Chris, out of habit, just acknowledging with just shrug.

A familiar voice dragged Chris from a brief power nap, his focus landing on Bog, rubbing his chin in front of a flip chart covered in arrows joining names in circles hung over a wardrobe door. Swigging tepid beer, he tried regaining the moment.

'We've definitely found links and trends Chris, and could do with a hand-writing analyst because from her doodles I reckon she's worried about something a lot bigger than she knows how to handle. We know it involves the military, and she's having second thoughts. There are loads of Milo entries, and question marks. Also, something happened eight weeks ago she's got an issue with. *Oh, no* scribbles everywhere. And look at these from her phone ... I'm glad I'm out of there. This can't be right.' Bog stopped pacing, alarmed at what he'd stumbled across.

Holding the mobile at Chris head height, he too baulked at the photo of a restrained human form. 'Christ. What's up with his scalp?' he winced, aghast at that cruelty displayed.

'Don't know. Worrying isn't it. ... So far, we've confirmed our climate bloke; his institutes link to Uganda, and a plane crash: which may not lead anywhere. Best get cracking. You Google Kampala's latest news; that drug you were on about and see what you can pull together. I'll start cataloguing these horrors.'

'Some fun evening this is turning out to be,' Chris moaned, trying to forget the disturbing image he'd just seen.

On a badly smudged iPad, Chris Googled odd shit happening in Kampala. Opening search result number ten — he hit gold.

'Bog. This didn't take long. Listen. "Uganda's Missing."'

When Chris finished reading his unsettling discovery, they were in agreement. They had to prevent this barbaric abuse from escalating.

Chapter Thirty-One

Kampala, Uganda

'The unusually high number of cases of the severe form of African Trypanosomiasis, more commonly referred to as African Sleeping Sickness, has left medical authorities throughout the East African community unprepared. The disease is normally responsible for approximately twenty-five thousand new infections annually. Doctors have confirmed those recently infected have contracted the acute form as their symptoms are showing much sooner than would be the case if infected by the less aggressive West African form of the disease, and in far greater numbers. Joining me today is Professor Peter Chang from the University College of London. He's an expert in the field of Molecular Parasitology. Professor, could you share your concerns with us regarding this latest outbreak of the sleeping sickness, and is it correct the World Health Organisation, only last year, downgraded the disease status off the critical research listing as the numbers infected over a decade have declined?'*

'Hello Joanne. Thank you for inviting me to discuss this worrying development. Firstly, for the record, funding for this debilitating disease has not been cut. Our research is paramount and our advances, while slower than we would wish, are progressing as fast as the scientific process will allow. But you must remember, when we make a breakthrough, we are often hindered by bacterial, viral and parasitic mutations which can override any successful advance we may have achieved. In the case of this sleeping sickness, our research shows the rapid increase in spread appears to be for that reason. The parasite has become more *virulent and faster developing. It has mutated, and this new variant has altered its surface glycoproteins, and can develop more rapidly than previously found, meaning the hosts immune system cannot fight back quickly enough. We are seeing those infected reduced to a coma state within days of the initial infection. The concentration of Tryptophol, which is the chemical compound inducing the sleep response in humans, has been found in greater density than we've ever known. All we can do is keep them well hydrated and hope they respond to the recognised treatment, which currently is Eflornithine.'*

'Do you have an explanation as to what might have brought on this mutation? Do you think it is excessive localised temperatures or because of an inoculation programme not trialled thoroughly? Can you give us any answers, Professor Chang?'

'How long is a piece of string? We just don't know. Following the successful release of sterile male tsetse flies, we had seen the numbers falling quite encouragingly. We thought we were making headway. Clearly this form of vector control hasn't done the job, and, to stress, we really don't know why. On a positive note, from the new cases data, we have identified a trend around an area. A parasitic mutation occurred within a 50-kilometre radius of a central zone. There's been a pocket of infection with an additional strand. This indicates a possible cross species jump. This area is our focal point and where our resources and expertise are being targeted to understand what has happened ... Joanne, I want to stress again ... science is a very rewarding and enlightening field, but at times, extremely frustrating.'

'Cross species jump. With what other species? Can you be more specific please Professor Chang?'

'No. Not yet. We've discovered an unusual complex arrangement of trans-genes. Not wanting to get too technical, but some form of GM strain or mutation is all I can say at this

stage ... If I may, I would like to clarify a point you raised earlier: The World Health Organisation has worked extremely hard and continues to do so for the health of the people in the areas affected. The organisation has secured, on a donation basis, the only drug presently available that has any effect against this disease. The manufacturer of the drug has continued to honour its pledge to cover the drugs production costs. This is a marvellous, self-less act on the part of a multi-national company and must be applauded ... Now, before you ask, I don't wish to speculate further on theories as to the possible species jump. However, I will say, at the start of the Ebola outbreak, someone ate a piece of fruit infected by a bat with the virus. It could be as simple as that. ... Just to clarify, I am of course talking about the Ebola virus. This sleeping sickness is not contracted from eating any form of fruit. As I said, science is fascinating, but equally, extremely contrary.'

'Fascinating is not a word I would have chosen to use in this context,' Joanne, the interviewer, added in a judgemental tone.

'Thank you, Professor Chang. Hopefully you, or one of your colleagues in the field, may be able to share more with us over the coming days.'

'Enough of that,' Siegfried muttered, aiming the remote at the wall mounted television, muting the infuriating chatter of the news presenter.

The first to be dropped at the muster area, a deserted administration building, he helped himself to water from a dispenser on a rickety table in the corner of the waiting room, wondering what on earth he'd signed up to. With a fractious agitation, recalling the grilling interviews; psychiatric assessments; the questioning and reams of paperwork to become part of ground-breaking neuroscience research.

Knowing he was in the running for lucrative months of work

maybe even years, Siegfried hoped it would prove worth putting his life on hold. And he made the grade.

Checking his mobile, having been told the remote facility had no regular internet or phone access, he still had a signal. Not yet cut off from the rest of the world, he thought, noticing four messages from his girlfriend, Greta. Choosing not to read them. She'd been getting on his nerves. If she's around on his return, so be it.

Thin privacy glass in the dated aluminium door rattled, announcing the arrival of two men and a woman. Each gave him a warm smile, choosing well-spaced seats. Clearly, they'd not met before today, he assumed. As an ice-breaker jesting, 'I take it you're waiting for the guys in black too? I'm Siegfried Acker. Neuroscientist from Berlin. I assume we're in similar fields?'

'Dr Sulaman Habib. Coma Research Centre Strasbourg. Pleased to meet you.' The tall, dapper one offered his hand.

'Dr Clare Cunningham from IBRO HQ in Paris.' The attractive women moved forward in her seat, giving him a casual nod.

'Pierre Lavigne. Cellular neuroscientist. CRNL, Lyon,' the bald man divulged, as the door again rattled. A slender, immaculately dressed lady entered with flowing grace.

'Welcome to the chosen few. Just running through introductions,' Siegfried offered.

'Hello. Some of you look familiar. I may have seen you at various related conferences. Dr Amal Najafi. I specialise in computational neuroscience. Let's hope we don't have to wait too long. It's stifling in here,' she exclaimed — fanning her face with a classy, grey leather traveller's wallet.

The noisy opening door signalled more action.

Led from the building, into a gleaming black people carrier, then driven at speed through the suburbs of Kampala, the group absorbed glimpses of the city through tinted windows; efficient air conditioning blasting clamminess from their skin.

A man in military uniform, with beads of sweat glistening on his face, raised a barrier, standing to attention, as they pulled into a well-tended campus. Lush carpets of Bermuda grass and dappled shade from eucalyptus trees made this destination far more appealing, Siegfried thought — spotting a familiar symbol: a rainbow coloured green, white and yellow on a directional sign mounted in a low bank. The same logo on the business card — still buried in his wallet — he'd been handed at the closing of a forum two years ago by a gentleman in a shiny grey Armani suit, appearing at his side bringing a waft of citrus scented aftershave. The discussion: The Way Ahead. Mechanism and Humanity had captured Siegfried's mood and imagination. 'Covertly recruiting neuro pioneers. If you're interested mail me,' he'd suggested without introduction, but with a magician's deftness flicked the card into Siegfried's palm as they shook hands. In the time it took Siegfried to read it: 'New Dawn', giving just an email address, and raise his gaze, he'd gone, lost in the crowd.

After much deliberation, Siegfried took up the offer. A good decision during uninspiring professional stagnation.

Leaving the coolness of the car, Siegfried noticed a man with a clip board stood in the main entranceway of a non-descript building beckoning them to approach.

Marched single file, brought to a halt outside a set of heavy wooden doors by the agitated man's up-stretched arm, Dr Siegfried Acker, ticked off against his list, was handed a note showing a seat number, then directed with a flick of an outstretched palm through the doors into an auditorium.

Forty or so individuals were already dotted around, sat separately, heads turning as he entered. Perhaps we're being kept at a distance in case we cheat at something, Siegfried wondered, finding his well-considered option.

'I hope you've told someone where you are, we might not make it out alive,' he joked to Clare Cunningham, sat three free-standing green velour seats away.

She humoured him with a smile. His attention then drawn to abstract paintings and copper foil art on the wall to his right. Noticing to his left, tinted mirror glass made up the entire area, dimly lit from behind, decorated with etchings of rhinos, elephants, giraffe, zebras and large cats: the big game animals so threatened by man. In awe of the craftsmanship taken to create the stunning safari scene, Siegfried much preferred it to the random blobs of paint thrown at the canvasses on the opposite side.

Not alone in his appreciation, the intricacy of the glass sketching also transfixed the others.

Half an hour past, and still they waited on tenterhooks, fidgeting, killing time playing games on their mobiles, and chit-chatting. The air of unease: palpable. Heads turning with impatient frequency to the repressive doors — eager minds willing them open to end the waiting game.

Four people went into the corridor huffing to find a bathroom, or question a person in charge.

Siegfried remained in his seat, lost in thought, keeping relaxed, wondering if the delay could be part of an impulsiveness test.

Scrapping his chair against the tiled floor, turning to face the etched glass, deciding he might as well study it in comfort without getting a crick in his neck. A few of the others followed his initiative: why face a blank wall with no projector screen, stage or lectern in place? Their expressions portrayed.

The discerning minds behind the two-way tint made their selections.

With a purposeful thrust of the auditorium doors, clipboard man returned, calling out eighteen numbers as he moved. Those not called were to follow him, the rest, remain seated. Siegfried, Clare, Amal, Sulaman and Pierre rose.

Maybe the easily distracted, the impatient had failed at this stage? Harsh, Siegfried thought. But then whoever was assessing could afford to be picky by first impressions from this room brimming with talent. 'That's assuming I'm not one of the rejected?' he wondered, looking at the glass wall, visualising eyes watching his every move. Following clip board man, Siegfried gave the thumbs-up to the decorative barrier.

The selectors behind appreciated his gesture.

A few smiled, wryly.

After much form filling, the waiting game continued in a sparsely fitted canteen — smelling of bleach — with thermoses of coffee and huge jugs of iced mint tea to keep them refreshed.

On clip board man's return, he read out just three names.

The selected hastily left, avoiding eye contact, crossing in the doorway with a very tall man wearing a creased white colonial suit, reminding Siegfried of his eccentric science teacher who wore an identical one all year. 'Barmy Bishop,' he murmured.

'Good day. Sorry about the delay. I'm Dr Rodrik Dreher and it gives me great pleasure to announce those of you remaining are invited to join the research and implementation team. Your induction will take a further twenty-four hours. You'll be spending the night here ready for your full integration tomorrow. We've a splendid inauguration dinner lined up to give you a flavour of the regional cuisine.' Harrumphing into a checked handkerchief, he continued: 'Please, in your own time, make your way out the rear doors for your identity card processing followed by a short briefing. I'd like to acknowledge your patience and look forward to seeing more of you over the coming months.'

The overheated doctor, face flushed scarlet with dark pools of sweat staining the armpits of his jacket was having problems acclimatising, Siegfried surmised, watching him mop his brow, hand a beige folder to clip board man, then saunter to the door, replaced by a skinny young adult at the lectern.

A gopher, Siegfried assumed as he launched into a monotone, breathless announcement without introduction.

'Because of the poverty in the area, The Government, in collaboration with the health authorities, has passed a law allowing the families of those critically ill, if they are the main bread winner, to be paid in line with the local wage for their next of kin's living body to be donated for medical science. This agreement will help them, and aid research into preventing the disease causing the recent fatalities and other long-term medical issues prevalent within the local population. The research will be undertaken at the institutes facility where you are going the day after tomorrow. If any of you feel uncomfortable with what you've been told, you still can leave. However, please be aware under contractual law you are obliged not to disclose anything you have seen, or heard up to now.'

The speaker swiftly left the lectern, throwing a furtive — perhaps embarrassed — sideways glance at those seated.

Siegfried's curiosity was finally fuelled. With crystal clarity he realised why they'd signed the reams of legal documents; disclaimers, and an Official Secrets Act before given a true insight into the nature of the work they were committing to.

If any dropped out, the organisation had every traceable detail of their lives. They'd be carefully monitored.

Big Brother and all that.

Chapter Thirty-Two

The window blinds on their coach closed with a whispering hum before they'd moved an inch. Another dropped behind the driver, blocking Siegfried's view ahead as the weighty vehicle lurched forwards.

Cocooned in twilight — for what seemed hours — eventually slowing, its chassis twisting and groaning as it lumbered off the wide tarmac road. Through a narrow gap at the base of his window blind, Siegfried saw a plume of red dust kicked up as the tyres met a crude track.

Nearing the research facility in the outback of Uganda, somewhere, he assumed.

Half an hour later, they came to a halt with a hiss of hydraulics. The atmosphere inside the coach, electric; a fraught silence prevailed, before the doors waggled open. The front seat passengers hesitated — looking behind for reassurance before stepping into the unknown. Siegfried took the initiative — launching himself out into the fierce heat, freed like an animal keen to explore its new environment. Shielding his eyes from the scorching sun, taking in the panorama: just barren savanna with a distant mass of greenery erupting from a valley, and an expansive hilly rock face in front.

The rest filed off, scattering like lost holidaymakers looking for signs of officialdom.

Noticing a black oblong shape appear in the well disguised stone work, a door Siegfried realised, as a figure stepped out, waving, heading towards them at a casual trot. Counting five larger doors painted to match: clever, he thought, as the stark realisation hit home: once he passed through those uninviting portals, he'd be incognito, making him wonder, 'For how long?'

'Hello. Please follow me. We have refreshments ready. Let's get you out of this heat,' a stout man wheezed after his brisk exertion. They obligingly followed to the sound of shoes and trundling luggage cases on concrete.

Stepping through the ominous doorway, the cooling relief was instantaneous. Rattled down flights of metal steps, further and further into the underground construction. Ushered past laboratories, operating theatres, countless wards and observation windows revealing nothing more than sinister inky blackness. 'Struth. Are they expecting a plague of biblical proportions?' Siegfried commented, louder than he realised, a few of the others glanced at him, their eyes transmitting unease.

'That's the common room. Please make your way back here in one hour after we've assigned your rooms,' the man instructed, as they paced past, pointing to a blue door at the top of a flight of concrete steps.

Matching the man's speedy stride, Siegfried was first in line to be allocated his room.

Throwing his holdall onto the crisp white bed linen of a single bed — displacing a grey fleecy blanket; his designated living space for the next few months smelt of wood: but not pleasant rosewood or cedar, one of urea-formaldehyde. The smell of bonded sawdust. 'Bloody MDF,' he chuntered — screwing up his nose in distaste.

Being subterranean, there were no windows: a metre sized modular roof seal provided the only natural light to brighten the place. Watching a few clouds drift by above, he scanned the frame for a catch: there wasn't one. He'd no way of ridding the air of its toxic under-tone. 'Bum,' he grumbled, before realising in the middle of nowhere, it'll be great for stargazing. 'Oh well. In for a penny, in for a good pay-out at the end of this,' he muttered, shoving clothing into surface dusty new homes.

Giving his face a quick swill, Siegfried headed back, as

instructed, to meet up with the rest.

Reading between the lines, the carefully selected arrivals were unattached extreme workaholics. Siegfried got the same answers to his prying questions as he killed time waiting for their briefing. The organisations quest for medical advancement allowed no room for personal distractions: these lone wolves were ideal.

'Ah. clip board man,' he murmured, as the door flew open; beady eyes surveying the room as he stepped up to the lectern.

'Hello again. I trust your rooms are fine?'

No one spoke.

'Your introduction to the programme will be gradual, allowing time for your immunisations to take effect. Please stick to the programme of procedural briefings, lectures and light duties found on the noticeboard in your room. Unless you experience severe side effects, you are expected to commit to your general nursing duties. I know these are well below your capabilities. But trust me, you'll be more than satisfied when your contractual tasks begin.'

Siegfried noticed him focus on Clare, sat in the front, for longer than she felt comfortable knowing, for definite, he'd found his foe. She pulled her skirt over exposed knees, looking away to break the unpleasant man's leering stare.

Chapter Thirty-Three

When their shift patterns coincided, Siegfried often spent time with Clare. She was OK, provided a sane distraction for his off-duty moments. Not that there were many: work and more work, being the order of everyday along with exhaustion fuelled rest.

Living like troglodytes, Siegfried noticed how the lack of fresh air and daylight was taking its toll on a few; relative to the life they normally led, he surmised. The ones with good physiques and skin tone on arrival — the out-doors type — suffered UV deprivation the quickest. Although the research station, designed with a large inner courtyard, stocked with trees and flora capturing sunlight throughout the day, provided a welcome respite to the realms of laboratory's and wards: it wasn't adequate.

Siegfried would sit with the others in the artificial oasis, usually in silence, facing skywards, probably sharing the same thought: not sure if I can handle months of this existence.

By day fourteen, given the medical all clear, things got real.

Mr Clipboard entered the seminar room hyped, sporting a cocky know it all expression, his gaze holding Siegfried's. Maybe he's detected my negative vibes. Just give me the slightest reason, he thought, knowing he'd end up thumping the short man syndrome sufferer.

Stepping onto a raised platform, Clipboard began: 'We would like to thank you, and assure you the work you've been doing is linked with what is to come. We hope you haven't been belittled by your introductory tasks.'

His seated audience, eagerly anticipating the next phase of their assignment, gestured in a not at all way.

Sub-consciously filtering Clipboard's words drifting from his soapbox, Siegfried replayed the recent chats he'd had with his new colleagues. They'd formed a speculation group, each having a theory what awaited them; even taking bets on what lay ahead. Siegfried pictured the wall chart pinned to the noticeboard in his room, showing their theories in code, the odds against each changing daily. He smiled, recalling their giggling fits, like naughty schoolboys wasting time with lad's banter; keeping their voices low in case they got caught and given extra shifts. This semi-normality served its purpose: it diluted the boundary between their oppressive work regime and basic functions of nutrition and rest.

In unanimous agreement they'd be making neurological modifications involving the donated; perhaps even linking the organic with the digital, bearing in mind the best in the field of computer programming were there. Whether their involvement was experimental or approved, was the subject of much heated debate, keeping them focussed and ready for more.

Drawn from his reverie as Clipboard's rapid burble ended, Siegfried felt an air of tangible disquiet hang, realising perhaps he should have paid more attention as to the cause.

The door then opened. The expectant group watched the facilities prime team enter, exuding authority. Taking their seats on the stage, critical eyes assessed their anxious audience. These were the white coats to impress; the innovators; the main funders of the enterprise who, up to now, they'd only caught fleeting glimpses.

On the edge of his chair, Siegfried rested his elbows on the back of the seat in front, supporting his chin on his hands, an oscillating left leg in constant motion.

One of their speculator group nervously giggled.

Siegfried threw the perpetrator of the infantile sound a withering look. His embarrassed colleague shook his head, with his hand over his mouth raised the other in apology.

In turn, the team explained their specific involvement within the project, before the last to speak stood, ambled as he spoke to a curtained area in the corner of the room.

'Esteemed colleagues. My name is Professor Leopold Fleischer. It has taken us three long years to reach this point of excellence. I will now introduce you to the paragon of our programme. Prepare yourselves for your first glimpse into the future of hybrid technology. Please welcome, Project GIMACV, Number 185.' And with a flourish, he whisked back the curtain.

Over-awed in reflex, Siegfried stood bolt upright, knowing he and the speculators had been partially right — but only when they'd taken their notions to the extreme.

In a split-second, their creation turned to face him.

After a combined loud gasp, the room fell silent.

Siegfried remained standing, asking, 'Where are the other 184?'

'An encouraging response. Please follow me, and I'll take you on a tour of the inner sanctum of our unique facility.'

Dumbstruck, and a little paler, Siegfried joined the rest, a few stumbling, the sound of chair legs scrapping against the floor, signalled their eyes were glued to the prime team's replicant as they filed from the room behind the Professor.

Number 185 dutifully followed, bringing up the rear.

Chapter Thirty-Four

River Valley Girls Boarding School, Alberta

'Jolie Brockman! It's way past lights out. What are you still doing in here? You'll ruin your eyes in this gloomy corner,' Mrs Jenkins barked.

'Sorry. I got carried away with this research. I promise I'll leave soon. If that's OK. I just wanted to finish these notes before I lose the link.'

'What are you researching, young lady? I take it not a homework project judging by your enthusiasm.'

'No, but something that's been bugging me at home. Can I tell you? Do you have a few minutes, please?'

With a comforting warmth, she offered, 'Yes, my dear. I'll get us a cup of hot chocolate, with extra milk for you. I know you girls like it that way, always so much nicer, creamy, late at night.' Mrs Jenkins face resembled a scary wrinkled clown lit by the blue glow of the library's vending machine. Jolie giggled.

'Right dear. I'm all ears,' she said, settling next to her in a study snug.

'OK. This may sound weird. But my granddad, who just died. Don't worry, I'm fine Mrs Jenkins, I don't need a hug or anything. Anyway, he kept talking to someone as if they were real, who none of us could see. He even described what she looked like and drew a sketch. Look, I've got it here. A bit Red Indian looking.' Jolie flattened the drawing onto the desk. 'He knew what this person liked and didn't. Mum, Dad, and me to be honest, thought she was an imaginary friend. But I've been thinking, maybe she wasn't? Maybe he was seeing a person who'd lived on the ranch, and perhaps it was her ghost? So,

I've researched how you trace people who've died, or can't be found, because granddad said she wasn't happy and missed her mum. I've been going around in circles with these links. Mainly Cyndi's List for the missing. I've entered loads of searches and gone off all over the place. I really need help focussing, pleeease Mrs Jenkins,' Jolie whined.

'Gosh. I think this will take some time. But, at least it's nothing to do with that controversial blood group project. It worried me you were going to drag me into a family parentage mystery. I was hoping the dust had settled on that. ... Poor Beatrice. She's still walking around looking guilty. Not that it's her fault, poor love. But some of you girls can be so cruel. Not you, dear. You're lovely. One of my favourites. Although we're not supposed to let on. Did you know her parents are divorcing? It's not right what happened years ago. But her mum obviously had her reasons to seek companionship elsewhere, what with her father working away so often. She should have told a little white lie. Then I suppose she was too busy thinking about other things Mums do. I understand that. It's like you all needing my shoulder to cry on and then of course—'

'*Mrs Jenkins.* I thought you were going to listen.'

'Oh yes. Sorry, dear. It's late and normally I'm off-loading to George. Right. My nephew Tony. I'm seeing him on Sunday. Such a nice boy. You'd get on with him. He loves horses and fishing. Sorry, off I go again. Well, he works in his local sheriff's office and is always saying he wants to make a breakthrough with an outstanding crime. So, write down all you have, and I'll ask him to search their records. You never know, he might even identify her. If not, it may put your mind at rest, your Grandfather's poor old brain was just playing tricks.' Mrs Jenkins comfortingly patted Jolie's knee.

'Maybe. Yes. You're probably right. Here, have this: what I know so far. It's not much. I think she's called Lucy. Had long dark hair, brown eyes, was pretty and looked native Indian.

She wrote poetry and didn't like where she was living. I'd really appreciate if your nephew could help. So would Mr Phillips, my maths homework is way over-due. I must get up early to do it before I get more minuses.'

'Sounds very intriguing, my dear. Leave it with me. And get to bed before you get us both in the Headmistresses bad book's,' Mrs Jenkins demanded — gathering Jolie's paperwork.

Chapter Thirty-Five

Rocky Mountain Resort, Canada

'What's eating you? Since yesterday you've been preoccupied. Come on, spit it out,' Milo coerced — stuffing belongings into a leather holdall.

'I'm fine. Just sad we're leaving.' Marie shrugged her shoulders with a weak smile.

'We can come back soon. Maybe the weekend after next? I'm at HQ for two nights, then I'll be free. What do you think? Milo playfully grabbed her, throwing her onto the bed. 'And, lady, you need to eat more. You weigh nothing. After all the food you've been waffling, I can still feel your ribs. Have you got worms? Should I get Ted to check you over the same time as the horses? Tickling her exposed tummy. 'That's better, laughter, you up tight mare. Perhaps that's it. You're in foal, with raging hormones. Are these tiny hooves, or are you constipated? It's a bit firm around this bit.'

'Don't Mi, I might have gas,' she chuckled — curling herself into a ball to stop his probing fingers. 'Seriously though Mi, we need to talk. But not now. Let's enjoy a last lunch at our fav' place and drive back at dusk,' she suggested, with a peck on his chin, before sheepishly adding, 'Would you mind driving? I fancy a teeny glass of wine. Is that OK?'

Milo took her head in his broad hands, dictating, 'On one condition. I want to see you eat a huge bowl of pasta, and a slice of that raspberry cake you were eyeing the other evening — deal?'

'Yes. No problem. Love you.' Marie puckered her lips for another kiss, her demeanour cloaking her mood.

The soothing CD, plus midday wine, made Marie soporific, reflecting about their weekend. It had been a success; they'd rekindled their passion: like lovers caught in the first rush of romance. Although undecided whether to taint the moment by unburdening her angst; of late, a dark car interior seemed to release Marie's soul-searching mechanism. And only half an hour from Red Brook she knew her dreaded conscience sharing couldn't be put off much longer. 'Mi. Where do I start—? You know I've had words stuck on the tip of my tongue for a while.'

Marie stalled.

Milo turned the mellow jazz music down, feeling a frown of intrigue form as he prepared for the worst. Glancing at the dimming shapes outside, convincing himself he'd shortly hear an alarming truth, made a swarm of butterflies take flight in his stomach. 'Carry on,' he said with reluctance.

Marie remained quiet.

She's going over her approach to whatever's the issue, he thought, placing his hand on her thigh. 'Get it off your chest. I'm sure we can deal with what's bugging you, Hun. Let me pull over. There's a rest stop soon.'

'No. Just drive, but Mi ... before you judge. I'll just say, I didn't know, and I still don't know for certain what my father has got involved in. I may be jumping to conclusions about the intended applications he's asked us to experiment with. We've been very successful; I'd like to add. Anyway, for a while we've worked with graphene. Do you remember I gave you a paper a while ago—? Scientists have theorised about this substance for decades. Mi, its properties are amazing. Because it's an allotrope of carbon in a 2D structure, we've focussed on its biological use as an interface with human tissues. With brain neurons, to be precise. We've found uncoated graphene is perfect as a neuron-boundary electrode. It doesn't alter or damage neural functions. There's minimal formation of scar tissue, and no signal loss. Graphene electrodes conductivity in

119

the body stay far more stable than tungsten, or silicon. They're biocompatible and cover micro-metre distances without scattering, even at body temperature. This material could restore lost sensory functions and aid motor disorders. It will be revolutionary for paralysis, or Parkinson's sufferers, solving any neuron issue, in theory. ... That was the easy bit. Now for where I think things have got out of hand. Obviously, there was only so much we'd learn from experiments on rats. So, we began working on donated neurological material from brain banks. To begin with, not a problem, we satisfied the Human Tissue Authority's ethical and scientific requirements. But, to take our research forward, we needed fresh — probably the wrong term to use — but fresh cadavers. This is where father and his cronies came up trumps. We were assured all was legitimate. He'd negotiated with hospitals, they in turn with the families. All we knew was, they were fresh and intact, perfect for our research advancement.'

Marie paused.

Milo glanced at her, chewing her bottom lip.

'We made such startling discoveries Mi, got so engrossed, and indifferent to the remains we were basically issued with—' Her voice trailed away. 'Mi. It was the amount, and ages of the bodies we received that rang alarm bells. I questioned Dad, who, as you can imagine, was dismissive telling me to focus, not to concern myself when asked to carry out experiments which appeared to have no link to the medical research we were undertaking; extract this, or that part of the brain, fuse an interface to this without that. Some neurologists started making a fuss. I fully understood where they were coming from when they demanded seeing the respective hospital release documents. To placate them, Dad produced the necessary. A few stayed. And however well they were being paid, some left. But most agreed, Donald had serious financial backing and his demands had to be met.'

In the gloom Marie glanced at Milo, concentrating on the

road ahead, his expression: blank. 'There's more. Just before you went to Paris, Donald insisted I work with the back-room team as he felt I'd be of no further use with the main team. I was bloody miffed, but accepted he is the head honcho and our professional relationship had to be respected. This was the same day a new batch of white coats arrived by helicopter, along with a fleet of official looking cars. These guys were active: came and went all hours. I got woken a lot as they didn't dip their headlights, floodlit the paddocks making the dogs bark.'

Marie exhaled, mouth closed, lips puffing outwards under pressure. 'Mi, the last time I was in the inner lab, before my entry card was blocked, I saw things that really shocked me. Don't ask me to elaborate. Not yet, anyway. But it's all gone. His new team must have removed everything. Goodness knows where too? The only proof I have is in my notebook and on my phone. But I'm not sharing that with you. I love you too much and want nothing to happen to you. Mi, please understand, I just needed to off load.'

Marie dropped her head, letting her frame collapse into the passenger seat — deflated by her disclosure.

Milo stopped the car on a verge.

'Marie. I'll support you. Whatever you feel is right and lets you sleep soundly; I'll be right behind you. If you suspect Donald has gone too far, if need be, we'll get police protection. I understand your dilemma and why you're not telling me everything. But you have a choice. If he's broken medical ethics — not unaided by the sounds of it — we should report him. You should have told me before. I knew something was eating away at you. I thought you were having doubts about us.'

Milo pulled her towards him. 'At least you're not dying. That was my worst fear, you were going to tell me you only had months to live.' Milo choked back emotion, kissing the top of her head, stroking her hair — holding her tight as she purged tears and pent-up frustration.

'Plausible deniability Mi. That's why I can't share with you what I believe they're doing. You're safer not knowing,' she said, her words muffled against his body.

In silence, they held onto each other, minds racing.

Regaining her composure, blowing her nose, she looked him straight in the eye, adding, 'To lighten the mood. There's something else you should know. I'm either going through an early menopause — probably through stress — or I may be pregnant.'

'That's the best news I've heard for a while. You're full of surprises this evening. Come on. Let's get you back and tucked up in bed. And no more wine! I'm surprised at you,' he chuckled, tweaking her cheek.

Chapter Thirty-Six

Red Brook Ranch, Edmonton

Driving past the main house, headlights off, guided by the moon's sheen on the tarmac; neither Milo nor Marie fancied an encounter with Millicent just yet. She was needy, highly strung at the best of times, but even more lately.

Unlocking the cabin door, she noticed the mat askew — one of her pet hates. Straightening it with her foot, turning up the heating as Milo carried their bags through and upstairs, she called— 'Mi, is everything OK up there? Oliver may have used our space for a sexual liaison.'

'Everything's fine. Bed as we left it. Perhaps they cosied up on the rug by the fire? Cheeky blighter. I'll let him know he's been rumbled when I see him. I'm running you a bath. Do you fancy a massage after your soak?' Milo asked — trotting back downstairs, through to the office. 'Just booking my shuttle flight, then I'm all yours. ... There's an odd smell in here, Hun. Marzipan, I think. And a gum wrapper on the floor. Bloody Oliver. That's kicking the arse out of our good nature. The loo seats up in the cloakroom too,' Milo's muted voice sounded in annoyance.

Marie shook her head, tutting.

Sat on the edge of the bathtub watching water flow over her hand, Marie relived her car divulgence. Although it changed nothing, by sharing her doubts, she'd halved her concerns. It then struck her: she felt guilty. Poor Milo had enough on his plate without taking on her issues as well.

Turning off the tap, an image of the fresh donates: the ones still breathing came to mind, making her shiver, knowing she'd never be able to tell him the extent of what she'd seen. And — more worryingly — willingly played her part in creating.

Encompassed by the warmth of the water scented with lavender bath oil Milo thoughtfully added; her present space was calm. Closing heavy eyes, shutting out her troubles, she relaxed before the sudden trill of the phone made her jump. Sliding under water — deadening the sound, wanting to stay in her chilled zone, get a good night's sleep, not prepared to run dripping wet likely drawn into a Millicent morose chat.

Surfacing, the ringing still apparent, Marie blanked the noise, comfort rubbing circles on her tummy, planning her morning. Memorising a grocery list, plus buy a pregnancy test before lunging Storm. She'd no intention of riding him until she was certain. 'Get you settled in first, little bean,' she mumbled, as silence prevailed. Judging by Milo's curt one-word answers, he'd chosen to suffer Millicent's depressing moans, giving Marie a further pang of guilt.

It had been good to get away. And yes, they must use their lodge more often. Add that to new beginnings starting tomorrow, she pondered, rising from her brief Zen refuge, drying herself, donning a white fluffy dressing gown.

'Bloody women. Although I can understand her angst. Seems your dad's done his usual, I'm off for as long as it takes. But that's not fair on your Mum. She needs more interests Marie. Can't you persuade her to join that bridge club again, or take up tennis?' Milo mumbled, face down in a pillow.

Leant against the bedroom door post, hair in a turban, she chuckled at the sight of him prone, naked on their bed. 'I'll see her in the morning. Suggest lunch, I suppose. ... Now for another revelation: *if* I'm pregnant, and *if* it's all right with you, I'll take a sabbatical and devote my life to our new little soul. If I'm not, I'll apply for a research post in Calgary. It'll do me good working away from Dad. And what I told you in the car; I've compartmentalised the whole thing; treating it like another finished assignment. It will only bring us aggravation running off to the police. He'd have covered his tracks. And who knows what government organisation his in cahoots with?

So, tomorrow, I'll destroy my notes, photos and move on. That's my decision.'

'Your call. But I have to agree. With everything else we've got going on, it's wise. And there was me getting paranoid when I couldn't get in the upper wing. At least you've solved that mystery: it wasn't personal, you'd been pushed out too. ... Maybe Donald's trying to protect you, Marie. Did you think of that?'

'Actually, no. I just became incensed. Makes sense. Thanks, Mi,' Marie, feeling heartened, said with raised eyebrows.

'Hun, as you're getting on, and if you are, perhaps we should get an abnormalities test done?' Milo teased, patting the bed onto which Marie obediently flopped.

'You jest, Mi. But I agree. One step at a time, though. I've got a real knotty bit under my left shoulder, and cover yourself up, my hands may wander,' she giggled — testing the massage oils warmth.

Chapter Thirty-Seven

A light pressure on top of Marie's head roused her from an early morning slumber. Thrusting her hand from under the bed covers, it met the suited leg of Milo, stood, kissing the only part of her visible. The clonk of a mug placed on a coaster accompanied his hushed words, 'Don't wake up. See you in a few days. Ring me later with any news. Love you.'

A waft of green tea and his toothpaste comforted Marie, continuing her doze.

After an hour, coming to, stretching herself, awakening from the fog of too much sleep, she drank the cold beverage, igniting a craving for blueberry pancakes. She was sure there were some in the freezer *if* Oliver hadn't eaten them; smiling, picturing him post-coital by the fire feeding his latest girly conquest. Then, before anything else, she must go the laboratory to erase the past seven months from her life; mentally it may take years, she mulled, wincing at the thought of taking her mum to lunch. Wanting to stay upbeat; hopeful, until the next inevitable incident comes along, Millicent's melancholy likely to entrap her, extinguishing that positivity.

Tugging on her dressing gown, heading to the bathroom, she wondered if she could postpone the midday arrangement Milo had made, sick of being a buffer for her mother's despondency, and the effect the women had on her well-being.

'Maybe I don't need that pregnancy test to confirm what I already know,' she mumbled to her distorted reflexion in the stainless-steel fridge door, sitting up too quickly, feeling queasy after pulling on thick socks and yard boots.

Selecting an apple flavoured cereal bar from the kitchen

cardboard, grabbing Milo's wax jacket from the back-door hook, she stepped out into the stimulating morning chill, feeling instantly better and wonderfully alive. Breaking into a skip, inhaling deep breaths of nourishing air, imagining the oxygen molecules enriching her developing foetus, she headed towards the builders' mound of virgin earth, piled high, next to the deepening water pond. Running her hand over the soil's lumpy surface — resembling a massive chocolate log with a dusting of crusty icy frosting — pleased with their progress, she scrambled up one side to get a better view of the trench. They'd exposed the bottom section of a subterranean wall having another forty metres of foundation still to clear. 'Don't come back yet Dad,' she muttered, knowing they wanted to crack on with the project before Donald returned: his reputation for awkwardness, legendary.

Skipping back down the corner of the crusty bank, walking in the mini digger's defined tracks to avoid traipsing over the frozen grass, Marie heard Pops' raspy voice in her subconscious reminding her: 'No Marie. You'll crush the delicate blades. Stay on thawed areas.' Looking up, she wondered if he was still critically watching her from another dimension.

A glance towards the yard confirmed Storm's frustration. Head nodding over his stable door trying to attract Oliver's attention; the dull thud of his hoof against wood emphasising annoyance. See you in a bit, she silently mouthed, heading through the laboratory's glass entrance.

Marie paused when she reached the doorway of the room where Crispin spent his last days at Red Brook to watch dust particles swim in a sunbeam at the edge of the vertical window blind. The thought crossing her mind: was an element of Crispin still trapped there? His detritus floating in perpetual motion, eventually settling, becoming earthbound again, unrecognisable in its new form? The shaft of light drew her in.

Twiddling her fingers, scattering the minute specks she'd

fondly named Crispinite's, Marie picked up a pillow from the bed — holding it to her nose, inhaling. Could she detect an elderly, nonenal scent? No. Betty's efficiency had removed any lingering aroma of Crispin from the laundered bedding. Marie blamed raging hormones that she felt emotional.

Closing the door behind her, she made her way along the corridor to her office.

Sat at her desk, looking around, she knew she'd reached a turning point in her career; without doubt no longer wanting to be part of her father's empire. She'd make sure the builders completed the work and when Donald returns, hand over the accounts and keys.

'That confirms it, you don't want me fully involved anymore. Your loss, you're on your own now *Dad*. I'm only kidding myself you've been trying to protect me. Time for change,' she muttered, gathering her favoured possessions, shoving them into a plastic bag, humming a song Jolie played repeatedly when home from school.

Moving items around her top drawer, looking for her notebook, her paper friend; a conscience offload that didn't object to what she wrote on its flimsy pages. It was time this pal was released from its burdensome role; be ceremoniously burnt on the log fire that evening, mumbling, 'It's always in here.' Yanking them out, searching the back of each insert, chuntering, 'It only contained the ramblings of an over-tired white coat. If someone's taken it, they've saved me the trouble.' But what if it's got into the wrong hands? The thought made her blood run cold.

'Phone. Where have *you* hidden yourself,' she then asked her elusive Android companion kept in the laboratory away from Jolie's prying eyes. Finding it, under folders on her desk, 'There you are, my cold flat friend,' she mumbled, connecting the charger. Still having enough power to bring it to life, she scrolled through her photo's: Jolie jumping Ziggy, Storm strutting around the paddock; the phone always to hand when she wandered as a respite from any horrors she'd witnessed. She must download these pleasurable images to her Dropbox, before deleting the sickening nightmare ones captured using the body of the device to block her direct view of an abomination.

'That's odd? Where *are* they?' Marie spoke to the room, realising perhaps she accidentally downloaded her lab' shots instead of the horses.

Opening her online storage account, 'Here we go,' she muttered. 'No. That can't be. Where the fuck, have they gone?' She was dumbfounded. Her heart skipped a beat. Her photos of Jolie, the horses, meals out with her family *were* there. 'How could the others have disappeared? The phone's been secure in my locker?' she wondered. But in hindsight — only an easily picked padlock had kept it safe.

Goose bumps rose on Marie's skin at the thought someone may have copied, then deleted them. Maybe that same person thinks I've shared them? No, my phone log would've confirmed I hadn't. Donald had left before we went to the lodge: it can't have been him. 'This is strange,' she muttered, wondering if he'd ordered one of his cronies to cleanse her data. If he had — they'd been thorough.

Gathering the rest of her possessions, Marie considered maybe a government agency had found her hidden hoard of worry, surmising, they'd done their job, she'd nothing to be concerned about.

'Still, shit,' she mumbled, resigned to the fact there may be consequences as once again her troubled mind filled with what ifs.

Leaving her office, overwhelmed by queasiness, bile rose in Marie's throat causing her to gag and run to the toilet, only just making it before vomiting. As she retched, thinking, maybe I don't need that tester. I already know.

Chapter Thirty-Eight

Kasese, Uganda

Showered, dressed, and ready for his next shift, Siegfried realised he'd been at this surreal location for just six weeks: it seemed much longer. The procedure, now tediously repetitive, meant he felt none of his initial euphoria, constantly giving himself a kick not to blow this opportunity to work with the best medical and technological advances available.

His pragmatism, and in-theatre suggestions having already impressed Professor Leopold enabling the procedural sequence to speed up, meant his future with the programme was guaranteed. If he didn't lose that edge. But, however prepared he thought he was; however rigorous his selection, he still felt overawed: knowing he wasn't alone feeling this way. Although no-one openly spoke about what was expected; they were only human, unsettled by the sheer scale of the facility and number of donates accommodated in ward, upon ward.

The deadening acceptance effect was Siegfried's chosen phraseology for their unease.

Pulling on his white coat, chivvying his mirror image, 'Keep pushing. Stay ahead of this fickle, unbalanced team.' With a clunk, his room door closed behind him: the time he recalled the professor's inspirational words: 'Radical. Incorruptible. Organic. Readily available resource. Synthesis. Payback. Unconditional subservience — The perfect solution.' The man was, without doubt, a persuasive genius. His words helping Siegfried make sense of the unnerving, alien environment he was now trapped within.

Joining the steady flow of medical staff striding towards the inner sanctum beginning a rota of four hours' surgery, with a two-hour break, followed by another session of surgery: this being their intense work pattern for five days, tirelessly repeating.

Siegfried had one more day to endure before his next recoup' phase. A long sleep, gym session, massage and chill-out with the guys beckoned.

The Org catered for their needs. A cinema, virtual gaming centre, spa, and lap pool kept them sane. The most popular haunt: the library, with its wall to wall oak shelving containing every genre of book they could wish for. An inviting open fireplace; cosy furs draped over day beds creating a medieval cocooned feel to the room, enhanced their relaxation. Under Gothic quarter-foils, windows with integral sofas, gave them stunning views of the river and greenery in the valley below: a favoured spot — hot seated. Sat there, Siegfried always felt like a king surveying his estate. The library was their comforting refuge away from an absorbing clinical environment, and gruelling daily commitments.

Siegfried took to the interfacing procedure quickly. But in the eyes of a few of the others: they hadn't, and were battling with their conscience's. To survive had learnt to disguise their doubts. But with no critical officialdom watching; they'd pretend to read — curled foetal on a day bed in the library — but turn no pages. Or in a window seat, distracted, knees tucked under their chin, staring longingly at the jagged rocks below. This behaviour gave them away.

Siegfried regularly checked the catches were secure. Accidents happen — intentional or not.

Alongside the supporting theatre staff, the intricacy of the procedure dictated they worked in teams of three. Siegfried reckoned they'd transformed twelve hundred donates over the past weeks. Desensitised, he'd given up walking around the recovery wards: something done passionately at the start.

After confirmation of Trypanosomiasis infection, the field

teams recognised the optimum time to gather those suitable for donation before their brains became too damaged. The donates, told they needed a small procedure to aid their full recovery and rid them of the disease: wasn't a complete distortion of the truth. The selected: stabilised with four drugs — Pentamidine, Melarsoprol, Eflornithine and Suranim, were then moved to the facility.

Only one drug was given to the unselected and supplied for free. An infected needing the combination to stand a chance of pulling through, which none of the families could afford.

Siegfried recalled the first question he'd asked Professor Leopold: 'Who was the first to undergo this procedure?' He'd replied: 'A willing scientist. One of the pioneers diagnosed with advanced pancreatic cancer. Amongst other things, we learnt a donate with intellect was not ideal. The wonders of the mind are such, we couldn't predict whether the essence of that person would fight back: whether a small part of what was left within the vital brain tissue would infiltrate, renew and try to take command. Consequently, we found lower IQ donates better. I can assure you, Siegfried, this hasn't been pleasant. Despite what you may think, we're not psychopaths. We knew what to expect throughout the trialling stage and have always endeavoured to make sure no-one has been in extreme pain and ended life quickly whenever that point was reached.'

Lead neurosurgeon for the first procedure of this shift, rinsing scrub solution from his forearms, Siegfried's mind wandered back to his training phase: to the experimental footage of a poor soul convulsing and screaming. The sickening stuff of nightmares, he'd thought, and still doesn't remember what he yelled before running out the room, heaving.

Siegfried wasn't alone: this reaction common place during those first weeks.

Surgical cap and face mask on — time to begin.

The next unsuspecting soul in position on the operating table was awake, scalp shaved, cleansed and locally anesthetized. Attached to drips, the incision area marked in violet and surrounded by clinical paraphernalia in the hell hole; brain lab; gore room; grey matter slaughterhouse – all terms they used to describe the surgical theatres.

'Just giving you a drug to help you relax. Preparing you in case we need to use a general anaesthetic due to a minor complication,' the anaesthetist conveyed to the anxious donate.

Siegfried watched his colleague slice through the delicate pale flesh, deftly creating flaps of skin and muscle, as if peeling a bizarre new fruit, before securing them back with large blue clips. The donates cranium, free from its natural mantel, resembled a glistening creamy pink, imperfect egg. With the team gently positioning the head, Siegfried glanced at the wall mounted display monitor broadcasting an enlargement of the gruesome unveiling to everyone in the room.

The fragile orb clamped ready; they effortlessly glided a robotic cranial incision instrument into position. 'It's OK. The process is about to begin. Stay relaxed,' they assured the donate as the automated instrument set to work making a cavity. The resulting high-pitched squeal as the machine made light work of creating a window into this person's living essence, giving access to 'The Organisations' lawfully acquired resource, always set Siegfried's teeth on edge.

A surgical assistant then carefully removed the bone flap, handling it like a precious archaeological find. 'Was this once part of a human, or perhaps a Roman bowl? How can this be right?' Siegfried again wondered, readying himself for his role in this unholy manifestation of medical perversity.

Using surgical scissors to cut through the dura and arachnoid maters: sympathetically folding them back, revealed the brain tissue. Next, Siegfried severed the brains ventricle, allowing any cerebrospinal fluids that hadn't run from a lumbar drain to be sucked out. Avoiding severe bleeds, he diathermied the major blood vessels before extracting the pituitary gland; part of the hippocampus; amygdalae; fornix; entorhinal and orbitofrontal cortexes, plus the anterior nuclei of the thalamus — removing the donates decision making; emotional response; and longer-term memory. Using an electrical probe to stimulate the frontal and temporal lobes, Siegfried determined the dominant hemisphere, and cortically mapped the exact areas controlling their movement; judgement; reasoning; learning and emotions.

'Questioning please,' he commanded, beginning further extraction, sucking out 'The Orgs' unwanted tissue, leaving room for extra hardware.

'Can you tell me who this is? Do you recognise this lady?' an assistant asked the donate. 'Count to ten and raise your right arm,' they continued.

The donate briefly co-operated, before becoming still and silent, meaning Siegfried had extracted enough tissue, so turned his attention to the parietal cortex and brain stem: the tricky part, the main graphene interface areas, once modified, should allow complete control of this donate, but allowing them to interpret touch, but feel no pain.

Preparing the graphene attachment points on the intraparietal sulcus; lateral intraparietal; ventral intraparietal posterior cortex and adjacent gyri, essential for guidance of their limbs and eyes. The brain stem — the brains hard drive — was then interfaced, meaning donates had autonomic abilities, just some overridden, as decided by their programming.

The Professor's theatre team created the specialist modifications — *the crème-de-la-crème* variants — left with more of brain tissue and advanced lens technology fitted into their orbits.

Happy all was going well with this procedure. Alongside Vince — one of the more serious techno-geek programmers — Siegfried began attaching the graphene interfaces, synthesising the organic with the electrical was done via Vince's laptop. The meshing: not always immediate: Vince gave the nod a signal was present, triggering a twitch and a limb movement.

Slipping up his magnifying loupes, Siegfried waited for Vince's final thumbs up before starting to rebuild this donate.

To successfully infuse the brain neurones an inflammation process was encouraged by injecting the body's own extracted bone marrow monocytes. This was carried out as Siegfried sealed the port download area, before suturing the dura's, replacing the cartilage flap, and affixing titanium screw plates.

Skin flap closed. Wound dressed — job done.

Watching this latest transformed human wheeled away, Siegfried recalled his amazement when the theatre team, hard and software producers achieved that first limb movement. Their elation had been overwhelming: now — just another part of the automated procedure with no cause for expletives.

This is how surgeons created a Graphene Interfaced Modified Awakened Coma Victim. A GIMACV. With advanced gaming software, they had complete domination of the modified donate, fondly referred to as a McVee, or a Frank. Depending on the donates skin colour, they identified them with a white or black number tattooed on the back of their neck next to a GPS implant. With the tap of a computer key, the donate will understand its purpose and how to react using the equipment provided. And know how to recognise a true threat, and what programmed action to take to shock, stun, or eliminate that threat. Post action: its programming sends a report to a nominated HQ, where the project control team relay a next action update. The donates vital signs, constantly monitored, and programmed when to drink, rest, due sanitisation, rehabilitation nourishment, and deep rest therapy, meaning replacement GIMACV's are dropped into zone, guaranteeing 24-hour cover for their designated task.

The programme was creating simple subservience in some McVee's: in others, fitted with advanced telescopic technology, the perfect snipers.

The result: a recyclable commodity, with low running costs

and constant obliging obedience. From a military perspective — excellence.

Before each GIMACV surgical procedure, Siegfried whispered the professor's philosophies: now his own work mantra: 'First, and fore-most, I'm a pioneering surgeon. I must dismiss any abhorrent, or negative thoughts. Progress is not always pleasant or understood by everyone. All positive change needs sacrifice. For the greater good, some need to perish.'

Chapter Thirty-Nine

Red Brook Ranch, Alberta, Canada

Lost in thought, cradling a cup of coffee, Marie starred out the picture window, recalling the thrill in Milo's voice when she'd shared the news about her pregnancy. She hadn't reacted the same. In the back of her mind, already planning the next stage in her life: a new position to feed her intellect. But, unless an abnormality was found, she couldn't bring herself to end its fragile existence. Marie was not looking forward to breaking the news to Jolie, whose arrival for a home weekend was imminent. She'd absolutely no idea how she's going to take it.

Ending her peace, the turbo drone of a powerful vehicle broke Marie's trance.

Chirpily, Marie went out to greet them — mouthing, 'Hi Abigail, Fiona, Jools.' Waving to their shapes behind blackened car windows.

In her usual haste, Jolie was the first to burst out a back door. 'Hi Mum. Is Dad back?' she shouted.

'Hi Jools. In a few hours. You'll have to make do with just me for a while.'

'I didn't mean it like that. I've made him a project which is already going floppy,' she said, reaching onto the back seat, retrieving what appeared to be a cardboard bird box.

'It's a sort of kaleidoscope that hasn't travelled well. You can use it too.' The inflection in her voice portraying guilt she'd not brought her mother a gift.

'I'll be here after lunch on Sunday,' Abigail shouted from the driver's seat. 'Is that OK with you?'

'Yes, of course. Would you like a drink before you head off?' Marie politely suggested: already knowing the answer, the woman wouldn't waste her time with no Milo in sight. Marie found it amusing how she'd swoon at his Peter Pan, boyish good looks.

'No. I'm running late. Have a dinner party to attend to. Thanks anyway. Perhaps another day?' she replied — letting the car crawl forward with Marie's hand still on the ledge of an opened window. You're looking at me as if I've got two heads again, she thought — giving the overly preened woman an obvious false smile before stepping away.

Marie had a problem gelling with most of the mums from Jolie's school, knowing it was probably her fault: she could appear disinterested, preferring to stand alone, observing. During attempts at conversation, their intense facial scrutiny for signs of Botox indulgence, or lip fillers, annoyed her the most. Marie dreaded attending education related events without Milo.

Giving Jools a big hug, before holding her at arms-length, checking the height their eyes met, then drawing her back for a tighter embrace. 'What's happening, Jools? You've grown a bit, I think.'

'Muuum. Are you OK? I normally have a nit check before any bodily contact. You're being weird,' Jolie squealed — pulling away with a puzzled expression.

'Actually. I do have news. And I've bought you new clothes.'

'Blimey Mum, are you ill? What's with the it's not even my birthday presents. Is there a catch? Not that I mind. I'm not being ungrateful,' she added — dragging her weekender bag up the cabin steps.

Marie followed her, blighted with pangs of guilt: all that growing up she'd missed, always too busy having more important things to do. It was no wonder Jolie was closer to Milo: he threw his heart and soul into their time together.

'Let's hope she likes my guilt shopping, and it fits. I've spent a fortune,' Marie chided herself, walking through the kitchen behind the lanky frame of her daughter.

'Muuum, what's with the big pile of earth by the lab', and who are those hunky builders?' Jolie called, sauntering to the living room window sipping an apple juice.

'We've got water seepage. They've started repairs while grand dads away. Don't get any ideas, one's married, and the other's going out with a girl from town. *And* you're too young for casual sex,' Marie shouted through from the utility room, sifting through Jolie's washing.

'I don't know what you mean,' Jolie called back with an edge of sarcasm.

'Yuck Jools. These must have been lingering at the bottom of your bag for months!' Marie exclaimed — holding a mouldy pair of sports shorts between her fingertips.

Jolie moved to the doorway: 'Sorry Mum. They're my favs'. I wondered where they were. Probably a bit small now. I'll give them to Amie. Just nipping down to see the ponies, then I'll try on my new stuff.' Then, in a flash, she was gone. Marie heard the loud clunk of a door being slammed.

'Fine by me. Looks like I'm busy with this lot for a while anyway,' she muttered — frowning at the heap of stale clothing.

Having set the machine for a sports wash, she noticed Jolie through the window, pacing towards the builders, who leapt into their truck without giving her a backward glance, driving off, sending mud splatters from their tyres high into the air.

'Ha. Maybe next time, Jools,' Marie chuckled.

Examining the fit of a white cheesecloth Bardot top in her full-length mirror, tweaking the lay of the hem over new stonewashed jeans. 'Are you and Dad happy, Mum?' Jolie asked, her face still flushed after running back from the stables.

'Yes.... Why do you ask?'

'It's just lately, I always feel there are problems. Like a vibe? One of my teachers says I'm very perceptive, so I'm demonstrating this skill to you,' Jolie cockily stated, hands on hips.

'Oh, shut up, little miss, I'm a teenager. Do you fancy a burger and chips?'

'Yeah. I'll dress for lunch in my new hippy chick frock,' she cooed, throwing Marie a beaming smile: one she rarely saw, lifting her mood, knowing their fleeting, natural fondness likely to evaporate with the news of a new sibling. Savouring the moment with a smile, 'Bugger,' Marie mumbled, heading for the kitchen.

Chapter Forty

'Do you still do that at your age? Don't you use contraception? Why do you want a smelly *baby* hanging around being sick and crying? I knew there was something different about you, *and* it explains the guilt presents. Will I still be able to come home for long weekends?' Jolie exclaimed — clutching her burger in both hands, tomato ketchup dribbling over her fingers.

'I thought you might react more maturely.' Marie took a sizeable bite of hers, chewing for a while, mulling. 'It's a bit of a shock to us too, Jools, but changes nothing. I realise it's a lot to take in and things won't seem the same for a while. But just think: you can teach your new brother or sister to ride. That'll be fun. And you won't lose your room, that's your space and always will be. We'll convert our dressing room or add an extra one off the study. You'll be loved by three people instead of two. They'll look up to you and want to please you. It'll be fun. You've just got to get used to the idea. It wasn't planned. And it's not because you're not enough. You Muppet. ... We want you to be part of this too, Jools. And enjoy our newcomer.'

In silence, they continued eating — avoiding eye contact.

'I'm sorry, Mum. I was wrong. I should've been nicer,' Jolie, repentantly broke the silence. 'Can I name it? Perhaps Cristina for a girl, or Christian for a boy, like Crispin. Or Krispy Kreme, if it turns out a mixture. I was reading the other day babies are getting messed up. Not one sex or the other,' she enthused.

'Why not?' Marie reached across the table to stroke her cheek — chuckling at her daughter's fickle moods.

'Good. Once I've finished this yummy burger, I'm off to my room to research child behaviour and other stuff. Because I know exactly what will happen. I'll have to play nanny, while you two are rattling around in wheelchairs. Is that Dad—?' she shouted, abandoning remnants of her lunch — dashing to the back door, leaving it wide open, running out to greet Milo.

Marie stopped herself shouting a lecture about letting the warmth out: instead, she savoured the blast of bitterly cold air on her legs. Closing her eyes, relishing the warming comfort from a shaft of sunlight on her face, as it penetrated the trees outside the door. The solid closure sound of Milo's boot, followed by their cheerful banter, made her smile.

'This weekend is going to be great,' Marie mumbled, nibbling her sesame bun.

Chapter Forty-One

'Life's a series of ups and downs. Mostly our fault, granted. I suppose it's the same for everyone,' Marie openly reflected, sipping her coffee, settled in Milo's arms on the sofa.

'You should go to bed. You look tired. I've a paper to finish. Shouldn't take more than an hour. And, my pregnant mare, stop being maudlin,' Milo jested, patting her tummy, gathering their mugs, mentioning, 'I forgot to ask the other night: did you get rid of your incriminating notes?'

'Sort of. Let's hope my ramblings don't come back to haunt me. But I feel I've moved on.'

Entranced by the open fire, Marie couldn't be bothered to leave the sofa's hug, aiming the remote towards the sound system. Lulled, into a reflexive state by Gregory Porter's soulful voice, deciding they might as well get the baby's room the right shade, she'd order a gender test in the morning. But what if it *is* a Krispy Kreme? What would you choose? Beige, yellow, perhaps a fresh pale green? She mulled, distracted by an odd scratching noise coming from the kitchen.

'Scamp. Has to be. As soon as his idol is around, he can't stay away,' she muttered, calling, 'Jools — there's someone at the back door for you.'

Picturing her ears prick up; her young mind conjure it could be one of the hunky builders come to take her for a drink. In a clatter of noise, she charged from her room, flattening a wisp of stray hair, rubbing an inflamed patch on her chin, checking how she looked in the hallway mirror, whispering, 'Who is it Mum?' Padding her way into the kitchen.

'It's definitely for you, Jools,' she chuckled, awaiting her reaction.

Silence. Before a cry, 'Muuuum. Daaaaaad. You need to come here quickly. Scamp's got something disgusting.'

'Is there no peace,' Marie muttered — rising from her couch haven, following Milo.

This doesn't look good, Marie thought, crouching next to the gruesome present Scamp dumped onto the wooden floor. Pleased with himself for retrieving the filthy object, he stood by it, tail wagging frantically. 'Jools, lock Scamp in the out-house. First thing he can take us to where he found it,' speaking authoritatively, she watched the canine/girly duo bustle out the door, then in a hushed tone, 'This looks human Mi. But not recent. I'll call the sheriff first thing. Pointless hassling him now.'

'Christ Marie. What next? I expect it's an old cattle bone he dug up from the excavation hole,' Milo huffed.

'He's not happy. I bet he howls all night,' Jolie, puffing and rosy cheeked, announced, her pussy cat print pyjama's covered in muddy paw marks. 'What is it, Mum —? I know it's quite a big bone. But what's it from?' she questioned, squatting in front of Scamps gift — pushing it about with a near to hand shoe.

'Out of the frying pan and into the fat,' Marie mumbled.

'What's that mean, Mum?'

'A saying Jools. When you think things can't get any worse, something always comes along to test you further. But don't worry. Old skeletons are found a lot around here. For centuries the natives migrated through this region and new burial sites are frequently found. Ask the builders: it's their worst nightmare,' Marie held the bone at nose level with a pair of kitchen tongs as she spoke.

'Best get to bed, Jools. Sling those PJ's in the laundry and make sure you wash your hands, thoroughly.' In silence, she complied. Now out of earshot, 'Mi. It looks like an ulna. Let's hope it's from an ancient. If not, we may have another storm cloud brewing,' Marie said, with an expression of despair.

Chapter Forty-Two

'Can you tell us anything yet? Is it an ancient, do you think?' Milo asked, stood next to Sheriff Sutherland looking into the earthy builder's abyss.

'Female. Mostly intact. Beyond that we'll have to wait for the forensic-anthropologist down there to fill in the gaps.' With a shrug, he pointed to a man on all fours wearing a hooded body suit, excavating the lower half of a skeleton. The moving human form, and remains of another, Milo thought, looked out of place in sharp contrast to the freshly disturbed soil around them. Calling, 'Hi.' A polyethylene-d arm gestured in response.

'I'll remind you; this is a crime scene. Please don't go beyond the cordoning tape. If your dog brings you anything else, bag it and ring it through. Your mutts had a good gouge around, and the builders must have damaged the skull. Probably happened at dusk, they didn't notice. Marie, I need to contact Mr Osborne-Maine. Also, your mothers refused to speak to me. It's procedure. The sooner done the better. And no disappearing, any of you, until we know more,' he told them brusquely.

'I'll see how mum's doing.' Without acknowledging his demand, Marie strode off towards the main house, leaving them to watch the forensic man's painstaking progress.

'You may have to put out an APB for Donald. That's the term, isn't it? The blokes gone off the radar. I'm not sure we can trace him any quicker than you. Best give her a bit of moral support,' Milo added, jogging to catch up with Marie.

'A POI at this stage, Mr Brockman. Hopefully we'll draw him in before taking things up a notch,' he shouted, without lifting his eyes from the job at hand.

'She's still woozy,' Marie announced, walking down the stairs.

'I'll give her another half an hour, then you'll have to bring her in. I'm sure she'd prefer that,' the sheriff tersely demanded — peering over the top of his glasses, adding, 'Let's hope it's an ancient. Although there're pros and cons to that. In theory, the law allows them to be re-buried, but also means it could be a multiple burial site taking months to excavate. Once the ancient tribal societies get in the know, it could mean an end to your building work for a while. If it's a one off? Well, that's a different story,' he concluded, sucking air through his teeth, rubbing his forehead.

'Would you like a drink?' The nervous wobble in Betty's voice turned all eyes towards the kitchen doorway.

'Sounds an excellent idea. Coffee. Milk with two,' the sheriff requested, putting his arms behind his head — relaxing his bulky frame into Donald's distressed leather reading chair.

'Me too please Betty, and Mi,' Marie asked, sitting opposite.

The sound of his heavy smokers breathing filled the quiet of the room; Betty's beverage preparation adding snippets of background noise.

'I've rung the builder. He's not happy. But said if you need the digger to speed up the process, it's not a problem. With Donald away, we wanted to get this project cracking. How long do you reckon it'll take for forensics to finish?' Marie rambled, breaking the silence, getting a blank look from them both.

After much coffee slurping and idle chat, Sheriff Sutherland launched himself upright, straightened his shirt, pulled up his trousers, stating, 'It's over to you Marie. Before the end of the day. Thanks for the coffee,' then headed for the front door.

'I've nothing to hide. I'll come forthwith and assist with your enquiries,' Millicent said tartly, from the top of the staircase, firmly gripping the bannister rail, thrusting out her chin in stately defiance, beginning an overtly controlled descent.

'OK. Perfect,' he barked, plucking his hat from the hall stand.

Chapter Forty-Three

'Come on, mum. Let's get this over with,' Marie chivvied, reaching across to the passenger foot well for her bag, getting out the car, her pale mother, having difficulty holding herself together, stayed stock still, staring ahead. Opening Millicent's door, Marie helped her to her feet. 'Do you think Donald had anything to do with this poor person?' Millicent mumbled as Marie aided her through the police station's double doors. 'I mean, judging from where it's been found. It's possible? That's what's concerning me the most. I know that sounds terrible. I don't even care who they were, I just don't want the shame of being associated with someone linked to their death.' With a tremulous voice she continued, 'I've thought back. And there were people who came and went around the time the laboratory was built. Do you think they didn't all go? And your father's been up to no good again?' She stared at Marie, unblinking.

'Oh, Mum, stop it. I'm sure this discovery has nothing to do with dad. Now come on, put on your brave face and let's have a chat with Sheriff Francis,' Marie tried reassuring her, guiding her firmly by the elbow.

Sat in the waiting room, a surge of concern hit Marie. 'Why had Millicent said again?' she wondered, deciding she'd rather not hear any more of her incriminating outbursts. She had no inkling who the remains once were, or how they came to be there and didn't want to be privy to any more of Millicent's doubts — cutting her short when she tried spilling more snippets from her past.

Marie felt sorry for her, though. The last few months she'd noticed Millicent shrink — not just in stature — she'd also lost her supercilious contempt; her holier than thou attitude. 'Perhaps her airs and graces were just a front? Maybe she's a lost soul coping with her lot by downing others? Maybe she keeps people at arms-length as a guard to her inner self? Because she feels there's not much to find?' Marie wondered, wandering off to find a loo.

Retracing her steps, she caught a glimpse of the anthropologist's assistant going into Sheriff Sutherland's office. Realising it was lunch time, the station quiet, Marie bent down outside the door pretending to tie her trainer lace. Finding it hard to decipher the unclear speech, she moved nearer. 'Initial findings a female, age approximately twenty. Height 1.68. Full dental recovery. No jewellery, clothing fragments or shoes in the near vicinity. Body in place around forty years, give or take, so not our favoured ancient. A fractured hyoid bone makes it a definite crime scene, plus — post-mortem foetal extrusion.'

The voice stopped.

Marie went lightheaded — losing her balance — supporting her squat with both hands on the floor, inhaling, assuming what she'd over-heard *had* to be about the find on their land. Attempting to rationalise, she hoped they *were* talking about another case. But deep down, knew the eves-dropped conversation was about this latest disturbing occurrence in their lives.

Moving quickly away, rounding the corner to re-join her mother, Marie paused. Millicent hadn't yet seen her, was staring sadly out the window like a limp grey rag doll, all hunch backed and forlorn — her outward demeanour pleading for someone to help her.

Hearing the sheriff's door open, Marie hurried back to Millicent, saying, 'Mum, the sheriffs on his way. Do you want me to come in with you?'

'Yes please. I feel terribly nervous. And guilty. Perhaps I should have helped some people back then. But I didn't. I turned a blind eye. Oh Marie, what's happening? Will I be arrested?' she feebly mumbled, bursting into tears.

'Mum, enough. The sheriff's here and wants a chat, that's all. You've done nothing wrong,' Marie assured her, rubbing her hand for comfort — watching the sheriff critically log Millicent's historic concerns.

Marie's request to support her fell on deaf ears.

Millicent was unaccompanied when she made her way back, clutching a screwed-up tissue pleading, 'Please take me home.'

Reversing out of their parking space, Millicent made a low groan, her eyes glued to the car pulling in beside them. 'That's Maddy Brandon. Gosh, she looks terrible. Keep driving, Marie.'

Rolling slowly backwards, gave Marie the chance to look at this Maddy woman, whose expression of feared recognition mirrored Millicent's.

Once clear of its tatty metal body, Marie swiftly sped away, worried an altercation was imminent. 'Who's that Mum?'

'Someone I've not seen for years. She was married to the laboratory contractor, Bert. Nasty bit of work, Marie. She accused Donald of all sorts of things. Said he was a pervert and spread rumours he hadn't paid them. She had a hard life though: often seen with black eyes and bruises. Once, she was found locked in their cellar. People started wondering where she was. After a week the sheriff went knocking.' Millicent wiped her nose and dabbed her eyes, before continuing, 'If it wasn't for their dogs digging at a hatch in the back yard, they wouldn't have found her. That Bert was crafty, though. Said he'd been away hunting, and the daft bitch must have shut herself down there. But everyone knew he'd rigged it. They just couldn't prove it. Sad, really, I suppose. She became as mean as him in the end. I still don't know why Donald chose him to do the work. I told him at the time I didn't trust the man.'

Looking vacantly out of the window, Millicent absent-mindedly shredded the tissue; disintegrating white flecks gathering on her black trousers. Before meekly adding, 'He was found dead in a ditch about ten years ago. Everyone thought he got what was coming. Oh Marie, my heads pounding. Have you any pain killers?'

Within seconds, her head drooped. The day's events having taken their toll: she fell into a stress induced doze.

Driving back to Red Brook, reflecting on the morning's unveiling, Marie wondered if she *really* knew her parents: having her doubts after Millicent's troubled admission.

But whatever happened for this woman to have ended up dead and buried on the ranch; her unfortunate child, dying before taking its first breath — was undeniably the innocent victim.

Chapter Forty-Four

With Betty fussing over Millicent, Marie decided she needed a brisk walk to settle her equilibrium. Heading for the stables, waving to Jolie, mounting Caramel in the enclosure, muttering, 'She's fast outgrowing you, little pony. Time for a new home.' She smiled at Jolie's booted feet dangling well below the chubby pony's belly. Before reasoning, she'll be suitable for our latest edition. Your fate is safe, Fatty Melly.

'Hi Mum. What's happening? Is grumpy Granddad going to get arrested? That's what Oliver said,' she chirped, trotting past Marie leant against the fence.

'Jools stop it. I'll have words with damn Oliver. He shouldn't be saying things like that.' Although in the back of her mind: it's possible? She mulled, from memory running over what Millicent said about this Bert character, who could be linked to the remains of the young woman being driven from the ranch in the forensics van; grateful Jolie was too busy coercing Caramel to a canter, puffs of surface dust flicking in front of her lazy hooves, to notice the grim scene.

'Muuuuum. I left another bit of person in the kitchen. Scamp brought me a finger,' she yelled, kicking Caramel hard to maintain her reluctant forward motion.

Great! Too late to catch them with another piece of skeletal jigsaw. I'll let the sheriff know, Marie thought, taking a moment to switch off from the turmoil to watch her blossoming daughter enjoy an uncomplicated slice of life.

'Jools—. You need to wear a bra. Tart!' Marie shouted in jest.

Cantering past, Jolie stuck out her tongue, breathlessly adding, 'I've a hunch Mum. I think it's Lucy.'

Marie smiled, toying with the idea: could be?

Drawing breath at the sight of the sinister metacarpal out of place against the gleaming stainless-steel sink, in disgust Marie muttered, 'Dogs really are the most basic of creatures,' examining the partially chewed bone fragment, the rest: probably half-digested in Scamps stomach.

'Perhaps I needn't give this to the sheriff. I suppose it's against a law, but would it matter? It's likely Scamp or foxes have scattered more around the ranch. And with the DNA testers in the lab,' Marie wondered, deciding she'd analyse this small piece of the unfortunate woman: see what it reveals about this once thriving soul.

Chapter Forty-Five

Kasese, Uganda

Spying spots of rain on the skylight, Siegfried leapt out of bed, threw on running gear and headed for the security office to collect a GPS tracker and sign out: the usual procedure when they wanted to use the tracks around the perimeter of the airfield.

His legs were heavy: his foot falls inert on the hard ground after the springy rebound of the gym's treadmills. It normally took five minutes for his physique to adapt; for an invigorated impetus to radiate through his trainers.

The light rain on his skin and pleasant humid breeze blew away the staleness of his subterranean life, making him grin as he ran, thinking about his next few days off. He'd a tour of the GIMACV kitting out area; the professor's question time; and a safari with hot-air balloon ride to enjoy. The moment tainted, passing the stationary grey hulk of a C5 Galaxy troop carrier on the runway, its nose cone open, resembling a beached basking shark, swallowing up McVee's filing into its cavernous depths.

No exchange of banter or laughter drifted on the air. No families were waving farewell. No one will write to these foot soldiers, or send them goody parcels to boost their morale, he reflected, stopping at the fence — grasping the wire mesh with an over-whelming sorrow for these altered souls. His handy work had created these camouflaged clad zombies heading for a combat zone, making him wonder, 'Would they adhere to politically correct stumbling blocks?' Probably not. They'd see their mission through to the end: either theirs, or their programmed enemies. Feeling a tad emotional, Siegfried saluted them.

'Thanks for your sacrifice. I'm truly sorry,' he said, before scolding himself, 'Get a grip.'

Showered and breakfasted, waiting with the rest of his tour group at the entrance to the McVee rehabilitation and kitting out wing; passing time, Siegfried reflected on the history of the site. He'd learnt, from an information pack left in his room, the new investors, 'The Org', acquired it from the Ugandan government who, in the 1960s, bought it from a Canadian mining company. Surmising, after reading the bias literature, The Org's exploitation of the local population meant they had to be in cahoots with the country's regime. Signs of copper extraction: deep groves cut into the rock from dynamite blasting, studding and traces of ore, could still be seen on the walls opposite where he stood.

'Good morning. Please follow me,' clipboard, their guide announced, setting off at a brisk pace. Siegfried stayed at the rear of the group, taking in the new surroundings. Filing along a rock lined passageway with a shiny black floor, resembling an uninviting motionless river, expecting disturbing ripples, or primeval snouts of slippery creatures below its surface to pop up; maybe even Tolkien's orcs to drop from the ceiling; Siegfried surmised this was not the place to be on your own.

'It took three months to cut this tunnel which links the two sites,' Clipboard stated, confidently nodding his head, using a beckoning arm to keep them moving.

*

Entering a well-lit cathedral sized cavern, an exclamation of, 'Wow,' filled the welcoming void. 'We're at the start of the recovery and kitting out zone. If you look through this viewing window, you'll see the latest batch of donates in post operation recovery,' Clipboard orated.

Siegfried looked down into the familiar sight of a dimly lit hospital ward at nurses checking pulses, glucose drips, dressings, and charts. The rooms serene glow created calm.

'There's got to be at least five hundred beds down there,' he mumbled, his breath condensing on the glass.

Along one wall, a bizarre coordinated movement of legs on a row of exercise couches caught his attention. A McVee on each was having its limbs mechanically flexed; to aid muscle tone in readiness for their duties, he presumed.

'You're bound to have a lot of questions. I'm sure they'll be answered during the open forum with Professor Leopold later. Make the most of the opportunity to get things off your chest,' Clipboard said with understanding.

Siegfried, noticing Victoria — a petite, shy doctor he'd not worked with — standing with her hands flat against the viewing window. Her pensive expression relaying hidden concern.

'Are you all-right?' he asked.

She didn't speak.

'Come on. Let's see what other delights they've in store for us,' he suggested, trying to break her trance like stare.

With eyes still glued to the window, 'Do you think they still feel anything? How do we know they're not in mental turmoil? I should have stayed in my room. I'm not sure this day will help me. Do I really want to witness the puppets we've created being dressed up and manipulated against their will?' Victoria frowned. Her eyes watered. 'What's the failure rate? And what happens to them if the procedure is unsuccessful?' she shouted with disapproval.

'At the start of the programme we had a fifty per cent success rate,' Clipboard called back, stopping in his tracks up ahead. 'It's repeated on the failures with a further twenty-five per cent successfully converted. Over-all, we achieve seventy-five per cent positives, which is still improving. Not bad, I'd say,' making his point with another cocky nod of the head.

'How *are* they helped on their way?' Victoria pushed.

'Dr Finlay isn't it?' He annotated something on his board. 'We're not an inner-city children's hospital. We're performing

156

a public service and making a difference. We don't let them suffer unduly. But, to be frank, most involved in this programme have gone beyond worrying about the welfare of the few. Do you worry about the demise of the chicken you eat that sustains you? But, to answer your unexpected concern at this stage in your contract, they're given a lethal injection, incinerated, and their ashes scattered in the valley below. Does that sooth your concern?' He threw Victoria a disdainful glance.

'Hey. There's no need for sarcasm. Some of us still possess compassion. You, arrogant little prick. Shall we continue?' Siegfried shouted — gripping Victoria's shoulder tightly to stop himself squaring up to the maddening man.

'Next. The testing area. They're up and about. Fine and dandy,' Clipboard stridently answered, projecting a sneer at Siegfried.

He ignored the goad. Taking hold of her hand, Siegfried gave it a squeeze, knowing she needed empathy. His reward: a twisted little smile. 'Thanks,' she whispered, head bowed.

Assessing her out the corner of his eye; curious she'd passed the assessment, not seeming to possess the bullish temperament required to survive this environment; a more discarded wall-flower type doubting her likeability. And she's on the edge, he realised. They all were, to be honest. For mutual harmony it was imperative they kept on an even keel for the sake of the programme.

Clattering down a small flight of metal steps, they re-joined the others.

'What's going on in there?' One asked, peering through a narrow window.

'The exercise area. Nothing much to look at. Now what I w—' Clipboard, cut short by their chorus of voices: they wanted to see. 'Very well. Stand at the top of the steps.'

By raising himself on the balls of his feet, Siegfried just made out a flood lit corral containing two massive circular structures like racehorse exercising contraptions. But no animals were being coerced into movement by the metal divide: a mass of boiler suited McVee's were being shunted forwards like humanoid automatons. Not one, looking around, wondering why?

'Human farming,' Siegfried muttered his summation of the unnerving scene.

The group went quiet, as the reality of what they'd become a part of hit home.

'You can try their kit on next. And see them perform their test phase, get their programming perfected,' Clipboard blurted — breaking the spell, directing, 'Please make your way in single file through the grey door in front of you and wait behind the rope barrier.'

Patches of sunlight streamed through windows in massive doors at the far end of the zone they entered, bringing the floor to life. The sense of space extinguishing what Siegfried just witnessed. The rest of the groups chit-chat, also now more buoyant.

McVee's must go from here onto the troop carriers, he presumed, taking in their last post before deployment; three-metre high partitions breaking the echoey expanse. But multiple conversations; silenced firing, buzzes, grunts, and other indescribable sounds still resonated.

An expressionless McVee, its mouth partly open, sat at a desk assembling a piece of equipment engrossed a calmer Victoria. An occupational therapist and a programmer were accessing its progress, speaking quietly, annotating achieved goals on a tick-chart.

'This is the last phase before they deploy these valiant chaps. Feel free to move amongst them,' Clipboard offered, pulling the barrier aside. 'You've got an hour. But please don't touch anything unless authorised by staff,' he called, heading off into the depths of the room.

Gently stroking the shaven head of a test McVee; intrigued, Victoria didn't notice Siegfried slip away to join Kirk: a fellow speculator.

Stood side by side watching one in virtual reality googles

battle an unseen enemy.

'A bit like Dad dancing,' Siegfried joked, moving behind the assessors, who fleetingly raised their eyes, saying nothing — fingers continuing to fly across keyboards, making them chatter like a swarm of locusts. From the war action being enacted on their computer displays, Siegfried easily worked out the figure representing the McVee: its super-fast reactions having the advantage. Battle-scarred buildings; helicopters, explosions and combat mayhem accompanied their conversions domination of the scenario.

'We're surgical conversion team,' Siegfried offered.

An assessor looked back, offering a brief semi-smile.

'It's impressive to see in action. I suppose there're no limits how you could programme them?'

'You're right. But we're strictly controlled. Must rein in our minds and fingers. It's too easy getting carried away with these guys. Whoa, hold your horses' young-un,' the programmer exclaimed, reining in the over-zealous McVee with the tap of a key.

'OK. My robot friend needs five and nosh. I've a few more to test run today. Best crack on,' he added, resuming his frantic keyboard zipping, with a forceful final bash, making the McVee stop, turn to its right shoulder and seemingly, search with its lips — like a baby trying to latch on for sustenance. 'Feeding time at the zoo,' Siegfried thought with pity.

Moving to the next zone, one was doing a weapons dexterity test; only a slight frown showing on its face; no other emotion or human sound was detectable.

Realising he'd created expressionless, alexithymia sufferers — perversely picturing this donate, smiling, laughing — perhaps playing with a child in his former existence, re-brewed Siegfried's maudlin. 'Even their basic nourishment and rehydration needs are programmed,' unprompted, an assessor, stood by his side said: both watching a McVee take a drink from a water dispenser.

Giving a shallow smile, Siegfried ambled towards a shelving

area stacked high with camouflage kit, helmets, and boots. The expected greens and browns were among an array of dappled colours, along with white, sandy, grey and black hues. And floppy wet suits hung on rails like empty rubber skins. 'These fellers are certainly globe-trotting,' Kirk said in surprise, before Siegfried rudely thumped in the stomach, doubled over, his hands landing on a hard object slammed into his mid belly.

'Try that for size. It's the latest Halo helmet from Matick with whatever add-ons we want. This one's got live-targeting; video drone surveillance; battle status displays, plus GPS route planning. The things bio-mechanically more advanced than any other similar product on the market. Marvellous what major investment can deliver,' Clipboard announced with smug arrogance.

'Christ. Thanks for the warning,' Siegfried barked, pulling on the surprisingly light helmet: through the transparent visor, sending a death stare to his arch enemy, before handing it back to the clothing technician intently waiting the return of his valuable charge.

'The display technology is powered by a mobile phone, is fully upgradable for new apps. Plus, it's linked to the solar power packs over there. Our guys are self-sufficient for up to ten days in theatre,' Clipboard enthused, pointing over his left shoulder. 'Perfect for their role, our out of Africa chaps are issued the general lightweight, advanced combat helmet with nape pad. We've the in-field nourishment and power pack to show you next. But first, feel this, the strongest Kevlar clothing available.'

Pulling a garment from the nearest shelf, laying it across his outstretched arms. 'Comfortable enough to reduce fatigue in the field, and five times stronger than steel on an equal weight basis. It's flame-resistant. Provides two-way thermal protection, insulating at night, cooling during the day. Nothing less for our boys.'

With a pride filled jut of his boyish chest, he chivvied them onwards to an armoury, eagerly continuing, 'Localised McVee's are issued a MP5SD sub-machine gun. A FN SCAR-H longer range assault rifle. A Glock 17 pistol, and a CN-600 Anti-Riot rubber bullet multi launcher plus a powerful Taser,'

Stood next to a dozen clothed and helmeted McVee's. 'This lot are waiting for their nourishment and solar charging back packs. You'll see those next.'

Marching them a short distance away. 'We had to have this stuff,' he began. 'Needs no rigid frame. Configured for our requirements and collects the most sun's energy in low-light situations, even on cloudy days, out-performing crystalline technology. It's the lightest, thinnest amorphous silicon available, made of flexible polymer paper thin substrate. Its monolithic construction makes these panels resilient to damage, and only individual areas shut down if that happens. Critical in the high stress environments our guys will be in,' Colin spieled, already on the trot.

The group ambled after him.

'Taste that,' he demanded, thrusting a plastic scoop at Kirk, containing an off-white substance scooped from a large stainless-steel vat.

'Err. It's like runny salty porridge,' he grimaced.

'Granted, you wouldn't choose it from the menu, but we still savour our food, our converts don't. It hydrates and nourishes with essential amino acids. We monitor their vitals and alter the mixture to suit. We load the prepared formula into their backpack up here, and they suck what they need until programmed to stop.' He pointed to the top of plastic jerry-can container with a chubby finger. 'If we detect signs of dehydration, we bring them in from the field for rehabilitation. Any questions?' he barked, with excitable, flitting eyes. In a flash saying, 'Good. You'll be visiting the wards later. But now The Professor is scheduled for a chat. Bet you can't wait?' Striding away, catching no-one's eye.

The group moved in quiet unison behind him.

'If anyone needs the rest room, there're on your right. Refreshments are in the auditorium,' he gestured to a white double door with a green light above.

'Make yourselves comfortable. The Professor will be here in ten.'

Best spend a penny. Don't want to miss the oracles revelations, Siegfried thought, following three others into the gents.

Chapter Forty-Six

Being the last to enter the auditorium, Siegfried smiled sheepishly, settling into the nearest seat. The professor consulted his notes before looking around the room, sarcastically greeting him, 'Ah, my star *protégé*. Nice of you to join us, Dr Acker.'

'Sorry. Beef curry from yesterday,' he offered.

'Now we're all present. I'd first like to thank you for your extreme hard work and dedication. I know it hasn't been easy. It's not gone unnoticed you've battled with your consciences, but on behalf of the board, I wish to invite you *all* to continue beyond your contracted time.'

Gauging their reaction, finding favoured faces amongst the ensemble. 'This is a two-way agreement. We will honour your desire to leave the programme, but urge you to embrace our intent, feel privileged to remain a pioneer in this exciting phase in our planet's history. I ask you now to listen and assimilate until the end of my address when you'll have ample opportunity to air your views.'

Taking a sip of water, he began, 'It's been a gargantuan task discreetly negotiating, networking and financing to reach an understanding with our major players, being the governments, security organisations and world health officials. Fortunately, without hindering media attention. Remarkably, we achieved this collective agreement; this collaboration of contributory will over five years, from the idea, to inception. The foundation laying process showed all were fully supportive of our motives, working hard with us to plan an appropriate implementation strategy. An axis of the willing have set wheels in motion for a better future for mankind; the planet and the creatures with whom we share this delicately balanced environment. Rest assured, the collective we, are not a bunch of controlling psychopaths; no despots are in the equation. Our decisions are democratic, made by our governing thousands, including the world's top intellects, all with the best interests of humanity at heart. We've firm objectives, and once we see results, we *will* alter our future programmes accordingly. We won't let our actions run amok. But we will achieve our aims. We have to, and nothing will detract us from our path to a fairer, more sustainable planetary future.'

Sighing, he cracked his knuckles. 'We see ourselves as the enablers of common sense; the enablers of the right way forward; the enablers of a strong, focussed, and at times, ruthless leadership which will not be popular, but the reason why the present methods of governing society are failing, having been tolerated for too long.'

The Professors train of thought momentarily de-railed. Hand on hip he studied his feet.

His audience: hooked, hanging on his every word.

'The world's population is expanding at an alarming rate. The resources needed to sustain this increase are depleting and opportunities decreasing. Anarchy *will* soon reign. Disillusionment *will* create civil unrest, and chaos *will* prevail. Increasing numbers of dispirited people will continue being brainwashed into following lost cause religious fanaticism creating utter turmoil. The present form of leadership is not coping and will not cope when that breaking point comes. Mark my word, tyranny *will* conquer. We must nip this bleak future in the bud. We must provide an effective alternative before it's too late. ... For too long society has been led by egoism, self-obsession and greed. Misled no other option exists but to follow the ethos of the political elite with their misguided correctness sensibilities and teachings of the religiously naïve. Society needs re-programming; re-setting, and we have hit that reset button. We will restructure, offering firm and fair leadership. We will realign our existence with the natural world, allowing Mother Nature actively to play her role in controlling our numbers. This approach works for other species: we just need to follow their example.'

He glanced around, holding a few expectant gazes, then carried on. 'There's been argument, as humans we dominate this planet and have a greater right to our place: but only evolutionary luck has given us that edge. All mammals suffer, feel emotions and pain. We all share the same needs, but through necessity other species won't tolerate imperfection, affliction or hindrance to their existence. They've the correct attitude, allowing the strongest of their species to survive and reproduce. Take a wolf pack: social, intelligent, and survive within the geography of a territory that can sustain their population. Ask yourselves, which species shows the greater intelligence — the one that poisons and decimates its environment and can't control its numbers, clutching to eroding life — or the one accepting of the natural way, living in harmony with the ecosystem? We're deluding ourselves; we are the most intelligent of mammals. The wolves are right. We are the ones out of kilter with our environment. ... Humanity must change. It must desensitise and allow the weak to pass naturally. Just because we can cure or prolong a fading existence, doesn't mean we always should.'

Gulping down water, he continued, 'At the outset of our programme a few of our collaborators argued by adopting this approach we were taking a step back in our intellectual evolution. We persuaded them humans are the only species that *can* make the changes necessary and must take responsibility for righting our wrongs: this is intellectual evolvement.'

Pacing, collecting his thoughts. 'Time to bring us back to the objectives of our current programme. For years, climatologists have preached that burning fossil fuels has led to global climate change. But we all know this is partly the truth. These sources were formed millions of years ago. Their unstable carbon 14 isotope has a half-life of around 6,000 years and tree ring analysis shows its atmospheric concentration is dropping. Humans emit carbon 12. The atmospheric concentration of this isotope is rising — fast. There's our answer, address the population explosion, get the birth death rate on a similar footing. Over a 24-hour period approximately 380,000 are born: around 170,000 die. We need to balance the two. We've already introduced the first of our monitoring programmes in areas of uncontrolled reproduction, engineering reflexive control, giving individuals a valid reason not to proceed with a pregnancy through fear of infant deformity. Ultimately, the decision is still in their hands: the mindset in ours. We've major pharmaceutical companies cooperating with our population decrease programmes. I won't elaborate further, but you'll be aware of the release initiative gaining far more support than we predicted. It achieved our aim, allowing a timely end to exhausted lives, changing the populations perspective. Our click of that re-set button is having an effect.'

The Professor looked around him, unsure how his speech was being received.

No one spoke. You could hear a pin drop.

'Time my friends, for an insight into your handiwork. I'm pleased to say our GIMACV's are already making an impact creating a propaganda blitz. We've deployed over one thousand to Syria and regions affected by the Islamic state destabilisation. They're doing their job way beyond our expectations. Fast and ruthless. No doubts cloud their programming; no conscience overrides their objective. They've become an infidel phenomenon, spreading rumour, if touched, they too will be transformed. We've helmet-cam footage showing the extreme fear on the faces of their enemy. They run and hide, my friends. Run and hide. We've created the perfect Nemesis.'

Clearing his throat, 'Now, turning to our essential ingredient:

our donates, and the ethics of our role in Africa — Uganda in particular. You may feel we're exploiting the indigenous population. Rightly you could say our programme is modern-day slavery: understandable opinion. But we classify this first phase as fulfilling a global conscription service. This call to duty the norm in times of conflict. However, we're not leaving families in a state of destitution. The donate would die of the mutated disease without the full complement of drugs. We've simply removed the angst of waiting, allowing them immediate closure with appropriate financial compensation. This seems hard, I know, but individuals have been exploited throughout history for a fight not of their making, merely at the whim of a greedy lord, baron or king. And, whilst governments squabble over whether to deploy ground troops to tackle the fundamentalist cause, we are acting and achieving results.'

Pausing without raising his eyes. 'If you've still got issues about our proactive solution to a global problem, think of it as utilising an abundant organic resource. Something we do daily, affecting millions of other species to supply our nourishment needs. Arguably, we're threatening the role of the military: but with line of duty compensation claims, pay, pensions, housing and the welfare needed to keep hundreds of thousands of soldiers ready for active service, we've created the ultimate in deployable, readily available, dispensable ground troops, who presently aren't governed by conventions.'

Addressing the room, the professor caught Siegfried's eye — holding his expression of understanding. 'It's important to win public approval. We've great plans for our donates beyond the ISIL struggle. For this reason, we are delicately handling their introduction to society, so they've been deployed to assist where they're most needed — where the benefit of their presence promotes the programme with noticeably positive results. We've sent them to assist the International Anti-Poaching Foundation in areas of escalating destruction of our big game animals. They're assigned to specific herds throughout the region, having already been effective in capturing prevalent poachers who, in turn, we've modified and sent back into the bush where their faces will be recognised providing the perfect Nemesis. The perfect pay back. You'll see these McVee's in the rehab' wing and observe their compatriots in the field from the safari lodge.'

He paced — watching his feet.

'Looking to the future, we aim to utilise our second and third phase donates for high risk tasks — deep sea and space exploration, plus, we've already deployed sub-aquatic donate variants throughout the regions contaminated by our scourge of plastic waste. They're providing 24-hour cover, filtering our toxic pollution from the worst affected river outlets in South America, India and Indonesia. ... If you need a breather, now's your chance, before I change tack,' the Professor offered, waiting for signs of chair movement.

No one moved an inch.

'No takers—? I'll carry on and ask you to consider the costs involved with creating human form artificial intelligence. You didn't see that coming?' he jested.

A few smiled.

'The manufacture is undeniably achievable, but again, ask yourselves, do we need this technology? Just because we can create it, should we? The huge investment into such projects is not timely. If these creations are to carry out repetitive menial tasks presently undertaken by humans; if we reduce the population enough to enable all able-bodied to be gainfully employed, by then utilising human form AI's, we'll be reducing those employment opportunities again, creating discontent and upsetting the balance. Humans need a purpose. They need to feel valued. We shouldn't aim to remove that essential ingredient from the hundreds of thousands. Our common-sense utilisation of an organic resource is timely. Investment into human form AI production, is not. This investment should go towards alternative energy research; cleansing our environment, our oceans, space exploration – the uses for this misplaced funding are endless. Which leads us back to greed and profit. The constant race to create the next piece of expensive technology. Because we can. Always cure. Because we can. Our collective is focussing on cleansing and purifying our planet. On promoting peace and stability for millions, creating a period of calm for humanity, at the cost of a few thousand.'

The Professor took a further sip of water as he paced, hand in pocket.

'You'll be pleased to hear we *have* persuaded many of those investing in AI research to do just this. An encouraging percentage *are* diverting their resources in line with our goals. We won our decisive argument: could AI's be fully controlled to stop them evolving and becoming a threat? We know, without doubt, we'll never face this problem with our donates.'

He grinned.

'I'd like to turn to another aspect of donate phasing. So far, we've manufactured the conditions to create an abundant source which is sustainable and multi-purpose. However, we're working with the worldwide judiciary and penal reform groups to change the sentencing laws for the most violent and heinous crimes committed – murders, paedophilia, class A drug dealing – having implemented our Graphene Interfaced Serious Offender Modification's. Utilising offenders who've no links to society outside their prison environment. We're covertly trialling this sentencing option until our second phase modification procedures become judicially lawful. They're out there now, repairing our roads, operating our sewage plants. Research has proven the public *are* supportive of severer sentencing for such offenders. Quite rightly, why should they have a comfortable existence cosseted in prison from where they still promote a criminal influence? These people don't deserve such treatment. They cost economies thousands. For what return? They messed up big style during the first phase of their existence: we're now utilising them, in modified form, for public service through their second phase. But this time, the system calls the shots, providing the right justice. Penal policy reform has long been over-due, and we've provided a suitable, well supported alternative.'

The Professor paused — gazing amongst their faces, before finishing his lecture.

'A person of intellect will understand what we are trying to achieve and accept the process ... I'll leave you with that thought and close with my usual mantra: progress is not always pleasant or understood by everyone. All positive change needs sacrifice. For the greater good, some need to perish. Thank you for your time. Please help yourself to a drink, then we'll begin the open forum.'

Chapter Forty-Seven

Did it make him a control freak, or a genocidal maniac, fully understanding the logic of the programme? Siegfried decided not, glad he'd uttered not a single a word during the heated forum debate. Although on reflection, the African race was being exploited. But an ethnic group not completely exterminated, just a selection engineered for a deniably worthwhile cause. You could argue a generation or two will be missing. But that's the whole point: to reduce numbers, he mulled, realising how small he felt: a mere minnow in a massive cog of change.

'OK. Everyone with me? Keen to see the rehabilitation unit?' Clipboard summoned the group gathered outside the auditorium. 'This way, please.'

Leading them back to the hangar, towards rows of McVee's patiently sat, fresh in from the field, their clothing covered in red dust; ashen faces highlighted by beams of sunlight. They watched nurses select them, one by one, and lead them by the elbow to a sanitising station. Soiled uniforms were removed, thick antiseptic cream applied to sores and grazes, before being coerced through a partition of hanging plastic strips into a walk-through shower wash, the escaping steam clouding their dark outlines. Their modesty: irrelevant, Siegfried surmised, taking in the scene — shallow breathing to avoid inhaling too much of the pungent combination of body odour, stale clothing and sickly undertone of lingering protein powders being pressure washed from nutrition packs.

A resource team creating a nifty production line of frantic manual activity, in another corner of the hangar, played their fiddly role in dismantling and inspecting weaponry before loading it onto trolleys trundled to the adjacent kitting out hangar.

'All self-explanatory here. The process to de-kit and sanitise a McVee — from the start of their contaminated arrival, being programmed for deep rest, then gurney-ed away for rehabilitation — takes a slick thirty minutes. So, unless anyone has any questions, we'll take a peep in a ward before a bite to eat. Please be back in the common room for your safari group designation and itinerary briefing in two hours. Bet you can't wait?' Clipboard enthused, for once displaying warmth in his smile, knowing they needed this break from an exhausting work regime.

Filing into a stark, enormous room, lined in military precision with rows of occupied beds, Siegfried was again hit by the enormity of the operation. Each having a computer display at the base and a drip feed either side attached to a rest mode, motionless McVee. The only discernible movement: the gentle rise and fall of chests and dripping motion within intravenous tubing. An occasional twitch of a limb drawing the eye to the McVee, whose nerve impulses had sparked an involuntary reaction.

There had to be another adjective, other than bizarre, or surreal to describe this vision from a Sci-Fi movie, Siegfried thought, walking amongst their resting creations; examining digital displays, stroking arms and fuzzy felt heads.

The ward was peaceful.

The McVee's cosseted and comfortable.

In here, Siegfried possessed no pity.

A few were thinner than others. When questioned, nurses assured they closely monitored them, ensuring they'd be ready for duty in ten days' time.

Through a set of swing doors into a second ward, it was clear these guys would be ready for action soon, their cheeks not so hollow, complexions healthier. On a row of toning tables, the limbs of these conscripts were being limbered up for the worthwhile challenges they'd face. Hydraulic hisses replacing grunts of exertion.

Looking around, Siegfried felt not one ounce of shame. This tour, and the professor's speech, settling any nagging doubts his instinct had been right to make that life changing phone call, joining the cause. His conscience soothed, reassured his work was making a difference. Sleep will be easy tonight, he thought, mumbling, 'Now time for some fun.' Imagining his room at the safari lodge; being immersed in the cooling water of a sunken plunge pool, cold beer in hand watching the sunset.

A sudden movement by the side of the bed nearest to the wards exit, then caught his eye. 'Was someone trying to hide?' he wondered, stopping in his tracks to watch two nurses push a rattling gurney carrying a lifeless McVee, towards the same set of doors. One entered a code. With a click, the door was released. The other trundled the body through. Hydraulic arms slowed their closure, giving time for the nurses and a stooping shape to pass into the adjacent ward.

'Oh Christ. It's Victoria. You really don't know when to stop pushing your luck,' Siegfried muttered, realising she'd bided her time to gain access to the prohibited area.

'You're on your own now, lady. Don't mess with these people,' he chuntered, willing the door to swing open and Victoria's anxious face re-appear.

He paced for five, maybe ten minutes before the two nurses returned. Giving him a sheepish look, they dropped their eyes, scurrying away.

Siegfried followed them, 'Excuse me. I'm Dr Acker. Conversion team. Can I go in there please?' He needed to know what lay on the other side of those doors — what Victoria may witness.

'Sorry. Off limits. Just end gamers,' the stouter nurse offered, looking behind her, not breaking her stride.

'I think my colleague went in there by mistake.'

'Didn't see anyone.'

Siegfried didn't push further. By the term used: off-limits, meant it had to be where they decommissioned McVee's. She'll freak out if she stumbles across a procedure. The phrasing: humanely and swiftly, had great sentiment. The reality: likely to be unpleasant.

Having no choice but return to the accommodation wing, he'd check her room in the hope she'd made her way back.

With a gentle knock, followed by one harder: no response. Maybe she's dozed off, or is taking a shower, he reasoned — starring at the pale cream Formica door. But no reassuring, I'm coming, confirmed she was safe inside.

'Crap,' Siegfried muttered, Victoria's capricious behaviour having unsettled his newfound composure.

Chapter Forty-Eight

'That's everything covered. To clarify: we've four hundred inbound, three hundred and seventy-five in field zone one, four hundred and eighty-six in theatre, two hundred and twenty-five in process, one hundred and seventy-eight in first stage rehab', three hundred and sixty-five in final. Plus, twenty-three decommissioned. Agreed?'

'Yes,' filled the small conference room, in answer to Professor Leopold. 'Back here in twenty-four for the security update re-Chang. Answers to the other outstanding's by close of play ... What day is it—? So damn easy losing track.'

'Wednesday Professor,' came an over eager reply.

'Thanks. By close of play Friday, at the latest.'

Rising from their chairs, gathering paperwork, the attendees were stopped in their tracks.

'Problem. We may have a problem—?' the professor barked, noticing a wall-mounted display monitor turn red, signifying a breach in an unauthorised area.

'The Twilight Zones been compromised. Check it out, Colin, and warn security,' he ordered, leaving at haste.

Chapter Forty-Nine

London, England

Chris: on time, smartly dressed and keen as mustard, waited in Pendleton's office. Their scoop could be explosive. He just needed to convince the Ed to take a chance with their, admittedly, speculative findings. They hoped, once they'd run their piece, juicier stuff would flow their way. Bog had done a superb job in Canada, got a few of the locals on side. Deducing the head boffins at the ranch laboratory weren't popular. The town's folk had worrying opinions about their activities.

'Come on. You, lazy fat bastard. I know you'll like what you hear. Just get your greasy carcass in here,' Chris chuntered, checking his watch.

'Ah. Golden Balls. Look at you all dolled up. I take it you're handing in your notice, on your way to a new job. Am I right?' the Ed chortled, barging in the door, carrying a large Starbucks with a bundle of newspapers stuffed under his sweaty armpit.

'Actually. You're completely wrong. You need to sit down. You're about to be impressed.'

The expression on Pendleton's face gave Chris confidence.

'Christ. Fire away,' he said, plonking onto his chair, taking a slurp of coffee, throwing Chris a piercing stare.

'OK. Here goes.' Chris then paused, reflecting how much like the workmen teetering precariously on the girder at the Rockefeller construction site he felt. The iconic image hung on the wall behind the Ed's desk.

Taking a deep breath, he began. 'It's our opinion, the characters living at Red Brook ranch near Calgary are linked to the release programme and a secret neurological research project with serious financial backing. We believe the location is a low profile off shoot from the US military testing place at Fairway in Utah, also with links to activities in Uganda, resulting in thousands of deaths.' Chris continued his spiel, uninterrupted.

The Ed, uncharacteristically quiet, absorbed every detail, his pen working furiously.

'Christ. Let me get this straight. You want me to publish this hunch piece, which might get us bumped off. But, by going public may provide protection, and who knows what else may materialise with these remains found at this ranch place too. Christ almighty. It sounds as if this Mrs Brockman is being pressured: is on the cusp. What security could we offer them? But if you reckon her husband is not in the loop with the neuro' stuff — maybe just her?' Through funnelled lips, Pendleton took a sharp intake of breath, slumping backwards.

Chris noticed globular beads of sweat developing on his forehead.

'Do you think Bogs ready to share this with the Sheriff in charge of this bones investigation? Back up from an official source would make a hell of a difference ... I don't know Chris. Leave it with me and keep digging. But well-done mate. Fancy a beer later? May be our last, if I give the go ahead for this huge bomb shell,' he suggested.

'Yes. See you in the Tavern around seven—?'

Chris rose from his chair, grinning — checking his pockets for money — thinking that couldn't have gone any better, flinging open the Ed's door.

'Drinks definitely on me, now I'm bosom buddies with Pendleton again,' he muttered, with a pronounced swagger, walking past the disorderly desks of his colleagues, getting the finger from a few.

Chapter Fifty

Red Brook Ranch, Alberta, Canada

'The wanderer returns. I'll give you half an hour, then it's time we talked,' Marie mumbled through the cabin window, watching Donald's car crawl along the ranch driveway, pulling up outside the main house. His distant figure stepped out, stretched, straightened his trousers, then opened the boot, retrieving his briefcase, before ambling to their porchway. She smiled, pleased to see Millicent hadn't run out to greet him. 'Good for you, Mum. Act nonchalant. Selfish bastard,' she said coldly, relishing the thought of him driven away in the sheriff's car. Although deep down knowing, if they link him to the skeletal find, he'd have covered his tracks.

'I've been calling you. Are you all right, Hun?' Milo asked, coming up behind her, stroking her shoulders.

Not breaking her intent stare, 'Yeah fine. Just want to get the snake on his own. Catch him off guard before he visits the sheriff.'

'Are you keeping secrets again, love of my life?' he asked, kissing the back of her neck, causing a pleasant prickle of goose bumps to stir. Reaching behind, she stroked his thigh.

'Stuff Mum came out with before her chat with the sheriff, aroused my curiosity. I think this may be the tip of the ice-burg, Mi.' Marie paused. 'I've been mulling. Do you fancy moving to Europe? There are promising research opportunities there. I know it's a major upheaval, but a fresh start with Jools and the baby. Sound exciting—?'

From his silence, Marie deduced: he's thinking here she goes again, off on another whim, best keep quiet.

Turning to face him, wrapping her arms around his waist,

resting the side of her face against his chest, topping up her inner strength with a dose of his manly confidence; all the time contemplating her daughter to father chat.

'Won't be long. Time for a few fire-works,' she assured him, pulling away.

'No problem. I've a few errands to run. But don't get yourself worked up, Marie. Do you hear—?'

To settle herself before their inevitable shouting match, she marched down the grass bank, squeezing the plastic bag of carrot peelings in her pocket for Storm. 'Collect yourself. Focus and stay calm,' she preached her resolve, questions buzzing wildly in her mind.

Donald had serious answers to give. And Mum. But who should she believe? And did she really want to get between them? She'd see how Millicent was today, and perhaps postpone. It wasn't her place to counsel them.

Releasing the catch of Storms stable door, revelling in the soft gentleness of his muzzle plucking the moist treats from her hand. 'Clearly, I'm already talking myself out of this. Why?' she posed her doubt to his warm, powerful neck.

With a heavy heart, dragging herself away from his comforting space, Marie headed for the main house.

'Looks as if the decision's been made for me. Not time for our confrontation yet,' she muttered, as Donald's car sped towards her. Drawing level, the hateful intensity filling those judgemental eyes: the sheer loathing oozing through windscreen in her direction, made her feel like a naughty schoolgirl. Marie's mouth dropped open: emitting an involuntary gasp as her determination dissolved. 'Why did he *still* have this effect on me?' she wondered. She'd only done his research; his laboratory repairs. She's not in the wrong. He's the one causing the problems; with the answers to the mounting riddles.

Following the path of his car, rear brake lights flashed — like demonic red eyes — warning her: keep your nose out, or else.

Chapter Fifty-One

'Not you again. I should report you for stalking, or clonk you over the head with this.' Milo aimed the fuel nozzle in Bogs direction, as he pulled up next to him at a gas station.

'For the last time, I don't have a clue who that person was. I was nowhere near the damned ranch when she was buried. Even the local press guys aren't hounding me as much as you. Bloody English: you're a tenacious breed, I'll give you that,' Milo added, throwing his stalker a sideways glance.

'I've grown on you, admit it,' Bog teased, offering, 'Fancy a coffee? Listen, I'm just a casual observer with the eyes and ears to help the righteous. Seriously, you should trust me. Granted, I seem to be in the right place at the right time, but that's fate. Simple as that. You've a right to know what I've heard. My contacts tell me something big is going to break soon, whether you like it, or not. I do the work I do because I want to find the truth. I'm not into sensationalism, but you deserve the heads up; to get your voice out there before you're forced. And yes, why should you trust this smartly dressed English man? But look into my eyes, I'm a good person. You must be intrigued. I bet you checked out my credentials after our last meet. You did. I can tell,' Bog chuckled — stretching across from the driver's seat — peering at Milo, trying his best to ignore him. 'I'm from good stock. My family are loaded, that should tell you I'm not here for financial gain.' Bog threw him an innocent smile before playing his trump card. 'I think Marie may need help. She may be in deeper than she thinks. You know where I'm staying if you want a chat. I'll be in the bar every evening at seven. Your call.' Bog kept eye contact as he slowly pulled away.

'What does he mean? What does the bloke know?' Crap. Paranoia's creeping back, Milo realised, paying for his fuel. Perhaps I should meet with him properly: get to the bottom of it. I'll say nothing. Let him do all the talking. 'What does he know about Marie? Lately, what do I truly know about her?' Milo wondered, battling with his doubts.

'Excuse me. Your card sir,' the cashier called, Milo having walked off leaving it on the cash desk.

'Sorry, thanks. I was miles away,' Milo answered, thinking — if only that were true.

Chapter Fifty-Two

'Bastard. How could he treat her like this? That's it, I'm not letting Donald intimidate us anymore,' Marie angrily muttered, after barging in the front door of the main house, appalled at the state of Millicent, sat on the bottom step in their hallway. She looked skeletal, thick layers of tear-streaked foundation smeared her face; no longer possible to disguise the deepening black shadows under her eyes.

After making her a cup of tea and settling her in the bath, Marie ran back to the cabin. Hearing the rattle of car keys in her pocket meant she'd be able to sneak off without Milo knowing. He'd only plead with her to calm down. She needed to get Donald on his own and unleash everything festering within her.

Jumping in her SUV, she tore down the drive, tyres squealing on the last bend before the highway.

Donald's car *was* still parked on the gravel next to the sheriffs.

Pleased she'd not encountered him on her journey there; the outcome of an anger infused manoeuvre, or worse, a crash — the impact unsettling her precious internal cargo, wasn't worth contemplating, she reflected, parking up the opposite side of the road.

Heavy rain splatters bounced off the bonnet, as she waited for his arrogant figure to strut down the steps of the police station; no doubt he'll be smiling, having sweet-talked his way out of another tricky situation — his forte. She planned ordering him to follow her to the out-of-town picnic area: the perfect spot for a shouting match nobody would over hear.

Chapter Fifty-Three

Kasese, Uganda

'Where am I? What happened?' Victoria mumbled, regaining consciousness, focussing on Siegfried stood at the foot of the hospital bed.

'They found you in a corridor leading from the rehab' wards. I last saw you disappearing into the off-limits area. I tried following, but I was denied access. Apparently, they found you unconscious. Do you feel OK?'

'Yes. I think so. I don't remember much, just the pain of the blow to my head.'

A nurse walked over to check Victoria's vitals, reassuring her, 'You're fine. We think a hormonal surge made you dizzy. You must have fallen and hit your head against a pillar,' she relayed in whispered speech.

Victoria sat upright — swinging her legs off the edge of the bed, assessing her stability.

'So, what did I miss?' Siegfried pushed.

Victoria hesitated, waiting for the nurse to move away.

'I saw arms flailing around on beds at the far end of that ward. People: not in white coats, were strapping them down, so I ducked, and hid. A McVee on a bed nearest to me said, "Where's my wife. Where's little Akia—" After that, nothing.'

Chapter Fifty-Four

Safari Lodge, Queen Elizabeth National Park, Uganda

'It must have been a trial one: before they perfected the procedure. That's got to be the reason it still had memories. Did she see the serial number?' Kirk asked Siegfried: both sat in wicker chairs at the swanky safari lodge sipping ice-cold beer, mesmerised by the stunning sunset.

'No, I don't think so. I'm positive she was coshed over the head. Deep down, she believes that too, but can't prove it. I warned her.'

'You know, research has shown neurons can regenerate. The brain can encode memories within the hippocampus, and even though we've removed part of the recall pathway, the retrieval process builds new routes to those memories. If an individual goes over a partial memory, it helps strengthen those connections. It's called synaptic plasticity. I read a paper on it,' Kirk said — glancing at Siegfried for a reaction.

'Yeah. I've heard that. Do you think we should mention Victoria's revelation? Perhaps we should, just to confirm at what stage of the programme they modified it. But then it was being decommissioned, so had to be a defunct earlier one, and we could cause more problems for her. She's bound to be seriously on their radar,' Siegfried contemplated, taking another refreshing sip of beer. Slipping lower into his chair, crossing his ankles, adding, 'For now, my friend, I want to enjoy this moment and chill. I'll have a chat with her before we leave in the morning. Saw her an hour ago set off for her night safari with those other lodge guests.'

'Yeah. Agreed. It's her call. We've been procedurally spot on since you helped perfect the bloody procedure — Golden

Bollocks,' Kirk exclaimed, giving Siegfried a clout on the shoulder.

'Cheers,' they chirped, clunking condensation sodden bottles.

'Let's toast all the awesome beasts we glimpsed and heard last night. And that our labours aren't in vain. Keep multiplying my friends,' Kirk rallied.

'Here's to the future. And rejuvenation.' Siegfried held his beer up to the amber glow of the setting sun, admiring the colours cast by the descending orb.

Chapter Fifty-Five

It was eerie: the green tinged low light on the tree trunks, dead grasses and occasional fleeting movement caught in the safari vehicles floodlighting. Victoria likened her first experience using night vision goggles to land based snorkelling. Enclosed in the face piece, she felt protected against the imminent danger her mind conjured from the prehistoric roars carried on the hot, strengthening breeze. Consoling herself, she was sat in a substantial Land-cruiser with ten others, an experienced guide and two rangers with rifles. But the nearby deep guttural grumbles from a pride of lionesses still sent alarming tingles through her body: a sensation she surprisingly enjoyed.

'The lions sleep for twenty-one hours' a day. It's already dark before the moon rises. The best time for them to catch their prey. At this watering hole they easily pick their target. The lions have the advantage with excellent night vision, much better than the animals they hunt. I think we may be lucky tonight and see a kill,' Saburo, their guide, informed them.

A flash of distant light, closely followed by the rumble of thunder signalled a storm was fast approaching, adding a dose of apocalyptic gloom to Victoria's experience. Another quick burst made her jump — her alarmed gaze drawn to the silhouettes of bush trees.

On the well-defined track, their vehicle pulled forward; all eyes within peeled for signs of movement. The upside-down guide prone on the roof — pupils as big as saucers, looked in the front windscreen, gesticulating with his hand off to the right.

Victoria's heart leapt into her mouth, as the cruiser spun

towards the hunting pride, bouncing over the terrain, past a herd of elephants ambling from the watering hole: their legs, through Victoria's goggles, creating an impenetrable wall of wrinkly moving limbs.

Judging from the bellowing and warning dust being kicked up by a lone straggler, the alarmed creature knew its survival was under threat.

Halting at a vantage point, for the group watched twenty or so, lionesses pacing, a few increasing their speed, starting their attack.

The small eyes of their target elephant reflected its fear. Making explosive snorts, it charged the nearest big cat before turning, trying to outrun the pride.

The lionesses concerted their efforts. Victoria held her breath, as two of them launched their muscular strength at each side of the animal's haunches — plunging their claws into its hide, clinging on before gravity dislodged them. The rest of the oversized felines ran, full pelt, to join the attack, two using its moving comrades as an aid to mount the rear and sides of the terrified creature. All claws and jaws were now in-bedded in its leathery hide. Even a virgin to the world of night hunting could tell the animal didn't have long to live. The writhing mass of fur, teeth, trunk and furrowed body plunged out of sight, crashing through the undergrowth.

The safari vehicle shifted position, allowing them to follow the action. Victoria again caught sight of the tormented animal buckling, being suffocated with powerful jaws clamped around the end of its trunk; the pride flowing over it like a bulbous, macabre fur coat, until the unfortunate beast fell onto its side with a muffled crash. With legs still kicking, the lionesses wasted no time ripping into its underbelly.

'These ladies are specialist elephant hunters. Look, the big male has now joined the feast,' Saburo described the drama playing out.

Driven away from the blood thirsty scene, he continued, 'To your left are the night patrol. The special men who help us with our poaching problem. These quiet ones know to keep their distance from their assigned herds. See how the elephants look back at them. They are very perceptive, have got used to their presence,' Saburo spoke in a hush, continuing, 'Sometimes these big animals come into our camp for treatment. We had a big bull with a snare around its leg last week. It was strong, got away from the poacher's traps and let us help. The majestic creature knew we would not hurt it. I tell you it was a marvellous feeling. We are so pleased numbers of these leviathans are on the increase in this area. Sometimes the special men cull an old animal. It is a quick end, they don't suffer. They are excellent shots, and this helps the local people who need the bush meat to feed their families. This way we can control the hunting and balance the population. They also carry powerful Tazers, and pistols with rubber bullets to warn off other wild animals. And rub themselves with dung — you can smell them before you see them!' Saburo quipped, as negotiating the undulating terrain, the vehicles movement bounced their bodies around. After a particularly bad wobbling moment, Victoria tried visualising the faces behind the goggle apparatus sat beside her. With a start: realising she was the only modification team member there. Recalling her pickup from the lodge: she'd been last to arrive in the foyer, ushered into this cruiser and whisked away. Transfixed by the duskily lit scenery, she remembered just smiling, saying hello to who she'd assumed were the facilities tour group. She then recalled three other cruisers were parked outside reception: perhaps she should've been in one of those? Maybe they'll be wondering where she is? These must be the other doctors working in the region who she'd had guarded chats with over lunch. The nice one called Peter is sat opposite, Victoria recognised his trousers. She quite liked him. Deciding when they got back, she'd ask if he fancied a drink. Perhaps a one-night stand was on the cards. Champagne, and a man to share her terrace jacuzzi. 'Why not?' she mouthed, amused by her urge to do something out of character. 'Enjoy. Live dangerously for once, girl,' she muttered, as the cruiser came to an abrupt halt, jolting her from inviting plans.

Saburo spoke in Swahili into his walkie-talkie, then to the group. 'We have to help the poaching team. I'm sorry, but we must transfer you to a different vehicle so we can give them back up. Your transport will be here in ten minutes. You have been lucky tonight with what you have seen. Please leave your night vision aids on the seats. We will need these. Thank you,' Saburo finished, sliding out his seat, still talking into his handset.

Victoria glanced around at the others; having taken off their goggles were rubbing their eyes, straightening their hair, released from the apparatus's sweaty confines.

In the shadow of the interior, Peter caught her eye.

She gave him a warm smile, before the thump of the guide sliding from the roof to join Saburo distracted him.

Muffled Swahili banter; chit-chatter of thousands of crickets; distant rumbles of an elephant herd and being way past midnight; with heavy eye's, the group waited in a quiet stupor.

Eventually, the drone of a diesel engine turned their weary faces towards the glow of approaching head lights.

'Your transport is here. Please wait a moment. We will let you know when it is safe to walk to the other track,' Saburo assured them through the window, the walkie talkie still pinned to an ear.

'Can't it come up behind us here?' A concerned member of the group suggested.

'It's OK. They have stopped on the one parallel, turning ready to take you back,' Saburo reassured them.

A flash of torchlight from their left confirmed the transfer could start.

'Please don't forget to leave your goggles. Follow my friend, he will lead you the right way. And walk slowly!' Saburo directed.

Tentatively stepping from the safety of the Land-cruiser;

instinct was telling Victoria to run for her life, to reach the metal security of the other vehicle. Knowing the others were close behind; reasoning, she wasn't last in line and only had to worry about an animal attack from the side, calmed her. But still, her involuntary murmur caused Peter to stretch back his hand searching for hers. She didn't hesitate in grabbing its clammy warmth. 'I can see the transport ahead. Don't worry,' he said in a comforting whisper.

Victoria looked back at the cruiser they'd left. Pale moon light glints on parts of its metal work disjointed the line, making it appear to levitate. Hearing the guides chatter; the clunk of heavy doors signalled these shining sections of security were about to leave.

'No. At least wait until we're safe before going. Aww, I don't like this,' Victoria shouted.

'It's all right. Nearly there,' Peter consoled.

Victoria's inner fear fired her courage. 'Do you fancy a night cap, *if* we ever see the lodge again?'

Peter gave her hand a squeeze: she assumed that meant — maybe?

The dark hulk of a large truck loomed in front of them.

Judging from the groups muffled comments: it wasn't quite the type of transport they'd expected. The guide leading them, then turned — crashing through the thicket to catch up with his colleagues. 'Oye. Where are you off to in such a hurry!' A few exclaimed.

'How do we get in? Where's the bloody driver with the torch?' Alarmed questioning rang through the ominous gloom.

'You climb in the cab. He must be in there. Hello. Hello,' another shouted.

A combined, 'Sssssshhhhh,' followed.

'This way please,' came a welcome response from the other side of the vehicle.

'Thank goodness for that,' Victoria squeaked — squeezing Peters hand tighter.

'Please form a line, and we'll help you,' the voice asked.

The low call of a nearby big cat caused fearful gasps.

'Quickly please,' Peter commanded, sensing Victoria's fear.

'Why's the engine not running, and the headlights not on? Surely that's wiser?' An impatient man offered, before climbing up the back, tugging open the rear tarpaulin.

Four male shapes then emerged from the gloom ahead.

Victoria noticed the moonlight reflecting in their night vision goggles, resembling trapped fireflies, as they stopped forty metres from the uneasy group.

'What are they doing?'

'I don't know. Let's just get in this flaming truck and where's the driver?' An angered voice shouted.

Victoria watched the male shapes space themselves ten metres apart. Recognising the outline of their backpacks, she assured the others, 'It's the patrol McVee's. They're fine. They'll only fire at a threat.' Dropping Peter's hand, taking a few paces towards the McVee's, giving them a childlike wave.

'I'd come back if I were you. They look like they mean business. How do they know we're not poachers? Come back!' Peter, along with the others angrily suggested.

'Because of our encoded wristbands,' Victoria answered with confidence, walking nearer, waving her right arm high above her head.

'I thought they were for free drinks at the lodge?' Peter jested, happy to follow her.

'Woah. That's not how they're supposed to react,' Victoria gasped as the four raised their weapons.

Instinctively, the group ducked. In a stooping run, moving to the off side of the truck.

Removing her wrist band, Victoria frantically waved it, calling, 'We're friends. Not foe.'

The McVee's didn't lower their weapons as she'd hoped. Instead, they adopted a stand alert posture — one notch up in their programming.

Victoria cried out, 'Why?' As the horror of the moment hit her like a brick. They had issued her with just the rubber housing. The digital insert, keeping her safe, was missing. 'Oh my God,' she shouted, dropping down, forcing herself low into the stubbly cover. 'Check your bands. Look inside, the part next to your arm. Is it flashing red?' she called. Panting, the scent of fertile soil filling her nostrils; her heart thumping so hard she felt it might rebound her across the compacted, dry ground.

Hearing the group compare, 'No.' 'No.' 'No,' their answers drifted on the night air.

'Stay very low,' she bellowed. 'Crap. We haven't even got our mobiles. We were told to leave them in our safes because of robbers,' Victoria whispered to Peter: elbow-crawling to her side.

Flipping over to lie on their backs; the splendour of the night sky unfolded in stunning awesomeness.

'If only under different circumstances,' Victoria reflected aloud. 'By mistake, or intentionally, we've been issued useless wristbands Peter. I think it may be the latter. What research *are* you doing in Uganda—?'

'Working on the cause of this sleeping sickness outbreak. Why—?'

'We're dispensable, Peter. In the way of something much bigger than you can possibly imagine. This has been planned. It's a trap, and there's only one outcome.'

A single, silenced warning shot was fired, defining the horrifying reality.

The startled group cried out: like frightened children a few screamed.

'Hold me please, Peter. We can't outrun them. And if we did, something is likely to hunt us. I think I'd prefer a quick bullet than being ripped apart alive,' Victoria wept — clinging to Peters tense body. 'Would you have had a drink with me? Please say yes. Why now?' she wailed, burying her face into his chest as heavy boots, crushing dried grass, neared, making her whimper, unabashed.

'Yes, I would. I was hoping for more. Sweet little lady,' he whispered, stroking her hair — holding her with a precious fondness.

The unleashed, multiple silenced shots made Victoria scream.

With the McVee's Heckler and Koch sub-machine guns capable of firing 800 rounds per minute: the tour group stood no chance.

The four McVee's; the special men; the quiet ones their mission accomplished, moved away, continuing their night patrol.

Waiting in a distant vehicle, a man, with cold blue eyes, heard the muffled report.

The McVee's having achieved their mission, he drove the clearance crew to the location, knowing what he'd find.

At the sound of the engine, a member of his team came out of the bush, jumping into the driver's seat of the empty truck. His wristband: emitting a small red beam, had ensured he survived.

Jewellery and personal items were removed from each slaughtered doctor and scientist, placed in zipper bags identified with the victim's name. Their culled bodies callously dumped into the back.

Victoria, Peter, Dr Chang and the rest of his researcher's left Kampala airport four hours later possessing their passports, wallets, mobile phones, laptops, luggage and a complete dossier of personal information containing PIN's, property entry codes, banking and car details. Plus, an itinerary for the next month to adhere to. Those with family links were flown directly to their new assignment: from where, an outbreak of the sleeping sickness would shortly manifest.

It was reported Chang and his team were trying to keep one step ahead to nip its devastating spread in the bud. In truth, they'd innocently fallen into a trap. Their identities and objective becoming conveniently exploited: they'd become posthumous pawns; unwitting accomplices in the grand re-set initiative, spreading vectors — creating further disease epicentres throughout the Continent of Africa, feeding the donate transformation machine.

Next to be targeted: The Americas and Europe.

The marvels of prosthetic make-up, paying the right people and irrefutable CCTV images meant the organisation could create, eliminate, or defer damaging exposure at will.

Dr Victoria Louise Findlay officially went missing en route to her parent's villa in Florence, Italy. She'd left her flat in Oxford and was last seen locking her graphite grey VW Golf near Zermatt in Switzerland. Carrying a multicoloured backpack, she'd set off alone.

Following unseasonal blizzard like conditions, they suspect she lost her way and with the paths becoming treacherous in inclement weather: also, her footing. Precipitous drops posing a particular hazard.

Only a parent can confidently identify their offspring from CCTV footage from a ferry terminal and petrol stations, as after months of hard work Victoria had left to enjoy a well-earned holiday. Only a mother could accept the woman she viewed, with a habit of tucking her hair behind her right ear and her strange shoulder mannerism, was her lost child.

Victoria's mother just wished she'd rung before setting off on her surprise visit.

She just wished she'd had the chance to hear her soft, sweet voice once again.

Despite extensive searches: Victoria's body has yet to be found.

Victoria spent a lot of time admiring the stunning view of the Great Rift Valley from the library's Gothic windows. Often wishing she could soar, like a bird, away from where she'd felt so trapped. This Jewel of Africa would absorb Victoria's, Chang, his teams, and the latest de-commissioned McVee's carbon compounds, feeding the land she so wished to fly above.

Siegfried and the others were told she'd been taken straight to the airport after her night safari, as she'd wanted no fuss.

It made sense. They knew she'd been plagued by inner demons. Toasting a fond farewell to her in the library, Siegfried and Kirk shared a pensive look, doubting this to be her true fate. But kept this to themselves.

Strolling back to their accommodation, Colin paced past, throwing them a cocky, knowing smile. 'Fresh batch of donates in from Tanzania. Best get cracking my friends,' he said, cuttingly.

Chapter Fifty-Six

Picnic Area Near Red Brook Ranch, Alberta.

'You've always been the same, sticking your nose in where it's not wanted. Why don't you ever listen when I say enough — that I mean it? Why do you think I demoted you? As you've phrased it, for this very reason. You didn't need to know more than I told you. So, for the last time, I know nothing about your office notes disappearing. To satisfy you, I'll take a look at the security tape. And as for photos stored in a personal box. How would I know anything about those? You've made it abundantly clear you copied them to someone else, so get a copy back from them. And as for the bones, Marie: the sheriffs leaning towards Bert as the prime suspect. The man had a police record; sexually assaulted a girl twenty years ago and thinks may have involvement with missing persons he's reopened. So, to stress, this skeleton has nothing to do with me,' Donald barked, sighing, rubbing his lower back, before angrily adding, 'I'm tired. I need a stiff drink, so, if you've finished with your false accusations, I'll be on my way.'

'No. Actually. I've just bloody started. You employ everyone in the lab' so, answer me this: the security guard must have known this person, yet, he went into my office and nothing dad, no reaction. Also, this person must have had an entry card. Plus, I worked it out — the bones — the woman. What equipment do we have? What would it tell me about her, *Dad?*' Marie yelled.

Donald went quiet. 'Have you mentioned this to Millicent?'

'No. Not yet. I wanted your reaction first.'

'Please, let's leave it at that, Marie. She's enough on her plate. Rather than stand here shouting at me, calm yourself, get back

to the ranch and spend some time with her,' Donald shouted —
losing his cool demeanour.

Marie fumed, 'You should be doing that. She's your bloody
wife. She's in bits, and you're solely to blame, going off, not
getting in touch. She's wasting away, Dad. You spend time with
her. Take her to the bloody Caribbean, anything, just
reconnect, cheer her up, give her a reason to bloody live,
because, quite frankly, she's close to the edge.'

Donald gave her a venomous stare.

Marie reciprocated.

Red faced, fuming and dripping wet, they stood by their
cars in the pouring rain.

Marie was the first to break the silence, 'I don't know who
you are any more. Or who you've got involved with. You've
hardened. So cold. What's really going on with these neuro'
experiments? What's happening, dad? I should go to the sheriff
with what I know. You can't stop me. It would put you back in
the frame. I'll tell him about all the stuff I've seen. You know
I've proof. I'm not letting you intimidate me anymore. I've had
enough dad. I suppose you might strangle *me* now and stick
me in a hole,' Marie screamed — wiping her nose on the sleeve
of her rain sodden trench coat.

Time froze before Donald spoke. 'Perhaps it's time you
moved on. I think it may be for the best. I feel our working
relationship will never be the same. You're not fully on side. I
need to know I can trust you. Yes, this is the right way forward.
I'll help you relocate. You'll get work easily enough with
glowing references. I want you out of my way, Marie.' Donald
looked up, rain running down his weary features.

Pacing in front of their cars, he added, 'I'll just say, be very
careful. Warn Milo he's being monitored. Seriously Marie, the
situation you're tinkering with is far bigger than a few suicides.
To be frank, it's bigger than I envisaged. Yes. I've played my
part, but I'm not sure I'll be of use for much longer.'

Marie watched his lips move, trying to comprehend the life

altering moment. Her world having been rocked on its foundations lately; she wondered how much more she could take.

'We're dispensable Marie. We're not the big fish we'd like to think we are. Go somewhere else and be happy. I promise I'll take care of Millicent.'

Ready to launch another verbal onslaught, Marie stop herself, overcome with racking sobs. Donald didn't try consoling her. Realising he felt nothing, he got into his car and drove back to the ranch, leaving Marie slumped on the wet soil.

He'd go through the motions with Millicent. What else could he do?

What else could any of them do other than keep breathing until fate, or a larger concern, made choices?

Chapter Fifty-Seven

Red Brook Ranch, Alberta

Millicent shared the news of their next grandchild with Donald, thinking he'd be thrilled — thinking it might lift the repressive cloud stifling them. Instead, he'd said nothing, just walked away, locking himself in his study; knowing this revelation had made his decision much harder. I've no choice. I'm obligated, he reflected, after sitting at his desk, head in his hands for an age. Marie had become a loose cannon: a liability. Donald knew this didn't bode well. Having been under surveillance for weeks, her pregnancy: not the secret she believed. The Org were stepping up a notch. Her development: making it easier to execute their plan. In a litter-strewn lay-by, through an opened car window, Donald had already been handed the necessary.

Millicent tried the office door handle. It moved in time with her simpering. With Marie fetching Jolie from school and Milo not back until late — the time was right.

Her whimpers fading. The flush of an upstairs toilet confirming Millicent's exact location. 'You've got no choice,' Donald muttered — glancing at the void of his open wall safe: at the container of golden pearls next to his Smith and Wesson taunting him with its toy like presence. He'd order flowers for Marie and Millicent; giving the impression he was sorry. Hand delivering a bunch to the cabin gave him the perfect excuse to go there alone and exchange the capsules. His associates could then play their part — take that final burden off his shoulders.

Telephoning the florist: lilies, large bunches would be delivered within the hour. Glancing again at the Smith and Wesson; Donald's second decision was not so easy.

Chapter Fifty-Eight

River Valley Girls Boarding School, Alberta

'Ah. Mrs Brockman. I'm glad I've caught you. Could you spare a moment? I've a few concerns regarding Jolie. Don't worry. She's doing fine academically, and we didn't feel it warranted ringing you,' the head-mistress apprehended Marie in the school corridor.

'Yes, of course. I'm a little early and planned sorting through her clothes to kill time,' she agreed, thinking, 'What now?'

The staffs' fleeting looks hit her on the back, like dull thuds, as she made her way through the bustling heart of the school behind the imposing figure of Mrs Warner.

'Please take a seat,' the head palm gestured, settling herself behind her desk, glancing at her computer screen. No doubt familiarising yourself with the exact details of Jolie's misdemeanour, Marie mulled, taking in the comfortable surroundings: pretty cushions on chairs lined along one wall; floral bone china mugs hung on hooks in a corner. A pleasant lavender or rose water odour pervaded the air.

'Now, I don't wish to alarm you, but we seem to be having a nightmare issue. Well, more talking loudly, screaming and teeth grinding to be precise. So, we've moved Jolie into the separate dorm' heads room. I'm sure you understand, it's a little unsettling for the other girls and appears these outbursts are getting more regular. My question is, Mrs Brockman, has something happened at home that could be worrying Jolie? Obviously, I'm not prying, but experience has shown these night terrors can be linked to adolescence, hormonal changes, that sort of thing, plus family traumas.'

'Gosh. I'd no idea. She hasn't mentioned anything when I've

rung. I'm so sorry if she's causing a problem. But to answer your question: yes, there's been odd issues to deal with lately which maybe unsettling her more than we've realised. I'm expecting. Although we thrashed this out. Her grandfather passed away. Which you know. Plus, there's been a discovery on our land involving the police. Do you think we should keep her home for the week and monitor her? Would that help?' Marie's left foot waggled violently as she spoke.

'Exactly what I would suggest. Give her time to open up about anxieties she may have. Please pop back before you leave to collect a lesson plan,' she said melodically, shaking Marie's hand.

In a daze, Marie made her way to Jolie's dormitory, mulling her troubling predicaments. An out-of-control father; a cover-up; a mother on the brink; human remains, and now a loopy fruit daughter. 'What next? My mental meltdown?' she muttered, waving to Jolie across the room strewn with teenage girl paraphernalia. Aromas of body sprays, sweets, and unwashed clothes made her nauseous.

'Hi Mum. Nearly done,' Jolie called over the hubbub of girly laughter.

'You need to throw open the windows Jools,' Marie suggested, giving her a warm embrace. 'By the way, I've spoken with Mrs Warner.'

Jolie pulled away, trilling, 'I'm fine, Mum. At least the pushy girls are leaving me alone. I've threatened them with Adam, my spirit guide. And yay, I've a week off. That's so cool. I'll miss the science test on Thursday and can school Ziggy ready for the mid-term show. I win all round. Yay.'

'To be honest, Jools, I find it rather disturbing. But I'm glad it doesn't seem to worry you. What have you been dreaming? Do you wake up crying? Let's hope it's just a phase, eh ... I thought Nathaniel was your spirit guide?'

'I changed it. Didn't like that name. Perhaps I've annoyed him, that's why he's invading my sleep? Anyway, Mum, you know my latest ranch history project. Well, I may have solved the bones puzzle: not on my own. A very reliable contact, unofficially, put the pieces together. So, we'll need a Jolie briefing at the main house. Will that be OK—? Once you've heard my theory, we could tell the sheriff. I might get a community award. Mum, I really do think those bones *are* Lucy,' she squawked, with her usual dose of confidence.

'I bet you haven't worked out who Lucy was though,' Marie mumbled, watching her hop on one foot, struggling to pull on a leather boot.

Chapter Fifty-Nine

London, England

'Chris. Get your arse down here, *now*. You need to see this,' Pendleton barked. The uncharacteristic panic channelling through the phone, Chris found alarming, forcing him from his desk. Opting for a stainless steel bannister rail slide to the boss's office: there in seconds. A nervous jitter manifested in his stomach at the sight of the Ed', sat, phone propped up against his chin, his face deathly white.

'This breaking news. This culling in Paris. Do you think it's another link? Christ all bloody mighty Chris, they reckon at least five-hundred druggies and rough sleepers were shot during the night. One bloke survived. He was sleeping under a pile of leaves near a bridge on the Seine where a load of that sort congregate. Just one bloody bloke. He's Latvian, or something, and watched these figures in black come out the drains and let off muffled rounds. Poor bugger ran to a taxi office, but they couldn't understand him, so made it to an A&E where he drew pictures on the bedsheets and they called the police. Christ. I reckon this might be the start of another bloody link. What the fuck!'

Pendleton scrabbled around in his desk drawer for a blood pressure tablet — downing it with a slurp of coffee.

Chris just sat, absorbing the gist of a broadcast on his huge flat-screen TV. An analysis panel were discussing who was behind the heinous act: a right-wing vigilante group being the shared opinion. 'Listen. It's happened in other capitals throughout Europe. Look at this footage, the mounds of bodies. Jesus H,' Chris exclaimed — his pallor now on par with the Ed's. 'It's been a slick, well organised operation. I think you're right, there's a link. We need to bring in our ranch friends. I'll give Bog the heads up,' Chris commanded, as Pendleton rocked in his chair, hugging his chest.

'I agree. I'll ring Jean. Make sure my life insurance is up to date. You said Bog's got a safe house prepped. We'll Fed ex what he needs. Can you pull this off? You'll get a fucking great pay rise if you do. That's if we live to see another bloody Christmas. Just don't let me down!'

Chris couldn't recall putting one foot in front of the other to reach his desk. Looking around the newsroom, at his colleagues noisily chatting on their phones, tapping on keyboards, he wondered: 'How is this happening? How on earth, have I got wrapped up in this? Are we being paranoid? Perhaps I need my head checked?' I suppose this was how the media reacted, with gut souring disbelief, at reports of the Nazi concentration camps, Chris reflected, studying the greasy display of his mobile — feeling numb to the core, yet oddly exhilarated.

His nearest colleague, noticing Chris's worried expression, threw him one of concern, mouthing, 'You OK?'

Chris contorted his mouth in response, before resuming his blank phone stare, muttering 'Time for action.'

Thumbing his log for their last chat — pressing call return — he got an irritating long ring before Bog's voice mail answered: 'Good to go, mate. FedExing today,' he said, his mind racing with the consequences.

Chapter Sixty

Red Brook Ranch, Alberta.

'Mi—, I'm popping down for a coffee with Mum. Jools is still asleep. Give her a kick in ten. I'll meet you at the stables in an hour,' Marie called up the stairs — yanking on her yard coat in front of the hall mirror, throwing the ostentatious bouquet of lilies on the table below a look of disdain. Although their scent was delicious: the false sentiment behind their delivery bit her to the core. She'd discard their unwelcome charm later.

Grabbing her Omega-3 supplements from the kitchen cupboard, popping two into her mouth, swigging orange juice straight from a carton to ease their passage, Marie opened the back door allowing a freezing blast to invade, making her shudder.

Pulling up her collar as a shield from the biting chill, striding towards the main house, testing the grass with the heel of her boot: it gave a little, not a problem for the horses, she felt, noticing the rear of Donald's car poking out his garage. The absence of exhaust gases puffing into the dank atmosphere meant he wasn't warming it up; his departure not imminent. 'Bugger,' she cussed at the thought of strained pleasantries for Millicent's sake.

Nearing the protruding back end of the Lexus Ramsey, Marie surmised it must have been exposed to the elements all night. Frosty white particles disguised the metals colour, and no footprints had broken the crunchy coating on the drive. This was out of character. Donald never left his pride and joy out to the mercy of the harsh climate. Perhaps Millicent clonked him over the head, and he's lying unconscious. Or, sneaked up behind his favourite reading chair and garrotted the evil old bastard, she contemplated, catching her smiling reflection in the glass pane at the side of their solid wood entranceway.

Marie always knocked before letting herself in: a habit she'd never broken. This courtesy she hoped would rub off on Millicent, who insisted on barging into their cabin un-announced. An image of Milo scooting into their bedroom, his manhood jiggling, made her chuckle, recalling his usual exclamation — 'Your bloody Mother. I thought you told her to ring first, or at least knock. I'm sure she does it on purpose.'

Marie got no response to her forceful taps on the door.

Slipping her key into the lock, opening it, calling, 'Hello.'

Still nothing.

Hanging her coat on a hook. Leaving her boots on the mat, she walked in thick socks through the hallway.

Everywhere was quiet — too quiet. 'Where's Betty?' She wondered, before remembering she'd been given a week off. This was clear when Marie saw the kitchen sink piled high with crockery; the marble worktops without their usual sheen. Un-plumped cushions; magazines left open on side tables; forgotten coffee cups in the living room. And no soothing classical tones playing confirmed something was definitely wrong. The only audible sound: the boiler firing in the basement, creating a gurgle in the pipes.

The unnatural silence was disturbing. Marie broke it, again calling, 'Hello.'

Silently tip-toeing over the polished wooden floor to the ajar door of Donald's study, she rubbed her tiny bump, settling an anxiety fuelled foetus flutter, whispering, 'It's OK little bean.'

The rooms distinctive sour wood aroma hit her.

The first thing she noticed out of place: a picture — its frame and glass undamaged — leaning against his filing cabinet. Her eyes flicked to where it hung, meeting the empty void of a small wall safe. 'Oh God. They've been burgled,' she muttered. 'Maybe they're bound and gagged somewhere? Perhaps dad was forced to open it?' she wondered in alarm, turning the key in the lock, securing her position from any lurking foe.

Standing, back to the safety barrier, assuming it happened yesterday evening, explained why the car wasn't garaged properly. With Millicent's obsessive tea drinking, she should have felt the kettle. It could still be warm and she's just gone back to bed to read, and dads decided on a walk. 'You, silly moo. Check it, make a hot drink and go upstairs to find her,' she mumbled. But why not have a look around in here beforehand? Why miss this rare opportunity to peek at Donald's stuff?

Sat in his chair, getting a feel for his space, she listened to the stillness of the house, noticing an empty glass tumbler on a wooden coaster. Burnt orange residue filled the base, drawing her eye to the spirit bottle on his barrel table. Knowing Donald wasn't a regular drinker, she pondered, why's his reserve whiskey drained dry? It had been two-thirds full when she'd last chatted with Betty as she'd dusted.

Finding nothing unusual in five of his desk drawers, with the bottom one locked, the safe being the obvious place for a key. She found it: tucked at the back.

The strengthening wind caused the house timbers to creak; listening for a moment, thinking she heard someone put her on edge, before mischievously unlocking the drawer.

The sight of the lap-top adorned with a Smiley sticker she'd last seen on Milo's desk took her by surprise, making her blood run a little cooler. Distinctly remembering at Crispin's *soiree*, overhearing dad tell Milo he'd taken care of it: now untraceable. 'Why's it still here? Is he hedging his bets, keeping it to take the heat off him? The keyboard having traces of Milo's DNA identifying him as the release programme trigger,' Marie wondered, muttering, 'Crap. They say curiosity killed the cat.'

She took a moment deciding how to play her unsanctioned discovery. Put it back in the drawer and keep the key? No, Donald could have a spare and may move it. Best take it. It should have been disposed of: he's not going to let on that it's now missing. She'd hide it in the woodshed. Collect it after seeing Mum, then stash it in the tack room, giving them time to sort out the final disposal.

Good plan, she decided — unlocking the study door.

Having crept back into the house, wandered the downstairs rooms concluding they hadn't been burgled because nothing was yanked open or out of place, and with the kettle cold, they had to still be in bed.

Looking up at their galleried landing made the hairs on her neck rise. 'Stop it,' she scolded, beginning her worrying climb up the elegant beechwood staircase.

Reaching the top, peering each way along the expansive corridor and into the lower hallway, invited memories of her as a child, squatting, looking through those bannisters. Picturing a younger Betty, laden with a tea-tray, calling up to her: 'There you are. Of all the places to play, you're up there again. Just don't slide down the rail. You know your mother hates it.'

There's a lot my mother hates, Marie mulled, struck again by their lack of mother-daughter connection. Although, Millicent often tried forging a softer bond, suggesting seemingly normal behaviour: complimenting new clothes; experimenting with make-up: Marie found excuses not to comply. It always felt so false; something she'd not the time or patience for.

Padding along the upper hallway, opening the familiar door to her childhood refuge. It smelt of stale hickory pot-pourri, making her wrinkle up her nose.

The same rug with its soft pile of greys, cool ivory's and brown lay on the wooden floor inducing a smile, remembering the hours she'd spent playing with her toy horses. Its creamy lines were bridleways; the border print, a mountain range; the inner design, perfect for corrals.

Closing the door, continuing her stealth mission towards her parent's bedroom, Marie called, 'Mum,' as she moved. 'Was that a faint murmur?' she wondered. Yes — it was coming from their room. Quickening her pace, hesitating outside, she saw nothing unusual through a slim gap in the doorway, before gently pushing it open.

The hinges creaked in complaint at her intrusion. 'Mum. Are you decent? Are you OK?'

Marie gasped at the room's reflection in their mirrored wardrobe doors. Millicent, sat on the floor in the corner nearest, was wrapped in a bed throw, looking at a large book, constantly muttering, wiping her nose with a handkerchief, and smiling oddly.

Pushing the door fully open gave Marie the right angle to see to the other side of the bed. The soles of gentlemen's leather slippers, she knew where Donald's — one laying on top of the other — made her heart miss another beat.

'Mum. It's Marie. What's happened? Are you OK?' she asked, kneeling beside her, placing her hand on Millicent's clutching a flimsy piece of pink cloth. Dainty initials — *M.O.M* — peeped from an exposed corner.

Knowing she *should* get help, she first had to assess the situation.

A patch of blood the size of a tea plate, stained the throw keeping Millicent warm. By its brownish tinge, not fresh. Wanting to check the condition of her mother before Donald: whose feet hadn't moved. No weak acknowledgement he was conscious. And the familiar sickly-sweet odour of death confirmed her worst fear. 'Mum. Have you cut yourself? Do you want me to have a look?'

'Marie. Oh, it's you. I've dug out the old photo albums. That's you aged one with your brother. You were both so adorable,' Millicent babbled — cooing, brushing her hand over a faded photograph.

Marie tugged a side of padded fabric away from the wrinkled, frail individual who bore no resemblance to her mother. Having seen her two days ago, Marie found it unnerving how someone could change so; from Millicent's vacant expression, assuming she'd suffered a mental breakdown. Tipping her face up by her chin — pulling down a lower eyelid — the inner colour still had a pinkish hue. With no sign of a wound, gathering the blood wasn't hers, light-headedness suddenly overcame Marie. Pulling the throw around her mother, relaxing her squat, letting her back slide down the high gloss wood of the bedroom door, closed it with her motion.

'Brother. What brother?' Marie wondered, holding her mother's free hand: the bony limb, icy cold.

Dismissing Millicent's confusion, leaving her gleefully viewing the poor-quality images, staying on all fours, she reluctantly crawled around the bed base, catching their surreal image in the mirrored doors; they looked like playing infants, one crawling away to hide a favoured toy. Weird, Marie thought, arriving at the grey silk sock, the scaly pale skin of Donald's lower shin: chilled to the touch.

'Oh Mum. What on earth happened?' Marie said, continuing her crawl to where his head lay on a cushion. Assuming he didn't fall this way, Millicent must have been with him when he died, or found him and made him comfortable. Donald's torso was tilted awkwardly against the side of the bed with a pillow in front. The crisp whiteness of the cotton fabric, garishly decorated with splays of scarlet brown, creating a form of death art. Although he'd died some time ago, Marie still checked for a pulse. And given the gravity of the situation, felt calm: pragmatism kicking in as she clinically evaluated the scene.

Donald had taken a fatal gunshot to the front of his chest.

A .45 handgun was lying by his right hand. The bullet, having hit his vena cava, caused catastrophic haemorrhaging in the wound space and the copious amounts of blood now soaked into the pillow and carpet. Marie estimated his death would have been quick: maybe as short as three minutes. The projectile exiting his back, taking part of his left shoulder blade, tissues and sweater with it. A fine mist of dried spots covered a mirrored door and their padded bedroom chair: confirming where he must have stood, facing the en-suite. 'Perhaps he'd disturbed someone? Maybe they made a run for it before he'd been able to stop them.' Marie wondered, needing to get sense out of Millicent before calling the emergency services. Or maybe not? It wasn't her responsibility to put the pieces together. She'd still heard no sounds from the rest of the house, any assailant having left.

Standing — willing the spinning motion to cease — Marie steadied herself, palms down against the cool white marble on top of Millicent's dressing table. It was no good, the buzzing in her ears was worsening, she needed to sit and get a grip of this horror of a morning.

The blood sprayed chair was her nearest option.

Sat on the very edge, avoiding the splattered life fluid that once pumped through her father, instead focussing on the wild-bird print by her thigh; the ceiling light — anything to avoid eye contact with his lifeless form.

Deep breathing helped.

Allowing her gaze to fall on Donald's wrinkled, age spotted neck, Marie considered covering him: deciding it pointless, no respectful shielding from gawkers was necessary. The sight of his corpse ignited no emotion in her. Confirming what she already knew: she'd reached that point in a relationship when there was nothing left. Surprised, even with a blood relative, to feel this way.

Her mind then wandered — maybe a delayed coping mechanism — but she recalled Millicent buying this chair. '.... its position means we can see right down to the stables, and it catches the morning sunlight. The perfect spot to relax and contemplate,' she had said, stood next to it, strong day light flooding in the window behind her highlighting an abundance of silver coiffured hair.

A sudden movement caught Marie's eye through that same window, severing the memory. A briskly moving black shape across the meadow. 'Aww. You sneaky wot-sit,' she muttered, realising Milo had let Storm run wild to expel his threatening energy, knowing it could take an age for her to catch him, always suggesting: why not ride reliable old Rustler or Toby?

Marie relished the distraction. Transfixed by Storms powerful image, she watched him gallop up the track to the woods, bucking and prancing to a trot, before jumping two cross country fences for the sheer fun of it. His unleashed free spirit was awesome: in stark contrast to the dark reality of death and questions that now surrounded her.

Shivering, deciding it pointless trying for any sense from Millicent whose crazy chattering filled the room, Marie plucked her mobile from a back pocket and called the sheriff. Then Milo, hoping he'd be in earshot of the stable phone.

'Here goes,' Marie mumbled, draping one of Millicent's shawls over her own shoulders, before aiding the confused woman away from the unexplained, to her childhood sanctuary.

Chapter Sixty-One

Georgetown, Washington D.C

You owe it to Milo. Keep her on side, it's the only way Josh lectured his image in the motel's bathroom mirror. Following the painful loss of Penny, the raw memories he was finding so difficult to deal with showed in his eyes. He'd been offered counselling, but wasn't prepared to go through the process for a psychiatrist to earn a fortune from his bad luck. No one was aware of his wretchedness: his inner turmoil. By working exhaustively; running hard and forcing himself to eat, he kept a lid on it. Sleep being the elusive element in his daily routine.

This repetition helped him cope with the loneliness; the dull, heart wrenching Penny void moments that overwhelmed him.

He just needed to pull this off before it was game over.

It took six weeks of covert delving to find the ideal patsy — Courtney Fielding, a trusted CIA Targeting Officer: as you'd expect of someone in her position at Langley — to confirm his suspicions about an undercurrent within his department. And establish what he'd feared: the Brockman's *were* a target. Josh had got wind through his other source, the order was being given tomorrow: wanting to know for certain before delivering Milo the news, hoping to avert their fatal destiny. Only Josh was aware of Courtney's addiction, which could destroy her career. This trump card: this unwholesome snippet of information he'd use against her that evening. Although not proud of his actions, if they help his dearest friend: that's all that mattered.

The sex was extremely gratifying. Satisfaction like this he'd never felt before. Courtney had an oral gift: amongst others. With the strong emotions he still felt for Penny, Josh assumed attempts at the act would be a non-starter. On the contrary, his body willingly complied. The past weeks' lustful night-time antics gave his complexion a healthy glow — had released an insatiable side to him he never knew existed.

Gentle knocking broke the moment.

'You OK in there? I'm ready and waiting,' Courtney's dulcet tones sounded from the other side of the closed metallic effect bathroom door.

'Sure. Just cleaning my teeth. Don't want you put off by my garlic breath. OK. Here I come,' Josh chanted, leaving the room naked and on the rise for another mind-blowing session.

The unleashed power he held over this beautiful, intelligent woman added to his sexual prowess. But this final time he didn't feel ashamed, he felt dominant, masterful, and not in the least bit guilty.

Chapter Sixty-Two

'Hoist by your own petard, my sexy bed-mate. Ketamine. Do you really think my occasional off-duty use of a horse tranquillizer will ruin me? Half the agencies on something, that's how we cope?' Courtney stated, pacing the motel bedroom with exaggerated hip movements. 'You're the one who's been played my friend. I've been observing *you* for months since you got back from Paris. Such a mug. Such easy prey. Don't get me wrong, I've enjoyed our time together. Who wouldn't with a Viagra fuelled widower? Yes, you heard me, I've aided your performance. So just listen. ... As you well know, what's going down is far bigger than minnows like us. We should be fine, *if* we play this game right. But to step out of line is unwise, my dumb politician.' Courtney sipped from a glass of white wine, continuing her sexy strut.

'You fool. Why did you agree to this? How could you have been so naïve? Why didn't you realise? You could have kept the upper hand, you idiot,' Josh silently admonished himself as she paraded in front of him.

'As I see it, you've two choices. Number one: take an L-Pill courtesy of The Agency. You know you want to end it,' she cruelly advised, removing a container of tablets from her bag, placing them on the bedside table next to where Josh was lying, bound by the wrists and ankles to the bedstead. 'Or, forget everything. Get on with the rest of your life and let me deal with the important stuff. What's it to be? Mr, on the fall, Secretary of State. Are you going to play nicely, or create an unnecessary fuss?' Courtney asked, straddling his torso, teasingly rubbing her vulva against his belly. 'Do you think if I stopped the field agents now, that would be that? It may delay the inevitable, but I'd end up dead too ... Oh, so you're aware, your other little helper from Homeland Security – he's on my side. Don't assume the cavalry will charge through that door to save you. I'm afraid it's just us. We've got to reach an understanding, all by our-selves,' she said, with child-like inflection.

'Shit,' Josh mumbled, closing his eyes, realising how out of his depth he was, how fucking dumb he'd been. 'Why hadn't he thought straight?' It was obvious *now* she'd planned the whole bondage thing to incapacitate him. 'You damned idiot, Hall,' he cussed.

Courtney, clearly on the edge, disguised it well. Josh never could have known the woman astride him, lying flat against his torso, humming, twiddling her fingers through his chest hair, pulling his nipples was a nut-job.

Christ, what's happening to me. How can I find this arousing? he thought, dismayed by the surge in his groin.

'Oooo. Hellooo. Why not, eh? Let's go out in style,' she crooned, reaching for the tablet container and wine bottle. 'But first, I'm going to ride the hell out of your loins, my foolish friend,' she commanded.

Josh could do nothing. In an out-of-body experience, he willed himself from the room as she writhed above him, hoping his housekeeper sticks to the plan: if he hadn't made contact by their agreed time each evening, she was to make the call. Trouble was, he'd rung her early before meeting with Courtney. Twenty-four hours might be wasted. Let's hope Milo's receptive to anything out the ordinary, he prayed – feeling warm tears roll down the sides of his face, pooling in his ears – watching the crazed She-Devil writhing on top of him with hedonistic abandon.

Having again enhanced his performance: he lasted fifteen minutes before shuddering to his final climatic experience.

Josh didn't resist as she jammed the tablet into his mouth, crushing the glass capsule against his molar. Grasping the wine bottle, she'd wedged between the pillows, yelling, 'Drink and ride.' She swigged straight from it without releasing his manhood from her death trap. Forcing Josh's lips apart, she then poured in a lukewarm stream of the sour fluid giving him no option but to swallow; accept his fate, as cyanide entered his digestive tract.

Through blurred vision Josh watched Courtney pop a capsule into her spittle covered mouth: a scrunch confirming she'd also consumed the deadly toxin along with the last of the cheap gas station wine.

The following morning the motel's cleaning lady clattered into the room with her linen cart, finding it odd the curtains were still drawn at eleven o'clock. With expert ease, whipping them open, turning, she screamed — clutching at her throat screaming at the grisly image of a naked woman slouched astride the body of a man, her arms dangling by her sides and features grotesquely contorted against the man's chest. A dribble of black substance ran from both their mouths onto the bed clothes. Their dark pink mottled skin and the smell of bitter almonds tipped the poor Latino over the brink. Crying out, she ran from the scene, reaching the motel lobby before passing out.

Chapter Sixty-Three

Red Brook Ranch, Alberta

Milo ignored the stable phone. Deciding not to give his mobile a try, gave Marie time to sort the situation while he and Jolie enjoyed their ride. Millicent was sleeping. She assumed an altered mental state had calmed her. Studying her relaxed features, you'd gather she'd not a care in the world. Perhaps that's it: she no longer does? Marie pondered, making her way downstairs.

Out of the kitchen window, she saw Storm charge down from the woods, so rang Oliver to make sure he was secured before the emergency vehicles arrived. Planning to tell the sheriff about her bone fragment discovery, she hoped he'd overlook her unauthorised testing. Also, she'd spill the beans of confusion invading the normality of her life.

'Was she doing the right thing, telling him everything?' she wondered: yes, she needed to purge. If she didn't share her fears, get her side on record, it could go against her if someone saw her arguing with Donald at the picnic area. And what if the initiative for their experiments got pinned on her? Who knows what these people may try with him out the loop? She had to think of Milo, Jolie and herself: their future was all that mattered. Wherever that maybe? Then she realised, get the lap top back in the drawer — Donald can take the rap for starting the pact. He'd have had no compunction bubbling Milo.

But she needed to be quick. The emergency services will be there soon.

Running back from the woodshed, Marie worked on a reason hers and Milo's fingerprints were on the device now tucked under her arm; when she'd first looked around the house, she'd checked to see if Donald had been used it that morning, and Milo gave it to him six months ago — simple. Just in time. Back in the house as the first emergency vehicle approached.

Marie took deep breaths, composing herself, calming her nerves, preaching, 'Stay strong.'

Stepping onto the front doorstep, 'Hello again, Sheriff. Whatever next?' she exclaimed, sporting her best mournful expression as he eased himself from the patrol car.

Chapter Sixty-Four

'Did you hear the one about the man who hospitalised with six plastic horses inside him? The doctor described his condition as stable. Dah, dah. What did the horse say when it fell? I've fallen and I can't giddy-up!' Jolie trilled, trotting off on Ziggy in front of Milo, shouting, 'Tally-ho.'

Ambling behind on Rustler, 'Enough. No more terrible horsey jokes pleeease,' he answered, reaching into his jacket pocket for his vibrating mobile.

Swiping the screen: the number not recognised, a stilted voice asked, 'Is that Professor Milo Brockman?'

'Yes. Can I help you?' He replied, relaying a sorry expression to Jolie.

She threw him a scowl with a 'Dad' through gritted teeth.

'You may not remember me. But Senator Hall left instructions if I hadn't heard from him to contact you and read you this short message. I do hope I'm not causing any inconvenience, but I don't know quite know what to do. I'm Diedre, by the way, Mr Hall's housekeeper.'

Milo brought Rustler to a halt.

'Is he OK? He's a good friend of mine. Do you think something has happened to him? Is that why you're calling?' The realisation hitting home, he'd not spoken to Josh for weeks.

'Please listen and decide for yourself. The message goes, "Tell Professor Brockman that he needs to get away and protect Marie and Jolie. Use new identities. And don't waste time tracing him, he'll be fine, and hopes to see you soon. He says, take care, man." I do hope this make sense and I haven't alarmed you unduly. I feel really bad making this call, but had no option. I hope you understand,' her voice wavered with uncertainty.

Milo took a moment. Who could he trust? One face came to mind.

'Thank you for letting me know. I suggest you contact his staff and take it from there. If they're concerned, they'll act. Your number's logged, and I'll be in touch once I've had time to think. Are you OK with that?'

'Yes. Fine. I hope you'll be OK. I remember you now. You seemed a very nice person. Let's hope this is all a terrible misunderstanding. Be careful my dear and goodbye for now.'

'Dad—, come on slow coach,' Jolie impatiently shouted, trotting around behind him, giving Rustler a flick on the haunches with her whip.

The horse flinched, thrusting pronounced teeth at Ziggy's shoulder.

'Sorry Jools. Something has come up. I've got to head back.'

'But Daaad, it's been ages since we've ridden out alone. You're getting really boring,' Jolie moaned, turning Ziggy sharply away, urging her into a willing canter, leaving Milo sat on his sturdy mount watching their unruly motion set off fast for the woods.

Milo's thoughts racing, reining the old horse towards the stables, without the slightest hesitation, he gladly obliged, breaking into a slow canter.

After the call he'd just taken, Milo's heart leapt into his mouth seeing an ambulance, patrol car, and two other vehicles outside the main house.

With doubts ricocheting, and the Josh mystery further ruffling his dwindling peace of mind, Milo knew he had to act. The time had come to accept Julian's offer of a getaway plan.

Mobile retrieved from his coat pocket, selecting Marie's number, he pushed Rustler faster towards the worrying array of vehicles.

Her device was off. 'Bugger,' he mumbled.

Chapter Sixty-Five

Black Ops, Alberta

Have a strong signal. Usual movement. Presently static. Feds. Possible sanitise, black bag job. On track for day after tomorrow. Perfect spot: was the live feed sent to their new point of contact at Langley.

Chapter Sixty-Six

Red Brook Ranch, Alberta

As an ambulance crew dressed a bullet graze on Millicent's arm, and the coroner took care of Donald, Marie sat with Sheriff Sutherland in Betty's snug — a small room off the kitchen that smelt of cinnamon biscuits — off-loading her facts, theories and worst fears.

She'd been stilted, reticent, not made coherent sense at first, but once in her stride, Marie's revelations couldn't be stopped. He'd listened, taking notes. In his experience, initial interviews were the most enlightening. Satisfied with her account, asked to remain with his sidekick, Sergeant Lambert, while he spent time with Millicent unravelling the puzzling course of events leading to Donald's death, Marie suggested, 'Coffee—?' to her imposing companion, whose unreadable expression she found unsettling.

The Nespresso machine buzzed as an accompaniment, as she leant against the worktop, switched on her mobile, casting the sergeant a pleasant smile. It pinged multiple times telling her Milo had called. Answering on her third attempt: 'At bloody last. Are you OK? What's happened, Marie? A cop wouldn't let me in,' he blurted with a voice overflowing with anxiety.

'I'm fine. But Dad's—' Marie cut short, Milo commanded, 'Good. Meet me at the cabin sharpish. We need to talk before Jools gets back.'

'I'd love to Mi, but Donald's dead. Shot in their bedroom. It appears it involved only the two of them. Mums away with the fairies. Completely gaga. The sheriffs with her, but I've got to stay put until her doctor arrives. They're working on getting her admitted to a psychiatric unit—' Marie's flow stopped. 'Mum only sustained a graze wound, but she's the prime suspect. And if they can't today, I've to be her surety. Beat that.'

'What! Blimey, Marie. I'm so sorry. Will they let me in if you ask?' Milo quizzed, pacing in front of the living room window, his mind buzzing with all he needed to achieve.

'It's *another* crime scene, they've cordoned the place. I'm here for a while with my uniformed friend,' Marie said, raising her eyebrows at the fresh-faced youthful man slurping his coffee. The gesture, he reciprocated.

'The forensic coroner is still doing his bit, and a homicide detective is on his way. The autopsy report will confirm the exact time of death, and how he died. Although it's blatantly obvious, and we'll be told the results of a toxicology test. Once I get the OK, I'll grab some bits together for Mum. Should be home in a couple of hours. Mi ... when I found her, she was looking at a photo album I've never seen and said stuff that made absolutely no sense. She was so cold: in shock I suppose and told me they'd agreed on a suicide pact. She reckoned she couldn't shoot herself, so asked him to kill her first. So, either he only wanted to finish himself off and made a feeble attempt at killing her, or, I don't know, maybe they struggled and she shot him. I knew she was down, partly his fault, but I didn't realise things were that bad between them. Obviously, I've informed The Sheriff of all this.' Marie gave her minder a reassuring smile, noticing him jot down what he'd heard in an official notebook.

Milo watched Donald's bagged remains carried on a stretcher to the coroner's vehicle, whilst listening to Marie. Stopping himself from telling her, he'd absorb the solemn scene on her behalf. The poor woman never would have envisaged Donald's last exit from Red Brook would be as a cold cadaver, culled in his place of rest. Or the cause — a fatal gunshot possibly inflicted by her mother.

Chapter Sixty-Seven

Rockies Roadside Diner, Alberta

'Be ready your end. I'll confirm good to go later,' Bog left a voicemail message on Chris's mobile, cursing, 'Dumb fuck. Where are you? Why aren't you answering? You really are a waste of space.' As he swigged green tea with sliced lemon: a drink he'd got hooked on over the past weeks' hanging around. Although his time hadn't been completely wasted: he'd written loads of articles and lost weight. Too much perhaps, catching his gaunt reflection, disguised by a week's beard growth, in the diner's smoked glass table division. A dark grey wall behind creating the perfect mirror image.

With expectant eyes peeled for a glimpse of Milo's Dodge pulling into the car park, he patted the canvas bag strapped around him containing the documents needed to bring in his whistle-blowers.

Bog doubted if Milo would ever agree for him to act as his press agent. When he'd made that first contact, in his haste to grab a pen and paper, he'd literally fallen off his chair. Manly embraces and carrying sports-bags off to enjoy a fitness session after not meeting for a while, was the impression Bog wanted to give when they'd first rendezvoused at a leisure centre. Milo, the bastard, made him swim twenty lengths before stopping, resting his arms over the drainage grids of the pool suggesting they grabbed lunch.

He'd quietly listened as Bog regaled his facts and theories, societies unfortunates being culled in European cities; the weird reports about the quiet men from Uganda, and the latest epidemic's fatalities. The whole disturbing picture would lead anyone to believe there had to be a link — a coordinated plan. But leading to what conclusion?

With each subsequent meet, Bog detected Milo's increasing edginess and hoped he wouldn't bottle this next liaison, which may prove the most fruitful.

Bog planned publishing his take on the suicide pact with Chris's tabloid, leaving a more credible broad sheet to run the scoop on Marie's revelations. This seemed fair and appropriate. Even with the constant threat from terrorism, it was worryingly easy to lay your hands on scrutable goods, Bog's National Crime Agency contact having contrived the Brockman's new identities from the UK's protected persons data base.

Martin, Wendy and Daniella Amos were the names on the passports burning a hole in his bag. They'd become the living substitutes for a family killed in a car crash years ago and resume their life in England. Bog's exfiltration plan: his clandestine operation to get Milo, Marie and Jolie out of harm's way, enabling them to spill the unsavoury beans in relative safety, he was keeping everything crossed goes without a hitch.

'Come on. I want this investment to pay off,' he mumbled, conscious he was over glancing at his watch; drumming impatient fingers against the sticky melamine table, scratching the back of his neck as the heat generated, from the odd smelling charity shop clothing used to baulk his appearance, increased his irritability.

Chapter Sixty-Eight

Red Brook Ranch, Alberta.

Despite this being a business arrangement, Milo hoped his gut instinct about Julian was right. He'd taken to the bloke. He seemed genuine. Maybe even a new friend. He could do with one? He considered flooring the Dodge straight over the meadow, avoiding the driveway past the builder's earth mound, noticing his decoy SUV parked outside the cabin still on its own.

'Good. They haven't left the main house yet. Perfect,' he muttered, the tail end of the old car slithering on the greasy mud surface; the momentary thrill of the out-of-control glide making him smile. Reaching tarmac, sticky mud splatters sounded against the Dodge's underbelly.

'Thanks, old girl,' he mumbled, running past the bonnet, giving it a pat then up the steps clutching a canvas bag filled with what he needed to execute their escape plan.

Pre-empting the sheriff's request to surrender their passports, Milo placed the superfluous items on the coffee table, hoping to tackle this issue while Jolie was still out riding.

Milo planned telling her coinciding with a conference he had to attend in London, he'd arranged a surprise touring holiday of Europe before Donald was taken ill. As Millicent was staying in the private clinic with him until he recovered, they'd insisted the family should go ahead with their plans. Once safely in England, he'll explain everything. He'll have to, she'll be devastated not being able to use her social media accounts.

Milo felt his brow furrow at the thought of her incessant questioning.

Marie wasn't such a problem. Having already mentioned moving, 'I've decided for us,' he voiced to the window, eyes glued outside for movement.

All too aware the schedule was tight; their flight in just two days, Milo again ran over the immediate details. Get Jolie tucked away first. Showering in her en-suite with loud clubbing music blaring normally takes her an age, giving me time to intercept the others. Make sure Millicent's upstairs, and get the sheriff out the way, asap. Tell Marie I'm concerned about one of the horses and reveal my plan as we walk to the stables, hopefully, while Jolie's still ensconced in her room. 'This is going to be one hell of a juggling act. Let's hope two days isn't too long?' Milo wondered, as the distant front door opened.

The figures of the Sheriff, aiding Millicent by the arm, followed by Marie, laden with a bag, made their way down the steps to the patrol car. In Milo's peripheral vision, he saw Jolie on foot, making his heart flip in hope she'd ridden up the ranch driveway, having no idea what's gone on. *If* Oliver hasn't wound her up with speculation, Milo cussed for her sanity not wanting her to know the truth about Donald just yet. He needed to get to her first. Now skipping on the perimeter fence path meant Milo *could* get to her first.

'Perfect. She won't see the sheriff's car. Get your arse in gear,' he chivvied, on the run, waving his arms above his head, catching her attention.

'Jolie's in the shower. Best we get Millicent settled in our room. You said she's being transferred in half an hour. It won't be too much taking her away so soon?' Milo queried for effect, watching Marie help her mother upstairs, one hand supporting her lower back, the other cupped under an elbow.

'It's procedure, Mr Brockman. Her doctor feels she poses a threat to herself and needs to be detained. The only suitable place is a psychiatric facility, and they've managed to get her booked in quicker than I'd envisaged. I understand your concern. But don't worry, it's for the best. She'll start receiving treatment straight away. You can visit, but not until the morning. I'll inform you when her interview with the homicide detective is so Marie can offer support,' Sheriff Sutherland briefed Milo, as he too watched their weary figures reach the top of the stairway.

'I understand. Sorry to cause confusion earlier. I want to keep Jolie in the dark. The only reason she's home this week is because of a nightmare issue, and the school thought it wise we thrash things out. You can appreciate our predicament,' Milo said, running a hand through the front of his hair. 'Makes me wonder what will happen next? What sort of family I'm embroiled with? Marie can be a loopy fruit: part of her charm. They say the highly intelligent are near the edge. I suppose Donald's actions have confirmed that theory. ... Just so you know, before today we'd discussed moving away. We feel it's not right for us here anymore. There's an unsavoury vibe tainting our lives.'

Milo turned to the window, breaking the sheriff's judgemental stare.

Standing in an uncomfortable silence, Sheriff Sutherland broke it with a bout of chesty coughs, accompanied by the loud blast of sound from Jolie's television as she threw open her bedroom door. A broadcast covering the death of a politician infiltrated Milo's subconscious.

'Ah ha. Sheriff Sutherland. Just the person. I've got something for you. Wait there please,' Jolie confidently demanded, holding a bath towel tightly around her skinny body, dashing back into her room, leaving a waft of coconut shampoo in her wake.

Milo shrugged his shoulders. He'd no idea what to expect either.

Donned in a hastily pulled on strappy t-shirt and jeans, she chirped, 'Could you have a look at my project please? It's a history of the ranch I've being doing in the evenings, with an additional chapter about the bone's lady. I think I could be right who she was. It was Lucy Delannay. She went missing. It all fits. There's even a sketch Pops did.' Jolie pointed at a crumpled sheet of paper. 'This is your copy, take it. The facts are there,' she proudly stated, thrusting a pastel green folder into the sheriff's hands.

'Thank you, young lady. It's good to see a child not wasting their time playing computer games. I'll give it the once over,' the sheriff said with a throaty chuckle, managing to exude genuine gratitude.

Milo caught his eye: thanking him with a grateful nod.

'Dad. There was something on TV about that Hall man, you know.' Jolie's elation at being taken seriously, reflected in her posture — head held high — she strutted back to her room. Watching her adolescent frame swagger away, her bony shoulder blades jutting through creamy white skin, made Milo smile with pride.

Then the penny dropped. 'Josh. Oh my God,' he cried.

Chapter Sixty-Nine

Sheriff Sutherlands Office, Near Calgary, Alberta.

Francis Sutherland sipped a calming mug of hot coffee, relaxing in his swivel chair. Using a booted foot, he spun himself around to face the window — his favoured position when trying to make sense of a case and collect his thoughts. He'd spend a quiet moment, eyes closed, processing memories of crime scenes. Pushing his mind to replay images; sort them according to their significance. Once satisfied, lids open, the view of the mountains lifted any air of malaise.

Today's habit reignited archived recollections of odd conversations he'd had with his predecessor, Bill Winterman. 'A word of warning, don't get drawn in by the Red Brook gossip. It's all hearsay. Just folks jumping to conclusions about a bunch of scientists they think are up to no good. My advice: drop it. They were drifters. Victims of bear attacks. They were living rough in the forests, on wacky-backy for goodness' sake, what else is likely to have happened to them?' Although thirty years ago, Francis could still see Bill's wary expression making his point, his dismissive comments, at the time, baffling Francis. They still did. The man had been such a stickler for doing things by the book; his attitude, so out of character.

Why *had* Bill refused to consider his hunches? He thought, knowing his memory would not let him erase those missing persons', their cases mysteriously leading to dead ends.

'Crikey, where's the time gone?' he muttered, glancing at a picture of his younger self hung on the wall; fresh out of training, keen as mustard.

Francis' mind had defined his unblemished reputation. His secret weapon was still sharp as a knife and never missed a trick. Impressive recall abilities had dug these archived doubts from his subconscious for a reason. Maybe he's being reminded he should have been more forceful, not just swallowed his bosses rebuff. Could those incidents be linked to the present?

Retiring, becoming a man of leisure in August, with no more mysteries to solve from gruesome clues, and no more late-night call outs disturbing Dorothy's sleep, made Francis chuckle, visualising her creased face, her groggy voice cussing. Was he looking forward to this next phase in his life? No, not really, he decided, flattening his notepad, firing up his computer, mumbling, 'Best get started.'

Waiting for the kettle to re-boil, he read his initial incident report, his concentration again invaded by memories of Millicent's ramblings during her lucid moments. Picturing her pained expression, her watery eyes, spittle in the corner of her mouth as she'd told him about Donald's joint suicide plan. Weeping, saying she couldn't bear to live with anymore of his verbal abuse yet couldn't live without him, and didn't have the guts to leave him. Burbling, Donald was being threatened by people he worked with and it was only a matter of time before they killed him, that's why he came up with a way out, on their terms. She'd just gone along with the idea.

Francis reached for the digital micro-recorder — the little black box Millicent thrust into his palm when led from the cabin to the ambulance — supposedly capturing Donald's abusive tirades. 'I couldn't get him to admit. But please listen, it may help you understand,' she'd whispered, clutching her comforting photo album.

Francis sipped his coffee and flicked play; recalling, during her interview following the bone's discovery, she'd mentioned then about their troubled relationship and asked his advice on recording devices: could he supply her with one? Not thinking she'd go ahead with her entrapment plan.

Listening for five minutes — rewinding when necessary — it was clear she'd been selective with the on/off switch: no sentence was fluid, just containing snippets of hurtful insults hurled between unhappy couples. 'Perhaps she'd ordered it online? Maybe Marie's in cahoots with her?' He wondered, remembering Millicent's claim as Donald lay dying, he'd confessed to killing the woman in the hole.

'Shame she'd not captured those words,' Francis mumbled. Surmising a lot of what he'd heard lately hadn't rung true; speculating whether Marie was right, or paranoid?

If she *was*: he could jangle powerful nerves getting involved in matters way above his pay grade.

Draining the last dregs of coffee, conjuring his last image of Donald Osbourne-Maine: undoubtedly an intelligent, influential individual. But prickly, unapproachable; with an air of irritancy.

Francis had never taken to the man, this now silent witness unable to reveal the riddle of his demise. Let's hope his remains provide the answer to his last life chapter. And the result of the investigation doesn't taint his professional legacy, Francis pondered, chuckling, 'Christ. Sounds like I'm writing the blokes obituary.'

Eyes drawn to the top of his bookcase, to the pale green folder, 'Ah. Crazy girl's theories,' he mumbled — foot propelling his chair across the room — the frame creaking under his weighty burden. Flipping open the front cover, giving the pages a quick thumb flick released a popcorn aroma, along with a few delicate paper flowers which fluttered to his desk. She must've been doing an art project, he guessed, undoing the metal retaining clip, extracting the intricate still-life pencil sketch of an exquisite face. From the lack of ageing facial lines, he reckoned this person would have been no older than her late teens' when she'd posed. The faint grey impression bore an uncanny resemblance: just the nose a smidgen longer; the cheekbones more prominent.

It's possible, he thought — recalling Marie's revelation, backed by DNA testing. *If* the link is confirmed, he'd give Marie's theory serious consideration.

'I wonder where you came from, bone lady? And how you ended up in a hole at Red Brook?' he murmured, continuing to browse Jolie's methodical handiwork with more belief; feeling a pang of guilt he'd initially dismissed her theories. The rejection he felt when his old boss reacted the same, springing to mind. If Jolie's right: we've found one of the missing. If Marie is: it explains why she never fitted neatly in the Osbourne-Maine household.

He just needed the motive, and who killed her.

Francis' focus returned to his main concern: Millicent, secure in a psychiatric ward. Convinced she wasn't as loopy as she was making out, she'll be served a Summons and Appearance notice in a day or so. The rest of the Brockman clan: on a promise to appear and not leave the territorial jurisdiction.

With a sigh, 'I've done my bit,' Francis reasoned, wondering how Milo and his family *were* holding up, picturing Marie's expression as she led Millicent down the cabin steps after being told the truth. 'Everything's best discussed. You can move on with your lives. Rebuild trust,' he'd advised — in his usual do the right thing spiel. It was never easy when relationship baggage got an airing.

But something else niggled at Francis: footage from a concealed security camera had captured Marie running backwards and forwards from the main house with a laptop tucked under her arm, before and after, she'd made the emergency call. Strange behaviour under the circumstances, he mulled. 'The detective in charges' problem to unravel. Thankfully not mine,' he muttered.

Noting down what lay ahead: missing persons; an unsolved murder; a police employee in breach of trust sharing confidential information; a family whose world might be turned upside down by the discovery of their daughter's remains identified by a tenacious teenage super sleuth. And a Government conspiracy. On reflection, this should keep me busy, no sitting on my haunches until August. 'All the better,' Francis spoke under his breath — letting out a guttural belch. 'That bacon sandwich, why will I never learn?' he chastised his mirror image hung by the office door, stretching his arms above his head to relieve a bout of indigestion. You're your own worst enemy: Dorothy's high-pitched nagging rang in his subconscious, as he swallowed two capsules of Divol dug from his drawer.

Depressing an intercom button, 'Ask Sergeant Lambert to come in please,' he bellowed. 'Let's hope my, can see the wood for the trees, sidekick has an hour free. I need him to work his magic with this lot,' he again spoke to his reflection, examining the wrinkly part at the front of his neck and grey receding hair line.

After a deep lingering look into his own eyes; feeling long diluted detective impulses rekindle, grip at the walls of his arteries, convinced there were more discoveries awaiting at Red Brook ranch, he'd appease his lingering guilt and reopen the missing persons, he decided. It will be his legacy to those neglected souls.

Sheriff Francis Sutherland intended going out with a bang. 'Before high cholesterol damn well finishes me off,' he grumbled 'But what if *I* vanish or get bumped-off walking home like Bill? Maybe he'd got in over his head too?' he wondered. What the heck. Better than getting on Dorothy's nerves all day, '... always under my feet making a mess. Sitting around with a twisted piss-pot face,' Francis imitated her usual gripes, sporting her downward mouth expression, sure she'd be happier looking at his urn on the mantle-piece than him drooling in an armchair.

Perhaps another of his legacies could be to rewrite The Government's Immigration and Citizenship website. 'It may limit the numbers flooding into the country,' he grumbled, smiling at the thought of a new advertising campaign:

beware of bears and wolves; local mass murderers; government sleeper cells and dodgy scientists — opposing the image of a safe and peaceful existence in the Canadian provinces.

Noisy hammering on his office door broke his contemplation. 'Yep,' he called, as Sergeant Lambert confidently strode in.

Francis watched him take a seat, hit again with a broody sadness he'd not had children. In a world brimming with spineless procrastination: a more dependable chap you'd be hard to find. To have had a son like Benjamin would have made him so proud.

With a broad grin, slinging the report across his desk, goading his favoured colleague, 'Jamin: you know that leave you mentioned? Well, my lad, it's cancelled. Get a load of this.'

Chapter Seventy

Kasese, Uganda.

Was he being asked to go to Kursk? Siegfried fretted, processing the implications of Professor Leopold's proposal with a forced smile; the rest of his words buzzed in his ears. Recalling his remark: 'Learn Russian, my friend.' He now gathered his advancement depended upon compliance. 'Shit,' he cussed, knowing he should have tried harder, annoyed with himself for the times he'd chosen extra gym sessions over language tutoring with Victor, the friendly Russian surgeon.

You need to react, he's getting out his chair, gesturing for you to join him through his impressive ebony carved door. With a strained smile Siegfried followed the professor into a cosy study, similar in decor to the facilities library. The comforting scent of leather, woollen rugs, a hint of nutmeg and mild cigar had a calming effect. Exhaling, the tension left his shoulders, as they continued through to a contemporary open plan room with a mezzanine sleeping platform. An animal hide, draped over a double bed, with a pair of brown suede moccasins discarded at its foot, confirmed he was at the heart of the great man's private lair.

Aiming a remote control at a shiny white wall to the left of where they stood: a view of the rehabilitation and kitting out area appeared.

'Woah. Electro-chromic smart. I've never seen its magic up close. Amazing stuff,' Siegfried commented in awe, walking over to the vast expanse of glass, stroking its chilled firmness as the image transformed back to milky white. All the better, he thought, feeling he'd come to a new mate's house to enjoy a beer, watch sport, play cards — maybe order a pizza. The unfamiliar surroundings, having transported Siegfried from the facility, made him wonder–, 'Will I ever enjoy a day like that again?'

'Please take a seat, Siegfried. An espresso, lager, something stronger?' Leopold offered, slipping off his clinical coat — discarding it on a sumptuous cream armchair, before moving through to a sleek minimalist kitchen.

Lost in his fanciful scenario, 'A beer and pizza would go down well, thanks,' Siegfried foolishly answered.

Taking off his own, he relaxed into the caress of the over-sized couches plush cushioning, slurping the froth from the top of a frosted tankard handed to him by Leopold, reflecting he could seriously get used to living here. After a hard shift, walking through the portal of intrigue into an environment the same as this appealed.

'Shall we cover the serious stuff, then fancy a game of chess?' Leopold suggested, rubbing his hands together with laddish enthusiasm.

Taken aback by The Professors familiarity, answering, 'Sounds an agreeable plan.' He stretched out his legs, gulping his cooling drink, watching Leopold stare at the opaque glass wall: collecting his thoughts, Siegfried surmised. 'I wonder where he was born? Where he trained? What he's seen through those knowing brown eyes?' Distinguished salt and pepper hair puts him perhaps ten years older than me? Strong jawline and broad forehead compliment his inner confidence. Siegfried continued his silent wonderment of his mentor, the man who encouraged his unconventional ways. A slight scar above his top lip was the only imperfection, adding an air of mystery. I bet he was injured on special ops' and just escaped with his life. And drives a big Merc', or Aston. I can see him in a silver DB9. He's got Bond manliness, Siegfried pondered, chomping handfuls of peanuts from a chunky wooden bowl sat on an industrial style coffee table.

'Siegfried, being entrenched out here you've lost touch, but the programme is going from strength to strength,' Leopold spoke abruptly, repositioning himself on the opposite couch.

'We've exceeded our initial expectations, couldn't have wished for a better start. This facility will keep churning out the vital cogs in our machine of change. Their contribution is paramount in maintaining a workable balance wherever they're deployed. But we must move forward and begin the third phase. This is where I need your help.' Leopold took a sip, droplets of condensation falling from his tankard hitting the dark matt floor.

Siegfried focussed on the translucent splats, his mind racing with what was to come.

'We'd like you to head our Transcontinental facility in Kursk. It's on par with this one. Lay out, equipment, the same. Skeleton staff are on-site test running. We've recruited five theatre teams. I'll accompany you at the start, then she'll be yours to develop. The procedures are the same, harvested from the European continent. I'll explain more as we progress. Sound good so far?' Leopold sported an uncharacteristic expression of doubt: a glabella furrow relayed his apprehension.

He *was* human. The overlord had emotions. This first glimpse of uncertainty empowered Siegfried. This influential man needs me: he sees *me* as an equal, and I'd assumed I was in for a telling off for pushing my popularity, not being offered promotion at a different frontier. A broad grin manifested as he replied, 'Thank you. Sounds an unbelievable opportunity. Not wishing to sound arrogant, I know I've stood out from my colleagues, not always for the best reasons, but I'd no inkling I'd impressed you that much. I'd be honoured to accept this chance of a lifetime.' Siegfried paused, mulling the man's words, continuing, 'So, Kursk. Reading between the lines you've attained Russian funding? With tyranny and terrorism stemming from the Middle East causing human displacement throughout Europe, the location makes geographical sense.

And with Russia being Russia, controlling their media, means you can crack on relatively unnoticed—' Siegfried stopped himself mid-sentence, carefully considering his phrasing: 'To be honest, what concerns me is your self-governing position. In theory fine, you know the personalities. But this is where I'm not entirely comfortable: who controls the controllers? If I'm being accepted into the fold and don't agree with a plan, or feel it's gone far enough and want to opt out, I gather that's the end of me? Will my demise be voted on by the rest? Your present hierarchy at times must disagree. Will you not eventually all get bumped off?' Siegfried knew he was taking a risk, that his words could lead to trouble.

Leopold suppressed his laughter with a snort. 'I understand your concerns. It's healthy you and I can question the ethics. We vote on every stage. No action happens without overall agreement. We must pass funding through a panel of over one hundred. You'd be right in thinking this causes brief delays. But, rest assured, any doubting individuals are still alive and kicking.'

They took a moment, sipping beer, holding each other's intent gaze. 'I could be lying Siegfried. This is for you to decide. But you've come this far, with the right temperament. And, to be frank, we'd value your input. You mentioned the issues in Europe. The region needs stabilising and holds a glut of harvesting potential. We aim to reform a harmonious society with a subservient controlling force produced from multinational conscripts being prepped on the Greek island of Kythira. It is under populated, has historic links to Russia and is the perfect location for staging to Kursk. We gained it with a substantial offer to ease Greece's debt, done on the hush hush from Brussels. This could be your baby Siegfried, *if* you've got the balls for it.' Leopold raised one brow, questioningly.

Siegfried said nothing: acting nonchalant, goading him to continue his persuasion tactic. He leant forward, scooping a handful of nuts, sending a few tumbling into the cushion recess by his side. He'd find them later.

'The Zika virus was first isolated in Uganda in 1947? Coincidence? Perhaps? Anyway, my point is, half the world's population is at risk from insect-borne diseases, so, as we've done in this region, we're working on halting medical advances by reversing the self-limiting strategies designed into insects to prevent the spread of disease, and genetically modify other indigenous ones to suit our purpose, covering our tracks by blaming horizontal transfers within species causing unintended consequences. If you agree to a future with us, you'll need further inoculations; we've more little nasties in the pipe-line.' Leopold linked his hands behind his head and stretched his back.

'As I see it: you've got me trapped. Head the new phase and stay safe. Or risk contracting an incurable mutation delivered by an insect's proboscis. Wonderful prospect,' Siegfried concluded, breaking into manic laughter. Given the gravity of their discussion, the sound provided light relief at a touchy moment.

Leopold smiled. 'Did you know rats — a supposed plague on the planet — will only re-produce when the conditions are right? We've an abundance of Homo-Sapien vermin too inane to realise theirs' aren't: their resources becoming limited and aren't prepared to embrace the bigger picture. Societies have created these lazy leeches, just as much a plague, who need educating, or eradicating.'

Leopold closed his eyes, frantically rubbing his scalp. 'We've such a long way to progress, it's exasperating my friend. We must stay committed, united and strong. That's why we need people like you to push the programme forward.' His stern tone and focussed core again prevalent.

'Still on for that game of chess?' Siegfried asked, attempting to exorcise Leopold's momentary resolve — wanting to encourage his softer, urbane side to return and be a normal human being for a moment in this crazy time.

'I'm black,' Leopold barked, pulling a chess board from the tables shelf.

Although beaten, Siegfried played his best game ever. 'Bravo. Same time next Sunday?' Leopold said, rising from his chair, making it clear he should leave by gesturing towards an unobtrusive black door at the far side of the room.

'Fine by me.' Siegfried turned away, hiding his self-satisfied smirk. Lightheaded, for stability, he braced a leg against the sofa, draping his coat over his shoulder, before following Leopold.

Walking in silence along a stark corridor towards a closed door, as they neared, Siegfried noticed three digital units mounted above. Red numbering in constant flux read: 7,000,354,010, increasing by ten digits as he watched. The unit below displayed: 167,200. The other: 75,563 also altering by the second.

'What do they signify?' Siegfried asked: reaching his own conclusion before Leopold answered.

The glowing figures represented the planets ever changing population, putting into perspective the enormity of their task.

'My answer's yes. On agreement, I take Victor Sokolov and Kirk Redman with me. And, I get a fuck off wooden door to my pad similar to yours.'

Siegfried's flippancy: acknowledged with a chuckle.

'My ploy worked. You understand the extent of our battle, my partner. These displays are in sync' with many others around the globe, reminding us so we don't slacken. Trust me, even I'm being monitored Siegfried. Best get used to it. And welcome on board.'

Chapter Seventy-One

Red Brook Ranch, Alberta.

'Why can't I do normal stuff like other girls. They go swimming, skiing, have parties and fun. But not Jolie Brockman. The weird kid who finds human bones; unravels mysteries; has to get her head around new babies and now has to miss the pony club show the one year she had a chance of winning a trophy for a grand tour of Europe. It's *so* unfair. No wonder I don't sleep properly,' she shouted, stomping to her room, slamming the bedroom door rattling the hallway mirror.

'At least it didn't fall off and give us more bad luck,' Milo winced, joining Marie clutching a glass of water on the sofa.

Loud rap music blared from Jolie's room, providing a convenient shield. 'Poor Jools,' Marie began. 'But we've decided and have to be strong. I couldn't sleep much last night, and despite what she said, didn't hear a peep from her room. That's an improvement. Do you think she's got psychic abilities? She *so* takes after Pops. Yesterday evening she said Lucy will let her rest now she'd shared the history and justice may be done. Weird eh. It's documented pubescent kids can become messengers for spirits. If you believe that sort of thing. We've come off lightly so far, I'd say. At least she's not been pinned to the ceiling, or vomited green gunge and something constructive could come of her messages from beyond,' Marie chuckled, twizzling her glass, bewitched by the water's swirling motion.

'You sure you're OK, Marie? I'll cancel the arrangement if you need longer.' Milo's concern evident by his tone. One arm around her shoulder, rubbing the top of her arm.

'I've known for a while Mi. Just didn't tell you. Don't know why? Perhaps I've been in denial. But when I saw the DNA result, it fell into place. Everything odd about my life: that answered. I was actually relieved, like a substantial weight had lifted. Millicent's admission yesterday, well it was good to hear her say, "she'd tried to love me as if I were her own, and she was sorry." But, in the grand scheme of things, it makes no difference. I want to find my twin brother. I need to do that. And learn what I can about my proper mum, how she ended up a pile of bones in an unmarked grave carrying what would have been my sister. Millicent clammed up when I delved ... It's so sad.

Momentarily starring out the cabin window, Marie continued, 'We shouldn't tell Jools: can't confuse her anymore. Did you disconnect the internet and take out her SIM—?' Marie's voice faltered; overcome with convulsive gasps, she sobbed like a child.

Milo stroked her cheeks, cradling and rocking her, kissing the top of her head, wiping away her steady stream of tears, their sweaters absorbing an abundance of salty run-off he couldn't stem. Until, in her usual stoic fashion, she got a grip, blew her nose, dabbing away moisture from her face with a soggy tissue, saying, 'Sorry Mi. We have to focus. That outburst didn't help.'

Milo continued stroking her hair, noticing blue veins at her temples: indigo streams flowing under her pale skin; dark circles under her eyes reflecting her inner exhaustion, and recent soft wrinkles formed around her mouth. For her own, and their baby's health, she needed rest. 'More sleep and spinach for you. You're looking tired,' Milo dictated, pulling down her lower eyelid to check the colour.

'I'm fine. Look at my tongue while you're at it.' Marie stuck it out — making an arr sound.

Using a light pressure, Milo felt no resistance coercing her backwards onto the sofa. Altering her position like an infant, placing her head on a cushion, lifting her legs, positioning her feet onto his thighs, he hummed a comforting melody, massaging the small pink extremities.

Lulled by the therapeutic sound and pose, Marie's words flowed. 'When Millicent showed me the photo album she'd kept hidden from Donald, I picked her out straight away. She was a beauty. Tall compared to the other flower power hippies, as she referred to them. He'd tell her off for taking photos and getting too friendly, "…. they are only passing through," she said he'd shout. A group of them shacked up in camper vans where the stables now are. They just appeared overnight. Donald paid them as guinea pigs for one of his genetics projects. Back then, his makeshift office was just an old Portakabin as the laboratory was being built. She said there was loads of noise and construction materials everywhere … that's so relaxing. Just what I need. Thanks Mi,' Marie purred, continuing, 'Millicent said it was a joyful time. The carefree bunch were always singing and playing guitars. Said she sat on the grass chatting with them, or watched them tending the vegetables they grew. Proper Mum, Lucy, turned up a few weeks after the rest.'

Sighing, closing her eyes, she fell silent, breathing calmly.

Comforted to see her features relax; the rise and fall of her chest slower, Milo's gaze drawn to her full lips when they again moved. 'Millicent assumed she was a runaway who Donald agreed to help while the sheriff traced her abusive parents, which she wasn't to mention. She did as he asked and thought nothing of it. She said she was different. Timid. Scowled at everyone but Donald and got up tight when the others tried making conversation.'

A noisy yawn broke Marie's flow. Cupping her hand over her mouth muffled her next few words. 'When their vans disappeared, she was sad. They'd been rays of sunshine, she phrased it, and missed their chirpy personalities. That's when she realised, she'd made a mistake with Donald: always grumpy and short, stifling her spirit, blaming her they'd not had children. A generation thing; ever the woman's fault. Stop if your bum's going numb.'

'I'm fine. I'm intrigued.'

'When Lucy was the only one left, Betty took her under her wing. Millicent said she noticed Lucy gain weight and assumed it was Betty's cooking. But remembered the afternoon she realised Lucy was pregnant. She'd been on her way to see Betty, and Lucy was walking in the meadow picking early purple Prairie Clover. Millicent recalled thinking the pink, and purple hues of the flowers matched her smock top. It was when she'd bent forward, awkwardly holding her lower back, it'd hit her: "Oh my God. They were supposed to be keeping her safe. What an earth will Bill say," she said she mumbled, assuming it resulted from a hippy liaison.'

Marie stretched, raising her arms, cracking her knuckles to ease the tension. 'Apparently, Lucy smelt of mountain mint. She made a deodorant spritz and showed her how to make it. That's so nice Mi, but we should be doing something constructive,' Marie chided, breaking the spell of Millicent's memories, trying to sit up.

Milo pushed her back, insisting: 'Another ten minutes won't hurt.'

Struggling to find her thread, recall competing with even louder irritating rap music booming from Jolie's space. Glancing at her door, Marie frowned, closed her eyes and carried on: 'Lucy had us at Betty's lodge. Millicent said she kept her distance: too guilty and jealous. Although she was a good, attentive mum. But when she realised Lucy was pregnant again: alarm bells rang. Lucy was infectious, had a perverse innocence Millicent found appealing, meaning she still spent time with her regardless of the new development. When they offered to adopt us, she found it odd Lucy didn't jump at the chance. She just threw Millicent an arrogant, knowing smile, one she'd never forget … Poor Millicent. She was an innocent pawn, Mi. Dad manipulated them. Perhaps he intended keeping Lucy as a second wife, a brood mare to provide more offspring. I don't know. Anyway, months later she vanished. Millicent said she'd written a note which they found at Betty's, saying she needed a fresh start with her new baby and wanted Betty to take care of us: Linus and Leanne. Millicent said Donald didn't want us both, only me. In his eyes, I was perfect. Not sure what she meant by that. They found a German couple, through Donald's contacts, for Linus, and I stayed here as Marie Osborne-Maine. Dah, dah.'

Yawning again, longer and louder, she said, 'Donald was a cruel man. Years later, during a heated row, Millicent said he told her the truth that he'd fathered Lucy's babies, and how proud he'd been of her beauty, intelligence, and mothering abilities: attributes Millicent lacked ... I'd like some of her photo's. She'll be drowsy when I see her tomorrow. I'll get the chance to take a couple. The way she clutched that album against her chest like a precious child, her eyes darting around. That image won't leave me for a long time. She will need a lot of help. Still, at least I now know why I wasn't embraced like a treasured possession in any of those photos. Right enough rambling, we've got to be positive,' Marie preached, rising from her relaxed position, taking hold of Milo's wrists. 'Let's leave noisy sulking girl in her den and get cracking. You take the cases upstairs. The horses!' The problem struck Marie hard, spinning to face Milo, grabbing one arm.

'It's OK. Oliver's not going anywhere. Just concentrate on the three of us. And don't forget we're being helped. You've not meet Julian yet. We'll be fine,' Milo assured her, breaking free of her grasp.

Chapter Seventy-Two

Struggling up the stairs with their cases, Milo heard Jolie's pronounced footfalls. The sound relaying she'd not quite got over her tantrum; was nearly back in her cheerful place, feeling his awkward burden lighten as she helped lift them from behind. She plonked onto the edge of their bed, kicking her feet around; she's coming to terms with the idea of an adventure but won't show her enthusiasm yet, he thought: reading her like a book.

They shared a smile beyond that, ignored her as they sorted their clothes, until, with a loud huff, she stomped out.

'Oh Mi. Josh! I'm so sorry. I've been self- absorbed, your turn to off load.' Marie flopped onto Jolie's vacated spot, stroking a red silk blouse.

Milo shrugged his shoulders with a not to worry expression. 'What I don't understand is the way he did it: in a seedy motel room with cyanide and a hooker. It dishonours Penny. And where would he have got it from? But then who knows with the underworld we're embroiled in. Figures, I suppose.'

'What do you mean? Why's that figure?' Marie pushed.

'Oh. Nothing, really. Just my imagination running wild.' Milo dismissed the notion, having not mentioned the house-keepers phone call. He'd heeded Josh's warning: they were on their way, that's what mattered. Wishing he'd not allowed himself get brain washed into leading the suicide plan. He should have stuck to facts and figures. The institute would still have been effective in the long run. What good came of meddling – of believing he could make a damn difference – his name likely recorded in history as the cause of millions of deaths. Bloody Donald. That's why. But think straight. If it comes to it, he'd say Donald sent the e-mail triggering the plan. Having threatened Marie, he'd simply acted as Donald's errand boy. But his gut told him there was more to Josh's warning: Marie's involvement. Her knowledge of the lab experiments and the horrors she'd tried telling him were the actual reason they were running. Play each hand as it's dealt. Distance and breathing space were still the best option.

'Mi. You're not answering me. The cyanide. Why does it figure?' Marie interrupted his troubled thoughts.

'What—? We shouldn't travel together. You should leave first with Jools,' he blurted.

'No way ... but I get where you're coming from, it makes sense. Your chap can change the one flight. But you and Jools go. I've got to see Mum and get my notes from the doctor. I'll need a bit longer and don't forget we're supposed to be calling the shots. Coffee break,' she insisted, slinging the blouse onto a chair, breezing from the room and the awkwardness.

Milo stood with his mouth open, holding a cashmere sweater as Marie's silk garment slipped to the floor in a fluid octopus' motion. 'What? Silly moo. Pregnancy notes for Marie Brockman won't be much use,' he mumbled, smiling.

'I know. Don't worry. A momentary blip,' she called from downstairs, heading for the kitchen, shaking her head at her reflection in the hallway mirror. 'You must take extra care before speaking, lady,' she admonished herself.

Adding fresh water to the coffee maker, fretting over everything they'd need to perfect to get away safely. Her forehead rested against a wall unit, arms spread wide, palms flat against the worktop. She listened to the bubbling appliance, realising she hadn't yet taken her daily supplement.

Plucking the container from a corner shelf, tugging off the stiff lid, she tipped a few capsules onto a white saucer, watching as they scattered. Rolling one under her forefinger, she gulped down another; with the thumb of her other hand squeezing the top back before adding it to the not to be forgotten items. Sachets of ginger tea; coconut lip balm;

lavender calming cream; spearmints; tissues and a packet of Paracetamol waiting to travel in her handbag. The sucking noise of the machine made her pivot. Her errant hand catching the supplement container, sending the golden pearls rolling in every direction. 'Arr. I thought I'd closed it,' she mumbled, gathering them in alarm wondering: 'What the devil's that?'

Pressing a capsule between her fingertips, holding it up to the sunlight as it streamed in the kitchen window. It looked like an insect trapped inside the innocuous vial of nourishment. 'Oh my God,' she said aghast, a flash of heat rising to her cheeks.

Grabbing her glasses from a pile of cookery books, Marie checked another: it was the same. So were three more. Slicing one open, she ran a slimy fingertip over the mysterious grain sized extraction. The oil acting like an adhesive stuck it to her skin, making it easier to examine. Achieving focus: wiring in a thin translucent coating puzzled her. Placing the oddity into her mortar, it yielded to pestle pressure. 'How haven't I noticed this before. What on the earth have I been taking?' she wondered, her mind racing with the consequences.

She needed a microscope.

Hearing Milo moving around upstairs, she grabbed her yard coat and entry pass before running out the back door. Trotting over the sodden grass, glancing behind to their bedroom window: Milo's concerned face wasn't observing her. 'Good,' she mumbled, assessing how she felt. No odd pains. Had been going to the loo fine. But what damage could they have done?

'Fuck,' she chuntered.

In the time it took her to reach the lab, she'd rationalised her predicament: an art perfected of late. It *had* to be an impurity sealed in during their manufacture.

Chapter Seventy-Three

Calgary International Airport, Alberta

Milo could handle tight corners; hold his nerve, think on his feet. He'd plotted and planned; held hundreds of awkward conversations, arguing his point with the best of them. But the last three hours had tested his mettle. Tense: he needed the shot of caffeine being prepared by the coffee shop girl. Glancing to where Jolie sat, bless her, he thought, impressed how she'd handled the unusual car swapping; luggage juggling and furtive glances — complying with raised hands and silent dah's cocooned in her ear-phone zone.

'She's a resilient cookie,' Milo mumbled, smiling at her adolescent legs swinging wildly under the table.

'Would you like anything else, sir? We do have a queue,' an irritated voice relayed, jolting Milo's attention to the well-lit food display.

'Sorry. A blueberry muffin and vanilla milkshake. Oh, and one of those cheese sandwiches. Thanks.' Milo said, peering over his shoulder, catching disdainful looks from impatient customers.

Jolie spooned the swirl of cream from the top of her shake, devouring it with gusto, nodding her head in time to mind-numbing music. When Marie gave her the MP3 player to download tracks from their CD collection, he recalled her tantrum: 'Muuum. This is from the arc. The memories crap.'

Milo smiled, shuffling the plated cake towards her elbow, gesticulating with his forefinger for her to eat. Her forced grin confirmed she'd taken the hint.

With the grease-proof wrapping pulled from one corner, she looked around the café, stooping to nibble the spongy delight.

Two lads tucking into baguettes at an adjacent table caught her eye. She straightened her posture, self-consciously pushed out her chest to improve her profile. They noticed, chuckling and commenting to each other. Youth and their preoccupation to impress: so glad I'm past all that, Milo reflected, replaying their escape, searching for flaws, gaps — any overlooked aspect of their planning as he slurped his scalding hot beverage.

He'd parked the Dodge at the back of the cabin. Loaded their cases under cover of darkness. Early morning they'd driven from the ranch, hoping, if being watched, not to raise suspicion. Milo had spotted Julian: inconspicuous, always in the right spot sticking to the rehearsed order. Speaking into his mobile was Milo's signal to activate the next phase of his subterfuge tactics, decamping them from this era of their lives.

Just one more hurdle: a final passport check.

Why did I agree to let you fly alone, Marie? The thought of living without you is unbearable, he mulled, shuffling forward in the boarding queue, taking their Amos passports from a smartly dressed member of the ground crew; extremely pleased their replacement identities hadn't caused a security alert.

Walking hand in hand along the gangway to an unknown future, Martin and Daniella Amos gave each other a self-assured smile.

Chapter Seventy-Four

Red Brook Ranch, Alberta.

The first rays of morning sunshine created a bejewelled twinkle on the frosty grass. Wrapped in a black fur throw, warming her palms around a mug of hot chocolate, Marie relished the landscapes breath-taking, transient beauty. She'd miss these early awakenings, hoping they'd return; that their running away would turn out to be a laughable mistake. 'The day we ran away from the Bogeyman. Splendid title for a book,' she chuckled, strolling towards a blackened area on the driveway: all that remained of Jolie's attempts at smoke signals.

Using her yard boot to grind the crispy charred remains of burnt paper into the asphalt left a dusty patch. Marie recalled her daughter's frustration: 'Just letting my friends know I won't see them for a while,' she'd shouted, frantically wafting a tea towel to break the upward spiral the way Pop's showed her. They'd watched from the doorway, chuckling. 'Maybe for the last time,' she muttered, glancing at the cabin, remembering Milo's warmth by her side.

To say Marie was lonely, unsettled — even lost — without her family, was an under-statement. Knowing she'd not hear their voices until she reached England: worsened that feeling. With no reports of plane crashes, she felt heartened they were safe.

Nearly making the mistake of checking their flight arrival on line and Googling human tracking devices: a clear give away she was on to them. Whoever them was? They'd targeted her. There was no doubt the lab photos deleted from her Drop Box *had* been the handiwork of Donald's associates. 'What had he got her into? What exactly *were* they running from, and how big is all this?' She wondered. Considering a normal, caring father would have given their daughter a choice. 'How damn selfish,' she mumbled, shuddering from the cold, tipping milky dregs onto the grass.

She didn't tell Milo of the intricate Nano-transmitters she'd swallowed, relaying her exact movements with no idea for how long. The MRI scanner in the laboratory was no help. Nothing she laid her hands on told her how many of the electronic parasites still lurked in her digestive system. She'd made herself vomit. Taken laxatives. What else could she do to expel the threat to her safety? And would she get through airport security? They'd think she was nuts; may inadvertently alert her foe if she mentioned her tiny, elusive travelling companions. Perhaps she should share her discovery with the sheriff? That's the answer. Tell him. Show him the proof. He'll help.

As instructed by Julian, via their landline: 'I've important information regarding Millicent that may be of help,' she relayed. 'Shame. I'd like to have shaken Jolie's hand. She did well, with her insider help, of course. Let me know when she's next home,' the sheriff answered, told Milo was returning her to school. Turned out, he'd news for her too, wanting to share it face to face.

Replacing the receiver, 'Coffee with a dash of brandy for courage, and, God, you're looking tired,' Marie muttered, using both hands to draw back the flesh on her cheeks, sticking out her tongue to the stressed women staring back from the hallway mirror. Was that Jolie's thumb print on the side? Marie imagined her sneakily straightening it after a bedroom door slamming episode. Placing her own on top of the smudgy reminder of her absent daughter helped diffuse the emptiness within.

Chapter Seventy-Five

Dressed in his girly disguise, Julian parked under the treeline outside Red Brook. Doubting he'd be able to stay awake for the next twenty-four hours, Milo's words: 'Promise me you'll get her away safely. You owe us that,' repeatedly ran through his mind. If Marie stuck to the plan: he intended honouring that deal.

He easily identified the surveillance vehicle; a woman running to a black Chevrolet Equinox with its engine idling, eyes glued to Milo's back as he'd left a store: let slip their ruse. Becoming sloppy, they'd under-estimated their prey, foolishly falling into Julian's trap to become the ones watched. Although, he found it odd, Marie: he'd assumed was their main target, wasn't always followed?

'Ah. Good morning Sheriff and your big tree of a sidekick. Time for a leg stretch,' he muttered, grabbing his camera, setting off along the track he'd first walked with Chris, breaking into an off-key whistle.

Enjoying the exertion, quickening his pace, reflecting on the undercurrent pulsing through social media. The public were spooked: asking questions. Not just conspiracy nuts. Normal people were wondering: Why the numerous viral outbreaks? The suicides? The culling's?

With the first stage of his plan in execution, Julian desperately wanted to get back to Blighty and solve the riddles. The Brockman's divulgence providing either logical answers to quell societies apprehension, or reveal an unpalatable truth.

Of course, they could end up dead like so many others.

Julian — aka Bog — stopped whistling.

Chapter Seventy-Six

Marie scanned the immediate area for tell-tale signs she was leaving. It looked lived in. More than normal, she realised, unsure whether it mattered *if* she goes ahead with her revelations. 'The next hour should be interesting. I might wind up in the nuthouse with Millicent,' she muttered, going out the back door to greet Sheriff Sutherland.

Reaching the warmth of the kitchen, Francis gave her an awkward consoling embrace. Feeling the permeating chill from his thickly padded jacket against her face; a damp car odour hung on the fabric, rustling as he put his arms around her shoulders. Marie quickly pulled away, suggesting a coffee.

Wandering into the living room, drawn to the welcoming fire she'd lit as a comfort for another strange day. Clutching hot mugs, they sat in silence, warming their hands.

'Is Sergeant Lambert not joining us?' she broke the ice.

'The lad loves to walk. He's exercising the patrol dog while we chat.' Francis then stood, placed his mug on the lintel above the fireplace, turning to Marie stating: 'The mother of the bone lady is still alive and lives in Saskatoon.'

For a time, she just looked blankly at him. 'Can she have a proper burial now? Will her mother wish to come here?' she asked with concern, knowing the timing not ideal.

'Yes. But it could be tricky. Where she's laid to rest follows the preferential direct line of succession which actually favours you, Marie. Her father's dead. And considering the last time her mother saw her was forty-three years ago, she'd like her buried in their hometown. You can understand it would give her closure.'

In his usual way, peering over his glasses at Marie, the sheriff took a noisy gulp of coffee.

Mindful she'd not be around: 'Trust me, Francis. It's not a problem. Only right she ends up near her. I'll sign whatever's necessary to ensure they release her remains asap. Can you tell me what you've found out about her?' Marie quizzed — wanting to stall him — wanting to relax before revealing her own unbelievable craziness.

'Any chance of another coffee?' he asked, taking a seat nearest the fire. Flicking open an aged buff folder, licking his forefinger, Francis searched the first few pages before stopping—. 'Here it is,' he called, as Marie returned clutching their mugs, settling on the chair opposite.

Assessing her mood for a moment, before reading aloud: 'Lucy was, Louanne Craven. An only child from a low-income family. Born 20th of June 1960 in the Riversdale area of Saskatoon. Got in trouble in her neighbourhood: antisocial behaviour, flaunting herself in bars, nothing major. She was seventeen in August 1977 when reported missing. Various sightings of her hitch-hiking on the Yellow-head Highway. Arrested for stealing groceries, booze and clothes just outside Edmonton and sent to a young offender's institute under the false name of Lucy Delannay.' Taking another slurp of coffee, he continued, '... was assessed, reformed and released after six months. You'll find this interesting Marie: she had a very high IQ. Probably the reason she turned bad: it wasn't noticed. They saw her as awkward. Poor kid. What a waste. Anyhow, says here they found her a work placement in the academic field and she didn't want to go home due to alleged abuse. Ironic really ... we're sat here talking about her and wouldn't be if the technology existed back then to identify her. She'd have been reunited with her family, offered the help she needed, and no you, Marie. Funny how things turn out.' Holding Marie's expectant gaze, they shared a silent, sympathetic moment for Louanne.

'You mentioned academic work. That's fascinating. She'd no influence over my upbringing, yet given my career, maybe genes *are* more complexly programmed than we realise? Perhaps there's a link with experiences on conception. Sorry. Carry on. I'm going off at a tangent. Was it around here?' Marie: keen to hear more about Louanne's brief life stopped her usual thought process diarrhoea.

'Have a look at this document. Signed by Jack Taylor, the institute Governor then. Take your time. What you notice?'

Francis handed her a musty smelling sheet of browning double-sided A4 paper. Examining the retro font, noticing the typist hadn't set the Certificate of Release form straight in the machine's roller, the paragraphs were askew. She began reading, frequently reciting its contents: 'Resettlement scheme ... on arrival provide orientation ... regular credit work ... follow modified plan ... advisory committee ... spend a semester at the institute. Upon satisfactory completion, eligible to enter the College of Applied Science. Wow. Great. They gave her a break,' Marie enthused, lifting her eyes to meet Francis' before continuing her methodical study of every inch, from the faded violet official stamps to the numerous signatures and dates. 'Assigned to the Misericordia Sisters for welfare purposes,' she read. Before two entries on the reverse side of the document struck her in the chest — like the gloved hand of a rude jack-in-a-box, — providing the link.

She'd found the fact. The indisputable evidence Sheriff Francis hoped she would.

Neatly written, at the bottom corner of the page, were two red letters — OM.

The girl had been assigned to OM — Osbourne-Maine — Donald. The institution had unwittingly condemned the poor girl to death.

'Oh my God! Millicent thought they were only helping the Sheriff. That she'd randomly turned up the same time as the other travellers. Turns out, it was planned. How come no-one checked how she was doing? How could she have disappeared from the system with no questions asked?'

Marie barked — throwing Francis a look of stern disbelief, exclaiming, 'This is terrible. My poor Mum. I hope she was happy for a while. Betty will know. I'll ask her when she's back. Shit. Not until next week—' Marie stopped herself short.

'I've wondered the same, Marie. I'll come clean. I believe my old boss was aware of issues linked to this ranch. I've reopened some missing persons, and I'm afraid Sergeant Lambert has found more links. He's unearthed fifteen more OM mentions from the same institution following a quick skim read of their files.'

A disturbing chill ran through her. It stunned her into silence. A worrying confusion bombarded her mind. Biting her lower lip, her gaze caught by the cerulean blue sky out the window, focusing on a hawk hovering above the meadow. Its small head assessed the ground, finding its target: a scurrying pika, or mouse. Marie watched it dive for the kill, landing on the builder's mound of earth that once covered her actual mother.

She was losing it. The dam holding back her emotions was about to break. Hot tears welled in the rims of her eyes: she didn't try stemming the flow. Allowing the salty droplets to topple down her cheeks obscured an image of the Sergeant walking back to the cabin, a darting black and white dog at his heels.

Saying nothing, Marie rose from the sofa and left the room, returning with the pot of polluted capsules. 'Sheriff Francis. I can't do this alone. Your turn to reach a conclusion.' Marie passed him the container. 'I have to go. I'll end up dead if I stay. I've proof now I'm not crazy. It's here. Can you help Millicent? Support her through the funeral? We're sure Donald was framing Milo. He'd an old laptop of Mi's we think he used to trigger recent events. I found it in his desk. He was involved with powerful people and asked me to do things in the laboratory that weren't ethical. I've told you this already. And can't give you any more answers. But need you

260

on my side. Please don't lock me up,' Marie pleaded.

Francis stayed silent.

'I don't know the truth behind Donald's death. What Millicent's involvement was. How Louanne ended up buried here, or anything about Donald's activities on this site when I was young. Please help me.'

Losing control, she sunk to her knees — not for effect or sympathy — but because every ounce of energy drained from her structure. She couldn't support the relenting pressure of the truth. Francis knelt on the floor beside her.

Fighting the urge to push away from his unfamiliar embrace, she instead relished the security his consoling frame provided. Tipping her head further down, avoiding the tobacco-y staleness of his breath; he's tired, she thought, as he continued robotically rubbing her back.

'It's alright,' he said, without genuine feeling.

Francis didn't doubt Marie.

Chastised by Dorothy for: '...still being in front of that damned computer at three in the morning,' He'd done enough research to know Marie was right: the technology existed to create the trackers she'd been covertly plied.

He would help her. He'd avenge the memory of Louanne, and all those unfortunate missing souls.

With events worldwide, and unravelling on his doorstep, he felt a change was happening, putting him on edge; suspicious, wondering what the future held.

Continuing to stroke the hair of the forlorn woman huddled at his knees, wiping a stray tear from his own cheek, Francis reflected: if Bill Winterman had done his job, Marie might not even be here. Whether that was a good, or a bad thing, recent developments considered, he wasn't sure. Convinced any skeletons their investigation's may uncover probably would not have.

Chapter Seventy-Seven

Stood in Storm's stable, a sudden stomach pain accompanied by a dull ache in her lower abdomen, made Marie cup her developing mound with both hands. Putting on his head collar, leading him out, she used her full weight against his powerful shoulder to slow him, chastising, 'Stop it.' Nearing the corral gate, struggling against his prancing frame, releasing the halter clasp, his muscular body took flight. Quickly sliding the pole into its housing; she'd neither the time, or energy, to play cat and mouse games with him today.

Watching him tear around, kicking up dust, tail flowing, she ran through the arrangements for the estate. Maintenance accounts for the horses, grounds and houses well in the black. Jolie's ponies would be exercised by the daughter of one of Betty's friends, who was over the moon. Oliver to ride Storm. Having already pushed her letter to Betty under the door to her lodge, telling her they're taking a sabbatical. And despite recent events, couldn't alter their travel plans, Marie felt comforted knowing she'd be safe by Milo's side when it's opened.

Knowing sleep unlikely, so pointless hanging around until morning, with growing apprehension and guilt, she changed her departure plan. Leaving that night, using Oliver's old shed of a car to travel to the airport, intending to doze in the car park ready for her early flight. Recalling Oliver's puzzled expression, then gratitude when handed the keys to her SUV, made her chuckle.

'Lunatic,' she shouted as Storm cantered by, bucking wildly, before slowing to a showy trot, letting off a peal of gas with each forward motion. Another uncomfortable twinge making her frown, reminding her to take it easy, Baby Bean wasn't happy. Storm watched her walk away, whinnying for attention, his alarmed sentinel head carried high, tendrils of hay dangling from the sides of his mouth. A few straggly wisps floated up on the strengthening breeze, like over-sized discarded insect legs, she thought, calling to him, 'Big Baby.' A dose of maudlin cutting short her fond gaze on a beloved equine companion.

Wandering further towards the main house, reliving her discussion with Sheriff Francis, she'd insisted nobody else's life should be put at risk; she needed him alive and well for Millicent and to keep an eye on the place, refusing his offer of a lift to the airport. The Sheriff didn't know exactly where she was going; only for her family's safety, she had to distance herself. Assuring him, after Milo dropped Jolie at school, he was flying to his HQ in Europe then returning. Francis' expression relayed his official conscience was struggling to comply with her request. And that he didn't truly believe her.

With sinister square eyes, the darkened windows of the house watched Marie approach. Playfully sticking out her tongue: 'You don't scare me,' she mumbled, catching her breath, realising her extra weight and vexatious state were taking their toll.

In the hallway's warmth, she looked for signs of the terrible event which last brought her there. Apart from a stray end of cordoning tape clinging to a bush in the driveway, they'd cleansed the place. Life within its walls could resume as normal.

'Tin foil. Photo's. Turn down the heating. Lock up,' she muttered, wandering into the kitchen. Dried coffee stained the bases of three white bone china mugs placed in the sink. Through habit, she loaded them into the stale smelling dishwasher, setting it to run. The fridge and freezer were emptied: Marie assumed by Oliver after a fretful Betty phone call.

Not allowing herself time to relive the recent nightmare,

Marie swiftly checked the bedrooms and collected her child-hood photo's. She'd add them to the ones pilfered from Millicent's album, concealed in the lining of her suitcase.

Halfway down the stairs, an unexpected creaking from the kitchen area made her jump and clutch at the bannister rail, goose-bumps rising on her skin. Tip-toeing to the source: Betty's snug, Marie paused outside the cedarwood door, picturing the cosy refuge the other side. Her rocking chair with worn pine arm rests and crocheted seat cushion. A grey tasselled throw hung over the back rest. Imagining Betty rocking it: that's the sound she'd heard.

Opening it a tad, she peered in.

Half-drawn curtains allowed a beam of daylight to invade the homely room in which there was no-one, and nothing moved.

With a firm tug, she closed it, wanting to leave the uninviting shell of a house, its beating heart long gone.

Stepping away, it resumed.

'A damn raccoon must have got in,' she muttered, before rationalising there'd be a hell of a lot more racket.

Armed with a rolling pin, she again opened the door, calling— 'Oliver, is that you?'

It was icy cold, and yet no windows were open.

Checking the cushion for traces of warmth: just the chill of abandonment met her palm; a waft of mint, her nose.

'This is weird,' she mumbled, turning from the Betty's space riddle, retracing her route to the hallway.

Closing the front door behind her, Marie found the moment poignant; as if she were closeting her troubled past; perhaps even saying a last farewell to the childhood home.

Walking along the driveway, looking back, raising a hand in adieu to her unhappy memories, she shuddered as a chilling sensation pulsed through her.

Pulling up the hood of her coat, a gentle spring of tears toppled over her cheeks. 'Where did they come from?' she wondered, assuming the biting breeze their cause. And yet, she wanted to smile. Twiddling her fingers through the air, turning a full circle, blowing kisses in all directions, recollecting Louanne's face from one of Millicent's photo's, she hoped one of her gestures may land on its target: the lingering spirit of Louanne Craven — her real mother, close by.

Chapter Seventy-Eight

A full moon. 'Perfect. Now for the strange bit,' Marie mumbled, unreeling a metre of aluminium foil. Holding the free end against her side, using the strapping of her bra as an attachment, she smoothed the metallic covering over her ribs and tummy.

'Now for my hat,' she muttered, finishing the binding process with strips of scotch tape, before moulding a head-sized insert. If this stops aliens, reading the thoughts of abduction nuts: it's good enough for me, she thought, chuckling at a memory of her as a child pretending to be an astronaut, sheathing herself with the foil Betty planned covering the Thanksgiving turkey.

Marie's core temperature soared when she pulled her jumper over the crispy body shield. 'No need for the car heater, England here I come,' she said exuberantly, knowing she needed to keep a positive frame of mind, and remember to remove the tin bandaging before check-in.

'Goodbye Marie Brockman. Hello Wendy Amos,' she prattled to her dimly lit reflection in the car's side mirror as she drove from the ranch, flicking on the headlights after a half a kilometre slow drive, realising how terrible Oliver's car stunk; the warmth from the engine kindling a cocktail of animal food, crisps and smelly boots from the debris-strewn carpet.

Opening the window, Marie pondered: let's hope he remembers to collect this heap and Pops' Dodge: visualising Milo and Jolie stepping from the old blue hulk now abandoned in a shopping centre parking area.

Deciding on Wendy's persona: a practical, tree hugger type with no hang ups about body image too interested in the bigger picture to waste time worrying over such inconsequential stuff, gave Marie an inner confidence; a perceived invisibility fitting for her secretive escape.

Choosing to wear old maroon corduroys, thinning at the knees. A huge moss green jumper, her scuffed paddock boots, two multi coloured scarves and one of Jolie's purple trapper hats; Marie's favourite tatty leather handbag, with a compartment for everything, completed the look.

Half an hour into the journey, with no lights tailing, cocooned in the darkness, Marie relaxed. The odd incident at the main house that morning, then came to the fore. 'Perhaps Louanne's dissipating energy had reached out to her? Perhaps they'd learn to communicate?' she wondered. Realising the strange event gave her a focus for her different life: a research project about experiences on conception. She'd get Jolie interested, guide her to follow the same career path. A pang of guilt then gnawed at her conscience. Julian will be concerned. He was supposed to watch her until she'd got through customs.

'Don't change the plan, Marie,' Milo and Julian had stressed.

Milo's expression of intent floated into her peripheral vision.

'Don't worry. I'll soon be parked up safe and sound,' she mumbled.

Feeling a sweaty moisture build between her skin and the foil, Marie loosened the scarfs and wound the window down further, imbibing in a blast of chilled air, exclaiming, 'Damn,' as out of habit, she'd pulled off the main highway and taken the loggers track shortcut running along a hillside through a housing development.

'I've only a few miles to go, pointless turning back,' she muttered, glancing in the rear-view mirror. With a smidgen of relief, no sinister vehicles had followed her mistake.

'I'll be OK,' she assured herself, the twinkling allure of Calgary airport's runway lights on the plain below drawing her on. Looming black shapes of unfinished houses briefly shielded the encouraging image, making her speed up to reach the other end of the sprawling construction site, feeling increasingly vulnerable: like she was giving away her position as the loud metallic pings of loose stones fiercely hit the underside of the chassis. 'Ah,' she mumbled, eyes flitting to the mirror.

'Christ,' she then cried, noticing through the windshield the lit outline of a broad vehicle coming at speed over the brow of a hill in front. Probably a delivery truck, she reasoned, as its full side illumination rose, highlighting the size of the metal leviathan.

'Shit. He can't have seen me,' she shouted — flashing the headlights, sounding the horn, knowing if it didn't stop, or slow, she'd be trapped on the narrow track they shared. On one side was a sheer vertical bank. The other: shrubs and trees before a steep drop into the valley.

The truck didn't appear to be slowing. She had to decide whether to turn quickly around, or reverse to a cut in she'd just past. But backwards in this car was hard to find, doubting she'd have time to avert an accident.

Screeching to a halt, creating a billow of dust haze in her lights, bellowing, 'How can you not have seen me. Come on, you heap of shit.' The preferred gear proved elusive.

With not a moment left to turn, Marie accelerated hard towards the wire fencing to her left.

Under the dire circumstances, her only viable option.

From the increase in red tinged particle plume caught in the truck's taillights, she could tell the driver hadn't slowed. He'd sped up — foot to the floor.

Squeezing her eyes shut, Marie yelled, aiming the side of the car at the chain linked barrier. The screech of metal against metal confirmed she'd made contact. A few upright poles relented under the onslaught, bashing against the wing in anger. Reaching the end of the secured section, Marie sharply turned the wheel to face the distant sparkle of the airport, illuminating the shapes of the trees and bushes, bringing them to life from an inky darkness.

Driving at a forty-five-degree angle towards a large mound of earth ahead, Marie knew she'd get stuck when she reached it. The full weight of realisation then engulfed her. She hadn't got away. This idiot driver wasn't there by chance.

Knowing her only hope was to get out and scramble away on foot, lose herself in the undergrowth, ignited an anxious nausea.

Hearing the hiss and squeal of the trucks air brakes controlling its weighty bulk on the incline, told her it was metres from hitting the passenger door: her cue to attempt an escape.

But she left it too late. The force of the impact made her grip on the steering wheel, tighten.

To jump out now would be pointless, she'd get dragged under its body.

As the car got shunted sideways, she tried wedging herself in position. Screaming, 'Why are you doing this?' To the taunting snarl of its front grill gleaming in the moonlight.

The trucks massive bulk favoured a victory.

The driver's door snagged on protruding rocks and shrubs, thwacking and waggling backwards and forwards, grinding in complaint at the harsh impacts. The perpetrators of this heinous act hidden in the shadows of the cab: their task soon to be over. Marie doubted their obscurity was for the sake of their consciences, so they'd sleep sounder.

The metal structure of Oliver's old faithful machine could take no more. Its rusting frame knocked off balance, with two further shunts, the gradient aided its point of no return. In a cruel slow motion, it tipped. The compressing action broke free the door as it began a noisy crushing roll. Marie supported herself within the compromised vehicle the best she could. Pushing her hands against the roof, forcing one foot each side of the door void.

The assailants would have heard her scream, 'Bastards. Why kill me?' She pleaded to their moonlit faces — one white, one black — before the moving angle of the cars frame blocked her view of the cab's interior. 'You idiot. Why didn't you listen?'

she blabbered, crying from the jolting pains surging through her limbs, and a terrible cramp in her lower belly. A sticky warmth running between her legs heightened her desperation.

Experiencing an unfamiliar sensation of being airborne, with no structural contact, before getting briefly knocked unconscious. Trying to regain her focus, it fell on the wreck of the car further down the slope back on its tyres. She couldn't move her right leg. Her head pounded and strong cervical cramping pains had worsened.

Managing to drag herself on her elbows over the hard ground, using her right knee to take the pressure off her baby, she crawled away trying to save them both. Looking around the gloom, the idle rattle of the truck's engine provided a back track to her futile escape.

Heavy footsteps then approached.

Marie turned to see two men picking their way through the low scrub. Pin pricks of light reflected in the eyes of the menacing assassins sent to do someone else's dirty work.

With no haste to their movements: Marie needed no convincing this was an accident. No call of, 'Are you alright?' accompanied their slow amble to where she lay.

Time was up for her, and her unborn child.

'Make it quick, you bastards. I've so much to bloody give. It's such a waste. And for what? Tell me that at least,' she screamed, clutching her cramping abdomen.

God, she was in agony. 'Not now,' she pleaded, instinctively pushing to aid the dragging sensation her miscarriage was creating. Was it still alive? She doubted. She'd fallen hard on the poor little mite. Her amniotic fluid ruptured on impact. If it wasn't dead: it soon will be.

Feeling their evil presence hover, bringing with it a smell of leather boots and cigarettes; damp dust and vegetation on the night air, mixed with diesel and petrol fumes: a toxic combination for her last olfactory experience, she contemplated, propelling herself to Red Brook. To the view from her bedroom of the Rockies; Milo's aftershave. His strong male odour she so loved to inhale with her face against his chest. To Storms stable: his warmth and sweet breath. Marie concentrated on arousing these aromas from her archive of the wonderful in her life as callous hands grasped her ankles and dragged her. Cruelly bumping her torso over the ragged terrain. A shooting pain soared through her leg.

Pointlessness and defiance wouldn't allow her to beg for mercy. Conjuring an image of Jolie: she's tough. Has her dad, she'll be fine. My Milo. Our first date. Our beautiful wedding. Making love with him — these positive thoughts Marie trapped in her closed eye vision, as she cried, detaching her mind from its broken flesh form, before being dumped, like a sack of rotten potatoes, her legs roughly arranged one forced under the car's wreckage.

Forcing herself to fleetingly witness the horror of her situation, Marie watched one of the shadowy figures examine the inside of her shoulder bag. 'You're not as dumb as I thought. Learn my language if you want to work with me again, or I get you finished off,' the others Russian voice said, stood by the side of his silent accomplice.

'Help me. You don't need to do this. Do you even know who I am?' Marie implored.

'Shut up,' came his hateful response. 'There it is, little missy. You thought you'd been so clever fooling us. You didn't look in your bag. Foolish missy,' the Soviet assassin mocked, holding a Nano-transmitter pearl between his fingers — waving it in front of her, the truck lights illuminating the liquid, revealing her fatal oversight. She'd only focussed on the capsules trapped *inside* her. She'd overlooked checking her bag. But who could have put it there? When she bought them, she always shoved the container in her coat pocket.

Marie battled with the thought as the Russian's boots moved away.

The man's quiet accessory watched her helplessness.

She knew she should shout, cuss at these men. But couldn't muster the anger; aware they were completing a questionable task: something she'd done regardless on many occasions in the laboratory. What goes around comes around. The cliché invaded her mind. Her gaze drawn to a brilliant moon seemingly held in place by indigo clouds. The normality of its familiar glow she found mesmerising.

Marie then worked it out. Donald planted the transmitters when he brought the flowers.

The betrayal: painful. But answering a puzzled recollection of her bag un-characteristically clasped shut.

'The Bastard,' she wailed, tears trailing over her cheeks.

The quiet one then bent, blankly looking into the depths of her eyes. Marie had seen his empty stare before. Those unreadable eyes were distinctive.

She helped create this scenario; had been involved with the process leading to this moment. Her handiwork had perversely come back to haunt her. They *were* using their creations in a way she'd feared. Her dabbling with Graphene had produced a mercenary in cahoots with this Russian thug. An altered human probably was about to end her life. The irony hit her like a stage comic's joke. She thought she was working on brain advancements to cure. And nourishing her developing foetus with vitamin capsules. Instead, her work, her care brought about their demise.

'Who are you? Who *were* you? Are you still in there? Remember your mother. Your family. What you liked. Fight back. Help me and I can help you. I know what to do,' Marie begged in a last-ditch attempt to persuade the controlled soul there was an alternative — he could disobey. 'Quick. Shoot him. He's your enemy. Please, I'm begging you. Shoot *him*,' Marie pleaded, convinced she'd ignite the quiet one's conscience to do the right thing.

He spun towards the Russian — then back to her — his face expressionless.

'Shoot him now. Don't hesitate. Please shoot him,' Marie again sobbed, as an over-powering stench of fuel made her retch.

A shot rang out.

Automotive urges took over, making her expel the pre-term baby's body wedged in its birth canal. A muffled ringing in her ears, silencing the moment.

'Thank God,' she cried out, shutting her eyes, giving a final push — jumping in shock as something heavy fell against her.

The altered man: the Russian had killed him.

Marie wept explosively. Placing her guilt laden hand on the limp arm of the abused soul, his corpse, quickly dragged away by the Soviet, muttering, 'Save the damn hardware.'

A rasp of red phosphorous against powdered glass filled Marie with dread. Whimpering pathetically, a swift blow ended the planned tragedy, releasing Marie from the pain and horror she was suffering.

The Org took advantage of Marie's error. Choosing the perfect time and place, preventing her part in the programme from ever being shared. She couldn't jeopardise their plan. She had to be eliminated along with her wealth of information.

Marie recognised her face being consumed by the flames, realising how similar her death had been to her birth mother's. Their life forces prematurely extinguished. Their innocent unborn lost.

An aroma of mint made Marie turn from her lifeless body.

A faint pulsing aura beckoned her.

Feeling unafraid, Marie cradled her baby boy and moved away from the scene, knowing she had push on. She had to find Milo and Jolie, somehow.

Chapter Seventy-Nine

Final Haven Cemetery, Alberta

'Perfect day for a funeral,' Francis Sutherland muttered, trotting down the station steps, glancing at the dull, snow filled sky. He'd Marie's promise to keep: aid Millicent through Donald's, and now her own cremation sharing an 11.30 service.

The chill on the air bit into his cheeks, making him pull up his fur collar as he eased himself into his patrol car, glancing around, fully expecting a whack around the head, or the impact from a sniper. Paranoia working overtime, he'd worn a bullet-proof vest since Marie's death.

With a heavy heart, he drove off, mulling his future. Perhaps he'd write a novel. Base his characters on the Brockman's and Osbourne-Maine's and the odd goings on at Red Brook: the disappearances, the riddles Sergeant Lambert was trying diligently to solve.

Waiting at traffic lights, locking eyes with his own in the patrol cars wing mirror; his tired, preoccupied gaze reflected his resolute frame of mind. They'd get to the bottom of the ranch mysteries. He'd absolve Milo and Marie: Donald—? Well, that's a different story. His control within the police and prison service and dubious past was slowly being uncovered. Too late for the poor unfortunates who'd crossed his path. But justice must be done, however long ago the back-hander deals and self-interest agreements were made.

Francis' thoughts turned to Marie: why did the foolish woman leave earlier than planned? And why on earth hadn't he followed his instincts, keeping their passports when Milo offered. Or at the very least, put Marie in temporary safe custody. Pointless dwelling. He couldn't have prevented her death, doubting whether securing her in a cell while they worked out what to do about the transmitters, would have kept her out of harm's way. If this organisation was capable of infiltrating his station, disposing of records so easily: realistically, what chance did she have?

At least poor Louanne's back home, he reflected, recalling the image of the hearse carrying her remains leave the forecourt of the coroner's office. She might not have wished to return to Saskatoon while alive: but probably wouldn't want to be anywhere else now. And her mother can regularly visit her grave. That's got to be better than remaining a lost soul in a worm riddled hole.

'It's not appropriate. I'll sell the place.' Francis recalled Millicent's dramatic tirade at the funeral director's suggestion they could bury Donald and Marie at Red Brook; dogmatically insisting on no newspaper announcements or official wake. They'd assumed she'd be in favour, would crave feeling near them and tend their graves.

This attitude hadn't gone unnoticed and wasn't helping her case.

Sheriff Francis sat with Millicent at the front of the austere chapel. Glancing behind, he counted thirty people paying their respects. Judging from their whispers and searching eyes: plain disbelief filled the room, Milo and Jolie weren't present.

Recognising all but two in attendance: a handsome, extremely well-attired individual sitting alone at the rear. In the opposite aisle, a younger casual man; edgy, uncomfortable being there, giving Francis the impression, he may know as much as him.

Aiding Millicent by the arm when she rose to sing hymns, also helped him achieve the desired angle to better watch his back; maintain a nervous vigil.

Betty cried inconsolably. Oliver hugged her, passing clean tissues, tucking the soggy exchanges into her handbag.

Frequently catching the eye of the casually dressed man, discreetly videoing the service with his phone, he'd offer Francis a sheepish grin.

The smarter one was controlled. Hardly moving his head. His features: familiar? Francis's heart skipped a beat when he delved into the inside pocket of a long navy coat to retrieve a smart pair of leather gloves, not draw a weapon.

Moment over.

Steadying Millicent's uneasy gait as they approached the two wicker coffins. She closed her eyes, placing her hand briefly on each. To Francis this seemed a forced gesture, done for effect, noticeably hesitating before again touching Donald's cedar coloured affair, fingering a fern frond from the wreath laid on top. Marie's pretty off-white basket, decorated with a purple band, complimented by the delicate splash of cream and violet flowers tumbling over the sides, perfectly matched her vibrant personality, he felt. Visualising what lay inside: charred bones and teeth; her skeletal arms cradling the minute form of her son.

Man-up, he scolded himself, coughing down the rising frog in his throat.

When Francis transferred Millicent's arm to the hospital warden, he told her he'd collect the ashes and take her to wherever she wanted to scatter them. She'd just given him her well-practised distant stare, before led back to her secure room.

Francis knew she'd lied. Just couldn't, yet, prove it.

Chapter Eighty

Sheriff Francis Sutherland's Office, Alberta.

Francis recognised the sleek silver limousine from the cemetery. And the smart chap with the gloves was sat in the driver's seat. Locking the patrol car, hearing a vehicle door open, then close, the bleep of a central locking device and scrunch of shoes on the fine gravel meant he was being followed.

'Excuse me. Sheriff. Could I have a word? Shouldn't take much of time. The names Professor Leopold Fleischer. I may need your help and thought it best to touch base. Pleased to meet you,' he said, extending his hand.

'Hello. I saw you at the service. Do you have information useful to our enquiries? If so, please come with me.' Francis offered his own, before leading the refined gentlemen into his office.

The Professor settled in a chair opposite the sheriff's desk, took an envelope from his suit pocket and handed it to Francis without saying a word.

Extracting the brief note: 'I'll always watch over you and do my up most to see you make a success of your life. You have my genetics, so you should. Maybe we'll meet under similar circumstances? That will be an interesting day. I'm sorry I couldn't keep you with me. Your sister being the perfect specimen. I just saw your deformities. You may think me cruel, but I know the way I am.' It read. Francis looked across his desk at Leopold, patiently awaiting a reaction. 'What deformities. You look fine to me.'

'This and this.' Leopold pointed to a slight scar on his lip and his left leg. 'I had an orofacial cleft and watch.' He got up, walked towards the office door, turned and pointed to his foot.

'Christ. The bloke gave you away because of a pigeon toe and your face wasn't right. What a bastard. We're not all like that around,' Francis exclaimed, dumbfounded by Donald's judgemental perfectionism.

'Mr Osborne-Maine's solicitor was the point of contact between my adoptive parents in Germany and himself. ... I remember seeing my genetic father at the establishment I presently head. My associates told me he was visiting in an advisory capacity from a research outpost. I recall our brief chats and wondered then: why the interest in my personal life, my ambitions? ... I'm disappointed I didn't grace the man with more of my time. I've so much to thank him for,' Leopold off-loaded.

They sat quietly, mulling.

'We will add the ranch to our patrols. I've a feeling we'll need access to the land, anyway. There are on goings we thought were dead ends and your inheritance may give us answers. Good luck with Millicent OM. You'll need it.' Francis paused, wondering whether to mention the man's natural mother: Louanne. Deciding against it. He felt sorry enough for him with his odd start to life. He'll leave Betty to tell him overtime.

'You'd have loved your sister. Very intelligent ... What a sad day. My wife and I wanted children. We weren't blessed.' As Francis spoke, Leopold maintained a stony stare which he found unnerving. 'Fate. Luck of the draw. Call it what you will, but you appear to be doing OK. Do you intend keeping it, do you think, the ranch—?' Francis pushed.

'Probably. No reason to dispose of it. The laboratory's top notch, perfect for my future needs. I understand there's a reliable couple keeping an eye on it. And, I've inherited a fabulous stallion. I'll be back when I get the chance. And I've a niece somewhere to work this out with. Exciting times professionally, and personally, I'd say.' Leopold momentarily lost himself, transfixed by the view of the mountains beyond where the sheriff sat. The moment broken by his mobile trilling a classical piece.

'Sorry. I need to take this. I'll be on my way. Thank you for your time Sheriff.' Leopold pushed the chair back with his legs, offering his hand, which Francis clenched firmly, conveying his message through touch: he wished this poor man all the best. Having come to terms with a few unpleasant truths can't have been easy.

Feeling empathy for the discarded man, Francis wondered what he did for a living? Leopold's steely eyes somehow transmitted unnerving images which Francis found rather unsettling. Very strange, he thought.

Chapter Eighty-One

Having lost focus, deciding to call it a day, Francis turned off his computer, made a coffee and sat back in his chair, losing himself in thought. He'd been right about the striking facial similarities. Leopold *is* Linus the other twin given up for adoption.

The man had done well: bequeathed the ranch house and laboratory. Donald had left instruction he should negotiate with Millicent about her future accommodation needs. Her hearing was in four days. This revelation wouldn't help her case, giving her the perfect motive for revenge. That's if she knew he changed the will three months prior to his tragic demise. Of course, it could go in her favour. She'd a roof over her head, a secure life while he was alive.

'And why wasn't Marie beneficiary?' he mumbled. Was Donald aware she may not live to hear its contents? 'Who knows? Not my problem,' Francis chuntered, rubbing his temples.

Chapter Eighty-Two

'Hi Siegfried. I take it you've arrived. Enjoying the cold, my friend? I bet it's freezing. Minus fifteen normally, by now. Go to Restaurant Nikolaevsky at eight. My colleagues will meet you there for a briefing ... Sorry—? Yes. Your Digi-counter is live. Best get to work.'

Having dealt with the niff-naff of life, Leopold needed to regain focus on who and what mattered. Although having fed his curiosity and gained an extremely useful asset: the laboratory, a future for which he'd already planned, this trip hadn't been a complete waste of his precious time.

Not sure where this adolescent niece fits in the plan. She could prove a thorn in his side. No doubt he'll find a suitable solution when the time comes. He contemplated, opening the car door, sporting a cruel smile.

Chapter Eighty-Three

Silver Vale Sanatorium, Alberta.

'Fools the lot of them,' Millicent muttered, sipping a warming treat of lusciously sweet sherry: the viscosity of the fluid soothing her parched throat. The aroma of date and molasses transported her from this sterile environment, with its lingering anti-bacterial scents which stuck in her nose, to the best times in her life. The fun. The parties she'd enjoyed while Donald had been away on business. All those admirers and sexually gratifying affairs with the husbands of her tennis friends: her book club plebs. 'What a bitch,' she murmured, raising her glass, toasting her reflection in the ageing mirror above a sink in the corner of her hospital room. 'Bottoms up,' she cheered with a flourish, tipping her head back to drain every drop from the dainty, sparkling crystal glass.

Easily persuaded to be her paid little pleasures of life accomplice while she's incarcerated in this place, Julia came in clanging a lunch tray against the door. 'How are you feeling? Was it awful? I've extra chicken and broccoli for you as you like it, Mrs Maine,' she said in whispered speech.

God. She's pathetic, Millicent thought, presenting her well-practised pleasant smile to acknowledge the woman's efforts.

There were five nurses for her to choose from. She needed one exuding an oppressiveness; who could be bought with the promise of a way out from the drudgery of clearing up after the clinically insane yet to be proven nut jobs.

Julia was ideal. Her slight frame, sloping shoulders and downtrodden personality: these ingredients made her the prime target to be moulded like putty with the false temptation of full-time employment as Millicent's personal assistant upon her release. 'How did the woman not realise she was being toyed with; was being manipulated? Working here, how an earth does she survive?' she wondered. Surmising, she surely can't be in contact with the highly dangerous inmates. She'd have had a knife at her throat in those hellish wings with the night screamers creating the heavy door clanging and banging.

Millicent would picture the restraining; the hypodermics being prepared; the relief when the drugs did their trick and silence resumed. Her sleep no longer disturbed.

'Why should I give a fuck where his toxic ashes are scattered? I'll sprinkle the bastard in the river. He despised water. The perfect end to his abominable existence,' Millicent cackled, pouring another sherry, hiding the bottle in a recess at the back of her bed locker.

She'd always been a plausible actress; having thoroughly researched the behaviour of mental break down sufferers, she wasn't taking her prescribed meds, needing no pills to aid her recovery. They got flushed down the toilet at night.

Entirely confident her trial would be a farce. She'd get pardoned. Be free to carry on living happily and alone.

Clearly Marie had no time for her. The ungrateful woman only came to visit her the once before carelessly driving off the road. She'd let Milo stay in the cabin if he wanted. *If* he returned. She enjoyed watching him run. 'If only I was twenty years younger,' she chuckled.

Jolie—? Well, she was OK in small doses.

The two sherries worked their magic. Millicent achieved her relaxed state of mind, comfortable in the faded light green winged back chair facing the rooms only window, observing squirrels flit through the trees, their tails jerking in annoyance at each other's presence. Smiling evilly, recalling Donald's shocked reaction when he realised, she'd got the upper hand. How he'd hated being belittled by anyone.

Millicent's mind then drifted further back to her time spent with his guinea pig hippy's: to a session in their barn with one called Maurice. He'd reached parts Donald never wanted to, or could. She sniggered, reliving the moment she'd seen the size of his cock. 'Woah boy. I know we're around horses, but what am I supposed to do with that?' She remembered laughing. She'd enjoyed him — a lot.

The skinny one who'd smelt of cheese and onion, was a disappointment, recalling their frantic sex session with distaste. Picturing her younger self wiping between her legs as he'd buttoned his cheesecloth shirt, thinking that wasn't worth the mess.

Sighing, pulling her beige lambswool wrap tightly around her slight frame, resting her head against the chair's firmness, she closed her eyes, soaking up the afternoon sun's warmth radiating through the glass. Igniting from her subconscious a vision of Lucy running through the meadow. Millicent clearly saw her long brown legs slicing through the tall dried grass against the pinkish tinge of her inward eye. You stupid girl, she thought, the serene scene replaced by one of Lucy's tanned face, surrounded by her gorgeous black locks creating a halo of glossiness, as she'd laid sprawled beneath her, pinned between Millicent's thighs.

'You can't take them. I won't allow you. After everything we've done for you. You little slut. You think you've been so clever. That I didn't have a clue what you'd been up to with *my* husband, and with this bulge, another product of your filthy liaisons. You bitch. You can scream as loud as you want. There's no one around. No-one will hear you.' Millicent recalled her verbal outrage. She hated that girl with a vengeance.

They say your strength grows when adrenaline flows.

Millicent's certainly had that day. Replaying how she'd used her full body weight to collapse the selfish cow's windpipe. The sensation of part of Lucy breaking under her thumbs had surprised her. She recollected the powerful, hate filled second when Lucy had gone limp.

Millicent had crushed the life force out of the oh so perfect one. She'd giggled manically, but panicked, realising the implications of what she'd done.

An image of her undressing Lucy's floppy frame. Having to dig the wet earth. And the struggle to move her dead weight into that hole. A storm had thundered over-head. The heavens had opened, and the rain had fallen with biblical force. Lightening illuminated the dead girl's lifeless features with every flash.

The scenario couldn't have been worse.

This unleashed nightmare regularly haunted Millicent, making her open her eyes to exorcise the memory. 'Justified hate and retribution,' she'd mutter, shuddering.

That frightful dream now had an addition: a recently formed companion to fuel its continuance and strengthen the horrors which also had to be relived before she temporarily capped them. Left them to fester until they breached her humanitarian guilt valve.

Her latest disturber of sleep took her back to the ranch house, to the other odious act she'd committed. Millicent saw herself in the darkness, sitting in Donald's leather reading chair, waiting for his study door to open.

He'd been drinking, would need the lavatory, his prostate not allowing him to hold the urge too long. She'd peeked over the head rest as he'd headed for the downstairs cloakroom, then made her move. Pulling on a thin pair of evening gloves, she'd silently padded into his haven, taken what she'd needed from his opened wall safe and tip-toed upstairs to their bedroom.

Having prepared the trap, she'd sneaked into their en-suite. And waited.

It hadn't taken long. She remembered the noise of his desk chair hitting something with a force and dull thuds of hurried footsteps ascending the stairs.

She pictured herself crouching, poised in the shadows, hearing him call: 'Where are you? What are you playing at?

Where have you put it? I need to know in case we get an intruder.'

The springy groan of their mattress meant her ploy worked. He'd sat by the body shape made of pillows and bed clothes.

She'd smiled, listening to him talk to the mound, bargaining on his sadistic streak, wanting her to know he'd planned killing her: that he wanted vengeance; wanted her to go to her grave knowing how she'd made him feel; recalling her frustration as he'd just talked about how they'd first met: what he'd hoped they'd achieve. Where had it gone wrong? She'd wanted him to react differently, to make the next stage of her plan easier.

Be strong, she remembered telling herself.

The sound of his voice had drowned the soft hiss of the en-suite door opening.

Inching back into the room, seeing his torso in the gloom facing towards the side window grasping a pillow — pleased she'd been right — he intended smothering her, but she'd out-witted *him*. Her mocking laughter had made him turn. He'd jumped. Stood bolt upright, mouth agape in surprise, as she'd moved nearer him, holding out her arms to invite an embrace while obscuring the weapon under the drape of her shawl.

Stood in the precise spot she'd planned; Millicent swung the pistol into position at the last moment, shooting Donald point blank in his chest. Recalling the deafening sound; the ringing in her ears and him floundering, falling to the floor at the bottom of their bed.

Weakened, she'd been able to force the gun between his fingers and aim the nozzle towards herself before squeezing the trigger. As intended, the bullet only grazed her arm.

'Were these tears of guilt? Or anger?' Millicent wasn't sure as they flowed. She let them, recalling his desperate final words: 'Christ almighty. Why Millicent? Isn't the cosseted bridge filled lifestyle I provide comfortable enough? Have you found someone else? Has one of your old conquests come out of the woodwork? I knew about most of them. You dirty whore.

... I loved Lucy. We planned to live together, but I wouldn't leave you. Don't ask me why?'

Picturing his face as a spasm of pain contorted his features, she'd thought then he was a handsome man despite his ageing looks.

It had only taken a few minutes for him to die. She'd laid his head on the pillow. And flushed her gloves down the toilet. It took three attempts to get the last black finger to disappear into the pipework. Away from his corpse, sat on the floor the other side of the bed with the photo album, she remembers telling herself: 'Time for crazy woman mode,' hoping her research was correct; the pistol, loaded by Donald, should only show traces of his fingerprint salts etched into its casing.

Millicent's fingers always crossed at this part of the memory replay.

'A joint suicide pact which hadn't gone exactly right. Case solved,' she mumbled, allowing her coping mechanism to archive these unpleasant memories for a little while longer, knowing she'd have to live in her post-traumatic prison of morbid self-infliction and reproach, with these horrors, for the rest of her life. Formal justice served or not.

Epilogue

One

Stanmore Hall Estate, West Sussex, England

'Once we're done, it'll do you good to get out of these four walls. You need to get familiar with your new character. Won't happen over-night. Trust me. Dad may be just short of eighty, but he's sharp as a tack. You'll get on like a house on fire. Done a few stints in counterintelligence. Lets nothing slip, even to me. He's helped me under similar circumstances and knows you'll be uneasy. ... We lost Mum eighteen months ago: crushed under her horse out hunting on her seventy-fifth birthday, of all bloody days. She was as mad as a hatter. That's blue bloods for you. Anyway, he'll know exactly what you're going through. So, go on, say yes. I'll get extra places laid for dinner,' Julian suggested, sat with Milo on a chintzy floral sofa in the living room of a pretty chocolate-box period lodge in the grounds of Julian's family estate: the safe-house.

'Let's work through these notes then I'll decide,' Milo answered with reluctance.

'Has to be said, Jolie's holding up better than you. It's amazing how she's taken everything in her stride. She'll keep you together, no doubt about that. It's as if she's always been here. She rode off half an hour ago with Emilia: who's chuffed to bits. She'd normally be moping around the house asking how much longer before she goes home. Anyway, let's crack on,' Julian cheerfully chatted, attempting to improve Milo's mood.

'It's a shorter piece. You should be happier. Reads: 'SUICIDES — THE TRUTH. The mass event with over five million participants, we can confirm, was a collaboration between leading worldwide supporters of a population reduction programme and the pharmaceutical industry. Enough is enough. We've proved our point. The desire is there to challenge the archaic suicide laws. The public are on side and must be heard. Change must happen. Yesterday, a spokesperson for the movement broke the silence to put to rest conspiracy rumours. Responsible for instigating the protest through action, although he did not sanction the inclusion of the unwilling. We have uncovered evidence that up to 300,000, in UK alone, we're administered the fatal drugs without their consent ...' Bog continued reading his article out loud.

Milo listened in silence.

'I take it you prefer how it now reads? I've taken loads out. Consequently, it doesn't have the same punch. But Chris's editor is waiting on tenterhooks. I've got to give him something for his investment,' Julian said, despondently.

'Yes. It's fine. I'm sorry, Julian. I don't want you to think I've let you down. It's just I've lost my way. Jools is the only reason I'm still sitting here. The times I've looked at your bloody lake. Pills. A few bottles of wine. Tie rocks round my ankles. In I go. End of.' Milo paused, holding his face in his hands, breathing deeply, trying to compose himself. 'Shall we run through what you asked me yesterday re the light aircraft incident—? I knew disease prevention measures were being decreased in that area. The doctor involved was depressed. Got drunk and crashed on purpose. But to stress, I knew nothing about what he carried in the hopper. If you reckon there's a link to this epidemic throughout Africa, you'll have to prove that through other channels. And, I've racked my brains, gone over the conversations Marie and I had about her work in the laboratory and only know she was very concerned. She told me on numerous occasions she planned getting a new post to get away from Donald. Truthfully, I know she had nothing to do with any experiments outside the lab; but it figures there's a link with the reports of altered men.'

Milo rubbed his scalp with both palms. 'Did you hear this morning's breaking news? An ISIL spokesperson says they've captured an infidel robot: is how they've reported it. Images on You-Tube keep getting taken down, but fresh ones are posted virtually straight away. The close-ups of their heads: it fits with the snippets Marie told me,' Milo paused, choking back emotion. 'Julian, at the start of their work with Graphene they convinced her it was to help humanity, not abuse the invention. She took photos. Said she deleted them. Shame. You'd have had your link. I wouldn't have consented to you using her name: Donald's, absolutely, with-out doubt.'

Through puffy sorrowful eyes, Milo looked at Julian: sat quietly, not knowing what to say.

'Nothing matters any more. It's nonsense. I'm not who I was. And what am I supposed to make of Josh's call, and the way *he* died? It wasn't suicide. Although, perhaps it was. I realise what he felt like now and wished—' The croak in Milo's voice prevented him continuing. Julian watched the broken man's body judder with the grief all- consuming him.

He'd not told Milo the images he'd stumbled across during his covert raid, provided the evidence he needed. The Red Brook laboratory *was* linked to a military experiment. They *were* using people, integrating technology into humans to tackle the more distasteful elements of present-day society.

Rubbing Milos back reassuringly, gazing out a tiny side window of the cottage, Julian saw the top branches of an old oak tree move in the wind; rolling media reports from the last few days through his mind. Terrorists had three of the robot men creations: more had been seen wandering before getting whisked away in military vehicles. In Uganda, one had even made its way home, telling tales of an abduction, before again mysteriously disappearing. I could expose the truth, if I dare? he considered, noticing a flock of crow's land on the branches, clinging tightly, wings flapping in synchronicity with the arboreal movement.

Julian couldn't put his finger on it, but felt an inner guilt override his normal desire to produce a sensational headline. Or show Milo the incriminating laboratory photographs. The man was in bits. What good came of seeing the horrors his dead wife had a hand in. And did he *really* have the drive to unleash the horror of a conspirical possibly government run underworld? The raging fire to push boundaries; to search for answers normally burning within him had lost its intensity. Let them get on with it. It makes sense to rid the world of despots, terrorists, *and* a proportion of the population. So, let whoever them is, use this technological advancement to better society. Give it five, maybe ten years. These creations may be accepted. We'll see them on street corners, perhaps even in schools taking control of a lawless generation. Why throw a huge spanner in the works? That's it. Time to stop. Maybe I'll pursue an art, or horticulture. Use the estate land to become self-sufficient. Or get into snail farming? I read the other day their slime is being researched as a revolutionary medical adhesive. I'll employ Chris: he's a crap journalist and can be my gloop collector. He's used to dealing with the grunge of life, Julian smiled to himself, rubbing Milo's back, which he'd neglectfully stopped.

Julian Fletcher Reynaud Spalding, a-ka Bog, embracing a sobbing Martin Amos, pondered, 'Maybe I'll get married. Have a few kids.' Deciding his future as together they watched the flock of unsettled crows take flight.

A comforting hug from Julian, added to Milo's emotional release, sparked a return of his rationale. 'Thanks for bringing the ashes. You can get them made into a gemstone. I might do that. Get it mounted in a ring. And you said Marie's twin came. Is that right—?'

Julian nodded.

'We must get Jolie's interest in the ranch documented. It'll be nice for her to go back, or at least sell her share to this Leopold. She can decide when she's older, and things are safer. It's encouraging you've got Sheriff Sutherland keeping you informed,' Milo said, blowing his nose. Julian remained quiet.

'I'd like to meet Leopold. See how similar he is to Marie. And it's good Betty and Oliver still have a roof. Not sounding promising for Millicent though, although she was lucky not getting charged. ... I never felt Red Brook was our home. I was a more long-term guest, to be honest. I'll not sell our ski lodge at Kicking Horse. Once the dust settles, we can go there, Julian. I need to keep occupied. Through your contacts, could you find me something low profile: perhaps a teaching post? I know my input hasn't been as lucrative for your article, so I insist on paying for our flights and new ID. Can you send the funeral video to my phone please? I will watch it, when I'm up to it. Thanks again. Thoughtful and appreciated,' Milo offloaded, grasping Julian for another chummy embrace.

'No problem. Right. Get showered. Change your bloody clothes, and be ready in ten,' Bog commanded, pushing him away as Jolie — a-ka Daniella — barged in the front door like a girly tornado.

Two

'Ventilation and fresh thinking. They never keep people in the field for long. A steady diet of CI can be dangerous for one's health,' Julian's father, Brigadier retired George Henry Spalding, chuckled, sat at the head of his imposing oak dining table. A meal, plated on fine bone china, in front of him hardly touched. 'So, young lady. Daniella, isn't it—? What does the future hold for you? What positive input will you make to this unruly world?' His gruff voice made her visibly jump.

'It's OK. Our kind host won't bite. Relax,' Milo assured her, placing his hand on top of hers as she looked like a rabbit caught in headlights.

'Erm. Well ... may be a scientist, or a physicist like Mum. Although, I'm not exactly sure what she did. But I've been researching the paranormal. You know psychic phenomena. People with special gifts. Maybe I'll study that and how it links to the conventional science of matter and energy. Sort of bridge the gap between the two. If that doesn't sound too weird?' Jolie sunk lower in her seat; aware all eyes were on her.

Milo gave her a proud smile, affectionately plucking her cheek.

'I'm going to work the land. Start snail farming with Chris Manning. You remember him, Pa—? He just got sacked. Is bringing the bumph with him tonight — *if* any-ones interested,' Julian interjected, causing raucous laughter to engulf the room.

'Feel free to begin your research in the upstairs hallway, Daniella. I'm sure Emilia's grandmother is still rattling around up there. She regularly trips me up, normally when I've had one too many of these,' Brig George chuckled, pointing to his wine glass.

She smiled, glancing at their cheery faces, uncertain whether she was the source of their amusement, or Julian. I'll show them, she thought, joining in the infectious outburst of uplifting joy.

'More brandy, my friend?' Brigadier George asked Milo, relaxing together in his drawing room. Nodding in agreement to a top up of his best quality stupor enhancer, enjoying the warmth and detachment it provided, he wondered whether he was on the cusp of his raw grief for Marie. Perhaps this evening had been a turning point for them both; an acceptance of their new existence, he reflected.

'Julian's a dutiful boy. Always wants to help and seek the truth. You've made a dependable friend there, my man,' Brigadier George began, noisily sipping his brandy. 'I do know a few details how you've ended up here. Don't worry, Mum's the word. You can use the cottage for as long as you like. Marjorie used to rent it in the summer months. Gave her something to do, fussing over people. Strangers buzzing around, popping up when you least expected. Bloody annoying, I always found. Julian's probably mentioned my late wife. Trust me. It'll get better. My advice: remember the fun, don't dwell on guilt or doubts, they won't bring her back ... And talk about her. Don't keep her name trapped inside. It'll fester. The emotion will flood out unexpected,' the Brigadier advised, in whispered speech, leaning forward, clutching his glass to his chest for emphasis.

Enfolded in the grasp of a burgundy leather, quintessential studded chair, carefully slurping his brandy, flickering flames from the open fire creating a dappled effect, like warming golden fingers against his weathered features, Milo studied his host as he spoke.

'I'll tell you one thing my friend, an acquaintance in The Lords reliably informs me they're shortly voting on an amendment bill to the Suicide Act. Says they'll agree, given the age of most of them and it'll fly through,' he guffawed. 'Just the lot in The Common's to get on side before Royal Assent. At least your countries progressive Government has legalised the process for the worst off. Let's wait and see if they also change the law for the incurably ill and the disruption to your life and your sad loss lead to a positive outcome, eh old chap.'

The Brigadier brusquely nudged Milo's knee with a gnarled, arthritic hand. 'If it happens here, it'll spread. You mark my words. Could be the catalyst this overcrowded planet needs.' Pouring another brandy, he continued. 'Not sure about these human bloody robot chaps, what that's all about? Seems far-fetched to me. I reckon it's a media ploy. If not, it's worrying who's behind that freakish nonsense. Just my opinion.' The Brigadier shrugged, sighing, stretching out his long legs, crossing his ankles.

Milo noticed a hole in his tartan sock. And in the drab khaki corduroy of his trousers, a worn patch on one thigh. On cue, Milo's host started a habitual leg stroking action: a nervous response to age or loneliness, he wasn't sure, but explained the distressed area of fabric.

Enjoying the tranquillity of the moment, without conversation, the crackle from the hearth; the gentle tick tock of a carriage clock and muffled laughter from the adjoining snooker room provided a contemplative accompaniment – a timely reminder of their future.

Milo closed his eyes, picturing Jolie unpacking, placing her favourite things into the old dark wood dressing table, glancing back at him, screwing up her nose at the musty odour that wafted from the wallpaper lined drawers.

They'd been two misplaced souls, longing for normality only weeks ago.

'Dad.' Milo recalled her squeaky girl voice. 'I found this in the zipper bit of my bag. I didn't put it there, did you?' she'd chirped. Milo recognised the manila protective cover she'd thrust at him. It was the document he returned to Donald's study shortly after they married. There you are, New Dawn. 'How did Jolie get hold of you?' he'd wondered, assuming

Marie must have put it in her bag the evening they packed. But why would she want her daughters view of her grandfather tainted? Maybe she didn't see it like that. They'd agreed in principle with Donald's views, so perhaps Marie hoped Jolie *would* understand and give him credit for pursuing his foresight to improve the planet.

'I'm not sure, Jools? Leave it there. I'll have a read,' Milo had answered, not wanting to dwell on its contents. Realising the past wasn't prepared to let them go just yet.

'You all right? Thought you'd nodded off. Sorry. Should have left you in peace. I'm off the bed. You're welcome to pop up any time, I need intellectual company. Help yourself,' the Brigadier said, rising slowly, pointing to the half empty crystal decanter.

'Thank you for a very pleasant evening. And, I will, that's for sure.'

In the room's stillness, Milo's thoughts again drifted. He saw himself sat with his back to Jolie, listening to her struggle to pull on a pair of borrowed riding boots, shouting: 'Bye Dad' and she'd slammed the cottage door. Picking up the document, he'd flicked through the pages, the woody essence of Donald's study serving as a reminder of its writer. Reaching the last, a notelet sized piece of lilac paper had fallen out. Recognising Marie's hand writing, he read her words out loud to the empty dwelling: 'Throughout your life exercise caution as the world is full of trickery. Always trust your instincts, never doubt them. You'll fall on your feet running. You're so gifted. Be brave. Be yourself. You'll go far, my beautiful girl. Love Mum xxxx'.

That was the first moment Milo couldn't control the breach in his dam emotions. Alone, in the strange old house, he'd cried, heart wrenching, painful sobs for two lonely hours. Marie knew deep down she'd be unable to join them. Had been aware her life was under serious threat.

Julian had been right. This evening had given him hope, his

optimism had returned, he thought, watching Jolie skip ahead towards their temporary, quaint home, breaking into a cantering motion, puffs of condensing breath floating above her head.

Glancing back, raising a hand in thanks to his host, whether he was watching, finding his silhouette in an upstairs window.

'There he is,' he muttered.

Recalling the Brigadier's historic spiel about the Arts and Crafts style manor house and medieval farm buildings, designed by an architect who'd made them naturally merge, as if seeded from the land, reminded Milo of the first time he'd seen Donald and Millicent's property at Red Brook. Same ethos, just a newer design. Fate may have sent us here? he pondered.

'Dad. Pleeeease come and see the horse's tomorrow morning. They've got one big enough for you,' Jolie shouted, running back, taking hold of his hand.

'Yes. I will Jools. Sounds a splendid idea,' Milo imitated the Brigadier's upper-class accent. 'Don't rush off without me. Wake me if you have to,' he added, ruffling her hair.

'Daaad. It's *Daniella*. Remember. Daniella, and you're Martin,' she scolded. 'It suits you. Accept life is different now. We've to make it fun and exciting. Emilia says I could go to her boarding school. She's a weekday boarder. I'd like that. If we can afford it?' she questioned with a beaming smile. 'I read that document, Dad. The one I found when we arrived that I gave you. I couldn't sleep the other night. Got a glass of milk and saw it on the coffee table. I finished reading it as the sun rose over those trees.' She pointed a mittened hand towards a ridge of poplars. 'It's weird. I had an epiphany. I think it's called. My future sort of slotted into place as I watched the crows and starlings flying about. I'll get you up early to watch it tomorrow morning. It's so beautiful. It was my New Dawn moment Dad. That sounds corny, I know, but it was. Everything will be OK. What's done, is done,' Jolie said, giving

Milo's hand a firm squeeze.

'You're my new rock. Right now, I don't know where I'd be without you. I love you Daniella Amos,' he answered, swallowing a lump in his throat, tears prickling in the corners of his eye's. 'Your Mum would have liked it here. She often said she wanted to stay in a stately home.'

'But she *is* here, Dad. And I don't mean her ashes in a jar on the mantelpiece, she's walking behind us, holding little Milo. Says she couldn't wait any longer for you to name him, so she chose. Just open your eyes, Dad, and you'll see.'

Three

In Kursk, a digital display read: 6,835,122,348.
One below it read: 143,876. The one next to that read: 95,938.

The programme continues.

THE END

Jay Warren is the pseudonym of Maureen Barkworth. A self-assessed borer-line autistic person with curly hair, who thought maybe she could turn the story in her head into a book; presently lives with her husband in a hot sunny place with a springer spaniel called Mattie, a garden full of house sparrows, geckos — occasional rats, snakes and toads!

Having dabbled with speech tweaking; writing work-related reports, legal documents and short stories as a child, she finally took the plunge to write Reset: New Dawn Challenge. Not realising in 2017, when the novel was started, how the tale may prove to be worryingly believable.

I hope you enjoyed reading Reset and will consider writing a review. Even just a few words could help others decide if the book is right for them.

Please visit the sales page, or revisit your Amazon orders to leave your comments.

Thank you in advance.

Revelation: New Dawn Discovery is a work in progress.

Return: Emergence of New Dawn will provide the conclusion to this trilogy.

Printed in Great Britain
by Amazon

62218025R00180

UK Immigration Made Simple

Taking the complexity out of UK Immigration rules

By Rajiv Immanuel

Note from the Author and Disclaimer

In this book, the words "UK" and "Britain" are used interchangeably to mean the same place. Where the information refers to England only and not to the rest of the UK (Wales, Scotland and Northern Ireland) that is indicated separately. The last UK Census was held in 2011. Data in this book that draws from the Census is therefore from 2011.

The European Economic Area (EEA) is the EU 28 countries plus Switzerland, Lichtenstein, Norway, and Iceland.

The material in this book is for general information only and does not constitute investment, tax, legal, career, financial, immigration or other form of advice. You should not rely on this information to make (or refrain from making) any decisions. Links to external sites are for information only and do not constitute endorsement. Always obtain independent, professional advice for your own particular situation.

Fees mentioned in this book for UKVI applications are correct at the time of writing. These costs may have since been revised upward by UKVI.

The Home Office publishes data after a time lag of about 1-2 years. Therefore, in 2019, the most up-to-date data may be from 2017.

ILR/ILE refers to Indefinite Leave to Remain/Enter and is the same as UK Permanent Residence.

Visa requirements are subject to change at any time. Before applying for any UK visa, you must ensure you read the relevant UKVI Policy Guidance in order to understand the full details and requirements at the time of application.

Contents

INTRODUCTION

Why this book?

You want a specific answer to a specific immigration question?

What you get instead is a massive UKVI website with links leading off to further links, clickable pdf documents that run into hundreds of pages.

The net result: you get stressed and develop a headache.

The UK Government Visas and Immigration website is a maze. The freedictionary.com defines a 'maze' as:

"a. An intricate, usually confusing network of interconnecting pathways, as in a garden; a labyrinth.

b. A physical situation in which it is easy to get lost: a maze of bureaucratic divisions.

c. Something made up of many confused or conflicting elements; a tangle: a maze of government regulations.

The net effect of a maze is to bewilder or astonish or to stupefy or daze."

Unfortunately that is what happens to most readers of the UKVI website. This is because material on the UK Immigration website is written in legal language by bureaucrats whose purpose is not to encourage UK immigration but to deter it. Vital details are often hidden in huge clickable pdf documents that the reader has to wade through to find out what they want.

Unless you have trained as a solicitor (the UK word for Lawyer) reading such hard and difficult prose can quickly give you a headache.

Don't lose heart, however. There is hope for those trying to make sense of UK immigration rules.

"There are some people who have the marvellous ability to take complex matters and make them appear quite simple. Such people can see to the heart of the matter. Such people can discard what is detail and what is irrelevant.": Edward de Bono in How To Be More Interesting (1998).

Do you get a headache looking at the UK Government Visas and Immigration website?

Were you planning to pay hundreds of pounds/dollars/euros to a UK immigration adviser?

Wait! This book makes UK immigration simple. It is continuously updated, so when you buy it you get the latest information.

It answers in simple English the typical questions foreigners have about UK immigration and student visas in particular. Do not get lost in the maze.

Aside from providing relevant visas and immigration information, this book takes the entire UK Visas and Immigration website and breaks down the hard legal prose into simple questions and answers.

This book also tells you about loopholes and ways around UK immigration rules that you will not see on the UKVI website.

For instance, you want info on how to get your non-EEA spouse into the UK legally despite your not earning the minimum £18,600 per year required. You won't find this easily on UKVI's website. In this book you will. Look for this question in the contents page: Is there a loophole to bypass the minimum earnings requirement? (in the section: "The Family/Partner Route to Settlement").

The UKVI website is not designed to make it easy to settle in the UK. They don't want to make it easy because they don't really want anyone to know about these loopholes in the system that they can't close because of EU law.

You want a specific answer to a specific immigration question? You get it in this book. No need to read reams of prose buried inside 75-page pdf documents to find out. Save your eyes for better things.

In this book the author, Rajiv Immanuel, answers most questions regarding UK immigration. This book answers questions relating to immigration, biometric residence permits, student visas, UK ancestry visas, work visas, spousal visas, investor visas, entrepreneur visas, UK nationality and citizenship and most importantly, permanent settlement in the UK.

The author, arrived in the UK from India in 1995 as an international student. Now he, a British citizen, is a writer of books preparing others for UK life.

This book is part of an 18 book series: Rajiv Immanuel's Preparing You for UK Life Series. Some major books in the series are

Complete Guide to Living, Working and Studying in the UK: Preparing You for Life in Britain

Study in the UK: All your questions answered

Best Scholarships for Studying in the UK: Study in the UK for free

What Not to Do in the UK: Save yourself failure, embarrassment, worry, time, and money

If you are a resident of a country outside the European Economic Area, are young, skilled and ambitious and are considering making the UK your home, then the first step for you is to find out how to settle down permanently in the UK.

This book tells you of conventions followed by the UKVI in granting permanent settlement. Such information could help you settle down in the UK. The author too settled down in the UK on the basis of one such convention. Find out in this book and profit. Find out about the 14 routes to UK Permanent Residency...

The other books in his series provide guidance on specific matters of interest to foreigners interested in the UK as a place to live, work and study.

Note: two new sections have been added after Brexit.

1. For EEA citizens applying for UK permanent residence.

2. How to purchase citizenship by investment in some EU countries and then eventually move to the UK.

People who get ahead in life often demonstrate excellent judgement. Show yours.

UK IMMIGRATION IN GENERAL

What is the UKVI?

The UK Border Agency (UKBA) was the old name of the division of the Home Office dealing with immigration and visa issues. Now the UKBA is called the UKVI (UK Visas and Immigration).

The UKBA was responsible for securing the UK border at air, rail and sea ports and migration controls. It was set up in 2008; two years after then Labour Home Secretary John Reid said the Home Office's Immigration and Nationality Directorate was "not fit for purpose." The plan was that the UK Border Force, the section of the UKBA that manages entry to the UK, would be a separate law-enforcement body reporting directly to the Home Office while the UKBA would be solely responsible for immigration policy work.

In March 2013, it was announced by the government that the UKBA would be split into parts focusing on the visa system (the UKVI) and on immigration law enforcement. The government announced that the UK Border Force - responsible for day-to-day operations - would become a separate law-enforcement body.

What does the UKVI do?

The UKVI deals with about 3 million applications every year from foreign nationals wishing to

- visit the UK,
- study, work, settle in the UK,
- or naturalise as British citizens.

How do I contact UKVI?

To contact

UK Visas and Immigration

By telephone: 0300 123 2241

Monday to Thursday, 9am to 4:45pm; Friday, 9am to 4:30pm

By post:

UKVI

Lunar House

40 Wellesley Road

Croydon

Surrey

CR9 2BY

U.K.

Website:

https://www.gov.uk/government/organisations/uk-visas-and-immigration

What is economic migration and what is the EEA?

The UK is part of the European free market under which goods, services and labour can freely move across borders. A person who comes to work in the UK is an economic migrant. Students are classified as economic migrants. Economic migrants come to the UK either from the EEA (European Economic Area) countries or the non-EEA countries (rest of the world). EEA migrants can work in the UK without immigration controls, just as British citizens can work anywhere in the European Union without immigration controls. The EEA includes all EU states plus Iceland, Liechtenstein and Norway and, for immigration purposes, Switzerland. Swiss nationals have the same rights to live and work in the UK as other EEA nationals.

The 28 EU states are: Austria, Belgium, Bulgaria, Croatia, Republic of Cyprus, Czech Republic, Denmark, Estonia, Finland, France, Germany, Greece, Hungary, Ireland, Italy, Latvia, Lithuania, Luxembourg, Malta, Netherlands, Poland, Portugal, Romania, Slovakia, Slovenia, Spain, Sweden and the UK.

How many foreigners live in the UK?

According to the 2011 Census, there were 7.5 million foreign-born residents in the UK, which was 13% of the total population.

Where do most foreigners in the UK come from?

The 2001 Census revealed that most foreigners in the UK came from:

1. Republic of Ireland
2. India
3. Pakistan
4. Germany
5. Bangladesh

By the time of the 2011 census, the picture had changed as follows:

1. India
2. Poland
3. Pakistan
4. Republic of Ireland
5. Germany
6. Bangladesh

The number of Polish-born residents rose ten times from 58,000 to 579,000 between 2001-2011. This is because of the UK government's decision in 2004 to allow free entry to certain new EU member countries.

In 2017, most foreigners in the UK come from:

1. Poland
2. Romania
3. Ireland
4. India
5. Italy

6. Portugal
7. Lithuania
8. Pakistan
9. Spain
10. France

Source: ONS

In 2017, the number of Polish-born residents rose to 35 times the figure for 2001. Most foreigners in the UK are now European.

What are the main reasons people come to the UK?

The four main reasons for people to come to the UK are to work, to study, to join family or to claim asylum. In 2016, 275,000 people came to the UK for work. This was lower compared to 2015, when it was 308,000.

In 2015, 280,000 non-EU student visas were issued by UKVI. In the same period, 169,000 work visas were issued. The top two reasons for people to come to the UK are to work or study.

About 450,000 higher education students arrive in the UK each year. The government is committed to reducing these numbers. It has no control over within-EU student migration so it has adopted tough new measures designed to curb non-EU student migration. While the numbers of visas issued to non-EU people who come to the UK for purposes other than to study has remained fairly static since 2000, non-EU student migration has increased substantially. This has been a major reason why the Government faces difficulties in hitting its migration target.

About 70% of students who come to the UK for study come from non-EU countries and about 55% are female. Most of these non-EU students came from Asian countries and the next biggest region is the Middle East. Most international students (81%) are heading to UK universities. The rest are aiming to study at tertiary, further education or other colleges (9%), English language schools (2%), Independent schools (7%) and others (1%).

People also come to the UK as visitors for tourism or to visit family, work, invest money, run a business, get married, join family/spouse permanently and to claim asylum. The least numbers of migrants to the UK are in the Asylum category. About 26,000 people or 4% of total inward migration are in the asylum category.

What is net migration?

Net migration is the difference between those arriving and those leaving. Official figures show that net migration was 196,000 in 2009. That figure includes British citizens returning from living abroad and people from inside the EEA. In 2010, that number rose to 250,000. Net migration to the UK was 333,000 in 2015. It fell to 248,000 in 2016 and fell further to about 230,000 in 2017.

Is the UK a net exporter or importer of population?

In the early 1900s the UK was a net exporter of population mainly to North America, Australia and New Zealand. After World War I the trend changed as many returned home. In the 1970s and 1980s the UK again became a net exporter of population as people migrated to Australia, New Zealand, and South Africa. This wave of emigration peaked in 1981 when 108,000 British and EU citizens decided to leave and only 28,000 people arrived to settle in the UK. But by 1983 more people were coming to live in the UK than were leaving. This reached a peak of 58,000 migrants in 1985, and the flow of people into the UK continued for every year for the rest of the decade, except 1988, setting a pattern that would continue into the 1990s. In 2017, the UK is a net importer of population.

Has Brexit affected UK immigration numbers?

Yes, according to figures released by the ONS in 2018, 130,000 EU nationals emigrated in the year to September, the highest number since 2008. Also, 220,000 EU nationals came to live in the UK – this was 47,000 lower than the previous year. Net EU migration - the difference between people arriving and departing - was 90,000, the lowest for five years.

What is the general attitude of the British people towards immigration?

The British people are sensible enough to realize that immigrants are necessary to pay taxes, to fund pensions in an ageing society, to do jobs like cleaning that locals no longer want to do cheaply, and to work in jobs like nursing that have odd hours of work. They acknowledge that many immigrants have a hard-working nature, and that they are needed to do highly-skilled jobs (like those in IT, medicine and accountancy) where there is a skills shortage. But they also realize that there is a limit to the capacity of schools, roads, housing, and hospitals to take in high levels of immigration.

Do Brits think that immigration is good for the UK? It depends on whom you ask. The young and highly educated are more likely to say that immigration is good for the economy, while older people and non-graduates are more likely to say it is bad.

The government is handicapped in reducing net-migration. It has no control over British emigration which is dependent on the world economy, and the inward migration of EU citizens, which is increasing. EU citizens account for 30% of arrivals to the UK. Polish is now the largest non-British nationality in the country.

The only tool available is to make bigger cuts to non-EU migration to the UK, which basically means to make drastic cuts or changes to the student visa system. The government is particularly looking at scrapping or modifying the post-study work visa system that enable overseas students to work in the UK after their studies. Overall, the government has said there will be 70,000 fewer student visas issued over a year. Only those offered a job with a recognised employer will be able to stay on after they finish their courses.

However, universities oppose any such move for two reasons. Firstly, many universities are short of cash (26 universities and higher education institutions are in deficit according to a report into the financial health of the higher education sector).

Secondly, because overseas students pay fees three times what the local students pay. Non-EU students bring around £9bn into the UK economy every year. The Higher Education Funding Council for England, the sector funding body, estimates that English universities make about £3.2bn a year from non-EU student fees. That constitutes 12.9% of their £25.6bn of income a year.

The universities also fear that overseas students will instead choose to study in the United States, Australia, Canada or Germany and the UK will lose out. The government faces this dilemma regarding immigration.

Which countries are deemed low risk by UK Visas and Immigration?

UK Immigration has designated some countries as low-risk from an immigration viewpoint. They are: Argentina, Australia, Brunei, Canada, Chile, Croatia, Hong Kong, Japan, New Zealand, Singapore, South Korea, Taiwan, Trinidad and Tobago, United States of America or a British National Overseas.

Which countries are deemed high risk by UK Visas and Immigration?

High-risk countries have been designated as: India, Pakistan, Sri Lanka, Bangladesh, Ghana and Nigeria.

What is the history of migration into the UK?

Foreigners have been around in the UK from the very beginning. Celtic and Pict tribes first colonised the British Isles (250-1066 AD). The Romans came in 250 AD and left in the 5th century. Then to southern England came the Germanic tribes - the Angles, the Saxons and the Jutes - from whom the English are descended. Four hundred years after these tribes the Vikings arrived in Northern England and present-day East Anglia. The Norman Conquest (1066 AD) was the most important of these immigrations. They brought with them French influences, which changed the English language and culture.

During the Middle Ages (1500-1700), there were not many non-white people in England. Britain's colonisation of parts of America led to its involvement in the slave trade and had the important effect of bringing in slaves into England. Britain became a wealthy country partly because of the slave trade. By 1770, there were 14,000 black people in England. It was only in 1833 that the British parliament finally banned the slave trade, which stopped the arrival of slaves in England. From 1830 to 1850, the Irish began to migrate to Britain as they tried to escape poverty and famine.

During the Spanish Civil War in 1937 about 4000 Basque children were evacuated by ship from the north of Spain to safety in Britain. Spain's General Franco asked the German Luftwaffe to carpet-bomb the historic Basque town of Guernica. Hundreds of people died in an indiscriminate attack that caused international outrage. There was a lot of concern for civilians. British volunteers raised money to send a ship to collect Basque child refugees and bring them to Britain.

The two World Wars brought in a large number of foreigners to Britain, most of them soldiers who had survived the wars. They formed small communities in port cities. About 1.3 million soldiers from India fought for Britain in World War I.

At the end of World War II, Britain found itself with huge labour shortages. Immigration was the only way out to cover these shortages.

Polish and Italian immigrants were the first to be allowed in. From 1948 onwards thousands of black people from the Caribbean began arriving in Britain lured by the promise of jobs. Then after the partition of the Indian subcontinent and the 1948 Indo-Pakistan war over Kashmir, many displaced Asians chose to emigrate and turned to Britain. As long as they had a British passport they were allowed in. Later, in the 1960s they were allowed in with work permits or to join family. The government, in response to public pressure, tried to curb black and Asian immigration by enacting legislation many times.

In 1972, the government of Idi Amin of Uganda expelled Asians in their thousands and since they held British passports they were allowed to stay in Britain. In the post-war years, the fledgling NHS badly needed trained medical staff, and it was the doctors of the Indian subcontinent who came to its rescue. They were willing to work in remote and rural parts of the country, and they became known as the doctors who 'saved' the NHS.

The government has continued to tighten immigration rules over the years. Until 1983 if your child was born in the UK, you were allowed to remain in the UK. Since 1983 that is no longer allowed.

There are plans to restrict visitors' visas to just three months from the present six months. New rules also require graduates to find a job earning at least £20,000 to be able to remain in the UK once their studies end.

What are the benefits of migration to the host country (the UK)?

According to Peter Sutherland, head of the Global Forum on Migration and Development, which brings together representatives of 160 nations to share policy ideas, migration is a "crucial dynamic for economic growth" in some EU nations. He argues that the future prosperity of many EU states depend on them becoming multicultural. In his view, national racial homogeneity cannot survive and states have to become more open states, in terms of the people who inhabit them, like the United Kingdom has demonstrated.

What advice and guidance is available about UK immigration?

You can get a lot of useful information at the UKVI website: https://www.gov.uk/government/organisations/uk-visas-and-immigration

Immigration rules keep changing. The current UK immigration rules are here:

https://www.gov.uk/government/collections/immigration-rules.

You can visit the Youtube channel of the UKVI ((http://www.youtube.com/user/UKvisas) or the website of the UK Council for International Student Affairs (www.ukcisa.org.uk). The UKCISA also provides guidance on making a Tier 4 (General) Application. This webpage has the information you need: https://www.gov.uk/tier-4-general-visa.

An introduction to UK Visas

UK visas. range from Tier 1 (for investors and exceptional talent), to Tier 5 visas for short-term voluntary and educational programmes. The two most common visas are the Tier 2 skilled worker visas and Tier 4 student visas. There is no Tier 3 (unskilled labour). Some UK visas allow people to apply to bring dependants (children and partners). Visas are issued on a points-based system. Applicants get more points for higher salaries or if their job is on the shortage occupation list. Most visas come with conditions, including knowledge of English and the need for a sponsor. UK visa applicants cannot claim benefits during their period of visa control.

Do I need a visa to enter the UK?

Three types of people do not need visas to enter the UK:

1. British citizens.

2. Commonwealth citizens with the right of UK abode

3. EEA nationals.

All others require visas to enter the UK.

Do I need a visa to visit the UK as a tourist?

Visitors from the following non-EEA countries: USA, Canada, Singapore, Australia, New Zealand, Hong Kong, Japan, Brazil, a British national overseas, a British overseas citizen, Israel, Malaysia, Mexico, do not need a visa to visit the UK for tourism, unless they have a criminal record. However, their documentation must be shown to UK immigration officials at the airport. The documents are:

- Passports plus previous passports
- One colour pp size photo
- Residence permit of country of application if not passport holders of that country
- Evidence of marital status
- Evidence of employment status
- Accommodation and return travel arrangements
- Bank statements
- Payslips for six months
- Tax returns
- Completed visa application form
- Supporting letter from your friend or sponsor in the UK
- Proof of travel arrangements within the UK

Do I need a visa to study in the UK?

You will need a visa to study in the UK if you are from outside the European Economic Area (the EU 28 countries plus Switzerland, Lichtenstein, Norway, and Iceland). If your course is shorter than 6 months, you can enter on a Student Visitor visa. If your course is longer than 6 months, you will need a Tier 4 (general) visa. The UKVI website also has a section entitled "Studying in the UK" which you can access for more information.

If you require a visa to study in the UK, the university that gave you admission can act as your sponsor. Visas issued under a university's sponsorship are valid for study at that university only.

Do I need a visa to work in the UK?

All non-EEA applicants will need a visa to work in the UK.

Do I need a visa to join my family or partner in the UK for a long stay?

This depends on where you are from, what kind of visa your partner holds and how long you intend to stay. If you are non-EEA and from the USA, Canada, Japan, Australia, New Zealand, Brazil, Hong Kong, Mexico, Malaysia and Singapore you do not need a visa for up to a six month stay. For more than six months stay, apply for a 'family of a settled person' visa if your family member or partner is a British citizen or they are from outside the European Economic Area (EEA) and settled in the UK. Apply as a 'dependant' of your family member's visa category if they are from outside the EEA and they are working or studying in the UK. Apply for a 'family permit' to join your family or partner for a short or long stay if they're living in the UK and are a EEA national.

If you are from most other non-EEA countries (including the UAE, Russia, China and India), and you are visiting family or a partner for 6 months or less, you will need a 'family visit' visa.

How do I apply for a UK visa?

If you are outside the UK, you must apply online for a UK visa to visit, work, study or join a family member or partner (spouse) already in the UK. This is the web address: https://www.visa4uk.fco.gov.uk/

You must register on the website before the application process starts. Most credit cards and PayPal are accepted for payments.

How long does the visa process take?

This depends on where you are applying from as well as what visa you want. Applicants from low-risk countries face less waiting times. Secondly, applying for simpler visas (visitors) takes less time to process. A visitor visa takes about 10 days, while visa applications for settlement can take up to 30 days to process for an applicant from a low-risk non-EEA country.

Applicants from high-risk countries (see elsewhere in this book for a listing) face delays of up to 60 days for settlement visas but only about 10-15 days for non-settlement visas.

What visa application fees must I pay?

This depends on where you are applying from as well as what visa you want (including the period of stay). Go to this webpage and find out for your country: https://visa-fees.homeoffice.gov.uk/

The rate structure tends to be similar for all visa types (business, entertainer, family, special - marriage, child, and sports visitors).

Will I have to pay tax on earnings in the UK?

Short-term visitors will not have to pay tax on their income, but long-term visitors will have to. Income includes wages, benefits, pensions, and savings interest. All income above the personal allowance of £11,500 per year is taxable. The tax year is 6th April current year to 5th April following year.

What is the PBS (points-based system) for non-EEA economic migrants?

Non-EEA economic migrants have to apply under one of the "tiers" that make up the Points Based System (PBS). Students are also covered by the PBS. The PBS awards points to migrants based on their skills, qualifications and experience The PBS has five "tiers." Tiers 1 and 2 cover highly skilled and skilled migrants respectively. Tier 3 was designed for unskilled workers but has never been implemented. Tier 4 covers students and the final tier covers temporary workers and special categories. Note: You can no longer apply for settlement using the Highly Skilled Migrant Programme.

Students make up the biggest number among economic migrants from the non-EEA countries. Among the skilled workers coming to the UK with jobs in hand, most are moving jobs within overseas companies that have now been set up in the UK.

UK visas are awarded on a points-based system. To apply for a student visa you need 40 points. These points come from:

• a Confirmation of Acceptance for Studies (CAS) number from the University (30 points)

• proof that you meet the financial requirements (10 points)

A CAS number will be issued to you as part of the admissions process. Once you have an unconditional offer from the University, your CAS number will be issued by the faculty office of the School you will be joining. Please contact them if you are eligible to receive a CAS number and have not yet received one. Apply for your visa as soon as you receive your CAS number.

You will need to provide evidence that you have funds to cover both your studies (i.e. tuition fees if you have not already paid them) and your living costs (about £800 per month for courses shorter than 9 months or about £7,200 for courses longer than 9 months). The living costs depend on which town/city you are going to. The living costs mentioned above are for outside London. For London the amount of living costs per month is about £1,000. The funds have to be in your account at least 28 days before you apply for your visa. During that time, the total amount in your account cannot drop below the minimum amount required by the UKVI.

You will also need to provide supporting documents including original documents relating to your existing academic qualifications for entry. Complete information about the documents required can be found on the UKVI website.

You must read the Tier 4 policy guidance [pdf] from the UKVI, which will give you detailed information about applying for your student visa.

Will I have to pay for my healthcare?

All non-EEA immigrants will have to pay for their healthcare if they are going to be in the UK for longer than six months. Non-EEA nationals already in the UK who apply to extend their stay will also have to pay. The health surcharge amount is £200 per person, per year of the visa for all, but £150 for students. Part years of less than six months will be charged at £75. Dependants will also pay the same amount as the main applicant.

Non-EEA nationals visiting the UK on a tourist visa will not pay the health surcharge, but will continue to be fully liable for the costs of any NHS treatment they receive. Foreign workers (non-EEA) often struggle to pay the health surcharge of £200 per family member per year for the duration of the work permit. A foreign worker's family of four will pay £200 times 4 times 3 (for 3 years). This will be £2400 upfront. The health surcharge is to increase to £400 in 2018.

What happens if I overstay my visa?

If a foreign national under visa control does not leave the UK after expiry of their visa or if their visa application has been refused they will be added to the Migration Refusal Pool (MRP), awaiting deportation to their country of origin. Most people in the MRP typically are foreign students.

The UK government says the problem of those illegally overstaying their visa is one of the biggest challenges facing the immigration system and target visitors from certain countries who present the greatest risk. These countries are: India, Pakistan, Sri Lanka, Bangladesh, Ghana and Nigeria.

Any period of overstaying for a period of 28 days or less will be disregarded and not treated as a violation of immigration rules.

Are sham marriages common among those seeking to remain in the UK?

Most sham marriages in Britain take place between an EU national with the right to be in the UK and someone from outside the EU. There have been many instances of desperate immigrants attempting sham marriages in order to remain in the UK, but this is illegal. Many people have been convicted of these offences and sent to prison. Marriage Registrars can report if they suspect a sham marriage or civil partnership under Section 24 of the Immigration and Asylum Act 1999.

The UK government has plans to introduce a minimum probationary period of five years for settlement to deter sham marriages. The Home Office estimates that some 10,000 applications to stay in Britain a year are based on a 'false' wedding or civil partnership.

Under existing rules, anyone who wants to marry must tell their local register office or church 28 days before the planned wedding date, and details of the union are then posted on a notice board.

The rules allow officials who suspect a bogus wedding may be about to take place to extend the notice period to 70 days - allowing them to investigate. Foreign nationals from outside the EU wanting to get married in a church will first have to go to the register office and get approval - ensuring the authorities are made aware of the planned wedding.

What is the trend in the numbers of foreigners seeking UK settlement/citizenship?

According to the ONS, 241,192 people were granted permanent residency rights in 2010, of whom 51 per cent were from Asia and 27 per cent from Africa. This was the highest ever recorded number of settlement grants. Since then the figure has been much lower.

The number of foreign nationals (non-EEA) becoming British citizens was

54,902 in 1999,

129,375 in 2008,

203,790 in 2009,

195,046 in 2010,

177,878 in 2011,

194,344 in 2012

104,057 in 2014

89,932 in 2015

Among those becoming British citizens by naturalisation in 2015, the largest groups by citizenship were from India (16% of the 2015 total), Pakistan (11%), Nigeria (7%), and South Africa (4%). 11% of grants were to EU nationals.

What is settlement?

Settlement or Indefinite Leave to Remain is a legal permission from the British government that grants the holder the right to live permanently in the UK without being subject to immigration control. It does not confer full citizenship status.

What is the most common category under which people seek UK permanent settlement?

Since 2008, employment has generally been the most frequent category of settlement granted. Settlement for family reasons was the third most common basis for settlement granted in 2015 after employment and asylum. Most people granted settlement for family reasons are spouses and children. In 2015, this was 99% of cases. Within this category, most cases are spouses of British citizens (85%) while those married to UK permanent residents was much lower (8%).

According to the Migration Observatory, there were 59,009 grants of settlement to non-EEA migrants in 2016. This is a drastic drop of more than 75% since 2010 and the lowest number recorded since 1998. In 2016, 40% of settlements were granted on the basis of employment and residency (including dependents of labour migrants), 22% were granted on the basis of asylum, and 11% were granted on the basis of family formation and reunification.

Which are the top countries whose nationals received settlement?

1. India (18%)

2. Pakistan (10%)

3. Zimbabwe (5%)

4. Nigeria (4%)

5. China (4%)

6. USA (3%)

7. Bangladesh (3%)

8. South Africa (3%)

9. Sri Lanka (2%)

10. Philippines (2%).

Note: Data is for 2015, the latest year data is available.

On what grounds were citizenship applications rejected/

According to the Migration Observatory, 9% of citizenship applications were rejected in 2015. The majority of refusals since 2002 have been because of failure to meet either the residence or the 'good character' requirements. English language requirements and the Life in the UK test account for a small percentage of rejected naturalisation applications.

Will my baggage/vehicle be searched at UK border controls?

Yes, it is quite possible. If a search of your baggage and vehicle at the border reveal items which demonstrate that you intend to work or live in the UK (while you have a visitor visa), then it may adversely affect your entry clearance.

At the border will I be asked further questions about the purpose of my visit?

At the border (usually airport), UKVI expects the applicant to be able to answer questions on what they plan to do in the UK. Questions will include plans for their stay. Applicants must provide information about this.

I plan to enter the UK through the Channel Tunnel, what documents must I produce?

You must provide evidence of your identity and nationality (usually a passport with a visa or an entry certificate). This is to determine whether you require a visa to enter the UK and, if so, on what terms leave to enter should be given.

On what grounds can my visa be cancelled?

Your entry clearance (visa) may be cancelled if you enter the UK before your visa starts or if you seek to enter the UK for a purpose other than the purpose specified in the entry clearance.

People with what medical conditions are not granted long term visas?

Active pulmonary tuberculosis. UKVI tests applicants in their home countries and on arrival to see that this tuberculosis is not present in the applicant.

What guidance can be given on completing visa application forms?

You must use a black pen to complete the form. Write names, addresses and similar details in capital letters. In the payment details and other sections where you give personal details and addresses, leave an empty box between each part of the name and of the address. Take care to complete all sections as required, including the Personal History section. You must enclose a letter of explanation if you are unable to provide all the required information or any relevant specified documents.

What is 'continuous residence'?

Continuous residence is time you have spent in the UK without gaps. You can leave the UK during the continuous residence for up to: 180 days at a time; or 540 days in total. You can't count time spent in a prison, young offender's institution or secure hospital; the Republic of Ireland, Isle of Man or Channel Islands.

Where can I get UKVI application forms?

All forms are available here:

https://www.gov.uk/government/collections/uk-visa-forms

There will be guidance notes with the application form.

In my country I cannot apply online, is there a way I can apply by post?

Yes, there is. All forms are also available in pdf format here:

https://www.gov.uk/government/collections/uk-visa-forms

Download the form and post it to the address listed on it.

Remember, if you are coming to the UK from abroad to visit, work, study or join a family member or partner, you must apply online. These application forms are for people in countries that cannot apply online.

I am disabled is there an alternative format in which forms are available?

Yes, email "alternativeformats@homeoffice.gsi.gov.uk" and tell them what type of assistive technology you use.

Why is it necessary to possess documents to demonstrate your right to be in the UK?

Recent changes to the law require anyone who wishes to work, rent property or have access to benefits and services in the UK to possess documents to demonstrate their right to be in the UK.

Are landlords required to perform immigration checks?

Yes, landlords of properties in England must check that someone has the right to rent before letting them a property. They must ask for original documents that prove you can live in the UK. They will check your documents to see if you have the right to rent your property. They will make and keep copies of the documents and record the date they made the check. Landlords who do not do such checks will face a fine (upto £3000) or go to prison.

Is it worthwhile to appeal against an immigration decision of the Home Office?

According to the UK Law Society, which represents solicitors in England and Wales, about half of all decisions by the Home Office on immigration issues concerning individuals that go on appeal are overturned. This could be because new evidence has been presented. It suggests that there are flaws in the way visa and asylum applications are dealt with. So yes, it could be worthwhile to appeal against an immigration decision of the Home Office.

Can the Home Secretary use his discretion to approve a waiver of rules?

Shreyas Royal, a 9-year-old Indian chess prodigy who was ranked 4 in the world in his age group, was granted leave to stay in the UK after the expiry of his father's work visa. The Home Office made an exception in the case due to his "exceptional talent". A number of British MPs had intervened in the case to urge the UK home secretary to make an exception in Royal's case due to his exceptional talent. The father could not extend his visa because he did not earn the minimum £120,000 a year. The family were allowed to extend their leave to remain on the Tier 2 general route despite this. This exception allowed Mr.Singh to apply for the Tier 2 work visa, which is valid for up to five years, without needing to leave the UK. Mr.Singh said he would eventually apply for UK ILR.

Applying for a UK visa from Australia - points to note

Do not contact the UK High Commission in Australia for a visa to the UK. You need to contact UKVI, and apply online (https://www.gov.uk/apply-to-come-to-the-uk). You must pay your fee; pay the Immigration Health Surcharge (if applicable); book and attend your biometric enrolment appointment; post your passport and supporting documents (Adelaide and Hobart only). UKVI aims to make a decision on a non-settlement visa application in 15 working days. For applying from Sydney, Melbourne, Brisbane, Perth and Canberra go to https://www.vfsglobal.co.uk/au/en/how-to-apply.

Travelling to the UK from Australia

You cannot apply earlier than 3 months before your intended travel date, unless you are applying under the Youth Mobility Scheme, where you can apply up to 6 months before. You must provide an accurate travel date as part of your application. If your visa is valid for more than 6 months, you will be given a 30-day travel window based on the information provided in the application form. If successful, your temporary visa will be valid for 30 days once you receive it and you will need to travel within this period. If you are unable to travel during this 30-day window, you will need to apply for a vignette transfer to change the dates.

How to apply for a UK settlement visa from Australia

There is a different process for submitting UK Settlement applications in Australia. Your application form and passport will be submitted at the visa application centre, or posted to UK Visas and Immigration, GPO Box 2718, Sydney NSW 2001, if you are applying from Adelaide and Hobart. Your supporting documents, including the appendix will be posted to PO Box 5852, Sheffield, United Kingdom S11 0FX, by the sponsor or the applicant. Information about applying in Sydney, Melbourne, Brisbane, Perth and Canberra is available on the VFS Global Australia website. Full details of how to prepare a settlement application can be found on the VFS website.

What is the Windrush scheme?

This scheme is for people who arrived in the UK from a number of Commonwealth countries after the Second World War and did not have documentation confirming their immigration status. They faced difficulties in proving their right to work, to rent property and to access benefits and services to which they are entitled. The Windrush Scheme helps people navigate the immigration system. It does not cover applications for a British passport. An application under the Windrush Scheme must be made on the relevant form on GOV.UK - the "Windrush Scheme application (UK)" for applicants living in the UK or the" Windrush Scheme application (Overseas)" for applicants living outside the UK. There is no fee for an application under the Windrush Scheme.

Applicants under the Windrush Scheme are required to provide their biometrics (photograph of face and fingerprints) unless they are exempt from that requirement. There is no fee for this. It is meant for Commonwealth citizens who were settled in the UK before 1 January 1973 and had been continuously resident in the UK since their arrival. The requirement to pass the Life in the UK test will not apply to them. They will also not have to attend a citizenship ceremony, unless they want to. The applicant will have to meet the residence requirements for citizenship and the good character requirement. If the applicant is lawfully in the UK and not liable to deportation on grounds of criminality or other non-conducive behaviour and has close and continuing ties with the UK they will be given indefinite leave to remain.

The rules also apply to a child of a Commonwealth citizen who was settled in the UK before 1 January 1973, where the child was born in the UK or arrived in the UK before the age of 18 and has been continuously resident in the UK since their arrival.

The rules also apply to a person of any nationality, who arrived in the UK before 31 December 1988 and is lawfully settled in the UK.

The rules also apply to a person living outside the UK: A Commonwealth citizen who was settled in the UK before 1 January 1973 but who does not have a document confirming their Right of Abode or settled status, or whose settled status has lapsed because they left the UK for a period of more than 2 years.

Special provisions for Afghan interpreters

The June 2018 amendment to the rules brought into effect rules that allow Afghan interpreters and their family members who have relocated to the UK to apply for settlement after 5 years' residence. It additionally implements plans to expand the ex-gratia redundancy scheme to recognise and honour the service of those made redundant before 19 December 2012.

Special provisions for Syrian nationals

The concession covers Syrian nationals who meet all of the following requirements are present within the UK; whose country of habitual residence is Syria; who either have limited leave to enter or remain or whose leave has expired but have applied within 14 days of that leave expiring.

If an applicant meets the above criteria they can apply to UK Visas and Immigration to switch from one category of the Immigration Rules to another, but they must meet the rules of that other category. The concession works by waiving some requirements of the Immigration Rules for switching.

Syrian nationals who entered the UK on short-term student visas on or after 24 April 2015, who apply for further leave to remain in that category will have their application considered as an application for leave to remain outside of the Immigration Rules.

Document flexibility is available under the Syria concession. Due to the civil unrest in Syria an applicant may be unable to provide the full range of documents required under the category in which they are applying. If so, an applicant must explain why they cannot provide particular documents when they make their application. If the Home Office is satisfied that due to the civil unrest in Syria a document required by the Immigration Rules, but listed in paragraph 6 or 10 of the Equality (Syria) Authorisation 2019 cannot be obtained from Syria, the requirement to provide that document may be waived.

To be eligible to be considered under the concession an applicant must be in the UK lawfully and have made an in time application, or apply within 14 days of the expiry of their leave, in line with the normal requirements of the rules in the category in which they are applying meet the requirements of the Immigration Rules for the category they are applying under, subject to the concessions contained in this guidance and pay the correct fee for the application they are making. Applications made after 29 February 2020 will not be considered under this concession.

WHAT VISA TO APPLY FOR?

What is a Biometric Residence Permit and do I need it?

It is a plastic card document that you need if you are going to be in the UK for longer than six months. It provides proof of your permission to be in the UK, for how long and the conditions attached to your stay (e.g. if you can access public services/benefits), and can also be used as identification. It is only for non-EEA applicants.

You must have a biometric residence permit (BRP) if you want to apply to come to the UK for more than six months; apply to extend your visa or settle in the UK; transfer your visa to a new passport; and apply for certain Home Office travel documents. The BRP can be used to show prospective employers/universities of your permission to stay and work or study in the UK.

You do not have to apply separately for a BRP. When you make your visa or immigration application you have to give certain personal data (your photograph, your fingerprints, and your signature).

If you are already in the UK you can provide your biometric info at certain Post Office branches (fees apply) (go to http://www.postoffice.co.uk/foreign-nationals-enrolment-biometric-residence-permit). You can also go to one of 7 premium service centres within the UK for a one-day service (fees £400) (go to https://www.gov.uk/ukvi-premium-service-centres).

If you applied from overseas you will receive a BRP upon arrival in the UK. You must collect your BRP within 10 days of arrival in the UK from the Post Office branch detailed in your decision letter. You can make your first trip to the UK without a BRP and using just a vignette valid for 30 days.

You do not need to carry your BRP with you at all times, only when travelling to and from the UK. You should take your BRP with you if you travel outside the UK otherwise you may be refused re-entry to the UK. You must apply for a new BRP before your present leave to remain expires.

If you are settled in the UK, your BRP will say either Indefinite leave to remain'; 'Indefinite leave to enter'; or 'No time limit'. Your BRP will last up to 10 years and will have an expiry date. Apply for a replacement around 3 months before expiry. Use the BRP replacement service to do this. You must tell the Home Office if you want to change the personal details on your BRP, such as your name or gender, or if your facial appearance changes significantly. Use the BRP replacement service to do this.

If your BRP is lost or stolen in the UK you must report the loss or theft to the police as soon as possible and get a police report and crime reference number. You must also report this to the Home Office by using the service on GOV.UK. The BRP will then be cancelled.

If your BRP is lost or stolen abroad, you must apply for a short-term single-entry visa to come back to the UK and then report it to the Home Office. You will then need to apply for a replacement BRP. Use the BRP replacement service to do this.

What is a UK Ancestry visa?

A UK Ancestry visa is a work visa for those who are Commonwealth citizens. You must apply from outside the UK; be able to prove that one of your grandparents was born in the UK; and you must be able and planning to work in the UK. You can stay in the UK for 5 years on this visa. You can apply to extend your visa. You can also apply to settle in the UK permanently after five years. You can work, study, and bring family members, but you cannot switch into this visa if you are already in the UK on another visa. You are not allowed to access public funds (benefits) while on this visa. A UK Ancestry visa costs £496. You will also have to pay the healthcare surcharge as part of your application.

You must prove that you are 17 or over; have enough money without help from public funds to support and house yourself and any dependants; and can and plan to work in the UK.

You must also show that you have a grandparent born in the UK; or born before 31 March 1922 in the Republic of Ireland or born on a British-registered ship or aircraft.

You can claim ancestry if either you or the relevant parent were adopted or were born within or outside marriage in the UK. You cannot claim UK ancestry through step-parents.

My family member is British/a permanent UK resident, what visa do I need to remain in the UK?

You need a 'family of a settled person' visa if you want to stay ('remain') with a family member who is living in the UK permanently. You must already be in the UK. You must be from outside the European Economic Area (EEA) and Switzerland. You can also extend your existing 'family of a settled person' visa. You can switch to a 'family of a settled person' visa. Your family member must be a British citizen; or have settled in the UK or be your partner who has asylum or humanitarian protection in the UK. You can also apply to remain with your child if the child has lived in the UK for at least 7 years. You must pay the healthcare surcharge.

You can stay for 2 years and 6 months. You will be able to apply to extend again towards the end of that. You can work, study and bring dependents under 18 years. You cannot claim benefits. You can also apply to settle permanently in the UK once you are eligible.

I am the partner of an EEA national, what visa do I need to come to/remain in the UK?

You can apply for a European Economic Area (EEA) family permit instead of a 'family of a settled person' visa if the person you will be joining is from a country in the European Economic Area (EEA) (excluding the UK) or from Switzerland. Applications must be made online. You will have to give your biometric information. These permits are valid for a period of 6 months from their date of issue. They are issued free of charge.

I am an EEA national in the UK, what document do I need to prove my immigration status?

You need a Registration Certificate as a Qualified Person. This applies if you are in the UK as a worker, self-employed person, self-sufficient person, student, or a jobseeker. You need form EEA(QP). A fee of £65 per applicant is to be paid. You do not need to give your biometric information.

I am extended family of an EEA national do I have an automatic right of residence in the UK?

Extended family members, including durable partners, of EEA nationals do not enjoy an automatic right of residence in the UK until they have been issued with a document by the Home Office confirming such a right.

I am the primary carer of a British citizen/EEA child in education in the UK, which visa do I need?

You need a derivative residence card. A DRF1 form can be used to submit an application. A fee of £65 per applicant is to be paid. All non-EEA applicants will have to give their biometric information. Applicants will need to show that the British citizen would be unable to reside in the UK or in another EEA member state if the applicant had to leave the UK. In the case of an EEA national child, evidence must be shown that the child would be unable to remain in the UK if the applicant had to leave the UK.

What is a Spousal visa?

This visa is for those who are not already in the UK. The spousal visa grants a person the right to remain in the UK for 30 months, after which they can apply for indefinite leave to remain.

The applicant must then pass an additional test on life and language in the UK. They cannot claim benefits. They can study and work in the UK.

Anyone from outside the EU applying for a visa to join their spouse or partner will have to prove they have a basic command of English, to help them get by in daily life, before their application is approved.

Visa applicants have to show that their marriage or partnership is genuine and that they can financially support themselves.

Is there a minimum salary I must earn before I can sponsor my spouse to join me in the UK?

Yes, under current rules, someone who is legally present in the UK can sponsor the arrival of their non-EEA spouse or partner providing they themselves are earning at least £18,600 before tax and housing costs. This rises to £22,400 for families with a child, and a further £2,400 for each extra child. Note that these controls only apply to workers from outside of the European Economic Area.

The new requirements have lowered the numbers of spousal visas issued. The couple must also demonstrate that they still meet the income threshold after 2.5 years when they apply to renew their visa. These rules hit females, the young and non-white applicants hardest as these groups often do not earn enough to sponsor a non-EEA spouse and one child and this becomes harder when there are two children involved.

Is there a requirement for knowledge of English language for spousal visas?

Yes, you must show that you can speak and understand English if you are a non-European migrant and you want to enter or extend your stay in the UK as the partner of a British citizen or a person settled here. If you are applying for indefinite leave to remain passing the Life in the UK test, which is also designed to check your English knowledge, will suffice. See the UK Home Office Youtube channel for more information.

How do I prove my English language ability?

If the visa you are applying for asks you to prove your English language ability you should use the list of approved secure English language tests and test centres that meet the Home Office's requirements.

The list of approved secure English language tests and test centres is available as a pdf document on the UKVI website:

https://www.gov.uk/government/publications/guidance-on-applying-for-uk-visa-approved-english-language-tests

Are English language rules and Life in the UK Test rules going to get harder?

Yes, in October 2018, the Home Secretary proposed a series of reforms to British citizenship. The reforms include tougher English language requirements for people applying for British citizenship and proposals to reform the Life in the UK test to give greater prominence to the British values and principles expected of those wishing to call the UK their permanent home. A public consultation will be held on the Life in the UK test, which is the test an individual is required to take as part of their application for British citizenship or settlement in the UK, and accompanying handbook. The proposals would ensure that the test is more relevant to daily life and culture in the UK. In addition, the level of language proficiency expected for adults seeking to naturalise as British citizens will be raised. He also outlined that powers to deprive individuals of their British citizenship will be applied to individuals convicted of the most serious criminal offences, where it is in the public interest.

I've been offered a skilled job in the UK, which visa do I need?

If the job is a skilled one, you can apply for a Tier 2 (General) visa. You need to be sponsored (i.e. have a certificate of sponsorship from a licensed sponsor) before you can apply to come to the UK to work.

A list of organisations licensed to sponsor migrants under Tiers 2 & 5 of the Points-Based System is available here:

https://www.gov.uk/government/uploads/system/uploads/attachment_data/file/664037/2017-12-01_Tier_25_Register_of_Sponsors.pdf

A certificate of sponsorship is a reference number which holds information about the job and your personal details. It is not an actual certificate or paper document. Your sponsor will give you your certificate of sponsorship reference number.

The work you do in the UK must relate to the work of your sponsor organisation. This visa is meant for those in shortage occupations, where is a lack of skilled people in the UK.

You can come to the UK with a Tier 2 (General) visa for a maximum of 5 years and 14 days, or the time given on your certificate of sponsorship plus 1 month, whichever is shorter. Your stay must start no more than 14 days before the start date on your certificate of sponsorship. You can apply to extend this visa for up to another 5 years, as long as your total stay is not more than 6 years.

You must be paid an appropriate salary (£30,000 or more per year). You must have the required level of English and £945 in savings in your bank account for 90 days before you apply. This is to prove you can support yourself. You cannot claim benefits in the UK.

I've got a great business idea and want to start a business, which visa do I need?

You can apply for a Tier 1 (Graduate Entrepreneur) visa if you are a graduate who has been officially endorsed as having a genuine and credible business idea. You must be endorsed by either the UK Trade and Investment (UKTI) as part of the elite global graduate entrepreneur programme (Sirius) or your current UK higher education institution (HEI) if it is an authorised endorsing body. UK Higher Education Institutions have been granted a central role in identifying graduates who have developed genuine and credible business ideas or entrepreneurial skills, and in endorsing and supporting them. UKVI has published a list of approved HEIs for this purpose. The full list can be found here:

https://www.gov.uk/government/uploads/system/uploads/attachment_data/file/467504/Tier_1__Graduate_Entrepreneur__authorised_endorsing_bodies_-_Oct_2015.pdf

You can stay in the UK for 1 year on a Tier 1 (Graduate Entrepreneur) visa and you can apply to extend this visa for 1 more year. You cannot settle down in the UK permanently on this visa.

What is the difference between a Tier 1 Entrepreneur visa and Tier 1 Graduate Entrepreneur visa?

A Tier 1 Graduate Entrepreneur visa was discussed in the previous question. A big difference of the Tier 1 Entrepreneur visa is that you *can* apply to settle permanently on this visa. But there are tough conditions to meet.

You can apply for a Tier 1 (Entrepreneur) visa if you want to set up or run a business in the UK. You must have access to at least £50,000 investment funds to apply for a Tier 1 (Entrepreneur) visa. Your funds must be held in one or more regulated financial institutions and free to spend on business in the UK. You can apply if you are in the UK on a Tier 1 (Post-study worker) visa or as a student.

You must meet the English language requirement; be able to support yourself during your stay; score 95 points on the PBS (explained earlier in this book) and be at least 16 years old. You can form an 'entrepreneurial team' with one other Tier 1 (Entrepreneur) applicant and share the same investment funds. You can switch to this visa from a variety of visa types. You can stay a maximum of 3 years after switching to a Tier 1 (Entrepreneur) visa. You must be in the UK to extend your visa. Your family members can come with you on this visa. You and they will have to pay the Health Surcharge. You must show that your dependants can be supported while they're in the UK. You cannot get benefits in the UK.

You can set up or take over the running of one business or more. You can't do any work outside your business.

You can come to the UK with a Tier 1 (Entrepreneur) visa for a maximum of 3 years and 4 months. You can apply to extend this visa for another 2 years if you're already in this category and 3 years if you're switching to it from another category. You may be able to apply for settlement once you've been in the UK for 5 years.

Only 1200 of these visas were issued in 2015.

I want to run a business in the UK, which visa do I need?

Assuming you are from outside the EEA, you can apply for a Tier 1 (Entrepreneur) visa if you want to set up or run a business in the UK. See previous answer.

What is the Tier 1 General visa?

It was for those wanting to switch from a current visa in certain categories (writer, composer or artist; self-employed lawyer; Highly Skilled Migrant Programme). Those on an existing Tier 1 (General) visa earlier could apply to extend it, but not now. One can no longer apply or extend Tier 1 (General) visas.

If you held this visa, you may be able to apply for settlement once you have been in the UK for 5 years.

I want to get married in the UK, which visa do I need?

You need a Marriage Visitor visa. It is assumed that you are not planning to stay or settle in the UK after your marriage or civil partnership. You can use this visa to visit the UK for 6 months.

Visitors intending to marry or form a civil partnership in the UK must give notice at a register office before the marriage or civil partnership can take place. In England and Wales notice must be given in person. In Scotland and Northern Ireland notice can be given by post.

An individual who is coming to the UK to marry or form a civil partnership will need to provide evidence they have made arrangements for their marriage or civil partnership to take place in the UK. Examples of evidence include confirmation of the church or register office booking (email confirmation or a receipt for payment of the marriage/civil partnership venue).

For visa applications, UKVI will consider the evidence submitted, including the arrangements for the marriage or civil partnership, the couple's relationship, future plans and living arrangements. If UKVI is satisfied from the evidence provided that the applicant is in a genuine relationship, the visa will be issued. If they consider the proposed marriage or civil partnership will be a sham, the application will be refused.

Which visa do I need for volunteer work in the UK?

The UKVI allows UK visitors to undertake volunteering (not voluntary work) provided volunteering is not the main purpose of the visit, it is for a registered charity and will be no longer than 30 days in total. Where an individual is looking to come to the UK specifically to volunteer they will be refused. Those who want to work as volunteers must apply via the Tier 5 Charity worker route of the points-based system.

I want to bring my relative to the UK to look after my children, which visa do they need?

A standard visitor visa. A family member coming to look after a child in the UK is permitted, provided it is for a short visit and does not amount to the relative being employed as a child-minder. The visit must be of a short duration and the relative must be a genuine visitor. At the border, all visitors are asked to explain what they are coming to do and for how long.

THE VISITOR VISA

What is a Standard Visitor visa and what can/can't you do on such a visa?

The Standard Visitor visa has replaced the:

Family Visitor visa

General Visitor visa

Child Visitor visa

Business Visitor visa, including visas for academics, doctors and dentists

Sports Visitor visa

Entertainer Visitor visa

Prospective Entrepreneur visa

Private Medical Treatment Visitor visa

Approved Destination Status (ADS) visa.

The standard visitor visa is for those wanting to visit the UK for leisure, for e.g. as a tourist on holiday, or for visiting friends or family who are not permanent residents in the UK or if they are donating an organ to a relative or friend. Only those from outside the European Economic Area (EEA) or Switzerland need such a visa. It is valid for six months. There are long-term visit visas available for those who can prove they need to make repeat visits over a longer period. Such visas allow you to stay for a maximum of 6 months on each visit and your visa can last for 1, 2, 5 or 10 years.

With a standard visitor visa you can study for up to 30 days, as long as it's not the main reason for your visit. You cannot take paid or unpaid work or live in the UK for long periods of time through frequent visits. You are not allowed to marry or register a civil partnership, or give notice of marriage or civil partnership. You are not allowed to get private medical treatment or access public funds (i.e. benefits).

You can also apply for a Standard Visitor visa if you want to visit the UK for business-related activities, e.g:

you're coming to the UK for a conference, meeting or training

you want to take part in a specific sports-related event

you're an artist, entertainer or musician and coming to the UK to perform

you're an academic and are doing research or accompanying students on a study abroad programme

you're a doctor or dentist and are coming to the UK to take a clinical attachment or observer post you want to take the Professional and Linguistic Assessment Board (PLAB) test or sit the Objective Structured Clinical Examination (OSCE)

you want to get funding to start, take over, join or run a business in the UK

A Standard Visitor visa costs £89. The fee for a long-term visit visa depends on its length:

2 years - £337

5 years - £612

10 years - £767

What is Access UK?

Access UK is a new digital visa application service for foreign visitors to the UK. Foreigners from over 180 countries can apply in any of 10 languages for a UK visa online. It is better than personally visiting a UK High Commission or Embassy because applicants

•   make quicker visa applications using an intuitive online form

•   use easy-to-follow checklists and steps which list the documents required to make an application

•   apply flexibly using any mobile device

You can apply by going to: https://www.gov.uk/apply-uk-visa

I have a visitor visa, can I settle in the UK permanently?

Yes, you can apply as the partner of a British citizen or person settled in the UK. You may be eligible for settlement if your partner is a British citizen or a person settled in the UK. You must be able to prove one of the following: you are married or you are in a civil partnership or you have been in a relationship for 2 years. You and your partner must intend to continue your relationship after you apply for settlement.

You need to have been living in the UK with a 'partner of a settled person' visa for 5 years or 10 years if you applied for your visa on or after 9 July 2012. Read the guidance below in the section entitled 'family/partner route to settlement' in this book for advice on the 5 and 10-year routes.

If you are 18 to 64 years old when you apply you must also pass the Life in the UK Test and an English language test.

Your application might be refused if, for example, you have a criminal record in the UK or another country, provided false or incomplete information to the Home Office or broken UK immigration law.

I need to visit the UK for a short time, which visa do I need?

Assuming you are from outside the EEA, you need a Standard Visitor visa if you want to visit the UK for business-related activities.

This is for those:

•   coming to the UK for a conference, meeting or training

•   wanting to take part in a specific sports-related event

•   who are an artist, entertainer or musician and coming to the UK to perform

- who are an academic and are doing research or accompanying students on a study abroad programme
- who are a doctor or dentist and are coming to the UK to take a clinical attachment or observer post
- wanting to take the Professional and Linguistic Assessment Board (PLAB) test or sit the Objective Structured Clinical Examination (OSCE)
- wanting to get funding to start, take over, join or run a business in the UK

You can study for up to 30 days. This visa lasts for up to 6 months. You might be able to stay for up to 11 months if you are coming to the UK for private medical treatment.

You, your spouse or civil partner and children might be able to stay for up to 12 months if you are an academic on sabbatical and coming to the UK for research.

You cannot marry, get benefits, get private medical treatment, or take up work not related to your job. You cannot live in the UK for long periods of time through frequent visits.

Can I get an extension of my visitor visa?

Yes, you need form FLR(O). A visa extension is granted provided you submit a valid application; meets all the mandatory identity and suitability checks; show that you are a genuine visitor; show that you intend to undertake only permitted activities and demonstrate that you intend to leave at the end of your stay.

The UKVI needs to be satisfied that you are not attempting to make the UK your home through frequent and successive visits.

You must have sufficient funds, maintenance and accommodation for the duration of your stay.

What criteria is used to assess the genuineness of visitor visa applications?

UKVI looks at the applicant's previous immigration history, including visits to the UK and other countries; the duration of previous visits; their financial circumstances as well as their family, social and economic background; their personal and economic ties to their country of residence; the cumulative period of time the applicant has visited the UK and their pattern of travel over the last 12 month period, and assess whether this amounts to 'defacto'residence in the UK.

They check to see whether the information and the reasons for the visit provided by the applicant are credible and correspond to their personal, family, social and economic background. They examine the political, economic and security situation of applicant's country of residence and/or country of nationality. If their country is a conflict zone because it has significant political or social unrest this will form an important part of the assessment of whether the applicant is a genuine visitor who has the intention and ability to leave the UK at the end of their visit.

If the applicant has few or no family and economic ties to their country of residence, while they have several family members in the UK, this will not be viewed positively.

Does my travel history matter in getting a visa?

An applicant's travel history as revealed in their passport (and, for visa applications, listed on the form) is relevant in securing a visa. A pattern of travel that shows the applicant has previously complied with UK immigration law is positive because it indicates that the applicant is a genuine visitor. Similarly, travel to other countries, especially the USA, Canada, Australia, New Zealand, Ireland, Schengen countries or Switzerland is viewed positively.

If an applicant has previously failed to comply with another country's immigration law, for example if they have been removed from another country, or if they have been refused entry to another country, this may suggest that an applicant is not a genuine visitor.

Travel history is not the only consideration used by UKVI in deciding whether the applicant is a genuine visitor.

How does UKVI assess whether an applicant is abusing the visitor visa?

UKVI is keen to prevent applicants whose intention is to abuse the visitor visa to make the UK their permanent home or place of work. They will note how long the applicant is spending in the UK and how frequently they are returning. UKVI also looks for evidence whether the UK is the applicant's main place of residence. This they can work out if the applicant has registered with a general practitioner (GP), or sent their children to UK schools. They also look at the history of previous applications, for example if the visitor has previously been refused under the family rules and subsequently wants to enter as a visitor. The objective is to prevent anyone using the visitor visa route to avoid the rules in place for family migrants joining British or settled persons in the UK.

If it is clear from an individual's travel history that they are making the UK their home their application will be refused.

What is a short-duration visa?

It is a visa for less than six months. This usually happens where an applicant has requested 6 months, but has been issued less leave for certain reasons. For example, if the applicant meets all the visitor rules, but UKVI has doubts about their intentions to return home after their visit, they could grant a short duration visa.

How much money must I show that I have to get a visitor visa?

The applicant must have access to sufficient resources to maintain and accommodate themselves adequately for the whole of their planned visit to the UK. There is no set level of funds required for an applicant to show this. An applicant will be asked where they will be staying and asked for evidence that they have access to funds to cover the costs they are likely to incur during their visit. The funds must have been in the applicant's account for a reasonable amount of time. If not, further checks will be made. Unaccompanied children will also have to show how their visit will be funded. This could be through access to their parents' funds or those of a third party.

What is the role of sponsors in applying for a visitor visa?

Only sponsors providing maintenance and accommodation are taken into account in the visitor visa rules. Sponsors send a letter undertaking support of a visit application. It is not accepted as evidence of funds.

Can I attend conferences and seminars on a visitor visa?

Yes, a visitor can attend conferences or seminars. However, these must not amount to the person undertaking work experience or longer study. There is no restriction on the duration of a conference but they must not last more than a couple of weeks. If a conference is longer, UKVI will check whether it amounts to a course of study, which will be grounds for refusal.

I plan to start a business in the UK, can I attend funding meetings on a visitor visa?

A visitor can take part in meetings and discussions to obtain funding for their business. Once funding is secured they must apply for a Tier 1 entrepreneur visa before they undertake any work as an entrepreneur.

I am an academic, I need to visit the UK for research, can I apply for a 12-month visitor visa?

An academic can carry out research for their own purposes such as for a book or for their employment overseas but the research should not be for commercial gain. Academics who are applying for a 12 month visit visa, or an extension for up to 12 months must be highly qualified within their field of expertise and working in that area before entering the UK. UKVI will look for evidence of a PhD. They will also check the applicant's university website.

What are the visitor visa rules for artists?

An artist can include anyone coming to the UK to undertake an activity that is connected to the arts. There is no restriction on amateur or professional artists doing permitted activities. Examples include poets, film crews, photographers, designers, artists, entertainers, stage managers, conductors, and choreographers. The personal staff of artists (bodyguards, make-up artists, press officers) can accompany an artist to the UK. The standard visitor visa applies to all.

What are the visitor visa rules for sportspersons?

A sportsperson coming to the UK to play for a British club/team must apply for a work visa under Tier 2 or 5 of the points based system.

Sportspersons are able to take part in tournaments or events, however if the applicant intends to participate in a professional domestic championship or league, including where one or more of the fixtures/rounds takes place outside the UK, this is classed as employment (paid or unpaid).

Technical or support staff for sports persons must be attending the same event as the sports person and be employed to work for them overseas.

The key question that qualifies them for a visitor visa is whether these support staff continue to be employed and paid overseas.

I need to visit the UK for work-related training; can I do this on a visitor visa?

Yes, the training should be in work practices and techniques that are not available in the visitor's home country. It should typically be classroom-based and/or involve familiarisation or observation. Practical training is however allowed provided it does not amount to 'training on the job' or the person filling a role. It is acceptable for a visitor to learn how to use a piece of equipment in the UK but if the duration is over one month or there is a risk the applicant may work for the training provider in the UK, then the visa application could be refused.

What are the visa rules for the PLAB test and OCS Examination?

A student visa is not needed to take the PLAB or OCSE or other medical examinations. The applicant should provide confirmation of their test from the General Medical Council or Nursing and Midwifery Council with their application. If the applicant successfully passes the PLAB test and wishes to remain in the UK they can only do so if it is for an unpaid clinical attachment.

Can I receive payment while in the UK on a visitor visa?

Visitors may only receive payment for their activities from a UK source in specific circumstances as set out in the visitor rules. This must not equate to a salary.

Can I study in the UK while on a visitor visa?

Yes, but visitors are limited to a maximum period of 30 days study. Study should not be the main purpose for which a visitor is coming to the UK. If the period of study is in excess of the permitted 30 day period, applicants should apply under the short term study route or Tier 4 of the points-based system. You are allowed to come to the UK as a visitor and enrol in a short course for say, diving, horse-riding, or dancing.

Can I get free medical treatment on the NHS while on a visitor visa?

UK visitors are not eligible for free treatment on the National Health Service (NHS). If they use the NHS, they may be billed for any NHS treatment received in the UK. The only exception is for organ donors.

My country has an RHCA with the UK, can I get free medical treatment on the NHS?

A RHCA (reciprocal healthcare agreement) generally provides access to immediately necessary healthcare for visitors from the contracting countries, when they are present in the other's country for a limited period. Treatment is provided on the same terms as for a local resident (free of charge in the UK). The majority of these RHCAs apply only to short-term visitors. RHCAs do not usually allow migrants to come to the UK for the specific purpose of seeking medical care.

What are the rules for granting a multiple entry visitor visa?

A multiple visitor visa allows multiple visits of up to 6 months for a visitor (standard) at a time over a period of 2 years, 5 years or 10 years.

The applicant must satisfy UKVI that they have a genuine intention to visit on a regular basis. A successful applicant will show a frequent and continued reason for coming to the UK, such as family links or an established business connection.

UKVI will reject applications from those who intend to make the UK their home. Warning signs are: visitors coming to marry or to form civil partnership in the UK, as well as unaccompanied children and those entering the UK for medical treatment.

They would like to see stability of the applicant's personal and economic circumstances. An applicant's financial circumstances and ties to their home country must be strong and be unlikely to change significantly during the validity of the visa.

Another check is travel history. A history of international travel which shows the individual's compliance with UK or other immigration laws will be relevant to deciding whether the applicant intends to leave the UK at the end of each visit.

Where the applicant meets the visitor rules, but does not show a need to visit the UK on a regular basis and therefore does not qualify for a long-term visit visa, UKVI will issue a visit visa for up to 6 months. In such cases, no refund (full or partial) is available.

What are the rules on children visiting the UK?

The UK Home Office has a statutory duty to have regard to the need to safeguard and promote the welfare of children in the UK under section 55 of the Borders, Citizenship and Immigration Act 2009.

Therefore, UKVI will only grant the application when they are satisfied that the child will be adequately accommodated and duty of care obligations have been met.

UKVI must be satisfied that care and reception arrangements are adequate and that the requirement for parental consent has been met. UKVI will make further enquiries to confirm the identity and residence of the host and make sure the child is expected. If UKVI remains concerned about the child's welfare in the UK, they will refuse the application.

If the applicant's parents are divorced, the consent for the visit must come from the parent who holds legal custody or sole responsibility. If the applicant provides information that the parent they will be travelling with is not the parent who holds legal custody UKVI will seek consent from both parents.

A child with an 'unaccompanied child visitor' visa may travel with or without an accompanying adult.

What are the rules for visits for private medical treatment in the UK?

Applicants must provide satisfactory evidence concerning their medical condition and treatment, expenses likely to be incurred, how they will be funded, and the likely duration of their treatment. Individuals applying for an 11 month visa for private medical treatment must provide medical evidence to support their stay in the UK for this period.

What special visa rules are there for Chinese visitors?

A visitor visa is normally for six months, but a new two-year visitor visa has been launched in January 2016 for visitors from China. It will help them to make multiple trips to the UK for longer periods. The visa is available for business people to attend conferences or to plan the setting up of a business, and also for tourists. This visa costs £85.

What is the British-Irish visa scheme for Chinese and Indian visitors?

This scheme allows Chinese and Indian nationals to visit both the UK and Ireland using a single visa when travelling on certain short stay and visitor visas. Some Irish short stay visas will allow onward travel to the UK and some UK visitor visas will allow onward travel to Ireland. This will help an Indian or Chinese visitor in Dublin/London to make a short trip to London/Dublin or Belfast or Cork without needing a separate visa. All Indian and Chinese nationals who hold an eligible UK visitor visa (except 'visitor in transit' and 'visitor for marriage or civil partnership') are covered by the scheme. Indian and Chinese nationals with any other type of Irish visa (for example a work or a study visa) will still need to apply for a separate UK visit visa to visit the UK from Ireland.

The following UK visas are eligible under this scheme: all standard visitor categories where the maximum period for a single visit is six months and Permitted Paid Engagement visas. To be eligible for the British-Irish visa scheme applicants for Irish short stay visas must apply at a UK/Irish visa application centre in India or China. Applications for Irish visas will continue to be determined by the Irish authorities and applications for UK visas will continue to be determined by the UK authorities.

THE STUDENT VISA

What is a Tier 4 General Student visa?

It is assumed that you are from a country that is not in the European Economic Area (EEA). This visa is for those coming to the UK to study a degree or college course for longer than 6 months (or 11 months if it is an English language course). You can apply for a Tier 4 (General) student visa to study in the UK if you are 16 or over and you have been offered a place on a course; can speak, read, write and understand English; have enough money to support yourself and pay for your course.

Has the student visa system been made tougher in recent years?

Yes, student visa rules are constantly being refined. New visa rules involve greater scrutiny about the student's study destination as well as on their English ability, and there are limits on their ability to work after their studies. The Home Office takes these measures to prevent abuse of the student visa system. These include cracking down on bogus colleges and they also plan to make it compulsory for students to have financial savings on arrival and not depend on working in the UK (by themselves or their spouses).

What are the new changes to the student visa system?

The new rules are designed to:

• Stop the 'perpetual student' who moves from course to course to prolong their stay in the UK. University students can study a new course at the same level but only where there is a link to their previous course or where the university confirms that this new course supports their career aspirations.

• Prevent students using bogus colleges to extend their student visa. College students are now banned from extending their Tier 4 visas in the UK unless they are studying at an 'embedded college' (i.e a college which has a formal, direct link to a university that is recognised by the Home Office).

• Prohibit visa 'switching'. College students are not allowed to switch visas from Tier 4 to Tiers 2 or 5 from within the UK. They must leave and re-apply from outside the UK.

• Control visa extensions. Visas for further education study will only be issued for two years maximum.

• Prevent students funding themselves by getting spouses to take low-paid jobs. Tier 4 student visa holders' dependants cannot now take low or unskilled jobs. They can, however, take part-time or full-time skilled work.

To make it easier for students to come and study in the UK the Home Office expanded the list of countries from which students would be able to benefit from a streamlined application process. Students from an additional 11 countries, including China, will be able to provide a reduced level of documentation when applying for their Tier 4 visa. All students from these countries still need to meet all requirements under Tier 4 and UK Visas and Immigration reserves the right to request this evidence in full and will do so for a random sample of applications.

What is a "course of study"?

According to the UKVI, a "course of study" is full-time studies leading to a qualification that is

at least level 6 on the revised National Qualifications Framework (NQF)

or an overseas course of degree level study that's equal to a UK higher education course and is being run by an overseas higher education institution

or a full-time course with at least 15 hours per week of organised daytime study leading to a qualification below degree level but at least NQF level 3

or a recognised foundation programme as a postgraduate doctor or dentist.

What is a CAS?

CAS is Confirmation of acceptance of studies. Your education provider will send you a reference number called a confirmation of acceptance for studies (CAS) once they have offered you a place on a course. You must enter this on your visa application. You must apply for your visa within 6 months after you receive the CAS.

I want to study for a postgraduate course in medicine/dentistry, which visa should I apply for?

Tier 4 General student visa. You must be sponsored to do a recognised foundation programme and you must have finished a recognised UK degree in medicine or dentistry, received that degree from a registered Tier 4 sponsor and spent your final year and at least 1 other year of studies leading to that degree in the UK.

How do I apply for a Tier 4 General student visa?

You must make your application online for the Tier 4 general student visa. You must not apply for a Tier 4 student visa more than three months before your course start date. As part of the visa application process, you will be required to supply biometric information (scans of your fingers and a digital photograph). You will need to visit a visa application centre in your country for this.

Apply online here: https://www.gov.uk/apply-uk-visa

or here: https://www.visa4uk.fco.gov.uk/ if you are outside the UK.

If you are from the USA, go here:

http://www.vfsglobal.co.uk/USA/applicationcentre.html

Where are the visa application centres in my country?

Go to this web page, click on your country and find out: https://www.gov.uk/find-a-visa-application-centre.

What documents must I provide along with my application?

This depends on how your country is categorised. If you are from a low-risk country then you need to provide fewer documents. Low risk countries are: Argentina, Australia, Brunei, Canada, Chile, Croatia, Hong Kong, Japan, New Zealand, Singapore, South Korea, Taiwan, Trinidad and Tobago, United States of America or a British National Overseas.

All others will have to provide the following information:

Passport/Travel document

A recent passport-sized photograph

Confirmation of Acceptance for Studies - CAS

Original certificate(s) or transcript(s) of results for any qualifications used to assess your application to the university

Evidence of your English language ability as stated in your CAS statement

Evidence that you can meet the cost of the tuition fees, maintenance and maintenance of any dependents

A letter from your parents (if you are under 18 years old)

ATAS certificate (if required)

TB screening certificate (if required)

You must submit all original documents along with a photocopy of each. Where a document is not in English or Welsh, the original needs to be accompanied by a fully certified translation that can be independently verified by the UK Home Office. You can find further information on the UKVI website. You are also required to pay £335 as application fee which is non-refundable. You must pay £335 per person for any dependants too. You will also have to pay the healthcare surcharge as part of your application, for yourself and your dependants.

How early can I arrive for my course?

You are allowed to arrive in the UK before your course starts. You can arrive up to 1 week before, if your course lasts 6 months or less and up to 1 month before, if your course lasts more than 6 months.

Can foreign students claim benefits in the UK?

No.

Can foreign students work in the UK?

Yes, for up to 20 hours per week during term time and full time in vacations. This is assuming you are not studying in a private educational institution.

Can a student bring their family members with them?

Your family members (dependants) might be able to apply to join or remain with you in the UK if they are from outside the European Economic Area (EEA) or Switzerland.

A dependant is either your husband, wife or civil partner; your unmarried or same-sex partner; your child under 18 years old - including if they were born in the UK during your stay. You can apply to bring a dependant to the UK if you are sponsored by a higher education institution on a course at level 7 on the Ofqual register or above that lasts 1 year or more

a new government-sponsored student on a course that lasts longer than 6 months

a Doctorate Extension Scheme student

They will also have to pay the healthcare surcharge as part of their application.

You must show that your dependants can be supported while they are in the UK.

Each dependant must have a certain amount of money available to them - this is in addition to the money you must have to support yourself.

The amount of money you need depends on the length of your course, where you're studying in the UK, and whether you've finished a UK course or are currently studying.

If the Tier 4 (General) student is studying on a course based in London you must have at least £845 per month to support yourself; if outside of London, you must have at least £680 per month to support yourself. This is for the duration of the student's leave up to a maximum of 9 months. If you are applying as the dependant of a Tier 4 student who is on the doctorate extension scheme, you will need to demonstrate maintenance for a period of 2 months. For example, a Tier 4 (General) applicant who is applying for leave to study in London at the same time as their spouse and 2 children would need to show that they have £845 per month for their spouse and a further £845 per month for each of their children, in addition to £1265 per month required for their own support. In total the family will require evidence that they hold £3800 in available funds up to a maximum of 9 months (3 x £845 = £2535 + £1265).

You must have proof you have the money, and that it has been in your bank account or your dependant's bank account for at least 28 days before you or they apply.

If your dependants are applying from outside the UK, they must apply online. They will need to have their fingerprints and photograph taken at a visa application centre (to get a biometric residence permit) as part of their application.

If your dependants are applying from inside the UK, you should apply for your dependants' visas at the same time as you extend or switch your own visa. If you can't do it at the same time, your dependants can apply to extend or switch their visas at a later date.

They cannot apply in the UK as dependants if they already have a Standard Visitor visa.

They cannot access public funds.

I am a student, can my spouse work in the UK?

Yes, employment is permitted where the period of leave granted to the student is 12 months or more. If you are the family member of a Tier 4 (General) student, you will not be allowed to work whilst in the UK if the main applicant's grant of leave is for a course of study below degree level, unless the Tier 4 migrant is a government sponsored student.

What about children born in the UK to foreign students?

Children born in the UK to overseas students will be treated as dependents of the student. They do not have any permanent right of abode in the UK. A foreign student will have to apply for their children born in the UK to stay in the UK as dependents. This is necessary if you want to travel in and out of the UK with your child.

Can I extend my student visa?

You can only apply to extend your leave to study if your current sponsor is:

a higher education institute (HEI)

an overseas HEI

an embedded college offering pathway courses

an independent school

You must include your dependants in your application if they're on your current visa, including children who have turned 18 during your stay.

It can be done on the UKVI website (go to the UKVI webpage where it says apply for a Tier 4 student visa). It costs £457 to extend a student visa. Add another £457 per dependent. Remember to apply before your current visa expires. It will be done within 8 weeks for online applications. If your existing visa expires while waiting do not worry, you are fine as long as you applied before your existing visa expired. Ensure you send all the correct documentation to avoid delays.

What are the chances of success of my application for student visa extension?

According to Home Office data, of those who entered in 2008 on a student visa (or as a student's dependent), only 15% still had valid leave to remain in the UK five years later in 2013. In 2014, about 85% of applications for student visa extension (65,900) were accepted, while about 15% (11,100) were rejected.

Can I do further studies in the UK after my present one?

Yes, you can. You must get a Confirmation of Acceptance for Studies (CAS) for the new course you want to study. You can only get a CAS for a new course if you are:

re-sitting exams or repeating modules

applying for the first time to a new institution to complete a course you started at an institution that's lost its Tier 4 sponsorship

applying to complete a PhD or other doctorate that you started studying under your last Tier 4 (General) student visa

studying for a new qualification at a higher academic level

studying for a new qualification at the same level and related to your previous course or career aspirations - it must be degree level or above at a Higher Education Institution (HEI)

applying after working as a student union sabbatical officer to complete a qualification you started studying under your last Tier 4 (General) student visa.

Can I switch from another visa to a student visa?

You can change (switch) to a Tier 4 (General) student visa if you are in the UK under any of the following visas or schemes:

Tier 2 (General)

Tier 2 (Intra-company transfer)

Tier 2 (Minister of religion)

Tier 4 (Child)

You should include any dependants who are on your current visa on your application to extend - including children who have turned 18 during your stay. You must apply within 6 months of getting a confirmation of acceptance for studies (CAS) and before your current visa expires - but no more than 3 months before the course start date on your CAS. You can stay in the UK until you get your decision. You will also need to provide biometric information and pay the healthcare surcharge.

Does the UK government fingerprint foreign students in the UK?

Yes, the move is to stop bogus colleges and bogus students. Overseas students (i.e. students coming to the UK from outside the EU) have to possess biometric identity cards. This also applies to those overseas students already in the UK seeking student visa extensions. This causes delays and difficulties for students already in the UK as their passports get held up with the UKBA for several months on end while their papers are being processed.

How can I prove my knowledge of English as a student?

You can prove your knowledge of English by passing an approved English language test. What level of English you need (in reading, writing, speaking and listening) depends on the course you are studying. The UKVI lays down the following requirements CEFR level B2 for courses at NQF 6/QCF 6/SCQF 9 or above and CEFR level B1 for courses at NQF 3-5/QCF 3-5/SCQF 6-8.

You can also prove your knowledge of English if you have an academic qualification that was taught in a majority English speaking country and is recognised by UK NARIC as being equivalent to a UK bachelor's degree. Your English is OK if you have successfully completed a course as a Tier 4 (Child) student that was at least 6 months long, and that finished less than 2 years before you got your confirmation of acceptance for studies (CAS). If you are considered by your sponsor to be a 'gifted student' that proves your English knowledge as well.

Who are exempt from the English knowledge requirement?

Are foreign students from certain countries exempt from the English knowledge requirement?

You do not need to prove your knowledge of English if you are a national of one of the following countries:

Antigua and Barbuda

Australia

The Bahamas

Barbados

Belize

Canada

Dominica

Grenada

Guyana

Jamaica

New Zealand

St Kitts and Nevis

St Lucia

St Vincent and the Grenadines

Trinidad and Tobago

USA

You do not need to prove your knowledge of English if you have completed a qualification equivalent to a UK degree in:

Antigua and Barbuda

Australia

the Bahamas

Barbados

Belize

Dominica

Grenada

Guyana

Ireland

Jamaica

New Zealand

St Kitts and Nevis

St Lucia

St Vincent and the Grenadines

Trinidad and Tobago

UK

USA

You also don't need to prove your knowledge of English if one of the following apply:

You are a national of Canada or any of the countries in the list above

you have studied in the UK before as a Tier 4 (Child) student

you are applying to come to the UK for a study abroad programme as part of a university degree course in the USA.

What aspects concerning foreign students does the UKVI require universities to monitor?

As part of their duties and responsibilities, a university in the UK is required by the UK Home Office to:

Ensure that you have the correct visa to study at the university on your chosen course.

Not allow you to enrol if you do not have the correct documentation to study here.

Keep copies of your visa documentation and passport (including when you extend your visa).

Keep up to date contact details for you.

Report to the UKVI if you do not enrol on your course.

Monitor your attendance and progression and report to the UKVI if you do not attend or progress from one part of your course to the next.

Notify the UKVI of any changes to your status. For example if you suspend your studies or withdraw from your course, if you change course whilst at university or finish your course earlier than expected.

Report to the UKVI if they suspect that you are breaking the terms and conditions of your visa.

What is a bogus college?

A college that is involved in a systematic attempt to get workers into the UK by helping them pose as students. The government wants to ensure that students in any college can actually speak English, that the courses are credible and that the college management are meeting immigration and visa obligations. The government is worried that there are many institutions offering international students an immigration service rather than an education and that many students come to the UK with the aim of getting work and bringing over family members.

What are the prospects for medical training in the NHS?

More than 95,000 foreign-trained doctors work in the UK. They make up about 25% of the total number of doctors. As a junior doctor you need to be trained in the UK in order to progress towards becoming a GP or a Consultant. There are about 9,000 training places in the UK and competition is intense with both British as well as a large number of foreign doctors competing. UK medical graduates and foreign doctors will be competing on equal terms as the courts have decided that giving local doctors priority is unfair. Some specialities such as 'surgery' attract about 10 applications per post.

I am an overseas student. Do I need to register with the police in the UK?

Not unless it requires you to do so on your student visa. If it does, you can do so through your university. In 2012 a change of rules meant that overseas students no longer have to register in person with the police. This change was brought in after thousands of overseas students from different countries queued all through the night in London in order to meet the registration deadline. This caused much embarrassment to the authorities and damaged the UK's reputation as a welcoming destination for overseas students.

Can I stay back in the UK after my studies?

For non-EEA students, it is possible to move from a student visa to a work visa. The rules require the applicant to have a graduate level job, with a graduate salary (a minimum of £20,800) with a licensed Home Office employer.

All foreign graduates from UK universities can remain in the UK after their studies if they get a graduate level job.

The possible visa options for the post-study work route:

- Tier 4 Doctorate Extension Scheme PhD students are allowed to stay on after their studies for up to a year and work in the UK (see Doctorate Extension Scheme on UKVI website).

- Tier 2 General- the standard work visa.

- Tier 1 Graduate Entrepreneur Scheme. Those who have studied for an MBA can apply to stay in the UK for a year after graduating under the Graduate Entrepreneur scheme which allows up to 1,000 foreign MBA graduates from British universities to do so. These graduates will be able to develop their own business idea, or work in a start-up, after which they will have the option to stay on in the UK as a skilled worker or entrepreneur.

- Tier 5 Youth Mobility Scheme. You can apply for a Tier 5 (Youth Mobility Scheme) visa if you're aged 18 to 30 and you are from:

Australia, Canada, Japan, Monaco, New Zealand, Hong Kong, Republic of Korea, or Taiwan.

- UK Ancestry Visa. Apply for a UK Ancestry visa if you are a Commonwealth citizen and can prove that one of your grandparents was born in the UK.

- Tier 5 Government Authorised Exchange visa if you: want to come to the UK for a short time for work experience or to do training, an Overseas Government Language Programme, research or a fellowship through an approved government authorised exchange scheme.

The government is concerned that abuse of the post-study work visa system is taking place by those wanting to settle down permanently in the UK. The entrepreneur route was intended to allow migrants to set up businesses in the UK in order to create jobs and growth. However, the government has found evidence from tax records that people on expiring student visas are transferring to entrepreneur status under the pretence of setting up a business when they are actually working in low skilled jobs.

To prevent abuse, students will now only be able to switch visas using funds from a government-approved source, and post-study workers will need additional evidence of their business activities. In addition, those who have not yet started businesses and who do not have evidence of a genuine business will not be able to switch from the old post-study route onto an entrepreneur visa.

Is a sponsor's permission required for student visa extensions?

An application for a variation of leave to enter or remain made by a student who is sponsored by a government or international sponsorship agency may be refused if the sponsor has not given written consent to the proposed variation.

I have a student visa, can I settle permanently in the UK?

Yes, you can apply as the partner of a British citizen or person settled in the UK. You may be eligible for settlement if your partner is a British citizen or a person settled in the UK. You must be able to prove one of the following you are married or you are in a civil partnership or you have been in a relationship for 2 years. You and your partner must intend to continue your relationship after you apply for settlement.

You need to have been living in the UK with a 'partner of a settled person' visa for 5 years or 10 years if you applied for your visa on or after 9 July 2012. Read the guidance below in the section entitled 'family/partner route to settlement' in this book for advice on the 5 and 10-year routes.

If you are 18 to 64 years old when you apply you must also pass the Life in the UK Test and an English language test.

Your application might be refused if, for example, you have a criminal record in the UK or another country, provided false or incomplete information to the Home Office or broken UK immigration law.

According to Home Office data in 2015, only 1% of student visa holders had received indefinite leave to remain.

WORKING IN THE UK

I want to work in the UK, how do I go about it?

Assuming you are non-EEA, you have to first choose the category under which you fit. If you are a sportsperson/entertainer /businessperson on a short visit, then you can come to the UK as a visitor. As a visitor, you are normally allowed to stay for a maximum of 6 months. If you want to stay longer than 6 months, you cannot come as a visitor.

If you are a skilled person and if you have a job offer and your prospective employer is willing to sponsor you, then you can apply to come or remain in the UK. You must pass a points-based assessment to be accepted. If you do not have a job offer, but you are an investor/entrepreneur/exceptionally talented/ you can apply to enter or stay in the UK - but you will still need to pass a points-based assessment.

Outside the points based system, there are a few categories of workers that can work in the UK: ·domestic workers; sole representatives of an overseas firm or representatives of an overseas newspaper, news agency or broadcasting organisation.

Foreign doctors wanting to take the Performance and Linguistic Assessments Board (PLAB) test must apply as a business visitor. They must be a graduate from a genuine medical school; intend to take the PLAB test in the UK; and provide documentary evidence of a confirmed test date or of their eligibility to take the PLAB test.

Postgraduate doctors or dentists should apply as a student under Tier 4 (General) of the points-based system.

What is a Skilled worker visa?

A 'skilled worker' visa may be suitable if you have been offered a skilled job in the UK, or role in your overseas employer's UK branch - the visa you apply for depends on your circumstances, a job in a religious community or a job as an elite sportsperson or coach. You can apply for a Tier 2 (General) visa if you've been offered a skilled job in the UK.

What is a Temporary worker visa?

A 'temporary worker' visa may be suitable if you want work in the UK for a short time in sports, in arts or entertainment, as a volunteer, in a work experience role, for a charity or for a religious organisation. You can also apply for an international agreement visa if you will be doing work covered by international law while in the UK (e.g. working for a foreign government or as a private servant in a diplomatic household).

What is a High-value worker visa?

A 'high value worker' visa may be suitable if you are an investor, an entrepreneur, a graduate entrepreneur, a leader in arts or sciences.

What are the prospects for doctors wishing to work in the UK?

Foreign doctors used to come to work in the UK under the Highly Skilled Migrant Programme, and they made up at least 50% of the applicants for training places in the UK. This category has now closed. They should now apply as a highly skilled worker (Tier 2 General) under the points-based system.

The UK Department of Health is concerned whether the British taxpayer must pay for the training of foreign doctors (£250,000 for every place), or whether some of these places must be reserved for British medical graduates.

Foreign doctors in the UK are to face a more rigorous assessment, after figures showed a high proportion of doctors who are disciplined are from overseas. During 2008-13, 63% of doctors either struck off or suspended by the General Medical Council (GMC) were trained outside the UK. Yet they make up only 36% of doctors on the medical register. The GMC plans new reforms including an induction programme, better checks and a review of the present testing system.

In June 2018 it was announced that doctors and nurses would be excluded from the 20,700 cap on skilled worker visas. There would be no restriction on the numbers of doctors and nurses who can be employed through the Tier 2 visa route. This decision was due to demand from the NHS, which accounts for around 40% of all Tier 2 places.

Are there special visa arrangements for young people to live, work and study in the UK?

Yes, you could try the Youth Mobility Scheme visa. This two-year visa is for people aged 18-30 from the following countries:

Australia

Canada

Japan

Monaco

New Zealand

Hong Kong

Republic of Korea

Taiwan.

You cannot apply if you have children who live with you or children you are financially responsible for or if you have already been in the UK under the scheme.

You cannot bring family members on your application, they must apply separately. You must have £1,890 in savings. You can enter the UK at any time while your visa is valid, and leave and come back at any time during your stay. You can work and study.

You cannot work as a professional sportsperson (e.g. as a coach), doctor or dentist in training - unless you can show you qualified in the UK, or extend your stay in the UK or get public funds (i.e. benefits). It costs £235 to apply. You must pay the healthcare surcharge.

Citizens of Hong Kong and the Republic of Korea must get a certificate of sponsorship reference number before they apply. A certificate of sponsorship is a unique reference number that holds information about the job you will do and your personal details. It's not a certificate or paper document.

Employees of which organisations can work in the UK without visa control?

Employees of international organisations like the following are exempt from visa control: African Development Bank; African Development Fund; Asian Development Bank; Commonwealth Secretariat; European Commission; European Community; European Coal and Steel Community; European Parliament; European Union; Food and Agricultural Organisation (FAO)*; International Atomic Energy Agency (IAEA); International Bank for Reconstruction and Development (IBRD); International Civil Aviation Organisation (ICAO)*; International Labour Organisation (ILO)*; International Lead and Zinc Study Group; International Monetary Fund; International Maritime Organisation (IMO); International Telecommunications Union (ITU)*; North Atlantic Treaty Organisation (NATO); Organisation for Economic Cooperation and Development (OECD); United Nations (UN); Universal Postal Union (UPU)*; Western European Union (WEU); World Health Organisation (WHO)*; World Intellectual Property Organisation (WIPO)*; World Meteorological Organisation (WMO)*; World Trade Organisation (WTO).

* senior employees only

What is an exempt vignette?

An exempt vignette is like a residence permit. It is for those who don't normally need a visa to work in the UK because they are exempt from immigration control. It can help avoid delays when they enter the UK. Applications are free. Applicants must provide evidence that they are coming to the UK as part of their job (if relevant), e.g. a letter from a UK or foreign ministry.

You can apply if you are:

a diplomat, or working for a diplomatic mission in the UK, and you were outside the UK when offered the post

an overseas government minister on official business, or travelling with one as part of your job

a member of Commonwealth or Overseas Territories armed forces posted in the UK or training in the UK

a head of state, or working for a head of state (e.g. on a state visit)

exempt from immigration control for any other reason

Some family members might also be able to get an exempt vignette.

What are the other ways in which one can work in the UK legally?

If you are the sole representative of an overseas company planning to set up a UK branch or a wholly owned subsidiary for an overseas parent company, or an employee of an overseas newspaper, news agency or broadcasting organisation posted on a long-term assignment to the UK then you can work in the UK legally.

You must apply from outside the EEA; have enough money to support yourself without help from public funds; and meet the English requirement.

What are the rules for sole representatives of an overseas company?

As a sole representative in the UK of an overseas company you must be recruited and employed outside the UK by a company whose headquarters and principal place of business are outside the UK; have extensive related industry experience and knowledge; hold a senior position within the company (but not be a major shareholder) and have full authority to make decisions on its behalf; and intend to establish the company's first commercial presence in the UK.

You may also be eligible if the company has a legal entity in the UK that does not employ staff or transact business. If your company has been working to establish a UK branch or subsidiary, but it is not yet set up, you can replace a previous sole representative.

What are the rules for newspaper, news agency or broadcast employees?

As an employee of an overseas newspaper, news agency or broadcasting organisation, you can come to the UK if you are being posted here on a long-term assignment.

What visa is available to undertake training and work experience in the UK?

The Tier 5 GAE (Temporary Worker - Government Authorised Exchange) is the principal visa route by which non-EEA nationals can undertake training and work experience in the UK. The route allows individuals entering the UK through this scheme to stay for up to 2 years. It is part of the new 'UKRI Science, Research and Academia' scheme, which allows non-EEA researchers, scientists and academics to work in the UK. It is operated by UK Research and Innovation (UKRI) and they, along with 12 approved research organisations, such as the Natural History Museum, will directly sponsor highly skilled individuals, such as specialist technicians, to work and train in the UK.

How do I prove my knowledge of English to work in the UK?

You can prove your knowledge of English by either passing an approved English language test with at least CEFR level A1 in reading, writing, speaking and listening; or by having an academic qualification that was taught in English and is recognised by UK NARIC as being equivalent to a UK bachelor's degree.

UK NARIC is the National Agency responsible for providing information, advice and opinion on vocational, academic and professional skills and qualifications from all over the world. Their web address is here: https://www.naric.org.uk/naric.

Are foreign workers from certain countries exempt from the English language requirement?

You will not need to prove your knowledge of English if you are a national of one of the following countries:

Antigua and Barbuda

Australia

the Bahamas

Barbados

Belize

Canada

Dominica

Grenada

Guyana

Jamaica

New Zealand

St Kitts and Nevis

St Lucia

St Vincent and the Grenadines

Trinidad and Tobago

USA.

What is the Tier 1 Entrepreneur visa?

A Tier 1 (Entrepreneur) visa is a visa for those (non-EEA persons) who want to set up or run a business in the UK. They must have access to at least £50,000 investment funds to apply. An online/postal application costs £1228. They will also have to pay the healthcare surcharge (£200).

They can come to the UK with a Tier 1 (Entrepreneur) visa for a maximum of 3 years and 4 months. They can apply to extend this visa for another 2 years if they were already in this category and 3 years if switching to it from another category. They may be able to apply for permanent settlement once they have been in the UK for 5 years.

They can set up or take over the running of one business or more; work for their own business, including being self-employed, but they should check their work meets the conditions of being self-employed. They can bring family members with them.

They cannot do any work outside their business, e.g. work where they are employed by another business or get public funds.

What is the Tier 1 (Exceptional Talent) visa?

A Tier 1 (Exceptional Talent) visa is for those ((non-EEA persons) who have been endorsed as an internationally recognised leader or emerging leader in their field in science, humanities, engineering, medicine, digital technology or the arts. They first need to apply to the Home Office for endorsement as a leader or an emerging leader in the particular field and then apply for the visa.

An application for endorsement is considered by Arts Council England; British Academy; Royal Academy of Engineering; Royal Society; or Tech City UK. There are 2000 visas available under this category. 1,000 visas are split between the 5 endorsing organisations. Additional places will be made available across all of the endorsing bodies dependent on need. In June 2018, the exceptional talent visa was widened to include leading fashion designers. They will have their application assessed by the British Fashion Council under the endorsement remit of Arts Council England (ACE), one of the existing 5 endorsing bodies on that route. This route has also been opened up to a wider pool of TV and film applicants, under the remit of ACE, thanks to changes to the list of eligible industry awards and how recently applicants must have won or been nominated for them.

Holders of this visa can stay in the UK for up to 5 years and 4 months if they apply outside the UK or 5 years if they apply inside the UK. They can apply to extend this visa for another 5 years.

They can do voluntary work; travel abroad and return to the UK; and bring family members. They cannot get public funds; work as a doctor or dentist in training or work as a professional sportsperson or sports coach.

What is a Tier 1 (Graduate Entrepreneur) visa?

A Tier 1 (Graduate Entrepreneur) visa is for graduates who have been officially endorsed as having a genuine and credible business idea. They must be endorsed by either the UK Trade and Investment (UKTI) as part of the elite global graduate entrepreneur programme (Sirius) or their current UK higher education institution (HEI) if it is an authorised endorsing body. They can stay in the UK for 1 year on a Tier 1 (Graduate Entrepreneur) visa and can apply to extend this visa for 1 more year.

They can bring family members; extend their stay in the UK using this visa; and switch into this visa from some other visa categories. They cannot get public funds; work as a doctor or dentist in training; work as a professional sportsperson, e.g. a sports coach; or settle in the UK on this visa.

Applicants must hold a UK-recognised bachelor's degree, master's degree or PhD awarded before their date of endorsement and hold an endorsement from an authorised UK higher education institution issued in the past 3 months; and have £945 in savings if applying from inside the UK, or £1,890 if applying from outside the UK - this is to prove they can support themselves and they must have had this in their bank account for 90 days before they apply; and meet the English language requirement; and have permission to remain in the UK from their financial sponsor if they're a government or an international scholarship agency and have paid their course fees and living costs in the past 12 months.

Applicants with the any of the following will not be considered: foundation degrees; honorary degrees; qualifications awarded in the UK by overseas awarding bodies; qualifications undertaken at overseas campuses of UK institutions; professional and vocational qualifications; postgraduate certificates or diplomas.

For endorsement by UK Trade and Investment (UKTI) applicants need all of the following to be eligible:

- a degree qualification that is recognised as being equal to a UK bachelor's degree
- to meet the criteria set by UKTI
- endorsement from UKTI issued in the past 3 months
- £945 in savings if applying from inside the UK or £1,890 if applying from outside the UK
- to meet the English language requirement

What is a Tier 1 (Investor) visa?

To begin with, you need £2 million to apply for a Tier 1 Investor visa. This is for a maximum of 3 years and 4 months. You can apply to extend this visa for another 2 years. This £2 million must be invested in UK government bonds, share capital or loan capital in active and trading UK registered companies. You can work or study and apply to settle after 2 years if you invest £10 million or you can apply to settle after 3 years if you invest £5 million.

You are not allowed to invest in companies mainly engaged in property investment, property management or property development or work as a professional sportsperson or sports coach or get public funds.

It costs £1561 per person to apply for this visa. You have to pay the healthcare surcharge (£200) as part of your application.

You cannot work as a doctor or dentist in training unless one of the following applies:

- you have a primary degree at bachelors level or above in medicine or dentistry from a UK institution that holds a Tier 4 sponsor license or is a UK recognised or listed body

- you worked as a doctor or dentist in training the last time you were in the UK

- neither of those conditions were part of the terms and conditions on a previous visa

You must be 18 or over to apply for this visa; be able to prove that the money belongs to either you or your husband, wife, unmarried or same-sex partner; and have opened a UK bank account.

Your funds must be held in one or more regulated financial institutions; and free to spend in the UK. Your money can be in the UK or overseas when you apply.

You will need to provide evidence showing that you have the required investment funds.

If you are using your own money to invest, you should be able to show:

- how much money you have and where it's being held

- where the money came from if you haven't had the money for at least 3 months, e.g. you inherited it from a relative

- that the money can be transferred to the UK and converted to sterling (if it's not already in the UK)

If using your partner's money, you will need to provide:

- a certificate of marriage or civil partnership, or in the case of unmarried or same-sex relationships, proof that you are in a long-term relationship (at least 2 years)

- a statement from your partner confirming that they will allow you to control the funds in the UK

- a letter from a legal adviser stating that the declaration is valid

You will need to provide a certified translation of any documents that are not in English or Welsh. In 2017, UKVI issued 355 such visas, up 56% from 2016.

What is a Tier 2 (General) visa

You can apply for a Tier 2 (General) visa if you have been offered a skilled job in the UK. You need to be sponsored (i.e. have a certificate of sponsorship from a licensed sponsor) before you can apply to come to the UK to work. The work you do in the UK must relate to the work of your sponsor organisation. It costs £610 per person to apply for this visa from outside the UK. This will be for up to three years.

You can come to the UK with a Tier 2 (General) visa for a maximum of 5 years and 14 days, or the time given on your certificate of sponsorship plus 1 month, whichever is shorter. You can apply to extend this visa for up to another 5 years, as long as your total stay is not more than 6 years. You will also have to pay the healthcare surcharge as part of your application.

You can

- work for your sponsor in the job described in your certificate of sponsorship
- do a second job in the same sector and at the same level as your main job for up to 20 hours per week
- do a job which has a shortage of workers in the UK for up to 20 hours per week
- do voluntary work
- study as long as it doesn't interfere with the job you are sponsored for
- travel abroad and return to the UK
- bring family members with you

You cannot:

- own more than 10% of your sponsor's shares (unless you earn more than £159,600 a year)
- get public funds
- start working before you get the visa
- apply for a second job until you've started working for your sponsor

You will need to make a new application if you want to do a second job that is not in the same sector as your main job.

You must have all of the following to be eligible for a Tier 2 (General) visa:

- a certificate of sponsorship reference number
- an 'appropriate' salary, usually £30,000 per year.
- the required level of English
- You must also have £945 in savings - this is to prove you can support yourself. You must have had this in your bank account for 90 days before you apply, unless you are exempt.

A certificate of sponsorship is a reference number which holds information about the job and your personal details. It is not an actual certificate or paper document. Your sponsor will give you your certificate of sponsorship reference number.

What is the register of licensed sponsors?

This is a pdf document of 1940 pages. It lists Tier 2 and 5 sponsors. It includes information about the category of workers they are licensed to sponsor and their sponsorship rating. It is available here:

https://www.gov.uk/government/publications/register-of-licensed-sponsors-workers

What is a Tier 2 (Intra-company Transfer) visa

You can apply for a Tier 2 (Intra-company Transfer) visa if your overseas employer has offered you a role in a UK branch of the organisation.

You need to be sponsored – i.e. have a certificate of sponsorship from a licensed sponsor - before you can apply to come to the UK to work. The work you do in the UK must relate to the work of your sponsor organisation.

There are 3 types of Intra-company Transfer visa.

Long-term Staff: This visa is for transfers of more than 12 months into a role that cannot be filled by a new UK recruit. You'll need to have worked for your company for more than 12 months, unless they're going to pay you £73,900 or more a year to work in the UK.

Short-term Staff: You can only apply for this type of visa if your certificate of sponsorship was assigned to you on or before 5 April 2017. Employers cannot give new certificates of sponsorship for this type of visa because it is now closed.

Graduate Trainee: This visa is for transfers into graduate trainee programmes for specialist roles. You need to be a recent graduate with at least 3 months' experience with your employer overseas.

You can

work for your sponsor in the job described in your certificate of sponsorship

do a second job in the same profession and at the same level as your main job for up to 20 hours per week

do voluntary work

study as long as it doesn't interfere with the job you're sponsored for

travel abroad and return to the UK

bring family members with you

You cannot:

get public funds

start working before you get a visa

You must have all of the following to be eligible for a Tier 2 (Intra-company Transfer) visa:

- certificate of sponsorship reference number
- an 'appropriate' salary
- £945 in savings - this is to prove you can support yourself and you must have had this in your bank account for 90 days before you apply

You must earn one of the following:

- Long-term Staff applicants - at least £41,500 or the 'appropriate rate' for the role (whichever is higher)
- Short-term Staff, - at least £30,000 or the 'appropriate rate' (whichever is higher). In November 2016, UKVI reduced the Tier 2 (Intra-Company Transfer) graduate trainee salary threshold to £23,000 and increased the number of places to 20 per company per year

- staff already in the UK on a Tier 2 (Intra-company Transfer) visa or work permit issued before 6 April 2011 - at least the 'appropriate rate'.

You can come to the UK with a Tier 2 (Intra-company Transfer) visa for up to the maximum stay allowed for your visa type, or the time given on your certificate of sponsorship plus one month, whichever is shorter.

The maximum stay for each type of Tier 2 (Intra-company Transfer) visa is:

Long-term Staff (if you earn more than £120,000 a year): 9 years

Long-term Staff (if you earn less than £120,000 a year): 5 years, 1 month

Graduate Trainee: 12 months

Short-term Staff: 12 months.

What is the UK Shortage Occupation List?

It is a list of jobs for which there is a shortage of workers in the UK. It is called The official Shortage Occupation List (SOL) for Tier 2 of the Points-Based System. There is one list covering the whole of the UK and an additional list for Scotland. To qualify under the Scotland list, the job must be based in Scotland. The present scheme for highly-skilled non-EEA migrants - known as the Tier 2 visa - allows 20,700 high-skilled workers into the UK each year. The current salary threshold for such visas is £30,000, and top priority is given to jobs on the Shortage Occupation List.

The following jobs fall under this category:

Production managers and directors in mining and energy

Physical Scientists

Civil engineers

Mechanical engineers

Electrical engineers

Electronics Engineers

Design and development engineers

Production and process engineers

Business analysts, architects and systems designers

Programmers and software development professionals

Environmental professionals

Medical practitioners

Medical Radiographers

Neurophysiology healthcare scientist, neurophysiology practitioner, nuclear medicine scientist

Orthotists; prosthetist

Consultant in clinical oncology; non-consultant, non-training, medical staff post in clinical radiology; CT3 trainee and ST4 to ST7 trainee in clinical radiology; all grades except CPT1in psychiatry; all grades in anaesthetics, paediatrics, obstetrics and gynaecology;

Specialist nurse working in neonatal intensive care units.

Secondary education teaching professionals: secondary education teachers in the subjects of maths and science (chemistry and physics only)

Actuaries, economists and statisticians

Social workers working in children's and family services

Quality control and planning engineers

Commissioning engineer; substation electrical engineer

Paramedics

Animator in visual effects and 2D/3D computer animation for the film, television or video games sectors

Dancers and choreographers

Arts officers, producers and director

Graphic designers

Manufacturing engineer (purchasing) in the aerospace industry

Welding trades

Aircraft Maintenance and related trades

Line repairers and cable jointers

Chefs

Physical scientists

The full list is available here:

https://www.gov.uk/guidance/immigration-rules/immigration-rules-appendix-k-shortage-occupation-list

If a job is placed in the SOL it means there is:

- No need to advertise the job to UK workers

- No need to meet the £35,800 salary threshold for settlement after five years

- Lower visa application fees for workers and their families

If the skilled labour cap of 20,700 is reached then occupations on the SOL are given priority.

HOW TO SECURE UK PERMANENT RESIDENCE

What is 'right of abode' in the UK?

'Right of abode' means the right to live and work in the UK without visa restrictions. It is also called "permanent residence" or "permanent settlement" or "indefinite leave to remain/enter (ILR/ILE)" in the UK. All British citizens have the right of abode in the UK. However, not all permanent residents are British citizens. Many permanent residents may still be citizens of a foreign country while having the right of abode in the UK.

Is there a checking service for UK settlement applications?

A list of local authorities in Greater London that offer a checking service for UK settlement applications is available here:

https://www.gov.uk/government/publications/settlement-checking-service-greater-london/greater-london-settlement-checking-services

I have ILR/ILE but do not have a document to prove it

If you have ILR or ILE but do not have a document to prove it, you can make a no time limit (NTL) application for confirmation of your status in the form of a biometric residence permit (BRP – see section on this topic earlier in this book). You can apply for NTL if your passport containing your status or previous NTL endorsement has been lost, stolen or has expired; you have ILR or ILE but you do not have any documentary evidence confirming this; you have legitimately changed your identity since being granted indefinite leave and want this confirmed on a BRP.

What are the benefits of having UK ILR/ILE?

You can work in the UK; access free healthcare in the UK; vote in an election and referendum; study in the UK; get a UK state pension (after 10 years of UK National Insurance contributions). Other benefits: your children born in the UK after you have ILR become British citizens automatically; your family members who are not British citizens may be able to join you in the UK.

What are the different routes to UK permanent residence?

Settling down in Britain is one of the most important questions that concern foreigners. On the question of settling down in Britain permanently, there are 14 main routes.

THE 14 ROUTES TO UK PERMANENT RESIDENCE

Family member/partner of a British citizen route

Family member/partner of a British permanent resident route

The work visa route

The UK ancestry route

The retired person route

The returning resident route

The discretionary leave route

The armed forces route

The 10-year private life route

The legal long residence route

The illegal long residence route

Through your child route

The investor route

The asylum route

THE FAMILY/PARTNER ROUTE TO SETTLEMENT

Who is a partner?

Partners are 2 people in a genuine relationship - you must be able to prove one of the following: you're married or you're in a civil partnership or you've been in a relationship for 2 years. You and your partner must intend to continue your relationship after you apply for settlement.

My partner is British/a permanent UK resident. Can I apply to settle permanently in the UK?

Yes, but first, you must be able to prove one of the following: you are married or you are in a civil partnership; and that you have been in a relationship for 2 years (for pre-2012 applicants). For others it is 5 or 10 years depending on your case. In 2012, there was a policy change which extended the time required before applying for settlement as a spouse or civil partner from 2 years to 5 years.

You and your partner must intend to continue your relationship after you apply for settlement. You need to have been living in the UK with a 'partner of a settled person' visa for 5 years or 10 years if you applied for your visa on or after 9 July 2012. The 5-year route as a partner or parent is for those who meet all of the suitability and eligibility requirements of the Immigration Rules at every stage.

Applications for leave on the 5-year routes to settlement can be made from outside the UK or in the UK. Applications for leave on the 10-year routes to settlement cannot be made from outside the UK. There is no financial requirement if you applied for your partner visa on the 10-year route (see 'minimum salary' question below).

Applicants must also pass the Life in the UK Test and an English language test. Applications might be refused if the applicant has a criminal record in the UK or another country; provided false or incomplete information to the Home Office; or broken UK immigration law. This visa costs £2297 per person if you apply by post. An applicant on a 5-year route as a partner will be eligible to apply for indefinite leave to remain (settlement) after a continuous period of 60 months (5 years).

Is there a loophole to bypass the minimum earnings requirement?

Since 2012, British citizens who wish to bring a non-EU partner to the UK to live with them must earn more than £18,600 a year. The **Surinder Singh route** is a loophole by which couples/families can avoid this minimum earnings requirement by moving to another EU state for a minimum of three months, have their partner join them and then move to the UK together under the EU's free movement laws. Relevant evidence concerning the sponsor's activity in the other EEA state must be provided with their application. This loophole arose because EU nationals are protected by EU law and not subject to the same restrictions as UK nationals. They can bring non-EEA spouses to the UK with no conditions attached. Sad but true: EEA citizens have stronger migration rights than UK citizens, since they can bring in family members from outside Europe in this way. Each year about 20,000 non-European family members come into the UK using this route. This route is completely legitimate at present but will become irrelevant when Britain leaves the EU, as she will then not be subject to EU law.

A British national goes to another EU member state purely to exercise an economic Treaty right so that they can come back to the UK with their family members. However, be warned: An application under this route can be refused if it cannot be proved the British citizen was genuinely engaged in employment.

Many UK nationals have turned to scamsters to abuse the UK immigration system and bring in non-EEA spouses illegally. The fraudsters they turn to often charge thousands of pounds to create a fake life so it looks like someone has genuinely moved to a European country (usually Ireland) while in fact they have stayed in the UK.

UKVI has moved to curb abuse of this loophole by British citizens. UKVI will now scrutinise the applicant's period of residence in another EEA member state as a worker or self-employed person; try to find out the location of the British citizen's principal residence; and test the degree of integration of the British citizen in the host member state. UKVI introduced new regulations in December 2016 which allows them to remove any individuals who abuse the system and ban them from re-entering the UK for 10 years.

What are the other ways to bypass/make up the minimum earnings requirement?

Applicants who have cash savings can make up for a shortage in earnings if the cash savings are at least £16,000 plus 2.5 times the difference. People without income can also qualify if they have cash savings of at least £62,500.

UK sponsors who are receiving certain disability-related benefits are exempt from the £18,600 threshold. The £18,600 threshold also does not apply to EEA citizens, whose free movement rights under European law allow them to bring non-EEA spouses with them.

UK citizens living in London are more likely to earn enough to sponsor a non-EEA partner. This is because salaries are higher in London than in other parts of the UK.

Can my non-EEA spouse's foreign income be used to calculate our family income?

No. The non-UK partner cannot count their income towards the threshold if they are working abroad, because they may stop working after they come to the UK. The £18,600 income threshold is based only on the income of the UK sponsor.

What is the difference between the parent route and the partner route to settlement?

The partner route is for couples with a child together who are in a genuine and ongoing relationship. If the relationship between the parents is broken down, then applicants in this position must apply under the parent route. An applicant cannot apply under the parent route if they are eligible to apply under the partner route. The parent route is for single parent applicants.

On what grounds are single-parent applications for settlement considered?

Single parent applications (assuming a broken parental relationship) for settlement can be made if

· the applicant has sole parental responsibility for their child; or

· the applicant does not live with the child (who lives with a British or settled parent or carer), but they have direct access (in person) to the child, as agreed with the parent or carer with whom the child normally lives, or as ordered by a court in the UK; or

· the applicant is the parent with whom the child normally lives, rather than the child's other parent who is British or settled.

Can a stepfather/mother be treated as a parent according to the immigration rules?

Yes, stepfather or stepmother as well as adoptive parents or those having parental responsibility are treated as parents.

I have a visitor visa, can I settle in the UK permanently?

Yes, you can apply as the partner of a British citizen or person settled in the UK. You may be eligible for settlement if your partner is a British citizen or a person settled in the UK. You must be able to prove one of the following you are married or you are in a civil partnership or you have been in a relationship for 2 years. You and your partner must intend to continue your relationship after you apply for settlement.

You need to have been living in the UK with a 'partner of a settled person' visa for 5 years or 10 years if you applied for your visa on or after 9 July 2012. Read the guidance below for the 5 and 10-year routes. If you are 18 to 64 years old when you apply you must also pass the Life in the UK Test and an English language test.

Your application might be refused if, for example, you have a criminal record in the UK or another country, provided false or incomplete information to the Home Office or broken UK immigration law.

What is the difference between the 5 year and 10 year family route to settlement?

There are two major differences: The 10-year route as a partner or parent is only applicable to in-country applications (you must be in the UK to apply). The 10 year route provides the basis on which an applicant in the UK who does not meet all of the eligibility requirements of the 5-year partner or parent route can qualify for leave to remain under the Rules on the basis of their family life in the UK.

I have been abroad during my 5/10 year period, is that a problem for settlement?

In applications for further limited leave to remain or for indefinite leave to remain in the UK as a partner, where there have been limited periods of time spent outside the UK, this must be for good reasons and the reasons must be consistent with the intention to live together permanently in the UK. Good reasons could include time spent in connection with the applicant's or their partner's employment, holidays, training or study.

If the couple have spent the majority of the period overseas, there may be reason to doubt that all the requirements of the Rules have been met, e.g. that the couple intend to live together permanently in the UK.

Will the Home Office revoke ILR granted due to too much time spent abroad?

Yes, the Home Office can revoke Indefinite Leave to Remain granted, if the applicant spends more than two years abroad.

My late partner was a British citizen/permanent resident, can I permanently settle in the UK?

Yes, you can apply to settle in the UK if your partner died and they had 'indefinite leave to remain' in the UK (or your partner was a British citizen) and you were their dependant. Your 'partner' could be your spouse, civil partner or someone you are/were living with in a relationship that is like a marriage or civil partnership.

You must have been in a genuine relationship with your partner and intended to live permanently with each other in the UK at the time of their death. Any children of the relationship under 18 can also apply as dependants.

Your partner must have been 'present and settled' in the UK at the time of their death, i.e. not living permanently in another country. You can apply any time after your partner's death. Download and fill in the SET(O) form and send it to the address on the form.

How can I get right of abode in the UK through my parents?

You can have right of abode through your parents if all the following conditions apply to you:

• one of your parents was born in the UK and a citizen of the United Kingdom and colonies when you were born or adopted

• you were a Commonwealth citizen on 31 December 1982 and continue to be so.

How can I get right of abode in the UK through marriage?

Only women who are Commonwealth citizens can get right of abode through marriage. You must have been married to someone with right of abode before 1 January 1983 and who was and continued to be a Commonwealth citizen on and after 31 December 1982. The person you were married to must not have another living wife or widow who is in the UK.

I am the partner of a work visa holder (tier 1,2 or 5); can I apply to settle in the UK?

You may be eligible for settlement ('indefinite leave to remain') as the partner or child of a person who's already settled using:

any tier 1 visa except Tier 1 (Graduate Entrepreneur) or Tier 1 (Post-Study Work)

a tier 2 visa

a Tier 5 (International Agreement) visa

If your partner or parent settled in another way, for example because they'd been in the UK for 10 years ('Long Residence'), you can't settle because of their work visa. You'll need to apply to stay in the UK with a person settled in the UK. Use form SET(O).

I am the partner of a work visa holder (not Tier 1, 2 or 5); can I apply to settle in the UK?

Yes, you may be eligible for settlement as the partner or child of a person who's already settled in the UK and they settled because the last permission they held was:

UK Ancestry

Work Permit

Highly Skilled Migrant Programme

Representative of an Overseas Company

Investor

Innovator

Businessperson

Self-Employed Lawyer

Domestic Worker in a Private Household given before 6 April 2012

Minister of Religion.

Use form SET(O).

UK SETTLEMENT THROUGH YOUR CHILD

How can I get UK permanent residence through my child?

Section 55 of the Borders, Citizenship and Immigration Act 2009 requires UKVI to have regard to the need to safeguard and promote the welfare of children who are in the UK. This means that consideration of a child's best interests is a primary consideration in immigration cases.

The UK authorities tend to grant permanent residence to applicants who can prove that they have lived in the UK legally for seven years and *throughout* this period, a child of theirs has lived with them.

It is essential that the child has not been away from the UK for more than two months at a time during this period and any absences have been infrequent and finally the applicant must prove that they have lost ties with their home country. This is done to protect the child's human rights because it would be unfair to send back a child who has become accustomed to living in the UK after over seven years of continuous legal residence.

What kind of evidence brings success to those seeking settlement through children?

You must prove that there are exceptional circumstances that warrant a grant of leave (permission) outside the Immigration Rules. UKVI will carefully assess the quality of any evidence provided. It is best to provide original, documentary evidence from official or independent sources, as these will be given more weight in the decision-making process than unsubstantiated assertions about a child's best interests.

What are the two routes for this visa?

There are two routes:

1. Family life as a parent (5-year route). Your child must be a British citizen or settled in the UK. You must meet the eligibility requirements for the parent routes and you must also be able to prove that: you have enough money to adequately support and accommodate you and your dependants without relying on public funds; you have good knowledge of English if you're 18 or over;

2. Family life as a parent (10-year route). You can also apply in this route if the child has lived in the UK continuously for at least 7 years. You must meet the eligibility requirements for the parent routes. You must also prove that it wouldn't be in the child's best interests to leave the UK with you.

You can apply using the form FLR (O).

SETTLEMENT AS A COMMONWEALTH CITIZEN

I am a Commonwealth citizen can I get UK permanent residence?

You must first prove that you have UK right of abode by producing a certificate of entitlement issued by the Government of the UK certifying that you have right of abode.

However, a Commonwealth citizen who has been given a limited visa to enter the UK may also later claim UK permanent residence if he can show that

(i) immediately before the commencement of the British Nationality Act 1981 he was a Commonwealth citizen born to or legally adopted by a parent who at the time of the birth had citizenship of the United Kingdom and Colonies by his birth in the United Kingdom or any of the Islands; and

(ii) he has not ceased to be a Commonwealth citizen in the meanwhile.

Advice for undocumented Commonwealth citizens (Windrush generation) in the UK

Those who have lived in the UK permanently before 1973 and have not been away for long periods in the last 30 years, have the right to be in the UK. They must apply for a permit card which proves their status in the UK. Those who came to the UK during the 1970s but after 1 January 1973 are not likely to have an automatic right to be in the UK. They may be allowed to stay in the UK permanently.

You must provide any of these documents that can help support your application for UK permanent residence: exam certificates, employment records, your National Insurance number, birth and marriage certificates, and any bills and letters.

For all enquiries contact Freephone: 0800 678 1925 (Monday to Saturday 9am to 5pm; Sunday 10am to 4pm) or email: commonwealthtaskforce@homeoffice.gsi.gov.uk

People who arrived after 1973 but before 1988 can also access the dedicated Windrush team so they can access the support and assistance needed to establish their claim to be in the UK legally. The Home Office will waive the citizenship fee for anyone in the Windrush generation who wishes to apply for citizenship – this applies to those who have no current documentation, and also to those who have it. It will also waive the requirement to do a Knowledge of Language and Life in the UK test and will waive the fee for the children of the Windrush generation who are in the UK who need to apply for naturalisation.

THE LONG RESIDENCE ROUTE TO SETTLEMENT

What is the legal long residence route to settlement?

Live in the UK legally for 10 years and then apply to settle down permanently (known as the 'long residence' route). This costs £2389 per person to apply by post. You need form SET (LR).

When does my 10-year qualifying period start?

Your 10-year qualifying period starts from either when you arrived in the UK with a visa or when you were given permission to stay in the UK.

What are the eligibility requirements?

You must not be an illegal immigrant. You must have a valid visa. This can be in any immigration category, or a combination of different immigration categories. You must also have been in the UK legally for 10 years; not have violated the terms of your UK visa, pass the Life in the UK Test and prove you have sufficient English language skills.

What happens if I do not meet the last 2 requirements?

Those aged between 18-65 years must pass the Life in the UK Test and prove they have sufficient English language skills. If you don't meet these requirement you can apply to extend your stay in the UK.

Why is it important to state all reasons for wanting to settle in the UK?

You have a duty to state all reasons to remain in the UK in your application form SET (LR). If you do not state any reasons or grounds for remaining in the United Kingdom at the time of your application and you tell UKVI later without good reason, you could lose any right of appeal you may have otherwise qualified for if UKVI refuse your claim.

Can I apply for settlement of my dependents as well?

Sorry, the immigration rules for Long Residence settlement cannot be used for dependants. Your family members ('dependants') can apply separately if they are eligible. A dependant is your partner or child aged under 18 years old. You cannot include your family members in your application.

How can my dependents apply separately?

If your application for settlement is successful your partner can apply to remain in the UK as the partner of a settled person if they are not eligible to apply separately. Your partner may be able to include their children under 18 in their application.

Do I need a biometric residence permit as well?

Yes, if you are applying for an extension of stay in the UK in the Long Residence category under SET (LR) you must also apply for a Biometric Residence Permit.

Does a period spent as a partner of an EEA national in the UK count towards the LR period?

Yes ,if your 10 years continuous lawful residence (LR) includes a period of time spent in the UK as an EEA national, or as a family member of an EEA treaty rights you must state this in your application. You must provide evidence to support these assertions. If you are the family member of an EEA national you should provide sufficient evidence to demonstrate when you became the family member of an EEA national, e.g. marriage/birth certificate. If you are married or in a civil partnership with an EEA national you should provide evidence to confirm this.

I have been out of the UK many times. How is long residence calculated?

Continuous residence is time you have spent in the UK without gaps. You are allowed to leave the UK during the continuous residence for up to 180 days at a time and 540 days in total. You cannot count time spent in a prison, young offender's institution or secure hospital; the Republic of Ireland, Isle of Man or Channel Islands.

What aspects of my personal history will need to be disclosed?

Application SET (LR) asks details about any criminal convictions, cautions, civil judgments or civil penalties against you or any dependants who are applying with you. It also asks for details of any involvement you or any dependants who are applying with you have had in war crimes, genocide, crimes against humanity or terrorism.

When should I apply for this form of settlement?

You can send your application as soon as you meet all the eligibility requirements. You do not need to wait until your current visa expires. You must be in the UK to apply.

Is there an illegal long-residence route to settlement?·

Yes, live in the UK illegally for 20 years and then apply to settle down permanently (not recommended).

THE ARMED FORCES ROUTE TO UK SETTLEMENT

You can apply for UK permanent residence if you served in the UK armed forces (including the Gurkhas) for four years and have left within the last two years. There are separate rules for Gurkhas. If you did not serve four years you should have been medically discharged. You should not have a criminal record in the UK or another country, or have provided false or incomplete information to the Home Office or broken UK immigration law.

THE PRIVATE LIFE SETTLEMENT ROUTE TO UK SETTLEMENT

This route is for those who are between 18 and 24 and have lived continuously in the UK for more than half their life. It is also for those who are 25 or over and had been in the UK continuously for 20 years. It can be used by those who are over 18 and had spent less than 20 years in the UK but had no ties with any other country.

This route can also be used by children (those who are under 18) and had lived in the UK continuously for at least 7 years, and it would be unreasonable to expect them to live in a different country.

You must have been living in the UK for 10 years from the date you started on the 10-year route to settlement for Private Life. You will not be able to apply to settle until 2022 at the earliest (i.e 10 years after this way to settle was introduced).

Your application can be refused if you have a criminal record in the UK or another country; provided false or incomplete information to the Home Office or broken UK immigration law. If you are 18 to 64 years old you must also pass the Life in the UK Test and meet the English language requirements.

Your partner must be eligible in their own right. They will be able to apply on the same form as you or separately. Your child may apply separately or on the same form as you if they are also eligible in the Private Life route. If they are not eligible themselves, they can apply as your dependant if they are not married, in a civil partnership or living an independent life; will be living with you and have enough money to be adequately supported and accommodated by you without relying on public funds.

You and your child's other parent must both be in the UK legally, or currently applying to enter, remain or settle, for the child to be allowed to settle.

Your child can also apply to settle in one of the following situations:

you have sole responsibility for your child, or the child normally lives with you

their other parent is dead

there are compelling reasons why they should be allowed to stay

Your child's application can be refused for other reasons: for example their previous immigration history.

THE DISCRETIONARY LEAVE ROUTE TO UK SETTLEMENT

This route is for those who have lived in the UK for 6 years if they applied on or before 8 July 2012 or 10 years if they applied from 9 July 2012. Your application can be refused if you have a criminal record in the UK or another country. Your partner and children under 18 can apply on the same form as you if they were given permission to stay in the UK as your dependants when you were given Discretionary Leave.

How you apply depends on why you were given Discretionary Leave. If you were refused asylum and given Discretionary Leave then download and fill in form FLR(DL). Send it to the address on the form. Check the application form to find out which supporting documents you need to send with your application.

It costs £811. You must pay additional fees if you are applying with a dependant. If your non-asylum application was refused but you were given Discretionary Leave, you can apply online. You can apply with form SET(O) instead. Send it to the address on the form. Check the application form to find out which supporting documents you need to send with your application. After you submit your application you'll be asked to provide a digital photo and fingerprints (known as 'biometric information').

THE RETIRED PERSON VISA ROUTE TO UK SETTLEMENT

This route is for those who have been living in the UK on a Retired Person visa for a continuous period of at least 5 years and have £25,000 annual income and proof that they can support themselves and dependants without using public funds and have close connections in the UK (family members settled in this country or long periods of residence). Those between 18 to 64 years old when they apply must also pass the Life in the UK Test and an English language test. Use SET (BUS) application form.

THE UK ANCESTRY ROUTE TO UK SETTLEMENT

A UK Ancestry visa was discussed earlier in this book. You can apply if you are a Commonwealth citizen; are applying from outside the UK; are able to prove that one of your grandparents was born in the UK; and are able and planning to work in the UK. The UKVI issued about 4000 Ancestry visas in 2015.

You can use this route to settle permanently in the UK. This route is for those with a UK Ancestry visa and who have been living and working in the UK for 5 years and spent no more than 180 days outside the UK in any 12 months (known as 'continuous residence'). If they are 18 to 64 years old when they apply, they must also pass the Life in the UK Test, and an English language test. You should not have a criminal record in the UK or another country or have provided false or incomplete information to the Home Office or broken UK immigration law.

Your partner and any children under 18 can apply at the same time as you if they're eligible. Your partner may qualify if all of the following apply: they have permission to be in the UK, provided they do not have a visitor visa; your relationship is genuine; you intend to live together; you have enough income to support yourselves and your dependants and you are not using public funds. They must pass the Life in the UK Test and meet the English language requirements.

Your child can apply if they have permission to be in the UK, provided they do not have a visitor visa; are not married or in a civil partnership; and will live with you and be supported by you without using public funds. You and your child's other parent must both be in the UK legally, or currently applying to enter, remain or settle, for the child to be allowed to settle.

Your child can also apply to settle in one of the following situations: 1). You are the child's sole surviving parent or you have sole responsibility for the child's upbringing or there are serious or compelling family or other considerations, for example you (if you are settled in the UK) or your child has a serious illness. If your child is over 18, they must apply either online (download and fill in a separate SET(O) form) or by post. You can apply with form SET(O) instead. Send it to the address on the form or take it to a premium service centre. Check the form to find out which supporting documents you need. After you submit your application you'll be asked to provide your fingerprints and a digital photo (called 'biometric information').

THE WORK VISA ROUTE TO UK SETTLEMENT

Applicants with a Work Visa who have been living and working in the UK for 5 years and spent no more than 180 days outside the UK in any 12 months (known as 'continuous residence') can apply for settlement on this basis.

If they are 18 to 64 years old when they apply, they must also pass the Life in the UK Test, and an English language test. You should not have a criminal record in the UK or another country or have provided false or incomplete information to the Home Office or broken UK immigration law. Applicants will also need a letter from their employer confirming that they are still required for the job and show proof that they were paid at or above the appropriate level specified in the Codes of Practice. The continuous residence of 5 years includes time spent on any of these visa types:

Highly Skilled Migrant Programme

Self-Employed Lawyer

Writer, Composer or Artist

Download and complete the SET(O) application form.

How many years as a work visa holder must I pass to apply for permanent residence?

Until 2006 this period was four years. This period is now five years. The five years includes time spent on any of these visa types: Highly Skilled Migrant Programme; Self-Employed Lawyer or Writer, Composer or Artist.

You should not have spent more than 180 days outside the UK in any 12 months during these five years. You should not have been claiming benefits in the UK. You must pass the criminality test (no serious criminal offences either in the UK or abroad). Note: The UKVI no longer issues work permits.

For Tier 1 (Entrepreneur) work visa; can I settle in 3 years instead of 5?

Normally, for settlement continuous UK legal residence on a work visa is 5 years. However, the rules are relaxed to 3 years if your business was new and either created 10 new full-time jobs or generated £5 million income.

You can also apply after 3 years if you took over an existing business and have had a net income from business activity of at least £5 million in a 3-year period.

The 3 or 5 years can include time you had either of these visas: Businessperson or Innovator. Download and complete the SET(O) application form.

How can my partner and children apply to settle on my Set (O) form?

Your partner may qualify if all of the following apply: they have permission to be in the UK as your partner; they have been living in the UK with you for at least 5 years if they applied on or after 9 July 2012; your relationship is genuine; you intend to carry on living together; and you are not using public funds. They must pass the Life in the UK Test and an English language test.

Your child can apply if they were previously given permission to stay in the UK as your child; are not married or in a civil partnership; and will live with you and be supported by you without using public funds.

You and your child's other parent must both be in the UK legally, or currently applying to enter, remain or settle, for the child to be allowed to settle.

Your child can also apply to settle if you are the child's sole surviving parent or you have sole responsibility for the child's upbringing or there are serious or compelling family or other considerations, for example you (if you are settled in the UK) or your child has a serious illness. If your child is 16 or older when you apply you'll need to provide proof of where they live.

If they are over 18 by the time you apply, they must pass the Life in the UK Test and prove they have English language skills. Your child over 18 must apply using a separate SET(O) form.

I have a Tier 2 (Intra-Company Transfer) visa, how can I settle permanently in the UK?

You can apply if you have a Tier 2 (Intra-Company Transfer) visa. You must have been living and working in the UK for 5 years and spent no more than 180 days outside the UK in any 12 months (known as 'continuous residence'); your employer (sponsor) still needs you for your job; and you get paid the relevant salary listed in the Codes of Practice.

To qualify, you must have had at least one of these visas in the 5 years:

Tier 2 (Intra-Company Transfer) issued under the Immigration Rules in place before 6 April 2010

Work Permit for an intra-company transfer

You can have had any combination of these visas during the 5 years:

Tier 2 (Intra-Company Transfer)

Work Permit in the business and commercial category or the sports and entertainment category

Representative of an Overseas Business

If you are 18 to 64 years old when you apply, you must also pass the Life in the UK Test and an English language test.

Your application might be refused if you have a criminal record in the UK or another country or if you provided false or incomplete information to the Home Office or if you have broken UK immigration law. You must apply using a SET(O) form.

Settlement via Tier 1 (General) visa

You can no longer apply for settlement using the Tier 1 (General) visa category. Applications closed on 6 April 2018.

I have a Tier 2 (General) visa, how can I settle permanently in the UK?

You can apply if you have a Tier 2 (General) visa. You must have been living and working in the UK for 5 years and spent no more than 180 days outside the UK in any 12 months ('continuous residence'); your employer (sponsor) must still need you for your job and your job pays £35,000 or more (unless you're exempt from the 'minimum earnings threshold'). You must be paid the relevant salary listed in the Codes of Practice.

The 5 years can include time in the UK on another visa if it was one of the following:

Member of Ground Staff of an Overseas Owned Airline

Minister of Religion, Missionary or Member of a Religious Order

Work Permit in the business and commercial category or the sports and entertainment category

Representative of an Overseas Business

Representative of an Overseas Newspaper, News Agency or Broadcasting Organisation

any tier 1, except Tier 1 (Post-study work) or Tier 1 (Graduate Entrepreneur)

Highly Skilled Migrant Programme

Innovator

The 5 years can include time in the UK on a Tier 2 (Intra-Company Transfer) visa if one of the following applies:

the continuous residence includes a period of leave granted under the Tier 2 (Intra-Company Transfer) rules in place before 6 April 2010

the continuous residence includes time where you had a work permit granted because you were the subject of an Intra-Company Transfer

If you are 18 to 64 when you apply, you must also pass the Life in the UK Test and an English language test.

You don't have to earn £35,000 if the main job you're sponsored for is a PhD level job listed in the Codes of Practice; has a shortage of workers; or was in the shortage of workers list in the last 6 years. To apply download and complete the SET(O) application form.

For those with a Tier 1 (Exceptional Talent) visa

You can apply to settle in the UK if you were endorsed in your field as either a recognised leader ('exceptional talent') - you must have been living and working in the UK on this visa for at least 3 years or as an emerging leader ('exceptional promise') - you must have been living and working in the UK on this visa for at least 5 years.

You must also have spent no more than 180 days outside the UK in any 12 month period (known as continuous residence); still be endorsed by the organisation that gave you the letter of endorsement to get a visa; and still be doing paid work in the field you came to the UK to work in. You must pass the Life in the UK Test and meet the English language requirements.

Your application can be refused if you have a criminal record in the UK or another country; provided false or incomplete information to the Home Office or broken UK immigration law.

THE RETURNING RESIDENT ROUTE TO UK SETTLEMENT

You can return to the UK to live as a settled person if you were settled before (given indefinite leave to remain) and it is less than 2 years since you left; and you were settled in the UK when you last left; and you are returning to live in the UK permanently; and you were not given public funds to pay the costs of leaving the UK.

Can Returning Residents who have been away for more than 2 years settle back in the UK?

Yes, they may still be able to return to live in the UK if, for example, if they have strong family ties here or have lived in the UK for most of their life.

UK SETTLEMENT THROUGH INVESTING MONEY IN THE UK

What are the three ways I can settle in the UK permanently by investing money?

You can eventually settle in the UK as an investor. In 2015, 1200 people settled in the UK permanently on this visa. The amount of time it takes depends on your level of investment. Your investment can be either cash or assets and a loan.

There are three ways to do this if you successfully applied for your visa on or after 6 November 2014.

1.**You have £2 million to invest.** To begin with, you need £2 million to apply for a Tier 1 Investor visa. This is for a maximum of 3 years and 4 months. You can apply to extend this visa for another 2 years. This £2 million must be invested in UK government bonds, share capital or loan capital in active and trading UK registered companies. After five years, you can apply to settle permanently in the UK.

2.**You have £5 million to invest.** If you invest £5 million, you can apply for your permanent residency after three years.

3.**You have £10 million to invest.** You can apply to settle after two years.

You must have made specific investments worth at least £750,000 for the whole time, except for the first 3 months. You must provide proof of where your money came from if you have not done this in a previous application.

You are not allowed to invest in companies mainly engaged in property investment, property management or property development or work as a professional sportsperson or sports coach or get public funds. You can work or study during this period.

You must download and apply using the SET (O) application form. If you are 18-64 when you apply, you must also pass the Life in the UK Test and an English language test. Your partner and children under 18 can apply on the same form as you if they are eligible.

How can my partner and children apply to settle on my SET (O) form?

Your partner may qualify if all of the following apply: they have permission to be in the UK as your partner; they have been living in the UK with you for at least 5 years if they applied on or after 9 July 2012; your relationship is genuine; you intend to carry on living together; and you are not using public funds. They must pass the Life in the UK Test and an English language test.

Your child can apply if they were previously given permission to stay in the UK as your child; are not married or in a civil partnership; and will live with you and be supported by you without using public funds.

You and your child's other parent must both be in the UK legally, or currently applying to enter, remain or settle, for the child to be allowed to settle.

Your child can also apply to settle if you are the child's sole surviving parent or you have sole responsibility for the child's upbringing or there are serious or compelling family or other considerations, for example you (if you are settled in the UK) or your child has a serious illness.

If your child is 16 or older when you apply you'll need to provide proof of where they live.

If they are over 18 by the time you apply, they must pass the Life in the UK Test and prove they have English language skills. Your child over 18 must apply using a separate SET(O) form.

For those with Investor, Innovator, Businessperson or Self-Employed Lawyer visa

You can apply to settle in the UK if you have an Investor, Innovator, Businessperson or Self-Employed Lawyer visa and you have been living and working in the UK for at least 5 years and spent no more than 180 days outside the UK in any 12 months. You're not eligible if you had a Tier 1 (Investor) visa.

You must have:

had £1 million with at least £750,000 invested for the whole 5 years

a personal net worth of more than £2 million and £1 million under your control in the UK (including loans from a Financial Services Authority-regulated lender) or £1 million of your own money

spent a continuous period of 5 years in the UK as an investor

made the UK your main home throughout the 5 years

housed and supported yourself and any dependants without using public funds or working as an employee

Additional criteria for business people:

You must have: worked full time in the same business; proof of audited accounts for 4 years and management accounts for the fifth showing you've had a minimum of £200,000 invested throughout the 5 years; created 2 full-time paid jobs for people already settled in the UK and spent a continuous period of 5 years in the UK in this capacity.

Additional criteria for innovators: You must have: the accounts for 4 years and management accounts for the 5th year showing your business is viable; retained at least a 5% shareholding in the business throughout your stay; created 2 full-time paid jobs for people already settled in the UK and spent a continuous period of 5 years in the UK as an investor.

Solicitors must be able to provide proof of their admission to the Roll of Solicitors from one of the following:the Law Society for England and Wales or the Law Society of Scotland or the Incorporated Law Society of Northern Ireland.

Barristers must be able to provide proof that they have been admitted to one of the following the Bar of England and Wales; the Bar of Scotland or the Bar of Northern Ireland or have a place in Chambers.

Consultants in overseas law must provide a letter from the appropriate UK law society saying whether there is any objection to the application being granted.

UK SETTLEMENT BY INVESTING MONEY OUTSIDE THE UK

Money can buy residence permits not only in the UK but elsewhere in the EU too. In the UK an investor needs to spend a minimum of £2 million to get permanent residence (after 5 years). However, there are European countries where you can purchase a residence permit with much less money. In Portugal and Spain investors have a minimum spend of 500,000 Euros on a property to get a permit, in Cyprus it is 300,000 Euros, and in Greece it is 250,000 Euros.

Portugal gives foreign investors who spend 500,000 Euros on a property in Portugal the right to live in Portugal. They are also free to travel around all the EU countries in the Schengen area and after six years they can apply for Portuguese citizenship. Foreign investors can also get a Golden Visa by investing a million Euros in capital or creating 10 jobs in Portugal.

Investors in Malta can obtain a passport for 1.15m Euro (£965,000; $1.3m) investment with one year residency requirement. Malta is a European Union (EU) nation. You can purchase citizenship here if you want.

Investing money in Cyprus: If you invest as part of a larger group whose collective investments total more than 12.5m Euros, then you can invest 2m Euros in Cyprus for citizenship. For an individual applying alone an investment of 5m Euros in real estate or banks is required. Applicants need to have a property in Cyprus but do not need to live there all of the time. Family members are included in the application.

Note: Although the British people voted to leave the EU on 23 June 2016, the UK will remain part of the EU till it formally leaves. These residence schemes will lapse when the UK eventually leaves the EU in 2021.

THE ASYLUM ROUTE TO SETTLEMENT

What is the power of the asylum application?

The UK Home Office treats asylum applications more sympathetically than other categories. Applicants are not deported without due process. In 2014, asylum seekers constituted 4% of permanent settlement approvals in the UK. ONS figures show that in 2017, the UK granted asylum, alternative forms of protection or resettlement to almost 15,000 people, 40% of whom were under 18.

Who can apply for settlement through asylum?

You can apply to settle in the UK if you have a residence card as a refugee or a person with humanitarian protection. Applications can be refused if the applicant has a criminal record or has been in prison. There is no fee for applying for settlement as a refugee or person who has been given humanitarian protection.

Your partner and children can apply to be reunited with you in the UK if your family was formed before you left your country. Your family members can apply to join you in the UK instead if one of the following is true they're not eligible to apply as a partner or a child or your family was formed after you left your country. If your application is successful, your family members will have permission to stay in the UK for the same length of time as you.

Do successful asylum applicants get immediate permanent residence in the UK?

No, the UK does not grant immediate settlement to refugees and other asylum applicants. Instead, applicants are granted limited leave to remain with the opportunity to apply for settlement after five more years of UK residence.

Where do most UK asylum seekers come from?

Top ten nationalities, UK asylum applicants, 2014

Country	Number of applicants	Share of total
Eritrea	3,239	13.0%
Pakistan	2,711	10.9%
Syria	2,081	8.4%
Iran	2,011	8.1%
Albania	1,576	6.3%
Sudan	1,449	5.8%
Sri Lanka	1,282	5.1%
Afghanistan	1,136	4.6%
Nigeria	875	3.5%
Bangladesh	742	3.0%

Source: Home Office, Immigration Statistics Table

More up to date Home Office figures reveal that since 2016, Iranians have made more UK asylum applications than any other nationality. In 2017, they made 9% of the 26,350 asylum applications.

OTHER WAYS OF SETTLING IN THE UK

You may also be able to settle in the UK if you have exceptional compassionate circumstances. You must explain in detail what these are if you choose to apply.

Contact UK Visas and Immigration (UKVI) if you want more information.

UK Visas and Immigration contact centre

Telephone: 0300 123 2241

Monday to Thursday, 9am to 4:45pm

Friday, 9am to 4:30pm

UKVI

Lunar House

40 Wellesley Road

Croydon

Surrey

CR9 2BY

THE LIFE IN THE UK TEST

What is the 'Life in the UK' test and is it easy to pass?

It is a 45-minute test on British society, traditions, customs, history and culture which an immigrant has to pass in order to be allowed to settle permanently or have full citizenship in the UK. 24 questions must be answered.

The test must be completed on a computer at one of 60 test centres around the UK. Introduced in 2005, the test is meant to help new arrivals hoping to make Britain their home integrate better into British society. Candidates must book their Life in the UK Test online at least 7 days in advance. It costs £50.

It covers topics such as Britain's constitution, the originating countries of previous UK immigrants, family life in the UK and where dialects like Geordie, Scouse or Cockney come from. More practical matters such as the minimum age to buy alcohol and tobacco and what services are provided by local authorities are also covered. According to the Home Office website, "studying for and taking the test will give you the practical knowledge you need to live in this country and to take part in society."

Candidates will be tested on information in the official handbook for the Life in the UK Test. They are advised that they should study this book to prepare for the test.

Passing the citizenship test demonstrates the candidate has "a sufficient knowledge" of the English language for the purposes of applying for settlement rights or a British passport.

Citizens of English-speaking countries tend to do best in this multiple-choice exam. Figures from the Home Office show that about 30% of foreigners taking the test fail to pass it.

Nationalities with a pass rate below 50% included Iraqis, Bangladeshis and Turks. High pass rates included Nigerians (pass rate of 82.5%), Zimbabweans (pass rate of 90.2%), Canadians (pass rate of 96.9%), Americans (pass rate of 97.9%) and Australians (pass rate of 98%).

The introduction of the Life in the UK test and more stringent English language requirements in 2004 does not seem to have changed the increasing trend in naturalisations, according to the UK Migration Observatory. Life in the UK test helpline: Telephone: 0800 015 4245

Where can I get the official study book for the Life in the UK test?

It is available at http://www.tsoshop.co.uk. It costs £12.99.

ISBN: 9780113413409

THE ENGLISH LANGUAGE REQUIREMENT

How do I prove that I meet the English language requirement for Settlement/Citizenship?

You can meet the English language requirement in one of the following ways:

·by passing an English language test in speaking and listening at a minimum of level A1

of the Common European Framework of Reference for Languages (CEFR) with a provider

approved by the Home Office;

·by being a national of a majority English speaking country listed earlier in this book

·by having an academic qualification recognised by UK NARIC to be equivalent to a Bachelor's or Master's degree or PhD in the UK, which was taught or researched in English;

Or by qualifying for an exemption.

If my degree was in English am I exempt from the English knowledge requirement?

Yes, produce your original degree certificate and one of the following:

a printout from the points-based calculator with the equivalent level of your degree and the level of English

an original letter or certificate from UK NARIC confirming the equivalent level of your degree, plus an official letter from your university with your name and degree confirming that your degree was taught in English

an original and official certificate from your university confirming the degree was taught or researched in a majority English-speaking country (except Canada).

Who else does not need to prove their knowledge of English?

You don't need to prove your knowledge of English if you're:

aged 65 or over

unable to, because of a long-term physical or mental condition

You must provide a letter from a doctor confirming your physical or mental condition.

I am applying for settlement; are there other exemptions from the English knowledge requirement?

You do not need to prove your knowledge of English if you're applying as:

a victim of domestic violence as the partner or spouse of a British citizen or someone settled in the UK

the partner or spouse of a British citizen or someone settled in the UK who has died

an adult dependent relative between 18 and 64 of someone present and settled in the UK or who is as a refugee or has humanitarian protection

a refugee living in the UK

someone living in the UK with discretionary leave

someone living in the UK for with humanitarian protection

someone who has permission to stay in the UK as a retired person of independent means

a Commonwealth citizen on discharge from HM Forces, including Gurkhas

someone in exceptional circumstances, e.g. as an orphan, widow or over-age dependant.

Will UKVI interview applicants for permanent residence?

Yes, an applicant for indefinite leave to enter or remain must, unless the applicant provides a reasonable explanation, comply with any request made by UKVI to attend an interview. An interview may be required to give the applicant a further opportunity to demonstrate sufficient knowledge of the English language and about life in the United Kingdom.

Even those with limited leave to enter or remain may be called for an interview to provide additional information and evidence to the Home Office.

EEA APPLICANTS APPLYING FOR UK PERMANENT RESIDENCE

When will the UK leave the EU?

On 29 March 2019.

What is a "valid application" for ILR/LLR in the context of EU citizens and family members? Paragraph EU(9)

A valid application is where:

(a) It has been made in the UK using the required application process;

(b) Any required fee has been paid in full in accordance with the required application process;

(c) The required proof of identity and nationality has been provided;

(d) The required biometrics have been provided.

These rules also pertain to the family members of a qualifying British citizen. If they apply under it to be granted indefinite leave to remain (ILR) or limited leave to remain (LLR).

The applicant will be granted indefinite leave to remain where:

A valid application has been made in accordance with paragraph EU9; The applicant meets the eligibility requirements for indefinite leave to remain. The applicant is not to be refused on grounds of suitability.

The applicant will be granted five years' limited leave to remain where a valid application has been made in accordance with paragraph EU9; The applicant does not meet the eligibility requirements for indefinite leave to remain, but meets the eligibility requirements for limited leave to remain in accordance and the applicant is not to be refused on grounds of suitability in accordance.

Where a person has been granted limited leave to remain under these rules they must continue to meet the eligibility requirements for that leave which they met at the date of application or meet other eligibility requirements for limited leave to remain.

What is the eligibility criterion for EEA citizens to apply for UK settled status?

To be eligible for UK settled status, you will need to:

be an EU citizen, or a family member of an EU citizen

have been living in the UK continuously for 5 years ('continuous residence')

have started living in the UK by 31 December 2020

If you have lived in the UK for less than 5 years, you will generally be eligible for 'pre-settled status' instead. If you are a non-EU citizen, you will need to show your relationship to an EU citizen living in the UK.

Which EU nationals do not need to apply for settled status in the UK?

You will not need to apply for settled status (if you want to continue living here after June 2021) if you are an Irish citizen or have indefinite leave to remain, but your family members from outside the UK and Ireland will. Rights for citizens of Norway, Iceland, Liechtenstein and Switzerland after Brexit are still being negotiated.

What is the implementation period?

The implementation period for EU citizens is the time until when they can continue to exercise their free movement rights. This will end on 31 December 2020.

Has the status of EEA nationals in the UK changed after Brexit?

There is no change to the rights and status of EEA nationals in the UK, and UK nationals in the EU, as a result of the Brexit referendum. The UK remains a member of the EU throughout the process of negotiations to leave the EU, and until these (Article 50 negotiations) have concluded.

Can EEA nationals be removed from the UK?

EEA nationals can only be removed from the UK if they are considered to pose a genuine, present and sufficiently serious threat to the public, if they are not lawfully resident or are abusing their free movement rights.

How many years must EEA nationals pass in the UK to apply for British citizenship?

EEA nationals who have lived continuously and lawfully in the UK for at least 5 years automatically have a permanent right to reside. EU nationals who have lived continuously and lawfully in the UK for at least 6 years are eligible to apply for British citizenship. There is no requirement to register for documentation to confirm this status.

What is the difference between a UK Residence Certificate and a UK Residence Card?

A Registration Certificate is for EEA nationals for confirmation of their right of residence. Since November 2015, this is required for citizenship applications for EEA nationals.

A Residence Card is for non-EEA nationals for confirmation of their right of residence. The latter is a document that you can apply for if you are from outside the European Economic Area (EEA) and you are the family member, or extended family member, of an EEA national who is a permanent resident. A UK Residence Card can help you re-enter the UK more quickly and easily if you travel abroad; show employers you are allowed to work in the UK; and help prove you qualify for certain benefits and services. It is not mandatory for family members, but for extended family members it is. They must have a valid EEA permit or residence card to stay in the UK.

After 5 years of living in the UK you can apply for a permanent residence card or certificate. Use Form EEA (PR). It is an 85 page form. It costs £65 for each person included in an application. A residence card is valid for up to 5 years.

I am an EEA national, on what grounds can the Home Office deny me a UK residence certificate?

EEA citizens living in the UK can be denied a UK residence certificate if they do not have a valid EHIC (European Health Insurance Card) issued by a EU member state or comprehensive health insurance. EEA citizens, without an EHIC and not in work or those looking for work must buy comprehensive health insurance. Since Brexit, many EEA citizens have applied for documents guaranteeing the right to live permanently in the UK. This document can, however, only be obtained by migrants who have consistently either worked, sought work, or bought the health insurance for five years. The Home Office will not remove people for failing to buy health insurance, but it will not issue those people with a guarantee of permanent residence.

Can my non-EEA partner enter the UK under EU law?

Non-EEA family members of EEA nationals must apply for a family permit if they wish to enter the UK under EU law, and they do not have a residence card issued by an EEA member state.

I am non-EEA. Can I apply for UK settled status as a family member of a EEA citizen?

You will need to provide evidence of your relationship to your EU citizen family member (for example, a birth, marriage or civil partnership certificate). You will be able to scan and submit this through the online application form. You will also need to provide evidence of your family member's identity and residence. You will need to provide your fingerprints and a photo of your face at an application centre in the UK. You will not need to do this if you already have a biometric residence card.

My family member is an EEA national, can I secure permanent residence?

A non-EEA national who is a family member of an EEA national can apply for a permanent residence card if they have resided in the UK in line with the regulations for a continuous period of 5 years.

Can the extended family of an EEA national reside in the UK?

Extended family members of EEA nationals must apply for a registration certificate (if they are an EEA national) or residence card (if they are a non-EEA national) if they wish to reside in the UK.

What evidence must I provide to show my relationship to the sponsor?

If you are applying as a family member or extended family member (other than an unmarried partner), or you are including family members/extended family members in your application, you must show how you/they are (or were) related to the sponsor by providing relevant birth, adoption, marriage or civil partnership certificates.

You must also prove your financial dependency on your sponsor. Show money transfer receipts from the sponsor to you, or bank statements showing receipt of money from the sponsor or sponsor's bank statements or other evidence of their financial resources or evidence of living in the same household as the sponsor, if relevant – e.g. tenancy agreement naming you/the family member and the sponsor, utility bills with your/the family member's name on, mobile phone bills, etc.

You must provide documentary evidence of living together with your sponsor. If you are applying as the unmarried (durable) partner of an EEA national, you must show that you have been living together in a relationship similar to a marriage or civil partnership.

Relevant documents may include the following:

- Letters or other documents from government departments or agencies, for example HM Revenue and Customs, Department for Work and Pensions,
- DVLA, TV Licensing letters or other documents from your GP, a hospital or other local health service about medical treatments, appointments, home visits or other medical matters.
- Bank statements/letters
- Building society savings books/letters
- Council tax bills or statements
- Electricity and/or gas bills or statements
- Water rates bills or statements
- Mortgage statements/agreement
- Tenancy agreement(s)
- Telephone bills or statements
- Photographs of you and your sponsor together – for example, on holiday or at a family celebration
- Evidence of how you have kept in contact with each other during periods in which you have not lived together – for example, letters, printouts of emails or contact via social media, mobile phone bills showing you have contacted each other, printouts of Skype (or similar) logs, etc.

Applying for a Residence card/certificate using form EEA (PR)

Use form EEA (PR) if you wish to apply for a document certifying UK permanent residence (if you are an EEA national). This form can also be used by non-EEA nationals to apply for a permanent residence card. This gives you confirmation of your right of permanent residence in the UK under the Immigration (European Economic Area) Regulations 2006.

To apply for this certificate or card you must normally have lived in the UK for a continuous period of five years.

This five year period can be as one of the following:

• an EEA national 'qualified person' (worker, self-employed, self-sufficient, student or jobseeker),

• a family member or extended family member of an EEA national qualified person or permanent resident,

• a former family member of an EEA national if you've retained your right of residence after the EEA national died or left the UK, or your/their marriage or civil partnership ended in divorce, annulment or dissolution, or

• a family member of a British citizen who worked or was self-employed in another EEA state

before returning to the UK.

You can also apply if you are:

• an EEA national former worker or self-employed person who has ceased activity in the UK

because you have retired, are permanently incapacitated, or you are now working or self-employed

in another EEA state but still retain your residence in the UK,

• the family member or extended family member of an EEA national who has ceased activity, or

• the family member or extended family member of an EEA national former worker or self-employed

person who has died.

Form EEA (PR) - Remember the following

- you can only apply as an extended family member if you have held valid residence documentation such as a registration certificate, residence card, or EEA family permit throughout the relevant qualifying period.

- Use a black pen and write names, addresses and similar details in capital letters. In sections where you are asked to give your personal details and address, leave a space between each name and each part of the address.

- If a section does not apply to you, leave it blank.

- You cannot apply in person. You must apply by post.

- Your biometric information will be required. When UKVI receive your application, they will send you a biometric enrolment letter. This will instruct you (and any non-EEA family members included in your application) to make an appointment at a designated Post Office to have your biometric information recorded. You will be charged an additional handling fee for this service, payable to the Post Office Ltd. You must pay the fee by cash or debit card when you attend your biometric enrolment appointment.

- Do not send the biometric enrolment fee with your application fee.

- EEA applicants include Swiss nationals.

What evidence must I send to prove my five years residency?

Your evidence must cover the 5-year period. The documents should be spread evenly throughout the 5 years and come from a variety of sources. UKVI recommend you submit at least 2 documents for each year of residence. If you are applying as the family member of an EEA national who has died or ceased activity, you must show that you and the EEA national were resident in the UK immediately before the EEA national died or ceased activity. If you are applying as the spouse, civil partner or durable partner of the sponsor, you must show you have been living together.

The following documents are acceptable to UKVI:

- Letters or other documents from government departments or agencies, for example HM Revenue and Customs, Department for Work and Pensions, DVLA, TV Licensing
- Letters or other documents from your GP, a hospital or other local health service about medical treatments, appointments, home visits or other medical matters
- Bank statements/letters
- Building society savings books/letters
- Council tax bills or statements
- Electricity and/or gas bills or statements
- Water rates bills or statements
- Mortgage statements/agreement
- Tenancy agreement(s)
- Telephone bills or statements.

Online application form for EU citizens in the UK

In December 2017 the UK government reached an agreement with the EU on the rights of EU citizens in the UK. They will need to secure their rights by applying online (form will go live in late 2018) to confirm their status in the UK. The application process will check 3 basic principles – identity, UK residence and criminal convictions. EU citizens will need to:

prove their identity and nationality with their EU passport or National ID card and provide a recent photograph of themselves

declare any criminal convictions – only serious or persistent criminality will affect eligibility for the scheme

Applicants they will not have to:

account for every trip taken out of the UK

show evidence that they held comprehensive sickness insurance

give their fingerprints

The application fee will be no more than the cost charged to British citizens for a UK passport. Applications will cost £65 and be half that cost for children under 16. For those who already have a valid permanent residence document, it will be free.

The Home Office will check the employment and benefit records held by the government which will mean the proof of residence check will be automatic. Those who have not yet lived in the UK for five years will be granted pre-settled status and be able to apply for settled status once they reach the five-year point. From April 2019, this second application will be free of charge.

The settlement scheme will open in a phased way (online, by secure post, and via a smartphone app) in late 2018 and will be fully open by 30 March 2019. Decisions on settlement are expected within two weeks or sooner. The deadline for applications will be 30 June 2021.

The scheme also includes citizens of Switzerland, Iceland, Liechtenstein and Norway.

I will have been resident in the UK for 10 years by 31/12/20 (the implementation period) will I get UK permanent residence?

All EU nationals who have been living continuously in the UK for over 5 years (without an absence of more than 5 years after that 5 years) immediately qualify for settled status, subject to criminality and security checks. You can apply for settled status under the new UK scheme once it is open in late 2018. You must apply to the Home Office by 30 June 2021 for permission to stay if you intend to carry on living in the UK afterwards.

What if I will not have the minimum 5 years on 29/03/19?

Brexit happens on 29/03/19. You may continue to live and work in the UK until 30 June 2021 without having to make an application. As soon as you have been resident for 5 years, you can apply for settled status which will allow you to settle in the UK permanently.

If you will not have 5 years' continuous residence when you apply you will get 'pre-settled status' instead. Pre-settled status means you can stay in the UK for a further 5 years. You can live and work in the UK, and will have access to public funds and services on the same basis as you do now. Once you have 5 years' continuous residence you can apply for settled status.

What if I will not have the minimum 5 years even on 30/06/21?

Apply to the Home Office for a temporary residence status by 30 June 2021 if you wish to continue to live in the UK. This will enable you to continue lawfully living and working in the UK until you meet the 5-year threshold. Once you have been resident for 5 years you will be entitled to apply for settled status which will allow you to settle in the UK permanently.

What are the rules for applying for settled status for children of EEA nationals?

You will need to apply on behalf of your child so they can get settled status, unless they are a British citizen. If you are eligible to apply, any children you have aged under 21 will also be eligible, even if they arrive in the UK after 31 December 2020. If you have a child after getting settled status, your child will automatically be a British citizen if they're born in the UK. You will not need to apply for settled status on their behalf.

I live overseas. I am a family member of an EU citizen living in the UK, can I apply for settled status?

If you are not living in the UK by 31 December 2020, you will be able to apply to join your family member here after that date if both a). your family member is eligible to apply and your relationship existed by 31 December 2020 and b). If you're a close family member, for example a spouse, civil partner, a dependent child or grandchild, or a dependent parent or grandparent.

I have criminal convictions, can I apply for settled status as an EU citizen?

If you are over 18 you will be asked about your criminal history in the UK and overseas. You will also be checked against the UK's crime databases. You can still get settled or pre-settled status even if you have convictions. This will be decided on a case-by-case basis. The government is concerned about serious and persistent criminality not parking fines.

Provisions for Turkish business people

In 2018 a new settlement category for Turkish business people, workers and their families who are in the UK under the EU-Turkey European Communities Association Agreement (ECAA) was announced. This means that Turkish workers and business people will be able to settle in the UK after 5 years as either an ECAA business person or ECAA worker (or equivalent points based system routes), as long as the most recent period of leave was under the ECAA.

BRITISH NATIONALITY AND CITIZENSHIP

What is meant by the term 'stateless'?

It means not recognised by any country as having a nationality.

Can a stateless person apply to stay in the UK?

You can apply to stay in the UK as a stateless person if you are not recognised as a citizen of any country. To be eligible to apply, you must also be in the UK and unable to return to another country as a result of being stateless.

If you cannot return to another country because you fear persecution there, you should claim asylum first. If you have already claimed asylum or have an outstanding human rights claim, you must wait until you have a decision. You can apply to stay as a stateless person if it is refused.

You can normally stay in the UK for 2 years and 6 months if you are given permission to stay (known as 'leave to remain'). You can apply for further leave when your leave expires. You need to include your family members ('dependants') in your application if you want them to stay with you in the UK. Your dependants must already be with you in the UK.

You must provide these documents, if you have them, for you and your dependants: current passports and other travel documents, e.g. visas; official letters confirming your immigration status (with the reference number ASL.2150, ASL.2151 or ASL.2152); birth certificates; and marriage certificates

You will also need to provide as many documents as you can to prove that you are stateless. You should also provide documents for your dependants if they are stateless.

These can include identity, immigration and travel documents, documents that prove where you lived before coming to the UK, e.g. school certificates, medical records or sworn statements from neighbours, documents from your applications for citizenship or requests for proof of nationality in other countries. You will find a list of documents you can include in the application form (FLR (S).

What is the difference between British nationality and British citizenship?

British citizenship is a type of British nationality. There are five other types of British nationality. They are:

British overseas territories citizen

British overseas citizen

British subject

British national (overseas)

British protected person.

What is naturalisation?

Naturalisation is the securing of British citizenship by someone who held (or continues to hold) foreign citizenship. There are several ways to naturalisation. Adults may qualify for British citizenship through at least five years of residence in the UK, or through marriage to a British citizen (with three years' residence in the UK as a spouse or civil partner). In addition to residency requirements, naturalising citizens must meet requirements of 'good character', ability to communicate in English (or Welsh or Scottish Gaelic), and 'knowledge of life in the UK' (as assessed by a Life in the UK test, also required for those applying for settlement). Children may qualify for either automatic or discretionary "registration" as British citizens depending on the country of their birth and nationalities of their parents. In 2015, 118,100 foreign citizens naturalised as British citizens.

I was born in the UK am I a British citizen?

If you were born in the UK before 1 January 1983, then you are a British citizen unless your father was a diplomat working in the UK for a foreign country. A child whose parents are not British citizens who is born in the UK is not a British citizen unless at least one parent has settled status (permanent residence) in the UK at the time. If Indefinite Leave to Remain (ILR) is acquired by the parents after the child's birth, the child will still not automatically be a British citizen. However, the child can be registered as a British citizen under section 1(3) of the British Nationality Act 1981 provided an application is made before they reach the age of 18. Alternatively, if the child lives in the UK until age 10, it will have a lifetime entitlement to registration as a British citizen under section 1(4) of the Act.

Is there a way to become a British citizen other than by birth or naturalization?

Yes, you can become a British citizen by registering as a British citizen if you fulfil one of these conditions:

you have another form of British nationality

you were born before 1 January 1983 to a British mother

you were born to a British father, even if he was not married to your mother

you were born in the UK on or after 1 January 1983

you are under 18 and don't fit into the other categories

you have a connection with Gibraltar or Hong Kong

you are stateless.

New rules on registration as British citizen for children of British parents

Before 1 January 1983, British women were not able to pass on citizenship to their children born abroad in the same way as British men. Children born before 1 January 1983 to British mothers can now apply for registration as a British citizen under section 4C of the British Nationality Act 1981.They will normally qualify if they would have become British citizens automatically under that Act had women been able to pass on citizenship in the same way as men.

Before 1 July 2006, a British man could not pass on citizenship to a child born outside the UK if he was not married to the child's mother. Children born before 1 July 2006 to unmarried British fathers can now apply for registration as a British citizen under sections 4G – 4I of the British Nationality Act 1981. They will normally qualify if they would have become British citizens automatically under that Act had their parents been married.

In addition, a person who would have qualified for registration as a British citizen had their parents been married can now apply for registration under section 4F of the 1981Act.

What is meant by British citizenship by descent?

You can get British citizenship by descent if you are one of the following:

A British overseas citizen

A British protected person

A British subject

A British national (overseas)

You need form B(OS) for this. If your application is successful, your children will not automatically become British citizens if born outside the UK.

What is meant by British citizenship 'otherwise than by descent'?

You can get British citizenship 'otherwise than by descent' if you hold any form of British nationality and either:

you have lived in the UK for at least 5 years - and spent no more than 450 days abroad during that time, and no more than 90 days abroad in the last 12 months

or you have worked in British Crown Service at any time.

If you get British citizenship 'otherwise than by descent', your children can also be British citizens. You need form B(OTA).

What are British Overseas Territories?

Anguilla

Bermuda

British Antarctic Territory

British Indian Ocean Territory

British Virgin Islands

Cayman Islands

Falkland Islands

Gibraltar

Montserrat

Pitcairn Islands

St Helena, Ascension and Tristan da Cunha

South Georgia and South Sandwich Islands

Turks and Caicos Islands

Who is a British protected person?

You are a British protected person if you are stateless and always have been so, and if you were born in the UK or an overseas territory and if your father or mother was a British protected person when you were born. You may be able to register as a British citizen.

Who is a British overseas territories citizen?

You are a British overseas territories citizen if both the following apply: you were born in a British overseas territory and, at the time of your birth, one of your parents was a British overseas territories citizen or legally settled in a British overseas territory.

You are also a British overseas territories citizen if one of the following applies you were adopted in an overseas territory by a British overseas territories citizen or you were born outside the overseas territory to a parent who gained British overseas territories citizenship in their own right (known as 'otherwise than by descent'). You may be able to register as a British citizen.

Who is a British overseas citizen?

You may be able to register as a British overseas citizen if you are stateless and you were born in the UK or an overseas territory and one of your parents is a British overseas citizen. You may be able to register as a British citizen if you are a British overseas citizen.

Who is a British national (overseas)?

This is a person who was a British overseas territories citizen by connection with Hong Kong was able to register as a British national (overseas) before 1 July 1997.

British overseas territories citizens from Hong Kong who didn't register as British nationals (overseas) and had no other nationality or citizenship on 30 June 1997 became British overseas citizens on 1 July 1997.

If you are not already a British national (overseas), you cannot apply to become one. You may be able to register as a British citizen.

Is there a checking service for UK nationality applications?

A list of local authorities in Greater London that offer a checking service for UK nationality applications is available here:

https://www.gov.uk/government/publications/nationality-checking-service-greater-london/greater-london-nationality-checking-services

EXCLUSION FROM THE UK

Can I lose my ILR/ILE?

Yes, if you are deported from the UK your indefinite leave will be invalidated. Indefinite leave can also be taken away if you: are liable to deportation but cannot be removed for legal reasons, such as the UK's obligations under the Refugee Convention or the European Convention on Human Rights (ECHR); obtained leave by deception; or were granted leave as a refugee and cease to be a refugee. Your indefinite leave will lapse if you stay outside the UK for 2 or more years (5 or more, if granted settled status under the EU Settlement Scheme) at a time.

Who has the power to exclude a person from the UK?

The decision to exclude a person is exercised by the Home Secretary. This is done on the basis of a recommendation which will set out why the use of the exclusion power is appropriate. A decision to exclude an individual from the UK will be made on the facts of the particular case.

What are the grounds for excluding a person from entering the UK?

UKVI normally excludes a person from the UK in circumstances involving national security, criminality, international crimes (war crimes, crimes against humanity or genocide), corruption and unacceptable behaviour.

National security grounds usually refer to terrorist activities. These could be:

an act committed, or the threat of action designed to influence a government or

intimidate the public, and made for the purposes of advancing a political, religious or

ideological cause and that:

involves serious violence against a person

may endanger another person's life

creates a serious risk to the health or safety of the public

involves serious damage to property

is designed to seriously disrupt or interfere with an electronic system

Can EEA nationals be refused admission to the UK?

Non-European Economic Area (non-EEA) nationals with past or present involvement in criminality, will normally be refused entry to the UK. European Economic Area (EEA) nationals or their non-EEA national family members can also be refused admission.

What are war crimes?

Those who have committed a war crime can be excluded. These include:

wilful killing

torture

extensive destruction of property not justified by military necessity

unlawful deportation

the intentional targeting of civilians

the taking of hostages

What are crimes against humanity?

Those who have committed crimes against humanity can also be excluded. These are acts committed at any time (not just during armed conflict) as part of a widespread or systematic attack, directed against any civilian population, with knowledge of the attack. This includes:

murder

torture

rape

severe deprivation of liberty in violation of fundamental rules of international law

enforced disappearance of persons

What is genocide?

Genocide means acts committed with intent to destroy, in whole or in part, a national, ethnic, racial or religious group.

Can those accused/convicted of corruption be excluded?

Transparency International defines corruption as 'the abuse of entrusted power for private gain'. The types of activities associated with corruption include:

tax evasion

money laundering

bribery and accepting kickbacks (part of an income paid to a person in return

for an opportunity to make a profit, often by some illegal arrangement)

extortion

asset stealing

fraud

match fixing in sport

A person does not need to have been convicted of a corruption related offence in order to be excluded. Where there is substantive, reliable information that a person has been involved in corruption this will be taken into account.

Can a person be excluded on the basis of past extremist activity?

If a person engages in unacceptable behaviour they can be excluded. This may include past or current extremist activity, either in the UK or overseas. A person who has engaged in unacceptable behaviour in the past may still be considered for exclusion unless it is clear that they have publicly retracted their views and it is clear that they have not re-engaged in such behaviour.

What is unacceptable behaviour?

Unacceptable behaviour refers to the behaviour of a non-UK national whether in the UK or abroad

who uses any means or medium including:

writing, producing, publishing or distributing material

public speaking including preaching

running a website

using a position of responsibility such as a teacher, community or youth leader to express views which:

foment (provoke), justify or glorify terrorist violence in furtherance of particular beliefs

seek to provoke others to terrorist acts

foment other serious criminal activity or seek to provoke others to serious criminal acts

foster hatred which might lead to inter-community violence in the UK

What kind of evidence will be used for exclusion?

Only reliable evidence will be used. Hearsay or evidence which is indirect, ambiguous, speculative or subjective is unreliable and will not be used to support a recommendation to exclude. Online research will be done by UKVI staff to examine grounds for exclusion. Direct statements made by an individual, together with the context in which they were made will be examined in unacceptable behaviour cases.

Will the human rights of the individual be respected in exclusion?

If the person has existing immigration status in the UK, UKVI will address any human rights considerations that may arise, whether on grounds of health or family reasons.

Can a British citizen be excluded from the UK?

It is not normally possible to exclude a British citizen from the UK. However, it may be possible in certain circumstances to deprive a person of their British citizenship under section 40 of the British Nationality Act 1981. If a person has been deprived of British citizenship, this will allow consideration of their exclusion.

Can an excluded person appeal against their exclusion?

A non-EEA national has no right of appeal against an exclusion decision. However, the decision can be challenged in the courts by way of judicial review. An EEA national has a right of appeal against a decision to make an exclusion order against them (regulation 36 of the EEA Regulations 2016) but that right of appeal can only be exercised outside of the UK (regulation 37(c)). A person can make a request to the Home Office to have the exclusion decision made against them revoked.

Complete Guide to Living, Working and Studying in the UK:

The material in the present book *UK Immigration Made Simple* has offered you some important advice on one aspect of your UK life. There are still many more things you could be aware of to maximise the positives of your UK experience. A more detailed book, with answers to over 400 questions typically asked by new migrants to the UK is available:

Complete Guide to Living, Working and Studying in the UK: Preparing You for Life in Britain by Rajiv Immanuel is that book. Following the advice in that book could save your life!

Over twenty years of living in the UK and several years of research produced that book

It deals with the following subjects:

1. Arrival in the UK

2. Immigration Issues

3. Accommodation and Property

4. Studying

5. Domestic

6. Schools and Children

7. Shopping

8. Motoring

9. Jobs

10. Community

11. Money Matters

12. Media and Entertainment

13. Crime

14. British Culture

15.What not to do in Britain

15. Is the UK the place for you?

Do you have questions regarding arriving in Britain, housing, renting a property, schooling for your children, studying in the UK, buying a car, crime, getting a job, money matters, and British culture and etiquette?

Then *Complete Guide to Living, Working and Studying in the UK: Preparing You for Life in Britain by Rajiv Immanuel* could be the book you need (available in print and digital form).

About The Author: Rajiv Immanuel

Dickens, Hardy, Hopkins, Chaucer, Wordsworth, Shelley, Keats, Shakespeare, Milton, Maugham, Emerson... you name it - we had it. Works by such authors lined our bookshelves at home in India. Our wealth was mostly in our heads. This was the type of home I was born into in 1965. Apart from being Christians, another way in which we were different from people around us was that we spoke English at home. In the India of those days that was unusual.

After a degree in Economics in 1982, I added an MBA in 1985. I worked for a while as a Civil Servant in India. I soon got bored with pushing files. In 1995 I arrived at Reading University, UK, to study for a Postgraduate degree in Economics. The scholarship I came on is listed in my *Complete Guide* book. I learnt a lot about UK university life.

As the years passed in the UK, we, my wife and I, found that our roots in the UK had become too strong to consider going back. Both our children were born here in the UK. We realised how much we loved this country and with the Home Office's co-operation decided to make the UK our home. Our English journey is available as a book called *The God of all Things*.

Meanwhile, I had found my métier in life: to be a writer. Since then I have been a professional observer of life in the UK.

While I have a great regard for this land, I am also aware that like any country there are problems here too.

I am an INFP. It is one of 16 personality types derived from the MBTI (Myers-Briggs Type Indicator). Those who belong to this personality type get a great deal of satisfaction from helping others grow and develop. My life's mission is to write books that help other migrants after me understand this country, make the most of opportunities here, contribute to UK society, and avoid nasty surprises. In short: to prepare new migrants for UK life.

In my books, I have put my nearly two decades of living in this country at your service. I hope you find my books helpful and the information and practical advice useful. Best wishes for your UK life. Please leave a review. Thanks.

Rajiv Immanuel.

Printed in Great Britain
by Amazon